FROM THE WINDO...
LONG LINE OF T...
AND ALMOST BLA...
WINDOWS SHOWIN...

Leaning on the broom, Kate permitted herself a moment's rest. Perhaps they had balls there, with guests and music and dancing, and one day she would be the lady's maid, attending to her, giving a last stitch to the hem of a satin dress, seeing a tiny pearl fall as she swept off to the sound of the music floating up. She stood and dreamed and heard the music and the rustle of the gowns and the ladies' laughter. She would be near, so very near, and her hands would be fine and white, as theirs were . . .

This was going to be the start of her new life and she need never again look into the dark face of Lord Liscombe . . .

ANNE GRIFFITHS

Liscombe Hall

SIGNET

SIGNET

Published by the Penguin Group
Penguin Books Ltd, 27 Wrights Lane, London W8 5TZ, England
Penguin Books USA Inc., 375 Hudson Street, New York, New York 10014, USA
Penguin Books Australia Ltd, Ringwood, Victoria, Australia
Penguin Books Canada Ltd, 10 Alcorn Avenue, Toronto, Ontario, Canada M4V 3B2
Penguin Books (NZ) Ltd, 182–190 Wairau Road, Auckland 10, New Zealand

Penguin Books Ltd, Registered Offices: Harmondsworth, Middlesex, England

First published by Piatkus 1991
Published in Signet 1992
3 5 7 9 10 8 6 4 2

Printed in England by Clays Ltd, St Ives plc

For my mother's late parents,
Will and Susan Bosher, who are
the Mr and Mrs Tranter of this book.

PART ONE

CHAPTER ONE

'Pa! You aren't going to leave the mangle behind! However will Mother manage the washing?' Kate Tranter, breath misting in the wintry night air, stamped a boot in exasperation at a father who considered women's work to be of no consequence.

'It don't fit nowhere on the load, do it, Carter?' In his Sunday and funeral suit, for removal day, Will Tranter sucked at the strands of tobacco on his lip and stood back to consider the mound of Tranter possessions piled on the cart.

'It don't,' agreed the carter, all bundled up in shawl and ear muffs, stumping round the dark shapes of his horses to heave himself upon the driving seat of the vehicle. A jingle of harness echoed down the village street as the beasts shook their massive heads and snorted out steam.

'Mother can't do the dairymen's whites without a mangle, Pa!' Kate slammed the lamp on the gatepost. Let her father work in darkness, the carter too; they deserved no help from her. Only men would wilfully misunderstand the usefulness of this modern invention that had meant no more days of dripping clothes in their kitchen.

'Mind that mangle, Kate!' Susan Tranter, finally dressed for departure, stood at the door of the cottage they were to leave with the rose of her black Sunday hat over one ear and a tangle of shawl about her sagging breasts.

'Pa's leaving it, Mother, but I shall see to it. Get Billy and Beth out here to help me, but only if they're prepared for leaving.' Kate looked with impatient love at her mother still standing helpless and fretful in the doorway. The candlelight from the kitchen behind Susan Tranter outlined her stout figure and the slump of her shoulders. She did not wish to leave this cottage, though there was damp in the parlour and bedrooms and the kitchen had an earth floor. She had become used to it. 'We got to have that mangle, Kate. However shall I . . .?'

'Yes, yes, Mother, I know. BOYS!' Kate put both hands up to her burning cheeks. There were hours yet before their journey's end and she must look pale when she arrived; pale and calm and capable. If she looked worn with work, they might only offer her a place in the kitchens. 'Bring my boater out, Mother, it's on the window-sill, Father's wanting to go.'

'Kate, I'm ready!' Beth Tranter, nine years old, with a mass of unbrushed hair under her hat and a black shawl of Kate's tied about her waist, held up her two story books to her sister, together with her blue bead necklace and a tiny square of looking-glass they shared.

'You put them things in your pinafore pocket,' said Kate, 'I want you to climb up to the top of the cart ready to help me and the boys to lift the mangle up. Pa wants to leave it. We got to hide it somehow in the mattresses and not let him see.'

'Yes, Kate.' Beth, accustomed to colluding in matters that had to be hidden from their father, went unquestioning to climb on to the cart's wheel and from there carefully over the cart's side with Kate holding her legs. She landed, giggling, on top of the mattresses. All three of them were piled up against the parlour settle and the kitchen table protecting the contents of their larder: rice and flour and dried herbs, Will Tranter's onions and the last of the potatoes, the suet and the bacon roly-

4

poly for supper. Tommy, their marmalade cat, showed a cross rump in the meat safe under the pine dresser that was jammed up against the wooden cage for Johnny's ferret Silky.

'I can bounce, Kate, look!' Beth swung her boots into the air and dropped the blue beads into the street.

'Pull them petticoats down, Beth. It isn't ladylike, and Mother hasn't mended the holes in your stockings.' Mrs Tranter was too worn in body and spirit to pay much attention to her children's clothes, but Kate felt their new place would improve matters even in that. She added the beads to her own possessions, a cameo brooch from Aunt Bessie and a pair of white gloves folded into the pocket of her good blue dress. They would cover her hands on their arrival, hands that for years now had been red and sore from work in soda and water, and marked her, she knew, as one of the lowly.

'Get them kids ready to leave, we'll be off shortly.' Will Tranter appeared out of the gloom behind the cart with his rope and knife and stopped by the carter's seat. The horses' hooves clattered and scraped at the flint-stone road and Johnny Tranter, thirteen years old and as swarthily handsome as his father, with a moustache beginning on his upper lip, ran round the beasts' heads to arrive with a clank of hob-nailed boots before his sister.

'Ready, our Kate!' he saluted.

'We must get this mangle up on the cart as soon as Pa's settled into the front seat. He's not to know, understand? Get on up and wait 'till I say.'

Johnny nodded and with a grating of his boots landed next to Beth. 'I'll drag it up from here, it'll go between the mattresses.'

Kate saw her brother wink and grin down at her in the lamplight and smiled back up at him. Johnny was a

5

scamp and a knowing charmer who could lift his mother's tired spirits and would do very nearly anything to help his sister. Similar in looks, both dark-haired and blue-eyed and standing as tall as their parents once had before labour and hardship had worn them down, Kate and Johnny had their reasons for being glad to leave East Purton and were anxious to be off.

'Where's our Billy?' Kate turned back to the cottage where their last candle glowed at the kitchen window for the last time.

'I'm here, Kate.' Eleven-year-old Billy, as pale and thin as his brother and sisters were dark and strong, dragged his too-big boots, already worn by Johnny, up to the gateway and his sister Kate. He, like his mother, had no wish to be leaving this safe cottage and village but he had no thought of protest or tears because he knew they would have been of no use.

'Pull your cap down over your ears, Billy, and wrap that shawl around. It'll be colder still when we start off.' Kate put her arm about his bony shoulders and hugged him to her. It was the only comfort she could give. 'Mother ready now, is she?'

'She's looking for your boater, Kate.' Billy put his face into his sister's bodice where the cloth was damp from the night air. Only Kate understood his fear of their new place.

'You said "on the kitchen window-sill" and it weren't,' Mrs Tranter grumbled, arriving behind her children and giving Kate her straw hat.

'Never mind, Mother. Listen – you get on up with Father and distract him while we get your mangle up.'

Mrs Tranter, grumbling still in the muttered monologue that was her habit although no one in her family ever listened to it, went to heave herself on to the front seat beside the carter in a muddle of shawl and skirts and involved herself in the talk of the journey and where they should stop for a pennyworth of cider. The Tranter children, giggling, and with muffled hoots and shrieks, heaved the mangle up over the cart's side and stuffed it between Kate's and Beth's mattress and the boys'. Somehow, it was done. Floss their sheepdog barked in triumph and Will Tranter shouted: 'You kids finish with that noise back there and keep that dog quiet. Check the cottage out, our Kate, and get ready to go.'

Kate, sucking at pinched fingers, ran back into the cottage and up the wooden stairs. There was a stub of candle left in her parents' bedroom. She put that in her pocket, for candles must never be wasted, and picked up a shoelace from a corner of the boys' room. Only bare floorboards and the spreading stain of damp under the windows were left there now. In the room she had shared with Beth there was just one hair pin by the door. From here, two years before, she had dressed at five in the morning in her first print dress with apron and cap to set off for a place as day skivvy to a farmer's wife. There was no manor house attached to the village nor any great hall where she might have found a better post. Kate flushed with remembered shame; she had hated it and Ma Hodden and the lowliness of it, and at night had sobbed in despair for the life stretching before her, which it seemed only marriage could take her from. And that would have made her like her mother.

But her father had lost his place yet again and now they were off and she was to have a new chance. If she were very lucky, they might take her on to train as a lady's maid at Liscombe Hall, or as a nursemaid, and then the whole world would open up before her. She flew down the stairs and defiantly left the piece of candle which remained on the kitchen window-sill and the potato which had rolled from its sack in the moving.

She locked the door and kicked her boot into the worn wood. It was a poor cottage. The one at Liscombe was going to be better. Kate felt her spirits lighten with hope. She gathered up Floss with a laugh and for the last time ran down the cinder path to lift her on to the cart. Johnny reached down to her and she too climbed up to land with her skirts around her knees and her boater slipped back on to her neck. Her hair, carefully pinned up that morning by candlelight, loosened about her ears but she did not mind; today was a day of hope.

They all rolled on the mound of feather down as the horses clattered and strained and set off along the village street. Other cottage windows were lit now by candle and lamp, and smoke drifted from chimneys as fires were stirred into life.

'Goodbye, East Purton,' Kate called.

'Good riddance, old Tompkins,' shouted Johnny, leaning across the pine dresser and kicking up his boots. 'No more school, our sis,' he said, 'no more cane.'

Kate smiled at her handsome brother's jaunty head with its cap at an angle. 'No more scratching on desks either, our Johnny, and fighting old Tompkins to get your six-blader knife back. No more red rages.'

'That were my six-blader and he took it and I never did scratch on no school desks.' Johnny grinned and rolled precariously round to turn his head towards the horses' rumps as the cart rumbled off down the street. Kate watched him joyfully breathe in the smell of horse and her heart lifted for Johnny. He was to have his first place on the Liscombe estate and hoped they would put him in the stables. Her brother lived for horses, was made to work with horses.

But Billy was not so happy to be leaving East Purton. She watched his pale pinched face under Johnny's old cap. 'It'll be all right, Billy,' she whispered, 'you'll see.'

8

'Shall I pretend I can't read nor write, Kate, at the new school?'

'Don't you dare, our Billy. You're cleverer and better than any of them, we all are, just don't you forget it. If you has any trouble, Johnny will go and sort them out.'

'Then he'll fight me to teach me to be brave, and I can never be brave, Kate,' Billy whispered. He would like to cry but Johnny would see and box his ears for being a sissy.

'We're all better,' said Kate again. At school, the Tranter children, each in turn, had been clever enough for the teachers to call to see their mother. But Mrs Tranter would never agree to the suggestion of scholarship or grammar school, even if the teachers promised help with clothing and books. Kate, listening in the scullery, had heard her Miss Otten ask Mrs Tranter for permission to enter Kate for scholarship, and had moaned with shame and despair to hear her mother refuse. Even then, at ten years old, Kate had longed for a life beyond a cottage and a village and the labour of poverty.

'Them kids all right, Kate?' Mrs Tranter called over the clatter of hooves.

'Yes, Mother.' Kate turned carefully around on the load and put her boots towards the front seat behind her mother's shoulders. She watched the long flintstone road turn and dip before her and the rumps of the horses, whitening now with dust like the hedgerows, swaying left and right in slow thumping steps. Their journey would take seven hours and Kate was glad of it. The more distant the place, the cleaner would be her start. No one at Liscombe should know the Tranters had ever been lowly. And it could be, if only her father would not lose his temper there; if only her mother could find the heart to keep the children's clothes mended. And if only the place should be a good one for her, Kate Tranter, to begin a new life, at Liscombe.

The fifth Viscount, Lord David Lonsdale Liscombe, a little younger than his new dairyman Will Tranter, stood as tall and straight as Tranter was bent and worn. He had thick black hair and a wide mouth which rarely smiled and narrow grey heavy-lidded eyes that to servant and estate worker and to his own family too often seemed angry. He was an unhappy man, though he had forgotten when his unhappiness had begun or indeed the precise cause of it, but his spirits always lightened when he was on Liscombe land, his land.

As the Tranters were rumbling away from East Purton and Ash Cottage, he was riding his favourite grey hunter, Jess, up the long sweep of Liscombe Hall drive, where the oaks his great-great-grandfather had planted led the way to the house. This was the moment he liked best, where the oaks, curving to the east with the prevailing winds, gave the lovely surprising glimpse of golden stone that was Liscombe Hall. This morning the maids' lamps still glowed along the mullioned windows. A first gleam of daylight picked out the brass ring on the oak door where Flanagan stood to take Jess, lathered from their ride along the top hills, and where Treeves waited to pull open the door that had withstood a hundred years of weathering. The butler had watched for his return from morning rides all Lord David's life, and each would have found it extraordinary for it not to be done.

'Fetch me the blue velvet case from my safe, will you, Treeves?' Lord David stepped into the dark hall where the sound of his boots echoed on the oak floor, and threw Treeves a cluster of keys. 'Hardy will come down for it.' Treeves bowed to his lordship's departing figure striding up the wide wooden staircase with its bronzed pillars, and past the flickering patterns of sunlight from the delicate tracing of window pane stretching twelve feet into the stairwell.

Within ten minutes Lord David Liscombe had stepped out of his hip bath and into the fine shirt and grey tweed suit laid out for him by his valet. Hardy brushed the back of Lord David's jacket and handed him the jewel case from the safe. He was already busy with his master's riding boots and riding clothes, sponging and cleaning them as he did each morning, when Lord David left his own dressing room and crossed the corridor to his wife's which he so seldom entered now.

'Is her ladyship up yet, Mary?'

Mary Smith, maid to Lady Blanche Liscombe, ceased her sponging of Lady Blanche's white silk evening dress encrusted around its corsage with tiny pearls, only long enough to bob a curtsey to Lord David.

'She is taking her coffee, your lordship,' she said and sighed over a smudge at the hem of the dress. Mary spent most of her life toiling in steam with sponge and flat iron over Lady Blanche's clothes.

Lord David passed into the adjoining bedroom lined in deep pink damask silk and there was his wife, lying up among lacy pillows. It was not to be a good day, for there were the two lines drawn down towards her mouth and she was clearly not going to make an effort, or not for him. Tomorrow, of course, for their guests, it would be different.

'Happy birthday, my dear,' he said and made his way around the tables covered in hand-worked cloths, where numberless tiny crystal animals, jade bowls and fine porcelain figures had each day to be dusted. Lady Blanche never gave them a glance although she knew the provenance and value of each.

She had spilt coffee on old Lady Liscombe's dowry sheets and a spot of butter was spreading under the corner of the breakfast tray which she had pushed aside. Lord David felt his usual irritation begin in a throb at his temples. Why did Blanche take so much pleasure in making work for the servants? But he knew he must not ask himself that question nor any other that would make him dwell upon his wife's faults. It would make such a bad start to his working day and he had had enough of bad starts caused by Blanche — fifteen years of them. He placed the jewel case on her knees.

'I hope you will have a pleasant day, my dear,' he said. He did not want to look at her.

'Aren't you going to kiss me?' Blanche raised her fretful face with its two hard lines and the wide blue-grey eyes he had once found lovely pulled together by a frown.

He bent and touched his lips into the dark blonde hair which had a bloom to it like his hothouse grapes. Blanche had been beautiful and her hair had been a crowning glory.

'Oh, pearls! Lovely, David.' She peered and frowned short-sightedly over them. Her nose seemed oddly long when Blanche showed her true nature, and she seldom bothered to disguise it to her husband now. It was strange that he had not noticed her nose when first they had been married fifteen years before. In profile, with that nose which he could not remember from their younger days, she looked like a bird of prey. Then, her youth had disguised it, and besides he had needed her dowry, to save Liscombe.

'I think you will find no flaws in them, Blanche, and I have had them fully insured.' A pulse was throbbing at his neck. He must not stay any longer or the day would be spoiled. He turned and left the room, feeling his teeth grind unpleasantly against each other. He should have given her nothing to mark her thirty-five years but instead he had searched London for fine quality pearls. It saved tantrums and trouble with servants, to keep her soothed. He wanted his life at Liscombe to be undisturbed by Blanche. Thank heaven, he thought, striding along to his own rooms, that it was to be a Friday to Monday. Her guests would keep Blanche occupied and give her the attention she needed, and which he had no taste to give her himself.

Lady Blanche Liscombe did not watch her husband leave her bedroom. She pushed aside her tray, knocking the hot milk jug on to the silk sheet which each day had to be changed for if it was not her breakfast she spilt then it was the hot brandy she took at night. It was not that she was clumsy. In fact her fingers, when holding jewellery, were skilful, but she liked to see those about her occupied by her needs and affairs.

She placed her new pearls in their box carefully between the Chinese silver brushes and ivory caskets on her dressing table. She was going to call Mary to dress her hair, but for a moment she wanted to be alone. This morning she was thirty-five years old. She wrapped a swansdown-trimmed gown about her shoulders and held up her hair into a coil at the top of her head. She was beautiful still and always had been. Watching her own reflection, Lady Blanche's expression softened. Gone were the two hard lines towards her mouth that only her husband and her children and the servants were allowed to see. She smiled to herself, remembering her father lifting her up as a child of ten to sit upon her first pony and boasting to house guests that she would make the marriage of the century. Only she had not, she had married David Liscombe because her father thought a viscount would serve well enough. Her father had not had to live with him.

She put the pearls around her neck and smiled to see the glow they brought to her eyes and the matt skin which belied her years. Her almond eyes, bluey-grey like the sea, smiled back at her and she remembered other compliments, other conquests. But dowagers wore pearls and today she had inexplicably reached thirty-five years of age. She pulled the pearls from her neck and threw them into their box. Her husband had done it on purpose: he had given her pearls to remind her that she was getting old.

'Mary! Mary! Come and see to my hair!' She must occupy herself or her day would end in gloom.

Mary, summoned from her flat irons, saw her mistress lean forward into the looking-glass and knew that it was not to be a good day.

Later, dressed in blue and cream, Lady Blanche rang for her secretary. Hicks always made her feel even more irritable. She could lose her temper with good reason on Hicks.

'Yes, your ladyship, did you want to see the seating plan for tomorrow night?'

Miss Hicks's narrow face with its pink nose and little button eyes looked at her over the ugly shade of fawn dress that she always wore, and Lady Blanche wondered vaguely how old she was. She must be forty, or more. But it would of course have meant nothing to her, the passing of the years, for she had certainly never had the glance of any man upon her. Only it was of no comfort to her, Lady Blanche Liscombe, on reaching thirty-five years, to know that, not today.

'We settled the seating plan,' she said, without her usual crossness, for it did not seem worthwhile this morning to be cross with Hicks. 'I want to see the bedroom list.' She would not make an issue of the fact that she did not want Lord Peter to be put opposite her own bedroom. She would not let Hicks see that she had tired of him. She thought, wrongly, that her secretary liked to spread that kind of information around the house. She did not know that Miss Hicks hugged such knowledge to herself as a sign of her privileged position as not quite a servant.

Lady Blanche threw the bedroom list back at her with a scribbled alteration. 'Send Mrs Baker with the menus,' she ordered.

Mrs Baker, with thirty years of loyal service at Liscombe, stood as stiff and proud before Lady Liscombe as she had held herself the day years before when Lord David's mother had promoted her from head housemaid to head housekeeper at £15 more a year and her own sitting room. Since then, her hair had grown white and a deep line had formed between her pale blue eyes which never missed a shadow of dust nor the tiniest spot of candle grease. Her back and her manner were each as they had been that day; her black dresses had hardly changed in their mode and cut and she still carried the jangle of keys around her in proud token of her position.

Lady Blanche had no idea what was in Liscombe store cupboards or stillrooms or china rooms but Mrs Baker knew, from the gold-embroidered silk sheets that would only have been brought out for royalty to the merest tablet of soap, maids for the use of.

'Cook and I thought we might begin with a hot consommé followed by a nice cold salmon mousse, my lady.'

Years of concourse with the aristocracy had hardened her Dorset accent to a clipped measured speech. 'With ptarmigan pie and braised leeks. Frampton says he has some nice baby leeks.' She did not add 'my lady' or 'your ladyship' as often as she had to Lord David's mother, old Lady Liscombe, in those better days before his marriage. Lady Blanche was of the aristocracy only on her mother's side; her father was a mere railway magnate.

'Yes, yes.' Lady Blanche gave the menus a glance. She did not care. Baker and Cook were better at menus than she was but one had, she knew, to keep the servants up to scratch. 'See if there are any pineapples ready for the centre table display. Ask Frampton to do something special.'

It was the final weekend of the season and she had not really needed to fit it in, but she had somehow to pass the last of the winter at Liscombe; only the company of others could help her through the short dark days and the hours when the wind whistled through the oaks and she had too much time to face herself in the looking glass. Soon it would be the London Season; she would see a little life in London. There would be admirers enough there, and no need to remind herself that she was beautiful.

She picked up the pearls. He still remembered her birthday and cared enough – surely he did care, David? – to offer her pearls. Pearls to lighten one's eyes, that's what they said. But dowagers wore pearls, and how was she to get through the day?

Perhaps she would take the motor out. David would have to notice her then for he hated her to drive. She would take his precious De Dion. He would have to come out of his study because of the noise it made on the drive with Flanagan bad-temperedly cranking it, he would not want her to dirty his machine – as if it were made only to sit gleaming in the coach-house.

Lady Blanche made up her mind. She would drive out to Dorchester or out to the Ramsays, who would be surprised to see her roaring up their drive; it would startle them. They were sure motoring would not last the decade.

'Mary! Bring my motoring veils and my blue hat and cape. And don't forget my gloves.'

The De Dion would almost certainly break down on her journey, Flanagan would have to go out to her with the phaeton and her husband would be furious. Lady Blanche felt better.

By afternoon, the Tranters were past Whitcombe and going on towards Welcombe. A watery sun showed up the drifting dust that would be in all their clothes and had already settled into their eyebrows and around the rims of their hats.

'A cup of tea will be nice, Kate, when we get there,' called Mrs Tranter for the tenth time. Kate, installed once more, after their stop at the inn, above her mother's shoulders, with the younger children dozing on the mattresses behind, said: 'If there's any kindling for the fire, Mother.' Since she had been old enough, Kate had little by little taken charge of the household, since the first time she had made tea, after one of her mother's miscarriages. Marriage and childbirth had dragged down Susan Tranter in spirit and body. Seeing her mother pull swollen feet about her kitchen, the child Kate had thought her heart would break with the pity of it, and it seemed like betrayal, her urgent desire not to grow as worn and tired as her mother was. She would find herself unexpectedly angry, watching her mother, though she hardly knew what she was angry at. She would not be angry at Liscombe. Perhaps her mother would not be tired at Liscombe.

Kate swayed with the moving cart and dreamed a dream of herself in a pair of black silk gloves over very white hands and someone calling her Miss Tranter. Miss Tranter, our governess, Miss Tranter, the lady's maid. There was a guinea in her reticule and a veiled hat upon her head.

'I hope the privy's not too far back,' Susan Tranter called again. 'But you'll soon be cleaned up. We'll soon be settled.'

They were all dozing, rolling with the cart and the beat of the hooves, when Kate saw it, a glimpse of a tower in golden stone at the top of the hill. The carter shouted, 'Whoah, my beauties,' and the cart thundered to a stop in the road, where a lane curved upwards. They were to climb the hill on foot whilst the cart with its load lumbered off the long way round.

'We're here!' the younger children shouted. Johnny threw up his cap and pushed his brother down past the mattresses where Billy's boots caught in the hook of the mangle. He landed with a squeal on the flintstone and Beth set up a wail of sympathy, sliding down behind him with her skirts about her waist.

'Wait!' shouted Kate uselessly. 'Look what you've done, our Johnny.' He vaulted over the cart's side to land on the dusty grass verge. Will Tranter gave him a cuff about the ear.

'Leave our Johnny, Father, he were only playing.' Mrs Tranter's skirt caught up behind her on the cart's front wheels as she slid down to join her family. Kate, seeing them all below her, dusty and dishevelled, quarrelling, put her face up to the winter sky and let out her own wail. Everything was going to be the same, even at Liscombe.

'Ahem,' a voice said. She had not heard him arrive. Kate looked with horror upon the dark head of a gentleman. He was dressed in a riding suit of the finest cloth and sat upon a gleaming chestnut hunter whose arched neck seemed to Kate to turn away from the Tranter group, but her family did not notice that, for Johnny had grasped the horse's bridle and was stroking its head as if it were a farm horse in a field and Beth was staring up at him with her finger in her mouth. Billy sat on the grass, wailing still. As if in a dream, Kate saw her father remove his cap and offer up a hand to shake whilst her mother gathered her dusty skirt to drop a curtsey.

'Tranter . . . ah, yes, of course. The new dairyman, for the new Jerseys. Well, well. Yes.' And Kate knew, before she heard her father say, 'Your lordship' that it was he and that their new start at Liscombe had been spoiled.

She tried to gather her skirts about her and shake away the dust. If he looked up now he would see her petticoat, but he must not look up for she was covered in dust and her good blue dress would count for nothing if he looked up now. She wanted him to turn away with his horse and not see her perched upon her family's worldly goods. There was about him a kind of shine, like his horse's coat, on his black boots and along the white of his breeches and the tan of his jacket and gloves. Her own gloves that would have hidden her red hands were still uselessly in her pocket.

'And this is your family?' Kate heard him say, and he looked up and saw her. He had a dark matt skin and black eyebrows frowning over eyes that were very clearly grey. His mouth seemed to give a twitch as his glance moved from her boots and the skirts of her good blue dress and her petticoats, now suddenly garments of shame for he had seen them and they were covered in road dust and up to her shawl where there was dust too, and her face. She felt herself lift a corner of her shawl to wipe at the travel dust, symbol of their poverty; his wife, she knew, would travel in a carriage and have veils about her head and Kate could not breathe. Her whole self seemed to be revealed to this man and her shame and the hopes she had had that were now as nothing for Lord Liscombe had seen her.

'Yes,' he said again, and put a black riding hat upon his dark head. There was a faint blue shadow about his chin and his mouth was tightly drawn.

There was a silence as the Tranters respectfully watched him turn his horse about and set up, to Kate, a welcome clatter as he galloped away. Nothing was to be different, even at Liscombe! She let her family argue themselves into some kind of order and watched the wobbling cart going off down the road round the hill with the chamber pots and their puffs of bedding and the mangle – the only things they owned.

In the lane, trees met over her head and gave welcome shade to shake out her shawl and blow the dust from her hat. She took out her white gloves, still dust-free, and put them on. She would not let her dream go so easily. She would still arrive standing as straight and proud as she knew she could. She must never meet his lordship again, and everything could be as she had dreamed it.

At the top of the hill, so steep and winding that even Kate felt her strong legs weaken, it was suddenly before her, Liscombe. There was a wide expanse of sky and stretches of the downs rolling to meet it and on the left an avenue of oaks leading to a great building of golden stone with two end towers. Here it is, thought Kate, gazing, this is the place where my real life will begin and I must not let anything spoil it.

Will Tranter pointed to the Liscombe vegetable gardens beside the Hall itself and the humble cow path leading past them, which they must take and which would lead them to their new home. Johnny gave a muffled hoot of pleasure, beginning to run from habit, but no one else spoke and there seemed to be no sound but the calling of late rooks, and a seagull trawling over the fields and a faint high whistle of wind.

Turning past the garden walls, the cow path led down into a valley behind the Hall. Kate saw a stream below them and the warm light from farm stables. A shout from the head carter drifted up and the clump of hooves on cobbled yard as the plough horses were being taken in to rest. Her father indicated a squat stone cottage lying past the stables before setting off on his way down and away from any complaint she or her mother might make.

Kate urged the younger children down into their new territory and searched for a word of comfort for her mother. Susan Tranter sighed for the walk that remained and the inevitability of the cold damp place that awaited them. Kate took her arm and said: 'We'll soon be settled, Mother.' It was as much for herself that she said it, for she felt only weariness at the tasks remaining to her before they could sleep. The sense of Liscombe as a dream place had quite gone, she thought, for this bumpy path before her, the path the cows took, and the chill damp air that would be in their new cottage, were all she could expect. That grand and forbidding building beyond its oaks would have nothing to do with her.

'It don't look too bad, Mother,' she said, steadying her across the planks that served as bridge over the stream. Mrs Tranter puffed, torn between keeping herself steady and inspecting her new home which seemed, Kate thought, to be looming at them without welcome as they approached.

The crooked blue door and the four blank windows gave no welcome either, nor did the rest of her family waiting for her orders to make this place their home.

'Will you go up to the Hall for some milk, Father?' she said. 'Then when the carter brings our things, we can make some tea.' She would say no word of blame to her father; they would stay until he had his next fit of rage over criticism of his new herd's milk yield, or used bad language in the presence of the land agent's wife. No one could foresee Will Tranter's behaviour. 'Can you leave your matches for the fire?'

He licked carefully along a strip of cigarette paper and spat out a strand of tobacco, lighting up with a Swan drawn across his boot. 'I'll get something out of that cook,' he said, jumping the stream and beginning to climb up the hill to the Hall at the top. He took a pride in his way with women.

When the carter had rumbled down the stream path with their load, Mrs Tranter and Beth rummaged about for the kettle and their cups. The boys soon ran down with armfuls of twigs for the fire and began their next task, dragging the mangle from the cart and into the back scullery to stand beside the boiler. Will Tranter would never set foot in a woman's work place nor take any interest in it. The mangle was safe from his eyes and ready for Susan Tranter's Monday wash of the dairymen's clothes.

Kate built up their first fire and sooty smoke was drifting from the chimney as Will arrived back with his offering from Cook: four cottage loaves, a two-pound cheese and milk in an enamel jug.

Grouped on the grass between the cottage and the stream, the Tranter family were festive, dunking new bread in steaming tea, considering their new home and the space about them and the novelty of Liscombe food.

22

'I'll get us in a pig.' Will leaned up against the cart wheels and cut the knob from the second loaf.

'And some chickens, Will.' Susan sat heavily in the damp grass with her skirts about her, cheese supper balanced in the folds.

'And rabbits, but not to eat them, just for cuddling.' Beth clapped her hands and the boys scuffled over the ownership of the last crumb of cheese.

'I can't start nothing yet, Kate, not without my things.' Susan Tranter gazed hopelessly at the mound of furniture and bedding still on the cart.

'We'll soon have them all in, Mother.' Revived by tea and bread, Kate jumped up with new energy. 'Find the buckets first, boys, fill them in the stream and fetch them up to me in the bedrooms. I'll start the bedroom floors first, Mother, so Father can get the beds up. You decide where to put your dresser and your nice things.'

Soon she was swishing water along the bare boards of the bedroom she had chosen for herself and Beth, for it faced the front and the stream and Liscombe Hill. From the window she could see the long line of the Hall, shadowy and almost black now, with the windows showing lamplight. Leaning on the broom, Kate permitted herself a moment's rest. Perhaps they had balls there, with guests and music and dancing, and one day she would be the lady's maid, attending to them, giving a last stitch to the hem of a satin dress, seeing a tiny pearl fall as they swept off to the sound of the music floating up. She stood and dreamed and heard the music and the rustle of the gowns and the ladies' laughter. She would be near, so very near, and her hands would be fine and white, as theirs were. Sometimes one might discard a dress that could be hers, with the necessary adjustments to make it suitably modest for Miss Tranter, lady's maid.

23

This was going to be the start of her new life and she need never again look into the dark face of Lord Liscombe; there would never again be dust upon her dress and around the rim of her hat.

'Bedrooms is ready, Father,' she called from the window. He and the carter had finished the unloading. Kitchen and bedroom and parlour furniture lay in piles amongst bedding and their clothes. Floss sat guard in the midst of it and Tommy howled from his cage, demanding freedom.

They all helped Will Tranter get up the iron bedsteads because Kate said there would be none of the cold suet roly-poly saved from yesterday until it was bedtime and they still had to lay out the kitchen, for their mother would not be able to settle until it was done.

By the light of their hurricane lamp and a row of candles on the window-sill, Kate and Johnny dragged the pine dresser to stand on the wall opposite the range and Mrs Tranter was able to line up her six Willow Pattern plates and pudding dishes. Beth and Billy opened the paper bundles of food and put rice and semolina, flour and baking powder, together with Mrs Tranter's dried herbs, into the cupboards by the range. She herself laid out the heavy black Bible and her much-read penny romances on the shelves, and they were all cheerful; the fire had warmed the dampness of the room away and the kitchen had begun to look like theirs.

'Where do you want this table, Mother?' Will Tranter called from the parlour. He, too, seemed cheerful this evening. Kate wondered if her father had his own dreams that Liscombe would be the start of a new life, if he had decided to himself that there would be no disagreements with Lord Liscombe. She hoped silently that it could be so and went to join him in setting up the table and laying out the green chenille cloth and her mother's photographs with the china blackbird on the mantelpiece where they always stood. It would be impossible even to begin to ask her father for his thoughts and he would be astonished that she herself had any outside washing and cleaning and the preparation of food.

It was quite late now. From the doorway, Kate could see the line of Liscombe black against the dark blue sky. The Liscombe family would be at dinner, no doubt, with salmon and duck to eat and wine in silver goblets. She imagined Lord Liscombe's frowning face transformed into a smile for his wife.

'Here, our sis.' Johnny came running and laughing down the path by the stream. He had tired of chores long since and had crept off up the back hill to explore his new territory. He had on his face a sparkling look of derring-do and carried a dead rabbit under his jacket. 'Hundreds of them there is, Kate, up there by the rookery. Just asking for it.' His favourite catapult never let him down.

'Kate, shan't we get into trouble with the keeper?' Mrs Tranter nevertheless held out a hand for the rabbit. 'Shut the door and windows, girl, let's get supper going. And mind you put the bricks in the range, or we'll be having cold beds to go to. I'll put this rabbit in that copper boiler in the scullery. We'll be having full bellies tomorrow.'

The Tranter family lay that night in their own feather mattresses, in a new cottage that had no mould and where the only sound was the faint tinkle of water from the stream and the last call of a late rook. Warmed by hot bricks, no one but Kate lay restless, seeing the shape of Liscombe Hall up on the hill. It seemed to her significant that it was on the top of a hill. Living up there must have something to do with your position in life; you could not feel at the bottom of things with so much light around you. No one would cast disparaging looks upon a family who lived on a hill.

Remembering Lord Liscombe's face looking at her, Kate let a tear fall into her pillow. Tomorrow she was to go up to the Hall for her place. Her good blue dress was sponged and her gloves drying from their wash in the stream. She would brush her hair into a pile upon her head. No one else from Liscombe should ever see her dust-covered and she need never see him again. She would put aside the memory of the moment on the cart.

Up at Liscombe Hall on the top of the hill, the three Liscombe children, Daisy, Lulu and Harry, were feasting on apples begged from Cook to supplement the plain bread and butter supper that was all their mother allowed. They watched from their schoolroom in East Tower as the cottage in the valley, once more occupied, showed a flickering candle taken first by Beth, then by the boys and Kate, and finally by Will and Susan Tranter, up to the bedroom window.

Harry, aged nine and not yet officially down on the schoolroom floor, left his window vigil and ran to sit beside Lulu, eleven years old and blonde and blue-eyed like her grandmother, the late Dowager Lady Liscombe.

'Do you think the new dairyman's children might play with us, Lulu?'

'They might.' Lulu took a bite of apple. 'The two youngest might. They looked nice, and Aunt Sarah said we could as they were to live so near.' She gathered her nightdress about her cold feet and picked up her copy of *Little Folk*. 'Help me with my reading, Daisy.'

Her sixteen-year-old sister sat still on the window seat regarding her reflection in the window pane. 'Not now, darling,' she said, twisting about her head the thick mass of her dark hair. Daisy resembled her mother and had the same almond eyes, only Daisy's had a gentle hazel light and a dreamy look in them that her mother's had never had. 'Do you think Mama might let me put up my hair for dinner tomorrow?'

'I wish I were old enough to go down to dinner. I wish I were pretty. I wish I could read.' Lulu sat up against her pillows and squeezed out a tear. 'I just wish,' she said again.

Harry snuggled himself against her. 'I think you're pretty, Lulu,' he said. He always tried to make her feel better about herself.

'Oh, come on. Let's get to bed, it's cold. Come on now, Harry, back upstairs.' Daisy asserted her authority as eldest child and the Liscombe children went comfortless to cold beds in cold schoolroom and nursery.

In the small dining room of Liscombe Hall, when Kate imagined him at dinner with his family, Lord Liscombe sat reluctantly opposite his wife for her birthday celebration. The Liscombe children never dined with their parents although on grand occasions Daisy was sometimes allowed down. The Ramsays were there, Caroline and Arthur, over from Welcombe, a couple of their own age. Arthur Ramsay had an estate smaller than Lord David's but as boys they had shared a Latin tutor and had gone up to Eton and Oxford together.

The conversation that evening had been strained, for Blanche was in her most coquettish mood. This meant that all her glances were directed at the unfortunate Arthur who, gentleman that he was, gamely responded whilst keeping sturdily loyal to his wife and best friend.

It meant that all the talk at dinner had been of love affairs and the London Season for Blanche did not care to settle her mind on more serious matters. David Liscombe knew that Caroline Ramsay, a grave and intelligent woman, would have preferred to talk of the planning of her new garden or of the education of women, for she was a school governor, and Arthur would have liked to discuss his new yearling and the condition of their stock after the hunting season. But when Blanche was in this mood it was easier to let her chatter; they all knew it though no one would have dreamed of referring to such a delicate matter.

They had reached the dessert and the evening had seemed to be interminable, when Lord David found himself staring across the table at the woman he had once thought would be his love and companion for life. How had he ever found her charming? How had he not been revolted by her knowing banter, her lack of grace, her frivolous mind? Tonight the almond slant of her eyes and the glossy pile of deep blonde hair, the flush of her cheeks and the way she leaned a hand across to artfully tap Arthur's, seemed part of a bad play where he was a bored spectator about to leave.

'Today,' he said, and he was surprised to hear himself speaking through Blanche's voice, 'I was out with Jess for an evening ride and came upon my new dairyman's family arriving.' He saw Blanche's smile freeze. She turned a startled face to him and opened her mouth. David thought: She is going to say, 'Really, David,' but I shall not allow it. I should like Blanche never to say anything in my hearing nor sit at this table again.

'Yes, David dear?' Caroline Ramsay joined her husband's, 'Really, old chap?' They both waited with absolute politeness for their long-time friend to go on, for he would have something of interest to say.

'Yes,' he said. 'They were all tumbling from a cart, several children, I think, and the man and his wife. All their poor things were piled up. There was a chamber pot sticking out and the mattresses were there. The wife curtsied to me. On the top of the pile was a girl.'

'Oh, David, when I see the poor like that, I so want to do something dramatic, though I know that social changes are coming, that there is improvement, education and so on, but I do feel I should like to do something personal.' Caroline Ramsay turned her grave and thoughtful face to her friend. 'It seems so . . .'

'You know it's a bottomless pit, old girl, one can only do so much. If David raised his dairyman's wages, the whole country would be up in arms for they'd all want rises and the whole thing would spiral into another agricultural disaster.' Arthur gulped the last of his wine and looked round the table for approval and agreement.

'There was a girl on top of the pile.' David Liscombe did not seem to hear Arthur. 'Her skirts were up and she was covered in dust. Why should they have to travel like that with everything on display, all their poor things?' He pushed away his porcelain plate where the almond ice pudding lay melted into a pool of yellow cream. 'The girl had the most beautiful face. If she were in our circle she would be fêted as a beauty. Under the road dust her cheeks were full and rosy. She had a pair of eyes as dark blue as bluebells. There was dust around the rim of her hat and her skirts were full of it and she gave me the most startled look. It seemed to say something to me.' He stopped, remembering the face of the girl on the cart. 'I suppose it'll soon be like the face of her mother, all life and health gone.'

'What did it say, her face, David?' asked Caroline.

'I don't know – something about her being there on

29

that cart and me on Jess. I don't know what it said. She was quite beautiful, you see.' He wanted to speak of it though he did not know why he had begun there at the table before Blanche who understood nothing.

'Really, David,' she said. She laughed. 'Really, I do think David's not quite right! I mean, a peasant girl, a rustic, whose face *said* something to him. You've been too stuck in the country, David. Thank God the Season won't be long coming.'

Blanche talked on. David saw Caroline and Arthur stare mutely at the remainder of their dessert and Treeves appeared with coffee and the evening was nearly over. He would be able to go to his study and consider his folly in trying to speak of the Tranter girl. But he could still feel the twist of shock he'd felt when he had seen her face. Soon it would be like her mother's and he could not bear to think of that. Probably Blanche was right and he had been too much in the country.

CHAPTER TWO

'There's a girl here says his lordship have promised her a place.' Letty Brown, scullery maid at Liscombe Hall, ran down the basement steps and arrived breathless in front of Cook.

Mrs Fellows, cook to Liscombe and queen of its kitchens, slapped a mound of scrambled egg into a silver dish and scattered parsley upon it. 'And what time do you think I've got to be seeing no girl?' She turned back to the ranges blasting heat into the big dark room where she spent most of her life. Her red hands, impervious now to the touch of hot or cold, turned strips of bacon on the griddle. Only six strips lay there today, in case his lordship or Lady Sarah should wish to take some. With weekend guests expected upstairs, she would soon have thirty or forty slices to watch over.

Letty breathed in the sweet savoury smell of sizzling bacon and prayed silently: Please, dear God, I'll be good and scrub them pans real fierce all day long, only please let them upstairs leave a piece in the dish for me, Letty Brown, and let Cook not see it.

Until she had been taken on at the Hall, Letty had never tasted bacon and indeed had rarely tasted meat. There had been little meat at the orphanage; they had had bread and lard and gruel made from cabbages.

In her good blue dress and her white gloves, Kate Tranter stood at the basement steps and breathed in the smell of bacon. Bacon in rabbit stew, she remembered, from the days they had kept a pig two villages before when her father had been briefly settled. But she felt none of Letty's longings for a taste of it. Now that she was here at Liscombe, what if she had to speak to her ladyship herself? Could it be possible that his lordship could have sent a message down to say that the Tranter family must be given the lowliest positions? Kate felt suddenly afraid. The spirit of hope that had supported her since her father had been taken on at Liscombe slipped away. Her mother said she must just do her best but it was no help; her mother had never been able to help her. She was alone in her hopes and her fears, and her mother would not have begun to skin the rabbit for the stew.

But the girl was coming back. Kate saw that her boots had a hole in the cap and there was a rent in her brown dress. She wore an apron made of sacking.

'Cook says as how she ain't got no time for no girls and you'd best see Mrs Baker.'

The two girls stared at each other with interest. Tiny Letty looked into Kate's anxious face with its rosy cheeks and thought she was the prettiest girl she had ever seen. Kate looked down at Letty's pinched ferret-like face and wispy ginger hair and thought she would like to take charge of her as she did Beth and Billy. This thought gave her a little courage. She would ask the girl who Mrs Baker was.

Letty rubbed one torn boot against the back of a bare cold leg and seemed to be wondering what to do next.

'Who is Mrs Baker, please?' ventured Kate. She was not then to see her ladyship and she was glad.

'Housekeeper,' said Letty. 'In charge, she is, 'cepting the kitchens, with that other one, the butler. Go down there to the end and past the stillrooms and the brush rooms and the laundry rooms but before the china rooms.'

Kate felt a moment of envy for the girl who knew so much about this great house and set off alone, watched by Letty who had almost forgotten her desire for bacon in the hope that Kate would be taken on and she would have a friend at Liscombe.

Kate heard her own boots echoing along the stone floor. The corridor was long and dark and full of shadows. There were cooking and beer and damp smells. She was glad to reach the end and turn as Letty said, for at the turn there were doors open to the passage and a new sound of voices with a welcome and familiar smell of soap and steam. She went on past the stillroom where she dared glance in at rows of shelving with jars and bottles around the walls and a woman busy at a table. There was food enough in there, she thought, to feed her family for a year. Next was the brush room with a man in a green baize apron working amongst rows of boots. Billows of steam told her the next room was the laundry. Calls and giggles from girls in there reached Kate; there might be friends for her at Liscombe, one day.

Now there was another long black stretch of corridor to face alone and a number of doors. Kate slowed her pace and hesitated. Should she dare knock, very gently, somewhere and ask for Mrs Baker?

She stood and shivered a little from chill and fear and wished she were back in the front bedroom with Beth still sleeping by her side. But she put up her chin and pulled back her shoulders. No one must see that she was uncertain nor that she had never been in such a place before.

Mrs Baker found Kate with her chin up, looking frightened just the same, and felt touched enough to speak first and even to tell her to sit down by the fireside in her room, which was not her usual habit with the lower servants. Village girls unused to society sometimes were too afraid to speak.

Kate sat on the edge of Mrs Baker's chair and crossed her gloved hands on her knees. She had, somehow, to make this lady see that she had something special to give, that she could offer more than the lowliest kind of work. She would work harder, try harder, than any other girl and soon her mother would not have to take in the dairymen's whites and the children would have their own new boots for school.

'Yes, madam,' she heard herself say, speaking with care as Miss Otten had taught her to do. 'I was general help for two years with Farmer Hodden's wife.' She wanted to go on, she wanted to say, 'I can do fine sewing. I can iron and fold and sponge, my mother has taught me.' Her mother did indeed know how to do things properly and surely that counted for something? But it seemed that before she had had time to say any of these things, Mrs Baker had risen and led her to the door and she had no choice but to make her way back down the long cold corridor and tell the girl in the apron, who was waiting by the basement steps, that she would be starting work tomorrow.

She had to stumble back down the hill to her new home that would not really ever be hers, not now, for she must live there, at the Hall, and that was not the only bad news she had to recount: she was to be kitchen maid. Mrs Baker had seen nothing in her but a girl suitable for kitchen work and it must be because his lordship had sent down to say that the Tranter girl would not be fit for upstairs work.

Mrs Tranter was sitting in her chair by the range with her tea, her black boots still unlaced and no apron on yet or the rabbit skinned.

'Taken on then, our Kate?'

'I have to live up there, Mother. I have to have two caps and two aprons and two print dresses and a trunk.' She could not say, yet, the words 'kitchen maid'.

A housemaid would have been so much better, for then you were already upstairs and upstairs was better than kitchen.

She sat opposite her mother with her own first cup of tea. She had not been able to drink anything before, she had been so excited, and now suddenly it was all gone. Kitchen maid. Skivvying. Not much better than Mrs Hodden's, not much better. Then she began to cry and the tears splashed into her mug of tea.

'You can stop snivelling, our Kate. I told you, you got to start low. Now, tomorrow you'll get on up there and show the lot of 'em what you're made of.'

'Why should it be, Mother, why should we have to start at the bottom?' Kate got up and threw her tea into the fire. 'We're as good as anyone else, better than some. And we're all clever. The teachers say we should go on with our schooling, me and Johnny and the others. Why can't we have something better than the very bottom of things?'

Susan Tranter sighed and sipped at her tea.

'Them two pink dresses you had at Mrs Hodden's, they'll do, and the aprons and caps is still good. Best get the irons out. I'll have a go at them and we can do up your bundle tonight. We've no money nor time to be getting no trunk just to carry them things up the hill.'

'Mother!' Kate sat down again and sobbed into her hands. 'I don't want to be a drudge all my life, and I don't want you to be either! A kitchen maid's no start, you know it won't. It must be because his lordship saw us in the road with our cart, and we looked so dirty and our things were all there.'

'What you trying to say, our Kate? How else is folks

to travel if it ain't with a cart and all? And the road dust falls on the high and mighty too, don't it, for all their fine ways.' Susan eased herself on to her feet and clumsily patted Kate's shoulder. 'You got no cause to be ashamed of your family, Kate. We're decent folk, and you're a Clarke on my side, remember that. Good as any, we are, even if your father is no church goer nor has had no schooling.'

Kate saw her bend to stir at the fire. Her drawn tired face with the strands of greying hair about her ears where she had been too tired to pin them up, and the way she leaned so clumsily to her task, touched her heart through her own pain. 'I'm sorry, Mother, I just want to have better things for us all.'

'I'll make us another cup of tea,' Mrs Tranter said, 'we'll sit and have it nice and quiet before we get going. Here, look what your Aunt Bessie have done up in London, a grand house, a good husband and all. There's no saying you can't do the same even if you do have to start low.'

Kate felt a little better and set herself to begin allocating the tasks for the day, organizing the chores between the three children, including Johnny for he had not to start work at Liscombe for a further week. He had his ferret Silky already in his pocket for a day's hunting and laughed at Kate's list for him. She knew he would fill the buckets and the boiler for the washing though he ran off up the hill with a hoot of joy for his freedom. She kissed Billy and Beth as they solemnly took their lists and read them through. They too would find life strange without Kate in the cottage to help them wash behind the ears and brush out tangled hair before school.

Moving about, in and out of the cottage that day, seeing the winter sun set a kind of halo around the line of Liscombe Hall with its towers on the hill, Kate let herself hope that there was still a possibility of achieving her dream, that she would be able to work her way out of the lowliest post. Up there was Lord Liscombe with his beautiful wife and children, who would never have to work. As she swept out the scullery and set up in it her mother's washing buckets and scrubbing boards and soap, ready for Monday's washing of the dairymen's clothes, Kate saw her own red hands, sore from soda and water, that she had wanted to hide at Liscombe with her cotton gloves. Her ladyship would wear silk gloves and never put her hands into water. Lord Liscombe wore gloves even for riding. They had been of the finest tan-coloured leather. If she had been taken on even as a nursemaid, Kate felt her hands would have become soft and white and one day they might have put her upstairs to work as lady's maid. Suddenly, it seemed to her, watching her strong red hands that had always worked, move about at the tasks she had set herself, that they would mark her for ever as someone who could only do the lowliest work. And yet she had worn gloves for Mrs Baker!

It did not matter; she would not let it matter. Tomorrow she would make her new life begin for herself and for all of them. She would not let her red hands count or any of the things that might set her in the usual mould of girls like herself. The very resolution, she thought, set her apart. All the other girls she had met in their different villages, the girls she had been at school with, had no dreams. They hoped vaguely for a good place in a manor house near their home, or perhaps they might dare to apply for a post in London. It did not much matter for they would find themselves a husband and begin the cycle of childbirths that their mothers had known. They called Kate hoity-toity and sniggered at her and did not understand.

Only Beth listened and dreamed too that her sister would one day have a fine place in the world. Her sweet and undemanding nature sighed with Kate over the stories they read together at night by candlelight; the quiet and clever governess no one at first noticed might be Kate, or the lady's maid who saved her mistress from drowning.

Helping her sweep the cobwebs from the privy and cut back the straggle of ivy round the door, Beth dreamed along with her sister that Liscombe's grandeur would touch them all.

Soon after dawn the next day, Kate washed at the china bowl on the stand by the window looking up Liscombe Hill, where her work would that day begin, her first and last morning wash in Stone Cottage. All those dreams of this fine place with a fine start for her, had not included moving into a servants' bedroom. She had been foolish. She deserved her low start. But it must be only a start. Her stomach seemed to be in knots, her jaw painfully tight when she tried to rub the salt against her teeth. She did not know whether it was from fear or determination. She could not drink the tea her mother had made and seemed to have nothing in her head but the feeling that she would never come home again, when of course she would, one evening each week and every other Sunday.

She could not say goodbye to the sleeping children whose lives she had hitherto organized; her dreams were for them too, and she must not fail them. Her mother stood in the doorway to see her leave. She had made an effort to show Kate that she would manage without her. Her boots were laced and her hair tidy and the porridge soaking ready to cook. Kate noticed these things with silent pity. Her mother's days would be long and hard without her, but harder still without her wages. She kissed her with no word of what she knew and her mother said no word either; it was how it had to be.

Tommy and Floss, told to stay by the stream, watched her make her way across the two stepping stones and on up through the damp grass for her second climb up Liscombe Hill, a servant there now, in her print dress with her servant's bundle. She thought, climbing up into the cold dark air towards Liscombe's lamps: Now I shall always be a servant. A kitchen servant, for who would recognize her worth in the kitchens?

Letty's voice, coming from the gloom of the basement steps, startled and cheered her. She was not to be quite alone.

'I bin getting the scullery boiler heated,' Letty said. 'Makes me job that much easier when they sends down the stuff from upstairs. I bin waiting for you. I'm glad you're come here.' She smiled up at Kate and Kate smiled back.

'What shall I do first, Letty?' She took in a deep breath. There would be no choice for her now nor any escape. She must make the best of it.

'You'd better go in and see Ada or Prissy. Cook 'ent up yet.' Letty pushed Kate into a passageway and on into a dark low room where Kate could hardly believe what she saw. The whole of Stone Cottage would have fitted into this kitchen. There were three ranges on the opposite wall where a woman was on her knees amongst kindling wood. There were copper pans as big as barrels hanging from beams and lined along the shelves. Sacks and jars and bottles covered every space against the walls and it seemed to Kate to be the most exotic place she had ever seen.

The woman with the kindling wood rose to her feet.

39

Kate saw boots as big as her father's and a sacking apron and a hot red face with smudges on it. 'If you're the new one, you'll be having this job tomorrow, and not before time. They promised us a new girl since I don't know when. You'd best get on up to put your things in your room and don't be tardy coming back neither.'

'That's Ada Roberts,' Letty whispered, 'best keep in with her and Prissy Hawkins, 'cause they both likes bossing us, being as Cook bosses them like. Pity there's no one for us to push around. We're bottom,' she said, but did not seem to mind, running up two flights of back stairs ahead of Kate and pushing her into a tiny attic room which held two beds, an iron washstand and two pegs for clothing behind the door.

Kate, regarding this small space and the nearness of Letty's bed to her own, thought: I shall stifle here. Between the basement and this attic room, there would be nothing that was hers, nor any space for dreams. Letty put her bundle on the bed under the window and offered: 'You can have my bed, if you like, by the door. It's not so cold in the winter.'

'No, thank you, Letty. I like to see the sky.'

'I don't want to see no sky. I hides my head under the bedclothes, I do, and pretends ... things,' Letty said, sitting on her bed and swinging thin legs in her orphanage boots.

'What do you pretend?' Perhaps this girl too had hopes?

'Food and things,' Letty said vaguely, 'custards and that ... and sometimes my very own mother standing there making dinner for me!'

Kate looked with pity upon the loneliness of Letty but the girl had quickly jumped from the bed and was running back down the corridor.

'You got to learn about Cook's tray first,' she called. 'Come on, Kate. You got to see how to lay it up and take it up to her room, and if she's already dressed you'll cop it.'

Kate was instructed in the art of cutting bread into delicate slices fit for a Head Cook to waken to, and how to lay the tea pot and the milk jug and the cup of porcelain on a tray. This tray, she understood from Ada, was now to be her first task in the morning after lighting the ranges. She stood beside Ada at the great table, watching as the woman's thick fingers worked. She thought she might do the job more carefully, that the butter should be thinly spread, that the teaspoon should be laid in a line with the cup handle and chided herself for her pride. Pride comes before a fall, she could almost hear her mother say it. But the tray could be laid more neatly; it could and she would do it. She must if she were to rise above such as Ada, and Prissy, second to Cook, who suddenly appeared beside her with her boots as big as Ada's and stout red arms crossed above her waist.

'You'll be answering to me,' she said.

'Yes, Miss.' Kate felt herself flush. There would be no place for her pride here.

'You go with that Letty into your own breakfast,' Prissy said. 'I'll keep you busy enough straight after.'

'Yes, Miss.' Kate found herself giving a little bob of a curtsey, and Letty dragged her across the room and into the passageway.

'You don't call any of them "Miss",' she hissed, 'they're no one, like us.'

Another long dark room now appeared before Kate, pushed by Letty, and this was, she said, the servants' hall. There were armchairs around a fire at the far side, and down the centre a table heaped with plates of bread

41

and butter and pots of jam. Behind and around her, as she and Letty stood in the doorway, was a bustle of people: housemaids coming in with hands smudged from Zebra grate polish, tossing at the ribbons from their caps and laughing, smiling hello at her and at the footmen. They all seemed to be laughing. It could not, thought Kate, be so very bad at Liscombe if there was laughter. The men were teasing the other two kitchen maids, Jane and Violet; small and pretty these two, unlike Ada and Prissy and with a twinkle about them.

Letty led Kate past them all to sit at their places at the foot of the table, beyond the footmen in smart fawn breeches and green striped waistcoats. There were three or four of them. They were throwing off their fawn coats with the emblem of an oak entwined by the letters L and H in green silk embroidery that Kate felt herself deciphering, so as not to reply to their banter at her, the new girl. One leaned back as she passed to pull on her apron strings. Letty poked him with a bony elbow, but Kate felt herself drawn to glance into his face where a little black moustache seemed to be painted on and his dark eyes, holding hers, were too close together.

She felt a little breathless, from nervousness and the crowd of people and the talking; she was so little used to chatter about her. She sat beside Letty and held her hands firmly in her lap, politely, as her mother had said she should, until this first meal should begin.

She saw Prissy come into the room, red-faced behind a pot of porridge and followed by Mrs Fellowes who must be the cook, waddling and puffing to her top place. The chatter stilled as hands reached out for the porridge she served into bowls and the sugar basins were passed around and emptied with a liberality unknown in the Tranter household.

Kate followed Letty in stirring her porridge into a

42

sticky mess and felt a little sick at the unfamiliar sweetness. She ate none the less and emptied her bowl for the pleasure there should be in it, and because she feared to waste it. Waste, her mother had always said, would bring want upon you. These other Liscombe servants seated along the table, however, did not seem to think of want, for they left bread half-eaten and rose, still chattering, to go again about their tasks.

'Getting ready for the guests upstairs,' Letty whispered through bread and butter, slices of which, in between mouthfuls, she folded into the pocket of the dress under her sacking apron. 'See him over there?' She gestured towards a thin youth in a black cloth jacket. His pale colourless hair seemed to blend with the colour of his skin and eyes so that Kate felt there was no life in him.

'He's the odd boy,' said Letty, 'and if I'm not careful he gets all the food scraps what's about. And when he goes into the other room, where the nob servants eat – the Pug's Parlour it's called, for the butler and that – when he goes in there, he gets double. It's not fair.'

'There seems to be so much here, how can you and that boy be hungry?' Kate put her third piece of bread and butter on to her plate and began to spread plum jam upon it. 'I don't think I ever had porridge *and* bread for breakfast before.'

'Orphanage,' said Letty, and that seemed to be enough.

'New girl?' Suddenly Cook was looking down the table at her. Kate put down her bread. She should not have eaten so much. It had been noticed. Here was her first mistake.

'You can start on them vegetables later, after Prissy shows you around so you can get things for me. Your job'll be a bit of all sorts, you might say, and when I

wants something, you gets it for me smartish and I
don't want you crying as how you don't know where it
is.' Kate saw that she had a tired air about her; her
shoulders were bent over heavy breasts which sagged on
to the table. Hair of a faded blonde escaped from a cap
that was not straight. 'I got twenty coming upstairs and
the fish not here yet and I told him I must have it early
for I got something special planned.'

Kate understood that she was not talking to the
remaining servants at the table, much less to her, and
that the amount of food eaten or wasted by servants
was not her worry; it was her work that concerned her.

The little maid called Jane sprang up from the table
and cried: 'Never mind, Mrs Fellowes, least we sees
some life when there's more upstairs.' She winked down
the table to Kate. 'And we gets a glimpse of them all
dressed up, Kate, and ooh, the handsome men sometimes! That Lord Dacre, Vi!' The two girls flounced off
to their tasks and Kate rose from her place though
Letty was still drinking cold tea. She began to clear her
plate and bowl, their familiar Willow pattern making
her remember the kitchen at home. She would not eat
her breakfast there ever again. How could that so suddenly be a fact when yesterday, still, she had not known
she would have to live at Liscombe?

'You leaves that,' Cook said sharply. 'Odd boy does
that. You tell Prissy to show you around.'

Kate found herself following heavy-footed Prissy
through the far door of the kitchen. 'Pantries,' said the
woman, airily waving her hand towards another set of
doors. Behind the first there were cheeses laid out,
round and triangular ones, some white, some a rich
yellow. A lower shelf held bowls of yellow cream and
custards, red jellies with a tracing of fruit in them, long
dishes holding bunches of black berries and orange

fruits Kate had never seen. In another room, golden-skinned fowls were lined in rows on marble slabs and hams hung from the ceiling. Kate thought that just one of those would have fed her family for a month. She breathed in rich smells of spice and fruit and roasted meat and had more to see for beyond that was a further room lined with marble which seemed to hold cold within it and had blood-red flesh hanging on rails and bare raw fowl on slabs.

'Cheeses and desserts first,' she said, 'then cold meats, Prissy, then fresh meat. Is that right?' She hoped for a friendly sign from this woman who claimed charge over her.

'Then there's fish next,' Prissy said grudgingly, 'only there 'ent any and she, Mrs Fellowes, is worried as we shan't get it in time.'

'Shall I have . . .' began Kate.

'You just does what I tells you and you'll be all right.' Prissy folded her arms in front of her and seemed prepared to be friendly. 'Fish just has to be real fresh otherwise it's no good, see?'

'Yes,' said Kate. 'Fish must be fresh,' she repeated. At home they had only ever had fish caught by Johnny and it was very fresh but she knew that there were other ways, that fish was caught from the sea and brought in carts around the countryside.

'And you'd better start learning the special words – cooking words. You just ask me.' Prissy walked back towards the kitchen and showed her another cold room with a stone floor and a stone sink. On stone shelves lay baby peas and tiny carrots in bunches. There was a smell of soil which lay amongst the roots of the vegetables Kate did not know spread along the shelving.

Standing behind Prissy, Kate noted cold and gloom for there was no window; her first work place at

Liscombe. She said, to show her knowledge: 'These are very early vegetables. Father does not plant his yet, not until Easter.'

Prissy heaved a basket of leeks into the sink. 'You wash these first,' she said, 'then I'll see what else is for you.' She had lost the tone of friendliness she had had in the pantries. 'We has glasshouses, for our vegetables,' she said. 'You get going on them leeks.' But Kate thought she was glad that Kate had not known about glasshouses, that she was ignorant of the ways of fine houses. She picked up the basket of leeks and put them back on to the floor. She would take one, two, at a time and open them up properly with the knife by the sink, slicing them straight down the centre and pulling open the leaves. She knew how to clean leeks, her mother had shown her, and it would not be the only thing she would be able to do well. The rest she would learn, beginning with glasshouses. She would very soon know all about them. Kate cut off roots and sliced and washed until all the leeks lay damp and clean along a shelf she had scrubbed for the purpose.

It might have been an hour before Prissy came stumping back from the warmth of the kitchen into Kate's cold place.

'You got to . . .' she began. Kate saw her face change as Prissy caught sight of her leeks lining the shelf.

'Oh, you done it,' the woman said. 'I'll see if they're right for Cook. I'll see if she . . .' She gathered them up in her plump red arms and said: 'Right. You get them peas opened up then.' Kate heard her sniff. Had she cleaned them the right way? Perhaps her mother's way was not right. There was no colander to hold the peas. She would have to slip out to find one.

Kate knew Prissy should have provided all that she needed but resolved to say nothing to her. She would simply watch and learn and be ready and help herself by learning. No one could stop her doing that. And there was much to learn, even, she thought, for a kitchen maid. There were the fruits and the meats to learn about after the vegetables and the glasshouses, and they were only the beginning. Cook was preparing food at the great table; if Kate turned around, she could see her rolling and pounding and calling for spoons and her fish knife and the fish kettle. There were fish kettles to be learned about too.

It was past servants' dinner, and Kate's hands were cold and sore in spite of the soft soap Letty had rubbed in for her before she began again on the sack of potatoes that had to be peeled. She had paused in her peeling to ease one aching foot from the stone floor when a voice, startling clear amongst the bustle and clatter of the kitchen work in the main room, said: 'You are the new kitchen maid?'

Kate turned to see a tall lady looking at her. She was dressed in grey with fair hair caught up in combs, and clear blue eyes in a sweet face.

'Yes, M'um, milady.' Kate bobbed a clumsy curtsey and wondered if this was Lady Blanche, wife to the dark man she had met on the cart. She was beautiful. She had known Lady Blanche would be beautiful.

'I do hope you will be happy with us.'

'Yes, my lady.' Kate saw three more pairs of eyes looking at her with interest; the Liscombe children, of course, she thought and they are staring at me. She backed away, towards her sink, where she belonged.

'I am Lady Sarah and this is Miss Daisy, Miss Lulu and Master Harry.'

Kate was glad the lady was not Lady Blanche; she felt she would rather not see such a grand lady, not here, in the vegetable pantry. Lady Sarah was the unmarried lady of the house, she had been told, the one who came to the kitchen and was therefore not too grand. But these were the children, and there seemed to be nothing grand about them either. The taller girl gazing at her wore only a brown stuff dress and the blonde girl was plump and smiling at her too shyly, too eagerly, to be grand. The little boy had a pale pinched face and was as dark-haired as his father but seemed strangely thin and sad. How could a Liscombe child be sad? Kate glanced from one to the other and held damp red hands behind her back. They were being kind to her as some of the gentry were. The lady said: 'I believe you have a sister and a brother, Kate? I shall see what we can find for them.' She moved away, smiling vaguely into the air, collecting the children, the very tall girl and the thin little boy with her whilst the plump girl lingered for a last smile.

Kate heard the words 'something for them' and felt a twist about her heart. It was not, then, going to be different. They were to receive charity. At the village before East Purton there had been a Lady who summoned Mrs Tranter to the kitchen entrance of the manor house and bestowed upon her some cast-off clothing. Kate had been eleven or twelve and could remember her mother being overcome with pleasure and curtseying to the lady who had offered them a gracious smile beneath her lorgnette. The clothes had smelt of lavender.

Kate leaned back against her cold sink and remembered. She had had to go to school in a dress of ivory satin with layers and flounces, and had been thoroughly mocked. Underneath there had been the shame of thick woollen combinations from someone else's winter wardrobe, to satisfy her mother's fear of draughts.

'Here, what're you standing there gawping for?' Prissy called across the kitchen as the group from upstairs left by the basement door into the gardens. Kate turned back to her sink where celery now lay waiting to be cleaned. With a surge of sudden anger she plunged her hands back into the cold water. Even this cleaning of celery she would do properly. She would clean leeks and celery and peel potatoes so well that no one would fail to notice her worth.

Somehow the day was over and the evening chatter in the servants' hall revealed to Kate that there was unhappiness in the Liscombe family; there were silences and quarrels and Lady Blanche was not quite a lady through one of the Worcesters on her mother's side. The servants longed for past days when Lord David's mother had been alive and he had not ridden the downs in a fury of anger.

Kate asked Letty, as the two sat well behind the others around the fire when everyone was gathered for evening cocoa, why Lord Liscombe should be angry, and why his children seemed so sad.

'Who can work that lot out?' Letty replied crossly, chewing on a stolen biscuit. 'They're all just miserable though they has enough to eat and to waste, that's all I know.'

At midnight, when the kitchen work was finally done, Kate lay sleepless in the iron bedstead under the window of the Liscombe attic room and watched the moonlight pass across the floor. It would be shining down on Stone Cottage, too, and on the room where Lord David Liscombe slept. How was it that he could be angry with the wealth and leisure that he had? She hoped he would never again look upon her. Lying sleepless, she could feel again the shame she had felt as he had looked up at her with a cold and disapproving glance. He would never go into the kitchens. At least there was that advantage to her lowly post. A lord would never look upon one of his own kitchen maids.

Kate turned about in the bed on the hard lumpy mattresses which must have served many kitchen maids before her; she missed being wrapped with Beth in a comfortable warm heap. And Beth must be missing her.

In this great house, the silence seemed strange. Kate could hear only a faint high sound of wind around the window, a frightening lonely sound; she was not used to being so high on a hill. She did not want to be on a hill. She put an arm about her face and breathed in the smell of Sunlight soap. She wanted to be at home on wash day, she wanted to be safe down in the valley with her father snoring and her mother grumbling as she got heavily into bed that it was going to rain for wash day.

Kate felt she had not slept at all when at last Letty stirred and announced it was almost five o'clock and time for her to begin her second day at Liscombe.

CHAPTER THREE

By the time Lady Sarah, younger sister to Lord David, rose from her bed along the corridor from Lady Blanche, Kate had already peeled forty pounds of apples in the kitchens of Liscombe Hall. Lady Sarah's bedroom was just above them, at the very eastern end of the Hall, below East Tower and the nursery wing, and well beyond the principal and guest bedrooms. This was fitting for the unmarried sister of the family, but Lady Sarah had not become eccentric like so many maiden ladies in her position; she visited the sick and poor of the estate and occupied herself with village affairs in the place of Lady Blanche who did not care for the lower orders. She also visited her nieces and nephew each morning, trying to supervise their education and see that they had some small pleasures in their lives.

Her window overlooked not the sweep of Liscombe lawns, but the valley where the Tranters now lived. The distant clatter of Home Stable horses being harnessed woke Lady Sarah each morning and the call of the rooks swooping for their pickings were a familiar part of her day. Unlike Lady Blanche, Sarah liked the country and its people and had been taught by her mother to fill the responsibilities of a position such as hers.

Today, Lady Sarah sat before her looking-glass in camisole and petticoats and dressed her own hair, as blonde as her brother's was dark, in the upswept style of the day. She did not need her maid to get out her grey skirt and tucked grey blouse. Often, Lady Sarah's maid had not enough to occupy her and had taken the habit of going out with Lady Sarah around the estate and helping her with the poor and the sick.

Lady Sarah regarded herself carefully in the looking glass. What bachelor spare man would Blanche have invited to the weekend this time, and would he very carefully keep out of Sarah's way? Her blue eyes filled with tears. Silly! Only she would rather not now have to make the kind of effort that was still required of her to find a husband. Soon she would be thirty and then they would leave her to the life she wanted, a useful, quiet, interesting life, with the estate and her drawing and music and the village school and the orphanage.

Emily, Lady Sarah's maid, was tidying the books in her mistress's sitting room next door. That was a house-maid's job, strictly speaking, but Emily liked to look after her mistress herself for she admired and loved her. She admired her pale blonde beauty and the stately way she held her head and her quiet clothes in their lovely pale colours. And she loved her because Lady Sarah had taken Emily from the orphanage, a poor girl of thirteen with only workhouse clothes on her back, and had dressed her and trained her how to behave.

'I am to go and see poor Mrs Beale today, Emily, and then afterwards to the village school where they are to show me their play. Will you fetch some broth from Cook, please, and I'll have some eggs and a little lean meat, that will be nourishing for her, if Cook can spare it. And some biscuits for the children, Emily. Can you remember all that?'

'Oh, yes, your ladyship.' Emily in her neat blue dress flew from the room and Lady Sarah went up the wooden staircase used by servants and children to the nursery and schoolroom wing in East Tower, where the Liscombe children were at breakfast.

There was no bacon in silver dishes here, or scrambled

52

egg sprinkled with parsley. The Liscombe children fared probably less well than the Tranter children as Blanche, in common with many women of her circle, believed rich food to be bad for them. Breakfast here was always porridge and bread and butter and milk. And the porridge was always cold, for Frank, the nursery footman, had first to carry it along the passages where Kate had walked, then the nursery maid had to take charge of it up the two flights of back stairs from ground floor to nursery and schoolroom.

Daisy, Lulu and Harry sat around the schoolroom table with Nanny and Mademoiselle.

'Aunt Sarah!' Harry ran to throw his arms around her skirts.

'Harry darling, let me hear your poem, and Lulu, I want to see your hemming.'

'Daisy has learned the passage from *Racine* I set her last week, Lady Sarah.' Mademoiselle, with her heavy accent and her heavy dark face, did not entirely please Sarah, but the woman had had some education and had come with good references. Was *Racine*, though, suitable for Daisy when the girl was clearly not going to have any academic interests? Perhaps she should speak to David about her.

Daisy was smiling anxiously at her aunt over her bread and butter. She was bored with the schoolroom. The girl needed an occupation, Sarah thought. It was good that she was soon to be out, London would be fun for her and she would be taken about. And she would be admired. Daisy did not yet know that she was beautiful with the ugly short stiff dresses Blanche made her wear, but with new clothes in the latest modes, and her hair up, and new people in her life, then Daisy would not be sitting in a schoolroom.

Lulu ran up to her aunt to offer her grubby piece of

hemming with its big tight stitches; the girl seemed to have two left hands.

'I am getting better, Aunt Sarah. I am, aren't I?'

'Yes, darling, you are. Try and not pull the thread too tight, then it will stay nice and straight. Let Nanny show you again this afternoon.'

'I do try hard, Aunt Sarah.' Lulu went sadly back to the table to finish her bread and butter.

And nothing I can say, my poor Lulu, can make you feel better. Sarah watched Lulu's rosebud mouth droop and her blue eyes fill with tears. Blanche was so persistent in her jibes at the girl, no encouragement from anyone else was ever quite enough for her. Of course, she was not going to be clever, but then nor was Daisy; one could not imagine either of them becoming the wit of their circle, or much in demand at parties and weekends for anything other than their youthful looks and their very solid position in society.

Lord Harry, nine years old, still in sailor suits and dark like his father, stood before his Aunt Sarah with his bottom lip trembling. He did know the poem, only now he would forget it. He fixed his gaze on the picture behind his aunt, which he knew in every detail. It was called 'A Little Child Shall Lead Them' and a boy quite like himself, wearing a nightgown, had by the hand a lion and a bull. Harry often dreamed he was that boy, bringing peace to the whole world. Instead, here he was in the schoolroom and probably in trouble again.

'"Crossing the Bar", by Alfred, Lord Tennyson,' he began. That part was easy for him though he could not quite say his Rs yet.

'Sunset and the evening star ... And one clear call for me.'

It came out in a rush. He was going to be all right.

'"And may there be ... And may there be ..."' He

had known it this morning and now there was nothing in his head at all.

'"No moaning, no moaning at the bar,"' whispered Lulu.

'"No moaning at the bar, When I put out to sea."' He had finished it; it was over for today. Harry felt very hot.

Daisy was crumbling her bread, uneaten, and Sarah knew she was saying to herself: Let Aunt Sarah not make me do the *Racine* today. I shall pretend I have forgotten, thought Sarah, she simply looks too grown up in that short dress with its wretched tight sleeves, for me to be asking her to do anything so infantile. I must speak to David about her; he should send her abroad to finish her education.

Lady Sarah Liscombe went downstairs to take her own breakfast from the piles of silver dishes on the sideboard in the dining room. David was already out on his horse. There would be twenty guests there the next day. She must make sure to come down early to avoid them. She sat alone that morning, for her sister-in-law never rose before luncheon unless they had guests. She ate only a little egg and toast with her coffee so that there was more than one slice of cold bacon returned to the kitchen for Letty Brown to hide from Cook.

Harry Liscombe, not yet down on the schoolroom floor, sat up in his nursery bed waiting for his sister Daisy to come and show herself to him in her grown-up dress. She was to go down to dinner with the Hall's guests. He was very fond of Daisy and sometimes she would be nice to him.

If he was good and did not rub the chilblains on his fingers and toes, if he did not even rub his toes against the sheet for comfort then she would come soon. He knew that if he held on tight to his bed rail, he would not be able to forget and start rubbing.

He decided to look at the pictures on the nursery walls to pass the time. Hours of his life Harry would spend thus for he did not go to sleep very easily. If he was not careful and glanced by mistake at the picture by the door of a dancing bear turning round on a chain with a nasty little dark man prodding him with a stick, then he would begin to cry and could not sleep and even when at last he did, the bear was in his dreams, sadly dancing round and round on the chain until Harry thought he would burst with the pity of it and woke up in a sweat.

His favourite one which he knew by heart, and that was lucky for often he could hardly see it in the lamplight, was beyond the foot of the bed. Soon Nanny would take the lamp away. If she had let him have just a tiny candle sometimes, then he would not have been afraid of the dancing bear.

He would concentrate very hard on the foxes picture. He did not really need to see it. There were grown-up foxes at breakfast in a house, sitting dressed as humans and behaving quite the same. But in the winter his father killed foxes and he must not think of that either. Harry knew Jesus would not want people to kill foxes, but he dared not say that to anyone for people always killed them; they dressed up in special clothes and took slobbering dogs to hunt them down. When he heard the bugle call and the dogs barking, Harry always tried to hide his head somewhere. He did not want to hear it for there might be a fox somewhere hearing it too. He must never let his father know he did not want to be a hunting man when he grew up for he would be disappointed in him. Harry knew he had been born to carry on the Liscombe line and Liscombe had a hunt. He knew he would never be able to escape the life laid out for him. He thought sometimes that his father knew he was afraid of many things and that was why he did not seem to love him however hard Harry tried to please.

But Daisy was coming. He could hear the rustle of her special pink dress, just as his chilblains had begun to torture him. Daisy stood in his room and he could see how lovely she was in the pink dress. There was black lace around the shoulders and it trailed on the floor behind her.

'Oh, Daisy, you do look lovely.'

She twirled before her brother in the light of his lamp. Poor little scrap, she thought. Nanny would soon take the lamp away and he would be frightened of the dark just as she and Lulu had been. 'It's not really a nice dress, Harry darling,' she said, 'and Mama will not let me have another although it's too tight across the shoulders. Look.'

Harry peered sympathetically at the mark on Daisy's bare skin. 'Aren't you cold? Will there be big fires downstairs?' He was hardly ever allowed a fire on the nursery floor; Nanny said heat made chilblains worse.

'Oh, big fires, darling, and lots of people so that it always seems very hot at dinner. You know that old Lady Augusta? Well, she wears the most frightful wig. It's far too big, and sometimes it begins to slip when she starts gobbling her food. She always gobbles as if she never had enough to eat at home. I am quite breathless waiting for it to fall off.'

Harry began to giggle. Now he would never be able to catch sight of Lady Augusta without having to run away to stop himself being rude.

He loved to hear Daisy telling him about downstairs. 'But, Daisy.' He had a sudden thought. 'What if it should fall off, the wig, into the soup or something, whatever would Papa do?' Now he had something else to worry about. His father hated to be embarrassed.

Daisy twirled before him again and laughed.

'There's the bell, darling. I must not be late or Mama will not let me down again for ages, you know she won't, and it's much better than having supper with boring old Mademoiselle making me say bits of horrible poetry with my milk.'

She looked, to Harry, as tall as their father, and she had on tiny shoes beneath the dress instead of her boots.

'I shall bring up some sweets for you and Lulu but do try and go to sleep. I shall wake you up, I promise. We'll have a feast together on your bed.' She was gone in a final rustle of pink silk. Darling Daisy, thought Harry. He had not dared ask for sometimes she could be contrary but he would have sweets to look forward to and that would make the evening easier.

But how would he pass the time? It might be one of Nanny's gin evenings and that would be another stroke of luck, if there were to be sweets too. Sometimes Nanny would sit in the nursery room next door and send for the maid to build up a fire for her. Then she would have a glass of what Daisy said was gin.

Harry crept out of bed and across the linoleum floor. It felt cool under his hot chilblained feet. He must leave the lamp behind. Nanny would punish him for a week if she caught him walking about with a lamp.

He edged open the door. Nanny sat by the fire with her head lolling against her chest. He could hear a tiny snore. It was a gin evening, and he must not think about her chest though it was rather big. She always wore a stiff blue skirt and a stiff blouse with a round ticking clock balanced somehow on the mound of her chest. It seemed to be Harry's first memory, that chest and the big silver disc sliding to and fro. He was aware that this woman did not always seem to love him either although he did everything he could to please her. He knew every line of her round plump face with the brown eyes which did not always smile and the mole on her chin with one black hair coming from it. He crept up to her now and saw the hair trembling slightly as she snored. He would like to tell her about it for it did not look very nice, especially when she was asleep, but of course he would not dare.

He turned away with a sigh and decided to creep down the nursery stairs to his sister Lulu's room. There was comfort to be had with her for each knew of the other's fears.

'Lulu?' She did not even jump. Lulu was not nervous at night as he was.

'Is it a gin night, Harry?'

'Nanny's snoring. Will you read to me, Lulu?' He climbed on to the bed and cuddled his head into her nightgown.

Lulu put a plump arm around her brother and began a story of *Cavaliers and Roundheads*. Harry did not mind if she stumbled over the bigger words and she did not mind if the pictures frightened him. When she had been small, she used to dream that the bear was going to leap out of the picture and chase her from the bed, but her fear now was of not being clever and not being so beautiful as Daisy. Harry often told her that she was just as lovely, pale and blue-eyed like their Aunt Sarah.

Harry slept. Lulu felt his head fall against her shoulder but she read on. She had promised herself that she would practise reading each night so that one day Mademoiselle would not have to tap her knuckle with a ruler because she said the K in know, and her mother would not be able to laugh and say she was stupid when she went down to read to her at teatime. Soon she too slept and dreamed she wore a pair of slippers and was sweeping down the stairs of Liscombe in a pink dress with a trail of black lace behind it. People stood in the hall and gasped because she was so beautiful.

Daisy, flushed from dinner and attention, left a handful of *petits fours* by Lulu's bedside and turned down the lamp. She thought her brother and sister looked sweet together; a blonde and a dark head. She, Daisy, had beautiful chestnut hair, Hadley Somerset had said so. He had smiled at her across the table and her mother had frowned.

Daisy dreamed that night that she had put up her beautiful chestnut hair into a halo around her face and a handsome young man, who had not quite Hadley Somerset's face, had pulled out all the pins, one by one.

At the age of nine, Johnny Tranter had not been in sailor suits like Master Harry. He had been in breeches and had killed his first rabbit with a stone. Now, at thirteen, he used lead shot like his father and killed rabbits with it, and pheasants when he dared. Today his ferret Silky was curled up inside his jacket with his catapult for he never went anywhere without his catapult. Mrs Tranter said he had to take Billy and Beth out with him to play, but that was not his own plan, although he liked to please his mother and get one of her tired smiles.

Kate had already been at work for two or three hours as the other Tranter children set off up Rookery Hill. Beth's warm hand was in Johnny's; he was her hero and today she was going to be lucky enough to go about with him on his business of catching things for their supper. Billy, trailing in his too-big boots behind them, thought he might prefer to be going to his new school than out with Johnny. Nothing he did was good enough for Johnny because he would not and could not kill although he had to put Johnny's kill into his keeper jacket.

When they had climbed up past the rookery trees where Johnny aimed a practice shot at the birds whirling up, and Mrs Tranter could no longer see them, Johnny shooed the two children down the other side.

'Keep going down to the bottom, our Billy,' he said. 'Follow the lane round to the village, there's a nice bit of bridge down there and the blacksmith's. Draw a map of it to show Ma or something.'

'Aren't you coming Johnny?'

'I got grown-up things to see to, our babe. Get hold of her hand, Billy and don't let it go. Meet me up here come four o'clock and don't be late.'

'Tie your shawl around, Beth, it's getting windier,' Billy said.

Beth obediently dropped his hand and fumbled with her shawl. It was her mother's and worried her where it wrapped itself around her skirts. Sometimes she felt she had so much petticoat and so much skirt and shawl about her, she would like to take them all off and run about in her shimmy, but neither her mother nor Kate would allow it.

'Here's your sandwiches,' Johnny called, and Billy had to run back for them.

'Don't be late,' Johnny repeated, 'and don't let go the babe's hand.'

Billy stumbled back to his sister and did not answer. A tear began to fall down his cheek, whipped away by the wind. It was a cold day. He counted up the hours to the moment he could be back in his bedroom, reading an adventure story by the light of a candle. He was only happy when he was reading.

61

Johnny, watching them go, threw up his cap for the sheer joy of being free and ran down to cut a hazel rod with his six-blade knife. He had string and wire in his pocket for the noose. He never went anywhere without being prepared for a catch. Soon he had the best rod chosen and fitted and was off down the lane away from Billy's and Beth's path towards the water meadows and the river where he had seen the pike lying, tempting him.

He skirted the water meadow and took the footpath which led over the stone bridge. The wind was not rippling the water and that would give him a chance; there was enough sun to bring them out. He took Silky from his jacket, giving her muzzle a kiss for luck. 'You'll have to go in the bag, old girl,' he said, 'till I've got the fish, then you'll have your chance.' He lay carefully into the grass and put his nose down near the water.

'I say . . . er, boy!'

Johnny had not heard anyone coming. It was a bad start. 'What is it?' He turned crossly to see a sickly boy in a sailor suit staring at him. 'Scarper,' he said. 'Can't you see I'm busy.'

'Are you poaching Papa's fish?'

Cripes, Johnny thought, just my luck, his lordship's son. 'No,' he said casually, 'of course not. I'm just looking about the place like.'

He stood up beside the boy. They both peered down into the water.

'Do the fish suffer when you catch them?' Harry said.

'Course they don't, fish don't have no feelings, they're not animals.'

'Aren't they?'

Johnny felt obliged to give the boy a lesson in natural history.

'Don't they teach you nothing?' He saw Harry's pale face look anxiously again into the water.

'Not much, I think,' he said. 'But I don't want to know about suffering.'

'Here, that's not facing up to life,' said Johnny. 'If you don't kill, you don't eat. And then there's the skill of it, see. Watch.'

He dropped to his belly in the damp grass and eased himself forward until he felt the chill of the stone against his hands and the grass had given way to reed.

'Do like me,' he said, 'and then keep quiet.' He felt the boy throw himself on to the earth and lie by him.

'Look,' Johnny whispered, 'in between the algae, there's two or three of them taking the sun. Now you got to be careful. Watch.' Johnny edged the hazel rod with its wire noose and string attached on the end. He inched it upstream and waited for it to float itself back down. 'If you don't get it round the fish first time, well, you try again.'

And he had to try again, he was a good hour at it. Cold was seeping into him and the boy was shivering, but he caught it, a three-pounder for their supper.

'See that,' he said, 'sheer skill and only a bit of rod and a twist of wire. See the skill of it?'

'Yes, I do see.' The boy's teeth were chattering like the pike's. 'I think you are clever, and if the fish don't suffer, if you promise they don't, I should like to learn to do fishing like that.'

'I'll learn you,' said Johnny, 'I'll learn you anything you like. That's if you're allowed to play with us, are you?'

'Oh, yes,' said Harry, 'Aunt Sarah and Papa like us to play with the estate children only most of them live the other side of Flush and that's too far. We've been watching you come,' he added shyly, 'I did hope . . . and I followed you.'

Johnny thought: I never knew. I'd better be more careful. Lucky it were only fish I caught.

'It's a fierce one,' he said, 'this pike, make a lovely supper it will. If I didn't catch us something we might only have dumplings and gravy.'

'I only have bread and butter for my supper,' said Harry, his teeth chattering still. 'Daisy sometimes gets real dinner now she's sixteen.'

'Bread and butter!' said Johnny. 'You'd do better to come and sup with us sometime. You ask that Nanny or someone.'

He felt sorry for the boy, so pale and thin. 'Here, hold my bag – and mind my ferret don't bite you.' Strange the gentry was, he thought. He had seen it at their last village but one. The children ate separately and had very little and their money never seemed to do them any good. 'Next time,' he said, 'I'll show you how Silky operates and maybe we'll get us a few rats' tails. Get a penny for them we do. Meet you up on the hill tomorrow morning. Cut along now, do, they'll be looking for you, the maids and that.'

Harry obediently returned Silky in her bag to her owner and cut along ahead of Johnny Tranter, his new friend.

Daisy and Lulu Liscombe, taking their cold walk through the village, saw Beth and Billy Tranter trail past the blacksmith's forge and saw Beth drop the primroses she had gathered. Lulu, stopping to pick them up, for she could not bear to see flowers die untended, said: 'Those are the new children, Daisy, shall we talk to them?'

'Umm,' Daisy said absently. 'You speak, Lulu, next time you see them. You mustn't be too forward even with the estate people, you know. You and Harry do

64

rush into things so.' She stopped to look into the forge which was throwing steam and flashes of fire into the winter air. 'Good afternoon, Blackie.'

'Don't stop here, Daisy. I don't like the sparks, you know I don't.' Lulu pulled at her cloak.

'We have a duty to speak to all the village people, Aunt Sarah says so.' Daisy smiled into the handsome dark sweating face of the blacksmith who smiled back at her deferentially through the black growth which covered his face but let his eyes sparkle through like the fire his hammer threw up. He thinks I am pretty, Daisy thought, and tossed her head to walk quickly away. How dare he! She felt her face flush.

'Shall we talk to them tomorrow then?' Lulu said.

Daisy did not answer but strode on her too-long legs up to the bridge where she sat on the stone wall and did not seem cold any more.

Lulu thought: She likes the blacksmith and we always have to come this way and Daisy is silly.

'I should like someone to talk to,' she insisted.

'Oh, talk to them, darling, they look nice, I don't mind. We'll talk to them tomorrow if you like. Or you do and I'll go for a walk on my own.'

Lulu watched her sister's lovely face turn towards the village street. She's soft on him, she thought. Now Daisy would talk to her even less as she did when she had liked the gardener's boy.

The two of them walked back up Liscombe Hill where Lulu looked for the hidden violets to add to her damp primroses. Perhaps the little girl would pick flowers with her tomorrow. Daisy had forgotten the girl and the boy. Tonight there were guests and she was to go down for dinner. If only her mother would let her have a new dress . . .

*

65

Beth and Billy were early at their meeting place with Johnny and it was not to be wondered at. There had been little for them to do on such a cold day. They saw the Liscombe girls walk up behind them through the village, and heard the blacksmith call: 'Good afternoon, Miss Daisy, Miss Lulu.' Beth whispered: 'They're from the big house, Billy, do you think they might play with us?'

'Depends,' he said, 'what sort of gentry they is.'

'Shall we try tomorrow if we see them?'

'If you like.' Billy held his sister's hand to warm it and they walked up to Rookery Hill to wait for Johnny who was late for he had found plenty to do. He had had a satisfactory day, spying out a rabbit set and some mole mounds which would give a penny a tail. By way of greeting, he threw at his brother a bundle of five sparrows tied around the neck with string. It was Billy's job to carry the spoils.

'We'll roast 'em after we've had our fish what Ma'll bake. Wowee!' He threw up his cap into the air and ran hooting down the hill to call out his good fortune to his mother.

The pike was good served with dumplings saved from Will Tranter's supper, and if Johnny Tranter did roast his sparrows round the range to torment Billy, it was only in fun and in the end Tommy cat ate them.

In the Liscombe schoolroom that same evening, Lulu Liscombe ate her bread and butter alone. Harry was banished to bed without supper for having muddied his sailor suit. Lulu, watching her flowers die in their jamjar, let a tear roll down her cheek for them and for Harry, supperless, and for herself, with nothing to do and no one to talk to. Daisy was allowed downstairs again in her pink dress with its trail of black lace while Lulu had years to wait before she would even be allowed down for luncheon, and she would never look as nice as Daisy no matter how many silk and lace dresses Mama allowed her.

She went sniffling and comfortless to bed to read by the cold light of a candle whilst the Tranters already lay in their feather mattresses, clutching to them hot bricks and the warm memory of fish supper.

CHAPTER FOUR

At 6.45 on Saturday evening Mrs Baker stood at the entrance to the dining room of Liscombe Hall. Frampton's pineapples lay amongst purple grapes in their silver bowls along the table, and today she had chosen pale gold candles to pick out the colour of the exotic fruit. These were set in high silver candlesticks between the bowls. Usually she chose a pink or a blue candle for the dining room table; since his mother's death, Lord David had had the room decorated in blue and pink as a fitting background for her portrait by Lenoir. This was fixed into the far end of the room and gave out a kind of blue glow, the colour of her eyes and her dress. She stood wreathed in blue with Liscombe a faint blue haze behind her and a pinky sunset in the Dorset sky. All the panelling in the room had been done in the same blue and the ceiling too, with gilt picking out the mouldings like the gilt of the picture frames. Even the chandelier was faintly rose-coloured to reflect the rose in the Aubusson carpet.

Mrs Baker liked to think that Lady Blanche hated the room and hated the vast portrait of her mother-in-law which faced her every time she entered. They had not got on.

The housekeeper stood admiring the table. Lady Blanche had had nothing to do with its artistry, whereas she and Frampton worked well together; they took the same pride in their work and had the same memories of a real lady at the Hall. It was a pity, she thought, that Lady Diana had lived to see Lady Blanche take over as mistress of it. It must have hurt her to see Lord David make such a mistake, even if the dowry she brought with her was needed for Liscombe after the farming depression of the 1880s.

Mrs Baker raised her eyes from the table to Lady Diana's glowing portrait. Each day she looked at it and remembered how life had been. If she had not been a woman of Christian faith, she might perhaps have wished evil on Lady Blanche. As it was, on a Sunday she led the servants into the Sunday service and she would pray for forgiveness for the wicked thoughts she had against her. Once, in a dream, she had seen Lady Blanche drowning by the village bridge and had woken happy.

Mrs Baker looked at the little gold watch pinned to her black silk dress. All the guests were safely in their rooms changing for dinner. As soon as they heard the ladies rustling down the stairs in their silks and their satin slippers, Mrs Baker's maids had to join the ladies' maids in clearing the bedrooms of their disorder. There would be hip baths to empty, jug by jug, abandoned tea dresses, flung on to day beds, to be sponged and hung. Combs and jewels, discarded on dressing tables, would have to be put away and the rooms then set for the night with mineral water and sandwiches, swansdown wraps and silk dressing gowns, and filled kettles set by the fires, to bubble a gentle steam about the rooms.

At every moment of the day and most of the night, Mrs Baker knew what was happening in each part of the Hall. There was little she did not discover on the activities of servants, family or guests. Her lips tightened now as she thought of the mystery of the weekend's bedroom list. Lord Peter had not been put opposite Lady Blanche. Was this to mean that she had a new man to flaunt in front of Lord David? Thank goodness Lady Diana had not lived to see her go that far!

*

Lord David, in his bedroom, was quiet and glad to be so. 'Just put out the suit, Charles,' he said to his valet, 'I shan't put it on to the last minute. I'm sick of high collars, and I'm heartily sick of dinner parties.'

'Yes, your lordship, I'm sure.' Charles Hardy had never sat down at a dinner party but it was as if he had, so much did he identify with his master, whom he had attended as valet since Lord David was down from Oxford. Within the bounds of their different roles, they were friends, though Lord David never quite stepped down from his position as lord of the Hall and Charles never dreamed of stepping out of his as valet and personal servant. Only they shared many experiences: travelling in Europe, the London Season, the races; even Lord Liscombe's clothes for Charles was of the same build though he stooped a little whereas Lord Liscombe held himself straight, and Charles's face was pasty and his eyes small and watery.

He was privy to many a secret early liaison of Lord David's and well aware of the little apartment his lordship had kept for a music-hall dancer. Indeed, Hardy paid the bills for it and had engaged the servant girl to clean it.

Even if Charles Hardy had not expected someone of Lord David's position to keep a mistress, every part of him rejoiced in the knowledge that Lady Blanche was being deceived. Charles hated Lady Blanche and especially hated the way she said he had a fine figure in his livery and looked straight into his eyes which a lady should never do to a male servant. It was unseemly, and Charles did not care for the unseemly any more than did his master.

The black suit was laid out carefully on the bed, shirt just so, ready to slip on, a high all-in-one collar beside it with the white silk ribbon he would draw into a tie later, when his lordship was ready. There were the brass jugs of hot water to bring up now. His lordship would take his bath and Charles would return just to tie the tie and give a last brush to the black suit. Then he would replace the cap on his lordship's cedar scent bottle, straighten the hair brushes and leave quietly until it should be time for his lordship to retire and Charles would take his brandy and hot water to him.

Charles Hardy left his lordship alone with a copy of *The Hound of the Baskervilles*. He was always reading, especially when it came to one of Lady Blanche's weekends, for then he had so much time to fill that was not his own.

Lord David sat on his window seat overlooking the valley where the Tranters lived and sighed over his novel. Another evening to get through for Blanche, another evening to waste. He would have liked to be in Home Farm stables perhaps, where there was a mare about to foal. He could see the glow of the stable lamps there down beyond the stream. The head carter would not get any sleep tonight.

The dairyman's cottage lamp was lit too. What was that family about this evening? he wondered. All these people were dependent on him and the estate. He sometimes thought he would like to be free of it, that he could have a simpler life without the responsibility, the constant demands through his land agent for the unkeep of cottages, the lowering of rents; farmers were always in the throes of some problem caused by weather or government regulation. And there were the problems put to him by his sister, for pensions for estate workers, for the care of the sick, for resources for the school and village hall. Without Sarah, the estate would be a poor one, though, for Blanche did not care for the servants or country people and he himself felt awkward in their presence. He did not have the common touch, as Arthur Ramsay had, and regretted it. He did care about them, he wanted the best for them. Today he had offered to pay for an operation for his head gardener's wife and it would cost him.

He stared down into his valley and scoffed at himself. He had not been able to see the woman himself so that she could thank him! He had baulked at that and had muttered something to Frampton. And yet others in a place like his own treated their people like one huge family; they had run about amongst the servants as children; they loved them. He watched the last of the plough horses being led into Home Farm stables. He could almost hear, through the open window, the sound of their hooves. The stable boys would be busy and the head ploughman shouting at them. The beasts would be warm to the touch, their lovely heavy heads lowered to take long drinks from the water troughs. He would like to be down there with them and the warm ammonia smell of them and their snorting breaths. Only if he went, everyone would be slow at their tasks, watching him and waiting for a cross word.

The devil of it was, he often found a cross word to say, some sharp comment that was unnecessary for he had not that touch which made his people feel at ease. He blamed his mother, a pious and grave woman who had tried to make him as grave as she. He had not been allowed to play about the estate but had to sit with tutors over books. And he had longed to be out and on his pony and later his horse. How he had longed for it! He smiled to himself, remembering the hours wasted over Virgil. All his childhood had been wrong as his life now was wrong. He should be happy; he had little enough cause to be otherwise, excepting Blanche.

The fault today was that he had too much time to wait for Blanche's guests to be entertained. He had too much time for staring from the window. Along from Home Farm stables was the dairyman's cottage and that was what he had been sitting there for to see if she were there, the beautiful girl. What a fool he had made of himself with that family, sitting on his horse staring at their goods as if he had never seen the poor travelling before. And that girl! He had looked up at her past her petticoats and worn boots. He could not forget the look on her face. Probably she had simply been horrified that her skirts were up. Country girls were very modest. Of course she was not there. A young boy was fetching water from the stream. There was a dog wagging its tail beside him. He was foolish to think that he would ever see her again, and if he did she would not be the same. It had been a trick of the light. She was simply a young Dorset girl like many another and his problem was that he had too much time to spend on such fruitless musing. The only time his days hung heavily was when he had to join Blanche's guests and when the Season came round again and he was obliged to spend hours escorting her about.

And this year, he had not Sadie. He had had to let her go. She was twenty-nine and soon it would be too late for her to find a husband. He had given her £100 to start up a dressmaking business for she was good with a needle and would soon find herself someone, especially with a steady income to offer. But he would miss her. He felt his sex stir under the dressing gown. He must get up, do something, call Hardy for his bath.

He pulled the bellcord. There was no point in thinking of Sadie, or of anyone else for that matter. And there were pleasures in abstinence, he had found, a certain pride in one's own will power. There was no shame in it, anyway, none of the tired guilt and mild depression he had when he left Sadie. A wife he loved would have been marvellous, only he could never have that now. He had made his mistake. There would have to be other Sadies, no doubt.

'Oh, Charles,' he called to the man now silently entering his room, 'I'll have my bath early after all. I want to have a walk down to Home Farm stables before dinner.' It would take his mind away from its muddle of thoughts on Sadie and the beautiful girl on the cart.

Lady Blanche Liscombe regarded herself dreamily in the looking-glass and adjusted the fine straps of her pearly evening dress. In the soft lamplight, her face was flushed and rosy, her pupils big and her lips full. John Encombe, she thought. They had played the delicious game of the look all last evening and today, and at tea he had brushed her hand, pressed it when he accepted his teacup. She was sure now that she would discard Peter Dacre. The boy was too young, was all pretty words and sweet notes, whereas John Encombe promised something more, something for a woman in her prime.

Mary Smith saw Lady Blanche lean forward in her looking glass and gaze into her own eyes. She looked as if she had had a drop too much already, Mary thought, and the clothes would be all over the floor in the morning. It must be because Lord Dacre was not about any more, not in her room anyway. Whatever could have ended that little business?

Lady Blanche thought, as she gazed: I am in the full bloom of my beauty and John Encombe and I . . .

Should she risk something this weekend? Today, tonight? Or should she wait for the Season and enjoy all of London with him. David could stay at Liscombe. It would suit him not to come up at all and she could tell him not to bother, not just for her sake.

She smoothed a suggestion of pink salve on her lips and rose from her dressing table. That silk magnolia flower in her hair ... Mary had not got it quite right, she knew, but it would have to do now. Treeves was ringing the gong and tonight it gave her a thrill just to hear it. She would be at her best tonight. Only when she and David were drearily alone did she hate the sound of the gong. Tonight it signalled talk and company and admiration and John Encombe. And Peter Dacre at the very edge of her attention, trying to catch her eye. Poor Peter. He just would not take the hint that it was all over.

Mr Treeves stood to the left of Lady Diana's portrait and behind the chair of the lady of the Hall, impeccably in his rightful place and bowing at the entrance of the Liscombe guests, old Sir John leading her in and his lordship leading in Lady Augusta who must be eighty-five and should be kept at home. He liked his position behind Lady Blanche's chair for then he could not see her nasty female wiles and her eyeing his lordship's male guests, right in front of him too. Sometimes, just to hear her trilling and coquetry was enough to make him signal the first footman out with him on some pretext so he could swallow a glass of wine in the serving room next door. Mr Treeves liked his glass of wine or port but he loved Liscombe Hall more and never let it show. Even when the family was away in London for the Season and had a temporary butler up there, the servants never knew Mr Treeves the worse for drink.

He saw that all the guests were seated now, the

widower Sir John and the widow Lady Augusta, lovely Lady Sarah opposite Mr John Encombe, and that nasty young whippersnapper Lord Peter Dacre next, mooning over Lady Blanche as he always did. Rumour said she had thrown him out of her bed but Mary Smith refused to confirm it. Little Jane Simester was opposite him but Dacre had eyes only for the mistress of the Hall so the poor girl would have to giggle and simper to someone else. The Ramsays were there. Lady Charlotte was supposed to be a friend of Lady Blanche's but she was too much of a lady to be truly friendly with one so indiscreet as her ladyship.

Mr Treeves gave the signal for the service of the hot consommé to begin and the footmen went into action. He saw there was a spot of something on the new boy Albert's white glove. He would have to have a word with him.

Of course, it was not the man's fault. He had been about to serve the cold salmon. He had the silver dish in his left hand, the silver fish servers in his right, and was just passing behind Jane Simester when she flung out her arm, caught at his right hand, the fish servers knocked against the salver and there it was, a piece of salmon lodged into Miss Simester's blue satin corsage and a deathly silence reigning over the table. If Miss Daisy had not snorted in her effort not to giggle, Lord David might have saved the moment calmly. As it was, Albert, in his inexperience, began to laugh too. His shoulders shook with his effort not to, and the fish servers rapped against the empty salver from which a trickle of sauce dripped on to Miss Simester's bare back. Then the whole table, save Blanche, began to laugh and Treeves came forward with a napkin and removed the fish, with impeccable discretion, for he somehow managed to do it without actually looking into the lady's dress. She herself lifted up her hands to her face and began to laugh too, a real laugh, not a laugh she hoped was attractive.

Lord David thought for the first time that she might be quite a pretty girl, and Daisy laughed with her in genuine sympathy instead of at her. Everyone was laughing now, even Mr Treeves and the new footman Albert who had had this unfortunate accident, for accident it was, and they all said how hungry they would be now for the next course and so well cleaned was Jane Simester, so discreetly well wiped, that she did not even leave the room, and suddenly Blanche stood up, pointed a finger at Albert and screeched at him: 'How dare you, you careless fool? How dare you make such an exhibition in my house, and in front of my guests. Treeves, get this man dismissed at once, get him out of the house. I will not have my guests humiliated in this way.'

There was a silence which Daisy afterwards described to Lulu as stunned. 'A stunned silence, Lulu. It was awful and Mama caused it.'

The man left. Mr Treeves followed him for the service of the next course, and the remaining footmen cleared the table of a debris which seemed to them now to be terrible, and the silence was terrible too.

'Servants,' said Lady Blanche, seating herself again calmly as if she had not turned their world upside down. 'They simply cannot be trusted. I shall have to see Treeves about training his men. Really I cannot understand it. He must be getting too old for the job. You'll have to see to him, David, pension him off or something.'

'Mr Treeves, Blanche,' said Lord David, getting to his feet, 'is not too old for his job. He trains his men perfectly well and what has just happened was an accident, a simple accident. It is unfortunate that I cannot say the same for your own behaviour. You may well have had a little too much to drink and I suggest that you retire to your room.'

He sat down again and horrified faces turned back to Blanche with one accord to hear her reply.

'Oh, you are far too soft with them, David, and of course I shan't go to bed, silly.'

She did not realize what she had done; only the middle classes humiliated servants in front of guests.

The service of the ptarmigan pie began and some kind of conversation started up. Lady Sarah stared at her plate and ate nothing and Daisy stared at her father and ate nothing. Lord David stared beyond Blanche's head at the portrait of his mother and the servants left his plate empty. His mother's gracious smiling face helped him make up his mind: he would have no more of Blanche.

Afterwards, they had to play cards for guests always did and then there was supper to get through before they could all thankfully retire from a painful evening. Sarah thought of the story those to attend the Season would have to tell. It would be across London in days.

Only Lady Blanche chattered warmly across the table with her partner John Encombe, during her four of bridge. She became a little fretful when he did not respond as he had the evening before. There was no brush against her hand, no glance held a little too long. She picked up his glass of whisky and playfully sipped at it, tapping at his cheek when he made a false bid. She nestled her skirts into his legs. Lady Blanche was in very good form that evening but the rest of the party was glad when Lord David managed to finish it all before their usual hour of midnight.

And then the guests lay sleepless in their four-poster

Liscombe beds with the fires in their grates dying out and the kettles the maids had kept boiling all evening growing cold at last, untended. Sleepless the guests were for they had a long Sunday to face the next day with church and an interminable afternoon if it should rain and a drive in the Panhard or the Daimler should be impossible. How could normal conversation and the ladies sewing cover up the disgrace of Lady Blanche?

Miss Jane Simester saw the dawn lighten the dark Liscombe windows for she had lain all night shuddering with remembered humiliation. Blanche had snubbed her before, Blanche had often snubbed Jane, though she went on inviting her to the weekends as a spare lady she could crow over and use as a foil for her own beauty. But this time Blanche had gone too far. Jane would not again come to Liscombe however many spare men Blanche would invite. They would all have heard of Blanche's gaffe; they would snigger over it, and Jane would be part of their sniggers. And tomorrow breakfast would be even longer, waiting for church, and then the whole of the day had to be got through somehow.

On Sunday morning, not one Liscombe guest ordered breakfast in their rooms. Each felt it their duty to assemble for a communal breakfast in the dining room to show that nothing had happened.

Lord David himself, who often had no breakfast, took his ride early so as to greet the guests who each came down in their turn and chattered, more lively than usual, as they met. He, watching them, saw the warm smiles offered to the Liscombe footman and butler standing by the sideboard where hams and tongues and galantines and ptarmigan pie were ready in case anyone should still feel hungry after they had been served from the silver dishes of hot kidneys and bacon and egg and haddock warming over spirit lamps. It seemed to him

79

that they had made a special effort for him, to show him that his wife was not his fault, an effort to show his servants that their manners were impeccably right.

They were all seated about him, talking of the shocking unruly demonstrations by the unemployed in London, when a distant door banged and Blanche appeared before them, becomingly flushed and with her hair loosely swept up.

'Darlings, am I late? Do forgive me.'

Lord David saw her seat herself beside John Encombe and girlishly pick from the man's plate a piece of bacon. Blanche never ate bacon and rarely came down for breakfast. What was she about now?

'It is unusual to see you down, Blanche,' he said drily. He felt all eyes turn to look at him. It would have been better to hold his tongue.

'I've come to see if anything has been done about that footman, darling. I cannot bear him in the house a moment longer. John dear, let me have a sip of your coffee.'

The whole table seemed to him to hold his breath. Not a fork or a cup moved. Lord David felt his teeth grind painfully against each other. What could he do about this woman who bore his name?

'Blanche,' he began, but did not go on for suddenly Charlotte Ramsay rose and said brightly: 'Hadn't we better be getting ready for church? I am sure I can glimpse the servants going down across the lawns.'

Of course it was too early for that, but David was grateful.

'Yes,' he said, getting up too, 'we mustn't keep everyone waiting. Sir John, should you like the wagonette up?'

Sir John got shakily to his feet and played his part.

'No, old chap. I shall walk with the rest of you.'

*

In the Liscombe basement, the servants were early in preparing for church; the upstairs drama which had involved one of their own, unpopular amongst them though he was, had inspired a sense of solidarity. There would be no laggards today or anyone too unwell to go to church.

Kate, assigned to help Letty so that she too could go to church, was bewildered by the confusion of people she had met at Liscombe, and by the upstairs events she did not fully understand. Letty was of the opinion that Lord Liscombe would not be pleased by the upstairs incident.

'He's the handsomest man you ever saw, Kate,' she said as together they heaved the porridge saucepan into the sink. 'But so cross and angry all the time, like he's going to burst into a rage. I wonder he didn't cuff that Albert.' She began to scrape at the porridge with a wooden spoon. 'I'd rather have that Lord Dacre. You should see him!'

'But they say it isn't Albert's fault, Letty.' Kate drew a bucket of water from the copper boiler. 'And why is he so angry?' She remembered his dark face, frowning up at her from his horse, and the feeling of shame that had spoiled her arrival at Liscombe.

'God knows.' Letty added soda to the hot water and poured it into the sink where a pile of upstairs plates, shiny with bacon fat and fish scales, also lay waiting for their attention. 'Oh!' She dropped the bucket with a clatter and turned away from the sink, raising skinny arms dreamily into the air. 'Sometimes I dream and I dream Lord Dacre's dancing with me and I'm pretty and we dance round and round and I'm wearing a gold dress.' She closed her eyes and began to hum the tune the footmen sang in the evenings: 'After the Ball is Over –'. Kate sang too and put up her arms to an imaginary partner to turn around the scullery with Letty.

'Here!' Cook's voice stopped their singing. 'You get on down to your mother, Kate. Tell her she must come on up to church if she wants to be seen to be respectable. She'd better start off right, tell her. Letty, finish that washing up and don't linger.'

Kate flew up the now familiar basement steps and heard the church bell tolling sweetly out over the Downs and across Liscombe Hill. Her heart lifted. It was a lovely misty day and the bell was singing out and she was allowed to run down the hill to home. There was the cottage and the stream and Floss and Tommy snuffling around the water's edge. Life at Liscombe was good.

'Mother! Kids! I'm home. You've to come up to the church.' She was surprised and deflated to find them already in full preparation for the event. Beth and Billy were sitting flushed from scrubbing at the kitchen table, their hair in its usual tangle and porridge about their mouths. Kitchen and scullery held a disarray of un-washed crockery and clothes waiting to be mended. She threw her arms about her brother and sister, making her old mental list: washing up, sweeping the bedrooms, scrubbing the kitchen table, leading the hearth, brushing Beth's hair. But they were not her work any more; she felt suddenly displaced amongst the familiar muddle of home and already out of touch for she had not heard of their visit to the school nor of the village children met nor of the Liscombe glimpses.

'Kate, my new teacher is nice, I think. She has gold spectacles and very fair hair and her name ...' Beth chattered on but Kate felt removed, very slightly, from these two whom she had nursed and cared for since her own young arms could carry them about. A sense of panic, of loss, made her kiss them again.

'I shall hear all about it on my day off,' she said, and

poured herself a cup of tea in her old cup that now felt different because she had become used to Liscombe cups.

'We're going to church, Kate, so as to start off right.' Susan Tranter called this redundant information down the stairs and added: 'Come and help me on with my corsets, do.'

Kate climbed stairs which now seemed narrow and cramped after Liscombe stairs, to find her mother amongst her camisole and knickers and the stiff casing of her pink whalebone corset. She took up the corset and wrapped it about her mother's plump waist. 'There, hold it and I'll do it up from behind.' A faint smell of lavender bag and moth balls came from the clothing her mother only took out of its trunk for church days. 'Are you managing, Ma, without me? Are the kids being good? I've so much to tell you, I don't know where to begin only Cook just sent me to say to come up to church.'

'As if I didn't know how to behave!' Mrs Tranter puffed out her breath and held herself in as far as she was able. Kate pulled with all her strength on the pink laces, as she had done so many times before, and tied them with a flourish. 'Are you managing, Mother?' She took up the strands of her hair and repinned them into her bun. 'Where's your hat?'

'You stop busybodying, our Kate, you've other work now. We'll manage as best we can, no doubt. Find me that hatpin.'

Kate felt disconcerted. Was she not needed now, after so many years? She passed her mother the black straw hat and the hatpin with a head in the shape of a swan, a gift from her sister, Bessie. Aunt Bessie had got on in the world and had a house in London. Today, Kate felt she could one day have the same. And if her mother did not need her? Around her the familiar pine dresser and the square of looking glass above it, the pink flowered wash jug and bowl, looked different; she saw them from the distance of Liscombe and knew she would not live amongst them again.

'There's that bell, Kate. Get on up to your place with the other servants. You'll not be going up with us, will you?'

'No, Mother. Cook says I must go up with Letty.'

'Yes, you'll do things right.'

'All right, Mother. I shall see you on Tuesday, for my evening off, and I'll tell you all about . . .'

'Yes, girl, get on now. There'll be time enough for telling.' She eased her heavy body from the bed and peered at herself in the looking glass.

Kate ran down the stairs and back to her brother and sister in the kitchen with a tiny feeling of pain around her heart. She had not expected to feel that her home would not be quite her home again.

'Goodbye, Beth. Goodbye Billy. 'Till Tuesday. Mind you're good.'

She flew from the doorway to kiss Tommy and Floss at the edge of the stream and jumped over it. Behind her, Beth called: 'Tell me about the fine ladies, Kate, and the hats.'

'Are there any books, Kate?'

She did not look back to see Beth's hand waving or Billy's earnest face blinking up at her. A blur of tears made her watch the grass beneath her feet until suddenly she was at the line of beeches and Letty was calling her. She was back at Liscombe, which was now to be her life.

Susan Tranter sighed for the daughter who ran so quickly away from home, though it was to be expected.

That she had waited for and dreaded this time had made it no easier.

She went slowly down the stairs and across to the stream. Billy and Beth had run to the top of the hill already, she could see them waving, but it was a steep climb for her. She eased a hand into her back and decided against the stepping stones. At her age, the bridge was needed though it was only a plank. Walking, her boots pinched. Johnny had promised her a new pair. 'When I gets my stables, Ma,' he'd said, but there'd be no new boots for her. She did not expect it. All her children were dreamers but they would learn that dreams were just that.

Puffing down past the stables and across the bridge and on up she had breath to shout up: 'Wait there, you kids.' She did not want them running round past the servants' area as if they were somebody. Estate people had to file up to the church behind the servants and with the villagers, and were expected to get the time right, though like so many of them, Mrs Tranter had no clock. But she knew what was right.

'Servants gone up yet?' she asked, breathless, at the top of the hill.

'They're just coming out, Mother,' Beth whispered, and there through the shading hedge of silver birch and beech trees was the long line of men and girls in the black Sunday cloaks they were not allowed to wear on any other occasion. Along the path to the church, the lords and ladies who must be the Liscombe Hall guests walked up together with stiff set faces under their hats. Mrs Tranter, watching, did not expect the gentry to be smiling. She knew that money had never made anyone happy, and the gentry had their places to play in the world just as everyone else did.

She picked out Miss Lulu in white, and Miss Daisy,

the lovely tall girl in brown. Behind them, the upper servants walked with the housekeeper in black and the butler as stiff as the gentry. Next came the upper housemaids and the ladies' maids with Sunday hats instead of caps.

Organ music was floating up across the lawns. Susan Tranter liked to hear music on Sundays. She cast a final disparaging glance upon the lower servants trailing behind Cook, the kitchen boy and the odd boy and scullery maids, looking somehow shabby in spite of their Sunday cloaks. Kate Tranter was not there yet.

No one could miss Kate, for her lovely dark hair under her blue hat and the proud way she held her head. Mrs Tranter knew her daughter would not be a kitchen maid for long. They would see she had something in her; it came from her side, she had Clarke blood as well as Tranter, and would certainly marry a butler or a head coachman.

The villagers were filing up now from the other side of the hill, looking shiny and well washed though their boots and skirts had the road dust on them. The single bell tolled a last note.

'Get on behind them, you kids,' said Mrs Tranter. 'Though not too close in, we don't know who they are.'

David Liscombe stood at the door of Liscombe Hall to see out his guests who had run chattering still up the stairs to change for church. All, every one of them, he could rely on to do their part; they were bred to it. Blanche had betrayed her breeding since the day he had married her to save Liscombe. Had it not been right though, for Liscombe? All that lay before him and for miles about was for his heirs and must go on as it had for generations past. Misty sunshine lay across the downs and on the little stone church beyond the lawns. The

86

bell tolling was slightly muffled, he thought, by the mist. In the churchyard his mother was buried and the father he had hardly known, killed out riding on his own hills.

He had come out to nod to his guests as they passed through the door and walked down the terrace steps. And he had come to see if he could catch a glimpse of the girl on the cart. He had woken with a pure image of her in his mind and wanted to know if it was a false one, if she could really have that face. If he thought of her, he kept himself free of the taint of Blanche and the problem which must be solved.

The servants were all filing along the lawns towards the church behind the guests. Caroline Ramsay was doing her best, nodding to everyone, with Sarah doing the work that Blanche should. He saw Treeves in his butler's best leading the servants along followed by Mrs Baker in her place, severe in black, and her maids and the kitchen girls in their black Sunday cloaks. The little scullery girl was late, he saw. She seemed to be running. He had a glimpse of her ginger hair and the cloak was slipping from her skinny shoulders. She was turning around. Mrs Baker turned around too. He could see the frown she gave towards the scullery maid and on to someone else running up. She looked very tall amongst the other servants. He had known she would be tall. She had on a blue hat, the same as on moving day when he had seen her first. It showed up blatantly against the black of the others. He smiled. A girl like that would always show up and he had foolishly stood there when he should have been at the front of the procession of guests, just to see if her face were the same. Well, he had seen her but could not see her face. That would have to wait for another day. He had another image of her now to haunt him: a girl in a blue boater worn proudly, standing out from the crowd.

*

87

Kate, breathless from her climb up the hill and running down and up the basement steps to collect hat and borrowed cloak, laughed at Letty's hissing. In the shelter of the beeches, she fitted the boater upon her head and drew on her white cotton gloves. This was her first time in public with a black Liscombe cloak about her shoulders. The Liscombe Hall guests were there by the church door and all the servants in double file behind Mr Treeves and Mrs Baker. She was one of them now. She held up her head and walked along the gravel path behind her friend. Letty scampered a little on her shorter legs. Lord Liscombe had not spoiled her beginning after all; she had tried to forget the look on his face, and the shame he had made her feel.

She turned to see again the long line of golden stone, as she had first seen it that day. Around her there was a shuffling of boots as the procession arrived at the church gate. He was there, by the great door, a dark and lonely figure staring across to the church. She knocked her arm against the gatepost and Letty nudged her and hissed again. But it did not matter for he could not have seen her, amongst the crowd of his servants, daring to turn around to look at him.

On Monday, Lady Sarah stood at the top of the Liscombe Hall steps to see off their weekend guests. She waved her hand and shivered in the cold air, and was grateful this was the last of the winter visits.

'Goodbye, goodbye,' she called, 'I so look forward to seeing you in London.' She would rather not go up for the Season but would certainly have to now in defiance of the whispers behind her back: a sister-in-law who was quite beyond the pale and unworthy of her position. They had whispered when George Gascoigne had died in the Boer War and Sarah had lost her chance at marriage; she had not forgotten how it had felt and how her face had taken on a permanent ache, from smiling.

'Is that the last of them?' David stood behind her and took her arm. 'For God's sake, let's have some breakfast on our own and rejoice there won't be any more of these terrible days.'

'Oh, I expect they'll be back, David, they are not likely to miss the Liscombe Hunt.'

'I shall not invite them, Sarah, never again.'

'David, you know it will all be forgotten in a few months. At first I thought: They will never come back. But, really, is it likely? They need not mention the actual incident.' Sarah stepped miserably over the stone flags of the terrace and in through the great oak door that David said needed replacing. She touched its worn cracked wood, carved for Liscombe three hundred years before, and thought: This can never be a happy place again with Blanche in it. She could never say that to David when they spoke of her, not directly; they had not talked freely of her since the marriage when Sarah had been thirteen.

'Sarah, I want to talk to you.' He led her past the bronzed carved pillars and behind the main staircase with its matching bronzed moulded banisters designed and made by Montague. Albert stood at the door to the small dining room and bowed as they passed. They would never be able to dismiss him now, though they had noticed his habit of looking directly at guests when serving at the table and even appearing to listen to their conversation. Albert, henceforth, would have to be constantly repaid for Blanche's terrible *faux pas*.

David took only a little bacon and scrambled egg from the silver dishes on the sideboard where the spirit lamps purred and blinked in their rows.

'Sit by me, Sarah, I don't want to be overheard.'
They set their plates near the foot of the table where all
the Liscombe guests had eaten their last Liscombe meal.

'Thank you, Albert,' Sarah called, 'we shan't need
anything else. I'll ring for you to clear.' She had never
liked the look of the man with his eyes too close and a
shifty look about him, but now she would have to pretend.

David sat frowning at his plate. There was a pale
look about his eyes and his mouth was set in that firm
unhappy line which was becoming usual now. He used
to be so handsome, Sarah thought; she had adored him
as a young man. He used to come and go from school
and Oxford and would take her riding even after he first
married, until Blanche put a stop to the innocent joy of
it. Sarah had heard her talking.

'It's not natural to go about with that sister of yours.'
They had been at luncheon and Sarah had been late
coming down for she had rather stay in the schoolroom
with her Mademoiselle. 'You can see the girl's in love
with you. If you're not careful she'll hang about here
instead of getting married and then she'll always be on
our hands.'

Blanche had such a talent for making everything into
something nasty. It was not the first time Sarah had
realized that and she had been only sixteen at the time.
Afterwards, riding with David had not been such a
pleasure.

Sarah toyed with her own breakfast and sipped at her
coffee. Her hand seemed to be shaking. Today David
was going to say something important, she could feel it,
and it was going to affect herself.

'Sarah, I don't think it can go on, do you?'

'No, David, perhaps not, not the way it always has.'
Were they at last going to speak of Blanche properly?

'I think I have a number of choices.' He looked up at

her and his grey eyes seemed paler and dulled. 'Only I cannot continue as we are.' He picked up his own coffee cup but did not drink. 'I cannot go on entertaining people I do not care for, and at the same time be humiliated because of my wife's behaviour. Blanche is not, you see, Sarah, quite to be relied on, is she?'

'No.' She took another sip of coffee and could not swallow it. The truth was not easy to listen to. It had been simpler to pretend that nothing could be done.

'So I will not entertain any more, but that leaves the problem of what she will do with herself. I have long turned a blind eye to her little flirtations, of course, but I imagine I might have grounds for divorce. She would then be free to do as she liked and we could live as we should at Liscombe.'

'A divorce, David?' Sarah caught her breath. A divorce was unheard of in their circle. 'Most people just pretend,' she said faintly. 'Look at the Bascombes, and the Gordons – they haven't spoken to each other for fifteen years they say.'

'Yes, but why should I pretend?' David stood up and pushed back his chair. 'Why should I? I am sick of it! Our whole lives are a pretence and I'll have no more of it.' He was shouting and Sarah had never heard him shout before. Usually when he was angry his voice would become stilted and cold. Once he had been angry with her when she had been eighteen and had wanted to leave Liscombe. She watched him stride up and down the room in front of her, slapping at the chairs as he went.

'I did make a mistake, we know that, and we know that most people of our kind keep up a pretence for the sake of their inheritances, for the sake of their social circle, – God knows why. But I, Sarah, do not care for society and as for inheritance, well, I shall repay Blanche some of her dowry. What do you think?'

He sat down again in his chair. His face had gone quite white.

'I think I want you to be happy, David dear, with Liscombe and all that you love, and I wish I never had to see Blanche ever again.'

There, that was the truth of it and she was glad it was said. 'Shall you just forget all the conventions, David? Be very unconventional for once. I think I hate the way we live, it seems to be so useless. So endlessly frivolous and useless. I think Blanche has made me hate it because she takes none of the responsibility that a position like ours must entail.'

David smiled at her and caught her hand across the table.

'We could become quite eccentric,' he said, 'they will all talk about us living at the top of our hill and not seeing people.'

'Only what will become of Blanche, David? And oh, I do not trust her! She will find a way to do you harm, she will not let it just happen.' Sarah took another sip of cold coffee. 'She will find a way to do something to you or to Liscombe.'

'Oh, she can get lawyers to get as much from me as she can, but is there anything else she can do?'

'She will find something, David.' It would not be anything so straightforward as money, she thought, Blanche would find a subtler, more painful way.

'Shall we just go on as we are then, Sarah? Is that what you want? Or shall I let her have the London house and make it a vague kind of separation? She would not be out of society then; perhaps she would find herself another husband if she could still move in the right circles and not be banished to the South of France with the other divorcees.'

Sarah leaned forward. David's happiness was what

counted. Why should he not be happy? He had never done a wicked or unkind action in his life, and Blanche had never ceased to cause turmoil and misery about her. Let it be Blanche who suffered.

'Divorce, David. After all, Mother is dead, there is no one to shame now. All our sisters will understand, won't they? And I am eccentric already since I have not managed to get myself married off.'

'Well, you cannot marry now, Sarah, you are needed here at Liscombe. I need you, the children certainly do, and the estate. You have always taken Blanche's place here.' He stood up. Suddenly, Sarah saw his face had altered. His eyes were smiling and his mouth, almost.

'Let's do it, Sarah. Let's dare to do it.'

She smiled back up at her brother.

'I feel quite changed, David, I feel somehow lighter.'

A distant door slammed and another flew open. Blanche entered the room. Sarah saw the look she knew only too well. There was a tightness about her sister-in-law's face, a drawing-down of the mouth that signalled trouble for her, or the children, or the servants. Blanche wore that look when she was out to hurt you by touching at something dear to you or at your weakest point.

'Good morning, Blanche.' David's voice was quite cheerful. 'Did you sleep well? Sarah is just going to order up the horses. Will you join me in a cup of coffee?'

CHAPTER FIVE

'Is that tea brewed yet, Kate?' Prissy sounded almost friendly. The continuing drama upstairs had made her forget Kate was a new girl. Kate poured her tea and laid up Cook's tray in the dainty way her mother had once shown her, very thinly sliced bread with butter evenly spread, placed in perfect alignment in triangles. Her mother had said, 'Do things nice,' and Kate had heard Cook say that presentation was part of the art of food, to no one in particular in the kitchen. It was the same thing, she thought, and if no one else listened to Cook she wanted Cook to notice that she strained to hear every word and moreover contrived to stand as often as possible near her at the big table, to begin to learn the way that ordinary mixtures could be transformed into magic dishes, soufflés and sauces and stuffings and pies that made sweet and savoury vapours drift about the room and mouths water. Ada and Prissy passed Cook her forks and mixing bowls but never gave so much as a glance as to what she did with them. They never asked for a taste nor seemed to take any interest in their sieving or mixing tasks.

Today, she wanted to be early with Cook's tray and so managed to avoid Albert, often waiting for her at the top of the stairs to try and pinch her cheek and say it glowed like roses. She hated the hot feel of his hand and the way he leaned his mean eyes right into her face. She would have liked to kick his ankle but dared not for fear of dismissal by Mr Treeves. She did not want to be dismissed; she wanted to learn to be a cook. She had decided that the day she had seen her first pie in which there was a bird, and inside the bird, some sweet stuffing.

There were pleasures even in a cook's room; two armchairs and a fire already lit and a polished cupboard for clothes and a mantelshelf holding *The Cook's Oracle* by William Kitchener and *Beeton's Book of Household Management*. Kate placed the tray carefully on Cook's polished table and looked with envy upon the lettering of the books. She had so few books in her life, only a copy of *Jane Eyre* as a composition prize and her mother's romances and the scanty libraries she had gone through at each school. Here were books that could tell her how to cook; she felt she longed to read them as much as she sometimes longed for a taste of Cook's dishes. How much *more* between those closed covers than in the sewing of silk underwear or the care of gloves that had once seemed to be the work of her dreams. She would have no taste now for becoming lady's maid. And they did not have £50 a year, as a cook did. If she did not tell Cook how she felt, about learning, Cook would not be able to help her.

'What you doing there, girl? Why aren't you down in your place?' Cook groaned from the bed and pushed off her mob cap. 'Bring my tray here do, and get off down. Tell Prissy to start the bacon.'

'I was just looking at your books up there, Cook.' Kate placed the tray with some daring on Cook's knees and stood back. With her heart beating uncomfortably, she ventured: 'I like reading, Cook, and I should like to read those books you have about cooking.'

'Then you're the only maid I ever knew as did.' Cook poured herself tea. 'I 'ent never met many as *wanted* to work, never mind cook.'

Kate held her breath and waited. Cook could be friendly. Kate felt sure she would appreciate someone noticing her skills.

'You mean you wants to read a cooking book? Did I hear right?'

'I should like to, yes. I would like to learn, you see, it seems so interesting and clever.' Kate hoped she did not sound as if she were pleading.

'You do, do you?' Kate saw her look up at her sharply. 'We'll see, one day, when I got less to do if that day ever comes, we'll have a talk.'

'Yes, Cook, thank you.' Kate ran downstairs to her tasks with her spirits high. She had not faltered, she had asked Cook and taken her first step; it had not been easy and she did not want to *creep*. Priss and Ada did that. It was shaming. But it was necessary, and done, and might mean that in years to come she would be able to take home £50 a year.

She felt happy, working with speed and skill, even over the servants' breakfast and one day it would not be bread and butter she had to cut but fine meats and fish and pâtés.

Already, ever since Cook had discovered Kate could write a clear hand, she had been learning the names, for she had to copy out each morning on to menu cards Cook's scrawled '*Consommé Fermière*' and '*Saumon Grillé Tartare*' or '*Ris de Veau Chicorée*'. She savoured the words, muttering over the sounds she heard Cook make. She thought she would never tire of it, nor of watching Cook transform plain ingredients into dishes for a queen.

Or for a viscount. Sometimes, she imagined Lord David reading the very words she had written, not knowing that the dusty girl on the cart had formed them. On the days Prissy or Ada had allowed her to rub through a sieve the split peas needed for '*Soupe aux Asperges*' or chop the onions for '*Soupe à l'Oignon*', she liked to imagine him tasting the dishes she had helped prepare, with his dark head bowed under the lamps and his cold grey eyes, cold no more, smiling at his wife and sister. She had hardly understood the tales she heard, brought down by footman and maid, of quarrelling and brooding and silent meals and did not know how Lady Blanche could not be a lady if her father had been a millionaire.

Johnny Tranter stood at the doorway of the small dining room of Liscombe Hall with the odd boy, Eric. It was Eric who vied with Letty in the collection of table leavings for their own consumption and Eric who was to instruct Johnny in his duties as lamp boy. They had that morning collected, filled, cleaned and returned the lamps of the ground-floor rooms but had to wait before this one for it was still occupied by upstairs.

Johnny was not comfortable. His uniform itched. He wished he were out snaring and could make as much at it as the few shillings they would pay him here.

'You two get away out of it.' Albert, on dining-room duty, pushed his fist into Johnny's shoulder. 'Get below where you belong.'

'Here,' said Johnny, pushing his fist into the man's shoulder, 'I'm not going to be shoved around.'

'Then you won't last long here, sonny. Scarper.' Albert resumed his position, chest out and gloved hands by his sides.

'You only wants to listen at doors, Albert.' Eric ran off behind the baize door before he should be cuffed, and up the back stairs.

'Wait for me,' hissed Johnny. He did not yet know his way about upstairs and did not care to let the weaker boy get the better of him.

'We'll start on the first floor corridors,' Eric said. 'And we uses paraffin oil for corridor lamps like for servants. Colsa oil's only for them upstairs in the big rooms and bedrooms and that.'

'Why does they have better stuff then?' Johnny put his boot automatically in front of Eric's feet so that the boy fell head first into a laundry basket. They scuffled amicably enough but Johnny's heart was not in it; he was not going to bother much with Eric.

'They has better stuff because they is better.' Eric pushed him through another baize door into the warmth and quiet of the first-floor corridors.

The wooden trays were heavy enough without the ten lamps they had to hold. Johnny had to stagger back down the stairs with them, turn down and round endless corridors of the basement to the room where Eric instructed him in the art of trimming wicks and cleaning lamp chimneys and judging the amount of oil left in each by tapping the sides, as if Johnny could possibly care about such a matter. Already he felt he stank of the stuff and by eleven o'clock his knees and wrists ached from climbing stairs and the carrying, up and down like a mountain goat, and in and out of rooms each seeming more splendid and more alien as he and Eric moved along the passage.

The carpets were so thick he felt as if he were walking on something not solid, they made his feet burn in his boots, and the walls were covered in silk with pictures that startled him, there was lace and perfume that made his head swim. He had to try and remember where he took out each set of lamps for he had to put them back. Eric and he had another scuffle outside a bedroom for he maintained the six lamps with a tiny flower painted on them belonged in there for the room had blue walls like the lamp's flowers. A lady in a black dress with keys jangling fixed him with a pair of cold hard eyes and Eric slipped away. Johnny knew he had only been

98

trying to get him into trouble. He apologized to the woman, from pride. He would not tell tales, not he, though two housemaids were giggling at him behind her back.

He felt he would quite like a scuffle with the fair-haired one, if he should ever catch her alone. She would soon see he was a man with a moustache already.

By twelve o'clock he felt like Billy, about to cry, but he would not, though he had reason enough, he felt. Still, he would not be a lamp boy for long.

At midday, he and Eric sat themselves at the very end of the long table in the servants' hall. He had helped Eric lay up for that was part of Eric's job, serving the servants here and the upper servants in the Pugs' Parlour.

'You got to help me,' Eric had whined, 'I helped you with the lamps.' It did not seem worth his while to argue about it although it was girl's work, and then Kate came in with the dumplings, a steaming plate of them, just like their mother's. She winked at him over the platter and he suddenly felt better. She looked nice in her cap and pink dress and apron with a gravy stain on it.

'Johnny,' she whispered, 'is it getting any easier?'

'It's all right,' he mumbled. He did not want the odd boy to know their business. 'Won't be doing it long, will I? I'll be in the stables soon as there's a place.

''Course you will, dear, they'll soon see your worth.' Kate came and sat beside him. She smelt of food. She always made him feel he could do anything, whereas their mother always looked on the worst side of things. She said he must keep his job whatever it was like.

'Can't we start? That stew'll be getting cold.' He must not tell Kate he was miserable, that his legs ached and that he could not stand the smell of the oil nor the smell of Eric with his nasty white skin.

99

'We can't start till the butler and the housekeeper comes in, can we, Eric?' He thought Kate probably felt sorry for the wretch and he was not worth it. She would do better to feel sorry for her own brother. He wished Kate would put an arm about him, for the comfort of it.

'And we got to stand up by our chairs,' Eric said, twisting his mouth into a grin. 'When the footmen and the maids is in, you stands up like I said.'

Kate smiled and winked at Johnny again. 'It's apple pie after,' she said, 'your favourite.'

Johnny knew she was trying to will her sympathy across to him. He felt tears prick at his eyes. He had not cried since he was a baby and must not do so now though he suddenly longed to and could not understand his weakness.

The footman Albert came in with his sharp oily face; if he gave him a cuff in passing, Johnny was ready for him. He was ready for anyone; he would fight the world because he was here, trapped as a lamp boy, and perhaps he would never get out and never be allowed to work with horses at all.

'Hello, my lovely rose, have you cooked me something good this morning with your own sweet hands?' Johnny saw the smooth shine of his black hair as the man leaned over Kate. 'Give us a kiss, darling.'

Johnny was on his feet in a flash, as soon as he saw the man's hand on his sister's shoulder. The swine was touching his sister and Kate was not to be touched.

'Take your filthy hands off my sister,' he could hear himself shouting, and he saw red, as he had when Tomkins tried to cane him. He saw a red haze instead of Kate and Albert but he gave the man a cut to his chin with his right hand. Kate was screaming: 'It's all right, Johnny, get away.'

He had time for one more before Albert got him with a thrust to his groin. Then the butler appeared and through the pain to his belly, Johnny heard him say he must go to his room.

He got three flights up the back stairs into the place he shared with three other boys. It was a bare room with rough blankets on the beds and a smell of feet and sweat. He had not liked it since his first night when the others had helped him undress and commented on the size of his member, shrieking about it, and Johnny had had to take it, for there were more of them; there was always more of everyone else.

The pain was easing. He sat quietly on the bed they had given him, then took off the fawn suit and the striped waistcoat. They could keep it. There was no point in waiting for Treeves to say he must go. He would go now and he would not tell his mother. She would make him go back. He must do without his mother now, and worse, she must do without him.

There were two pennies in his inside pocket. They would have to get him somewhere and then he would give his wits a chance. He was worth more than lamp boy. He was made to work with horses. Someone would give him work in stables; it would only be a beginning. One day there would not be anyone he had to kowtow to.

'Johnny's a hundred times better than Albert and everyone knows it, Lett.' Kate helped Letty lift the stew pot on to the sink.

'A thousand times handsomer, Kate.' Letty gazed mournfully into the stew pot where fat and strands of meat and carrot were congealed. 'This'll take some doing. I better get the water boiled up.'

'But, Lett, what'll happen to him? What'll happen to all of us? Shall we be dismissed too, me and father and all?' Kate looked unseeing into the pot and felt fear, mixed with resentment, for Johnny's sake who was worth so much more than Albert.

'I don't rightly know.' Letty lit the taper under her boiler. 'But that Mr Treeves, he won't stand no nonsense.'

'But it wasn't Johnny's fault, Letty.' Kate, seeking reassurance, began the story again. 'He was just . . .'

'Kate,' a cold clipped voice interrupted her, 'would you come to my room? Letty will finish the pots.'

Kate saw Letty's face grow pale over the stew pot and her light green eyes look up at her with the same thought: Mrs Baker. Kate was to be dismissed.

Making her way blindly down the corridor that was now so familiar to her, Kate wondered if it would mean dismissal for her father too. What would be his rage this time, and how would they stand another move?

Liscombe was not to be the place where they could begin a new life: she would not be able to bear it.

She hardly noticed that she had found Mrs Baker's room and the woman had begun to speak to her in a kindly tone that could not mean a sacking.

'You see, the boy needs someone who will be kind to him for a while. It seems he has been most unhappy and – well, shall we say not as well treated as he might.'

Suddenly she understood. She was not to be sent away with Johnny. She was to be offered upstairs work. Her old dream was given back to her.

CHAPTER SIX

Lady Blanche took another sip of brandy. What should she do? What was to become of her? She stood at the window of her bedroom and pulled fretfully at the lace curtains. Dreary Liscombe Downs! Her husband had never given her what she needed, he had always bored her, and now he had the effrontery to say that he did not want her. It would be all right, of course, she would bring him round, she would find a way.

All because she had been sharp with the lower orders. Really, it was too much. David had always been too soft with them, and as for Sarah, – she treated them as equals. The two of them were going to stay at Liscombe together. It was unnatural.

But now what should she do? There was the Season she had so looked forward to. She would go to London, up to the house there as if nothing had happened and go about and entertain as usual. No one would know yet. She could carry it off. She took another sip of brandy. The things he said to her! They must not know, none of them. She would go down to tea as usual and send for Harry. She was still his mother.

Half an hour later she sat among the remains of drawing-room tea with Harry beside her in a ridiculous Norfolk jacket Sarah had ordered. She slapped his wrist.

'What a boy! Can you not see the word is awkward? There it is, a-w-k . . .'

Harry let the book slip from his knees and scrambled to retrieve it.

'And that is just what you are! Now sit there quietly and let me hear you say a poem. Which one have you learned today?'

'Kate and me have been rather busy today, Mama, I haven't learned one today. We had to go into Dorchester with the cart and get some new clothes and, oh, Mama, it was . . .'

'Too much for you, yes, I can see that. It was too much for you and now you are worn out. Only Mama knows what is best for you, darling, doesn't she?' She stroked his dark hair, so like his father's. There is nothing of myself in the boy, she thought. She could take him up to London with her, keep him with her, and never come back to Liscombe, not even if David begged for his precious heir. She could take him up to London. What was there here for her? It was all dead to her and she had a boy who was a weakling. She longed for a real son, a son who adored her, a handsome son, fiery like her own father and brother, who would pay her court and treat her as a son should. She would put him in the Guards and his wife would come second.

'Well, don't just sit there, say the poem you learned yesterday.'

'Yesterday, Mama, we were busy too. I did some writing with Mademoiselle, then I got all my sums right, and then Kate and me had to go about. Papa said we were to and we like it very much.'

They had taken him out of sailor suits and put him in a jacket that was too big, but it was not her concern now. Her husband meant to cut her off from her own children and it was to be her punishment.

'Then it seems you have not been working at all hard enough. Now –' She picked up a copy of *Palgrave's Golden Treasury* and flicked through it.

'– this is short enough: "Crossing the Bar", by Alfred,

Lord Tennyson. You must go over there and sit quietly and learn it, and then you shall have a piece of cake and go back upstairs to Nurse.'

Harry walked stiffly across the room in new boots. Old Nanny, she thought, would never have allowed boots at his age, but she had been dismissed behind her ladyship's back. They had given him a village girl who would pass on rustic ways.

Lady Blanche crumbled a piece of Madeira cake and let her mouth droop. She could take the train up soon for the Season but did not feel her usual pleasure at the thought. Her husband had spoilt it with his concern for servants and Liscombe tradition, as if all that mattered today. Only she saw that he had that closed look on his face, now that they had stopped shouting at each other. He would not quite look at her, his own wife. When had things changed between them? She could not remember. Peter Dacre and the others had only been for fun, to pass the time. All the ladies in her circle flirted a little.

Lady Blanche, forgetting past passions, thought of letters and roses and pretty words. It had been quite harmless and she loved her husband. She would show him she loved him. No man could resist her if she really tried. Her heart began to beat a little faster. That was how she would do it.

'I know the poem, Mama.' Harry was standing in the middle of the room ready to recite and he would make mistakes and would not get any cake. She had not the patience for him. She needed to think.

She leaned over and pulled at the bellrope by the fireplace.

'Not now, Harry. Very well done, but Mama has not the time to hear the poem now. Let Nurse hear it. Come and give Mama a kiss.'

*

She waited until two o'clock that night when there was darkness and silence in the passage outside her room. David's apartment was beyond the landing with the alcoves and his precious pictures. The door made no noise as she opened it. The curtains of his dressing room were drawn; she could see nothing. She felt carefully along the walls, running her hand along the chests and the window trunk. No light came from under his door. She must slip quietly into the bed and he would be lost. No man could resist her. No one but David ever had. She should have walked straight across the centre of the room for on the window trunk was a book and she knocked it down. She stood still as a statue but her husband heard her. There was the sudden light of his candle under the door and now it would not be quite so easy.

'Blanche! What are you doing here?'

'Oh, David, I am so glad you are awake. I was wondering if I might have a word with you, only I did not know that you were asleep.'

'Of course I was asleep, Blanche, it's well past two o'clock. What on earth is it you want to speak to me about at this hour?'

'David dear, nothing really, only I have been rather worried about Daisy.' She would have to try and start some kind of conversation.

'Blanche, the day you spend sleepless hours over the children . . . What do you really want to speak to me about?'

He put down his candle and Blanche moved towards him. She must do something straight away.

'Oh, David, I do love our children, if only you would love me as much. David . . .'

She leaned against him and opened her robe a fraction, putting her hand into his shirt. His skin felt cold, but she could not stop now. She lifted her left leg and rubbed it against his.

'David, you don't know how I have missed you. Sometimes I should so like you to come to me again.' She let her other hand play about his shoulders. 'Remember how it used to be for us? We are man and wife and always will be, promised to each other, bound to each other. David!'

'Blanche, really, you know very well there is nothing like that between us nor has been for a long time. What can you be thinking of?'

'Oh, David.' She undid her robe and quietly slipped the chemise from her shoulders. She would abase herself completely. Her life depended on the next few moments and he would not resist her.

But he moved only to bend and pick up her robe.

'Blanche, do not embarrass yourself. I am afraid that I cannot, do not . . . please, Blanche.' He was pulling the robe about her though her breasts were raised and ready for him. He was made of stone.

He was leading her to the door, he was refusing her outright, throwing away what other men sighed for. Blanche grabbed her robe and tore open the door.

'You are a heartless man, David Liscombe. If only the world knew what you are.' She paused, hugging the robe to her. She was quite lost now. 'Well, I shall tell them. You will be the laughing stock of our circle. I shall tell them you haven't been to my bed for years. I shall tell them you moon over your own sister. You'll see! And you'll be sorry!'

'Whatever you like, Blanche. It is of no import.'

If he had not said those calm quiet words, if he had screamed back at her, she would have been all right.

'Beast! Beast!' She felt herself beating at him and

107

shrieking. It could not be all lost, it could not be. What would become of her?

'I'll tell them all, the whole world and your precious servants, I'll tell them you're no real man. I'll tell them you can't manage to make love to me. They'll laugh at you behind your back. I shall say you like footmen . . . I shall say I caught you in Albert's room!'

'Very well, Blanche, as you wish.'

And he left her there. She had fallen to the floor, shouting at him, and he walked through the door and there was no one to hear her.

But it would be all right. She would be all right. Blanche stopped sobbing when he was gone and went back to her room.

She sat up against the high silky pillows of her bed and sipped at her brandy. There must be a way to get at David somehow. And she would find it. Then he would not dare divorce her.

David Liscombe lit the lamp in his bedroom and put on his breeches. He would not, he knew, find sleep again that night. How was it that his own wife was repugnant to him, that the strong female scent of her seemed to linger unpleasantly about him although he had not embraced her and would not embrace her again? He pulled absent-mindedly at the bell which would call his valet from his bed and waited until Hardy slipped soundlessly into the room, he too in nightshirt and breeches.

'The fire, Hardy, and some brandy and hot water.'

'Your lordship cannot sleep?' Hardy took up the fire irons and stirred life into the fire he had tended all that day between his other duties. The kettle had boiled itself almost dry. Soundless still, as light on his slippered feet as a dancer, Hardy moved to and fro between water jug and scuttle whilst his master stood gazing into the growing flames.

'Shall I be making some inquiries, your lordship, as to Miss Sadie's position? It may be she's still . . .' Only years of unspoken secrets shared could have permitted such a suggestion, as Hardy knew, and it was only his guess that marital problems once more kept his master sleepless.

Lord David, absently, used to his valet's knowing all of him, thinking for him, said: 'No, Hardy, thank you. We must leave Sadie, let her have a chance of a proper marriage, you know.'

'Yes, your lordship.' Hardy set a glass to warm before the fire for Lord David's brandy.

'Get two glasses, old chap, since I've woken you.'

His face as set and smooth as always, Charles Hardy showed no sign of the pleasure he felt at this invitation, rare enough though not unknown, something to be treasured.

Absently, Lord David took the warm glass his valet offered him and as absently said: 'You've really never thought of marriage, have you, Hardy?'

Charles Hardy stood beside his master and took a gulp of brandy, spluttering, 'Oh no, your lordship! The very idea. Why, I couldn't do my job with you if I had some woman behind me. There'd be nagging and no end of trouble, sir, there would, with a woman. And there's no woman . . .'

Lord David turned to look at the man who had shared years of his life. 'Quite right, old chap, no end of trouble. You're better off heart-free and celibate.' There were men like Hardy at Eton and Oxford only they gave themselves finer airs about it than poor Hardy could do. He passed him his glass. 'I think I'll take a turn about, it might help me sleep.'

'Very well, sir.' Charles Hardy watched Lord David leave the bedroom before turning back to the brandy carafe and pouring himself another draught. He drank it in one mouthful and wiped at his face with one of Lord David's old silk handkerchiefs. He folded it fussily and pursed his lips into their habitual tight line and moved about the room with his usual quick way: tidying, straightening, smoothing the bedlinen, laying out a clean nightshirt. And how, he thought, would you be doing without me, you fine fellow? Lucky I don't need women, I'd say, he told himself. Lucky I don't.

He pulled crossly at the unused side of the bed where once Lady Blanche had occasionally slept. He was glad that the days were long past when he had sometimes come upon her making up to her husband.

'Shameless hussy,' he muttered. 'Shameless!' And with a last look about the room, tidied now to his satisfaction and newly warm from his built-up fire, Charles Hardy went his dancer's way back to his own room beyond his lordship's gun store where he kept himself very comfortably in a manner not unlike that of Lord David himself, with fire and kettle and fine nightshirt.

Lord David, leaving his valet to his tidying and hearing the clink as Hardy served himself a second brandy, turned into the long corridor where the lamp he took up threw shadows along the pictures from his grandfather's collection. It was sometimes his habit to linger there on sleepless nights and study the masters by the dim light. He had once had a fancy to paint himself but had failed to put in the necessary study. It was into Liscombe itself that his time and energy went. The Liscombe life was the one he had been born to and one day Harry would follow.

He was at the last picture on the south wall, by

Sarah's room, when he heard a distant shriek sounding from East Tower. It must be Harry, he thought; the girls were too old to cry out like that. He went through the service door and up the back stairs. All was quite still from the schoolroom floor but a murmur of voices came from the nursery. Harry was not then past the nightmare stage.

A fire burned in the nursery grate and through the open door to Harry's bedroom, he could see the girl. He had learned that morning that Sarah had taken his advice and appointed the Tranter girl as the new nurse-maid and had deluded himself that he had climbed the stairs to see his son and not this girl who would take the taste of Blanche away. She was sitting on the bed and holding Harry to her.

'But the dancing bear's been saved by the man,' he heard her say, 'he's been brought over here from Canada and he's happy or he wouldn't be dancing, would he, Master Harry?'

'What's all this about the dancing bear? Has the picture been giving him nightmares?' He walked through into the light from Harry's lamp and saw that what he had waited to confirm was really so. She had a remark-able face, softly beautiful with a perfect oval form and in it dark blue eyes. He felt himself smile. He had wanted it to be true.

'Oh, your lordship!' Kate stood up, pulling her shawl about her nightgown. She had the same intense, startled look that he remembered.

'I used to have nightmares about that picture when I was a boy.' He laughed, watching her face. 'I was full of pity for the poor thing. I used . . .'

'Then if I may say so, your lordship, it's hardly sensible to let the boy suffer as you did, and hardly kind either.' The lamplight made blue shadows under her eyes. By

Jove, he thought, she is beautiful and she has pluck. No one had spoken to him like that since he was ten years old.

'No sense in it, you think . . . er, Kate, isn't it? Kate Tranter?' He knew her name very well, had learned it the day after her arrival.

'Yes, your lordship.' She seemed to bob a kind of curtsey to him in her bare feet.

Harry stuffed several fingers into his mouth and leaned his head against Kate. Lord David saw that his son was frightened.

'It's all right, old chap. Papa isn't cross. I'll have the picture taken away, Kate, if you wish. You're right, of course, only I had never thought of it. You know how it is, family tradition, things are just left as they have always been.' His voice seemed to hang foolishly in the air.

Kate said nothing, staring back at him as Harry did, waiting for him to speak again. That look she has, he thought; she has intelligence, there's no doubt of it. She is judging me.

'And . . . er, is there anything else? While I'm here, although of course you may always speak to Lady Sarah or Mrs Baker if you need anything.' There was purity there too, and honesty. A sudden picture of Blanche's artful face made him shudder.

'There is something, your lordship, and I have spoken to Lady Sarah and Mrs Baker. They say it has always been like that but I don't see why it should be.'

'Yes?' He saw her rub one foot against the other. She must be getting cold but he did not want to leave. It was pleasant standing there in the lamplight and the warmth from the fire and this girl with his son.

'It's the mutton, your lordship. Every day he is given it, and he hates it. Mutton is far too fatty for a child. We would never have it at home, not for young children, sir.'

Lord David could see the shape of her body under

her gown. She was slender as a reed and stood beautifully tall and straight. He would not release her yet, though he had not the right to stand over her and look at her as if she were Sadie. What was he about?

'Oh?' He felt a warmth about his loins and was ashamed.

'Yes, your lordship.' Kate had to go on because he did not answer her properly. 'Children should have eggs and vegetables and a little fish without bones. My father grows vegetables if we have enough garden. You need vegetables to keep healthy and strong.'

'And where did you learn such things, my dear? At school?'

'At home, your lordship. Mother knows what food we should have. If there is enough money to buy it, or if we have chickens and a pig and garden.'

'Perhaps we should ask you to manage the Hall for us then, Kate?' He felt himself laugh and was ashamed. He would let her go now. 'Very well, then, you see Mrs Baker and Cook and order meals as you would have them at home. If there were money enough and chickens and so on. Will you do that?' He saw her nod. Harry still had the fingers in his mouth and was looking at him with horror.

'How are you, my boy? Doing well at your sums and writing?'

'Yes, Papa.' Harry pushed his head farther into Kate's nightgown.

'I'll come and see you again another day.'

'Yes, Papa.'

He heard the murmur of their voices as he left. They were no doubt glad to be rid of him.

'You were very brave, Kate,' Harry whispered, looking up at her.

She hugged him. 'Shall we take the picture down now? Shall we move everything about and have it just as we want it?'

'Oh, Kate!' Harry jumped off the bed. 'Let's lift it down ourselves, but not to put it right away. Someone must see him sometimes, the bear. I do not want him to be lonely.'

'We'll put it at the top of the stairs where he can see us coming and going. He won't be lonely.'

They moved all the pictures, putting Harry's favourite fox one at the foot of his bed as near as possible to where he lay.

That done, they were too exhilarated to sleep and Kate put the kettle on so they might have one of their talks and Harry could free himself of the fears and dreads of his short life.

They sat by the fire, Kate in the chair with her arms around the boy's thin frame.

'No one speaks to Papa like you do, Kate.' His head lay heavily on her shoulder and his Liscombe eyes began to close. 'Shall I really never have mutton for luncheon again?'

'Never again, darling, it's to be hoped.' She put both arms about him and stroked the dark hair that was so like his father's. 'I shan't give in. I shan't let them tell me it's always been mutton in the nursery. I shan't.'

Her voice went on, soothing Harry, but her heart said: I have seen him, he has looked on me and does not remember about the cart. He cannot remember about the cart for he has smiled and spoken kindly and not frowned as he did that day.

His face was not the angry one he was supposed to have, around Liscombe, as the servants said. He had smiled at her and at his son and his face was different, without the dark shadows in it. And his eyes were not a cold grey as she had thought but almost blue with his smiling. His eyes were a blue-grey that changed with his mood.

The next day she crept early down the back stairs as soon as it was light for it was to be her afternoon off. She was in the kitchen before Letty for the milk and porridge for nursery breakfast. That had been her first innovation and no one had bothered to question it. Frank no longer carried cold porridge along the basement corridors and up two flights of stairs. Kate made it herself over the nursery fire, and toast too, holding yesterday's bread up to the flames on long forks. She liked their breakfast together, liked to see Harry's cheeks flush with food and warmth. She felt, making Harry well and happy, that she was in charge of her life. She felt a kind of freedom and rejoiced in it, though she missed the kitchen life and the fascination of watching Cook turn ordinary things into extraordinary dishes. When Harry was to go to school, she might ask to go back to Cook, who was willing to take her. She had lent her the new cookbook by Mrs Beeton that Kate had once longed for and sometimes let her try her hand at dishes in the quiet afternoons.

'Goodbye, Kate, don't be late.' After church and luncheon, Harry stood at the top of the nursery stairs and waved goodbye to her. Daisy and Lulu and Mademoiselle, dressed to take him for a walk, laughed from the bottom of the stairs, on the schoolroom floor. But Harry did not mind their laughing and thinking him a baby. Kate knew it was a kind of courage and admired him for it, though she wondered how she would toughen him enough for him to go to school. He must not show emotion in front of other boys. Her brother Billy's experiences at school had taught her that.

'I shall expect you to be in bed and asleep before I get back,' she called and ran on down the stairs towards the kitchens, thinking already of home and Johnny.

'Here!' Martha, the schoolroom maid, was clattering down the stairs behind her. 'Did you get to hear yet whether it's true, about the divorce, Kate? Surely you must hear something from the boy, and his lordship's been up, hasn't he?'

'How could I know, anything, Martha? And as if such a thing as a divorce was likely with their sort. Harry knows nothing and I don't want you going asking him, neither. They don't speak hardly to him anyway, as you very well know.' Kate swung round the last banister and began to run along the basement corridor.

'I hear as how you been telling his lordship what's what,' Martha called behind her.

'I hear as how you ent got enough to do, Martha Dewbury.' However could downstairs gossip have spread so quickly?

She passed into the kitchen where the remains of upstairs luncheon were being cleared away.

'Any news, Kate girl, about upstairs?' Cook, standing at the big table, called out to her. Kate stopped, as she always did for Cook.

'I know I'm upstairs, Cook, but I don't know nothing. I'm not real upstairs, am I?' She put a finger mechanically into a soufflé bowl and licked it. 'Any one of them footmen or maids must know more than me. I don't hardly see Lady Blanche, and she's only spoken to me once. She said, "Take the boy away", just as if he was a pile of dirty sheets.'

'There's no accounting for the way gentry treats their kids, girl, I ent never understood it, so don't you try.' Cook passed Kate a spoon. 'Here, taste this lemon pudding I made this morning. Now you tell me what's in it, aside from the lemon.'

It was half an hour before Kate was out in the open air and could run with the warm breeze on her face down the hill to Stone Cottage and scoop up golden Tommy cat and let Floss lick the skin from her.

'Any news, our Kate?' Mrs Tranter was standing in the doorway with her most hopeless look. Around her, her flowers were spreading; sweet pea tendrils reached up along the window-sill of the kitchen and into the geranium pots. 'Any news of our Johnny?'

'I think he'd come straight back here, Mother, if there was any chance of him coming back. He wouldn't go up to the Hall now, would he?' Kate took off her shawl and led her mother into the kitchen. She had to clean that and sweep out the bedrooms, see to the washing. Her mother did not seem able to turn her hand to anything since Johnny had run away.

'Tell your mother to stop her fretting.' Will Tranter sat with his Sunday pipe by the kitchen fire. 'The boy can look after himself. He's a smart one, like I taught him to be. He'll get on for a bit, then he'll find he'd rather be at home where he belongs, and he'll come back with his tail between his legs then go back up there and ask for his place back.' It was a long speech for Mr Tranter.

Kate stirred the fire and filled the kettle. 'You sit down, Mother,' she said. 'You can have a rest now I'm here.'

'Heard anything about them divorcing? Cook run down yesterday and said it were all about upstairs. Them's been rowing and the footmen have heard the word divorce,' Susan Tranter whispered, watching her daughter move about the kitchen.

'Yes, Mother, but I don't really know nothing.' Kate felt suddenly tired, as if she could sit in her mother's chair and sleep the day away. 'Where are the kids?'

Will Tranter shot a look at his wife. 'She've sent 'em off down the village again, looking for him, as if he'd be strolling about down there. Foolish, ent it?'

'He must be somewhere,' Kate said, pouring tea for three at the table. 'And probably not far, either. What if I were to walk as far as Dorchester later, Mother, and call in at the police station?'

'It'd take you a fair time, girl.' Susan Tranter's face brightened. 'But there must be someone somewhere as have seen him.'

Kate flew about her tasks and felt recharged. She would be doing something practical and active, instead of mulling it all over yet again with her mother.

Of course, Kate found no one who had seen Johnny. It had been a hopeless thing to do, but they had taken a description of him at the police station. Afterwards, she had been lucky for the village carter was on the road from town, bringing his wife back from a Sunday visit. It was therefore only midnight when she stumbled, with both heels blistered under her boots, back along the stream towards the lamplight she could see burning from their kitchen.

Her mother was waiting at the open door, Kate could see her outline. Her poor mother was waiting for Johnny who would not come, who perhaps would never come home again. But it was not for news of Johnny that Mrs Tranter was standing there. She had news of her own and it was for Kate.

'Hurry up, girl,' she was calling out to her before Kate had passed Home Stables. 'His lordship's waiting up at the Hall for you. The boy have gone. Master Harry's bin took.'

*

Kate stood before Lord Liscombe in his study overlooking Liscombe Valley. A few stars glinted beyond the blank of the window where he stood, watching her.

'Did Master Harry ever say anything to you about going with his mother on holiday?' The shadows of his face moved and changed in the flicker of lamplight. The room was warm. All about the walls were silver cups and the heads of dead deer. A long silver fish in a glass case was fixed over the desk where one of the machines that sent the sound of voices over the air sat amongst a scattering of papers.

'Well? You have a voice, I know. I have heard it, haven't I?'

Kate saw him move across the room towards her, past his male things, trophies of hunting and shooting, business things that she would never have any part in. 'No, your lordship,' she said, 'not once.' She could hear the soft fall of his boots as he paced the carpet and came and stood before her. She could smell his cedar scent and his cigar. A drift of smoke was being caught up by the lamp.

'Did he ever speak of his mother?' She saw there was no blue in his eyes now, only a hard grey.

'Only sometimes, when he worried that she would be cross with him at tea time when I took him down to her.'

'She was often cross with him?'

'It seemed so, your lordship.' Kate thought: And so was this man, his father, and angry with her too, for leaving Harry. 'He expected people to be cross with him, but I never was, not once, and I am so sorry to have left him, even to go home. He never wanted me to go home and leave him.'

She felt weak tears begin and forced them back. She was tired and worried for Harry, but she must not cry before this man. He was so close to her that she could see the fine dark hairs that grew along his arms below his shirt sleeves. 'The boy lived in fear,' she said. 'I had only just got him to sleep without calling out. How a boy of such a young age should be so frightened of life, I cannot understand.' She forgot her need not to cry and this man standing before her and spoke out, for Harry's sake. She could perhaps still do that for the boy. But he took away her growing anger for he smiled at her, a tired smile that seemed to fill his face with sadness.

'Yes, yes,' he said, 'you were doing very well with him, Kate.' He stood very still before her, looking down, dark in the lamplight. Kate felt she could hear his breathing as she could hear her own. She looked past him and towards the window. She thought he must hear her nervous heart beating. It seemed to be a long time before he spoke again. 'He'll be in a fine state of nerves, when we do find him.' He moved away from her and Kate, with relief, interrupted him: 'Yes, your lordship,' she said eagerly, 'he'll be very nervous and he . . .'

'And he'll need you, so I want you to come to Paris with me. I have reason to think my wife might have taken him there.' Kate heard his words with a start of shock. His lordship was to take her abroad.

'Hardy!' she heard him call.

Charles Hardy, waiting soundless and attentive in the corridor, led Kate from the room. At the bottom of the stairs she found her voice. 'Charles, I haven't been to France before. However shall I manage? His lordship is to take me abroad.'

'I been all over with him,' said Charles, 'I'll see you're all right.' Charles, with his light voice and pale looks and soft skin like a woman's, could be trusted. Kate felt she would have to trust him. The knot in her chest relaxed. She was going overseas. His lordship had chosen to take her with him across the sea, like an upper servant. She was going to travel on train and boat, across England, across the water, with him.

Soon the black leather bag Mrs Baker had given her lay beside her bed packed with a print dress for when Master Harry was found and her mother's second-best black silk from her younger days when she was less stout. Mrs Tranter's black hat with the rose and her own Sunday cloak from church days lay at the foot where she and Letty, woken too, had put them. They both lay sleepless, talking of a France they could not imagine.

The lamps of Liscombe Hall shone out down the valley all that night, for hardly anyone slept. Mrs Tranter sat watching the shadows move to and fro across the Liscombe windows as clothes were found and folded and messages went up and down the back stairs. Lady Liscombe had run away with the boy and his lordship was fit to bursting! Divorce, shame, scandal was in the air. Mrs Tranter imagined the whisperings and the running about and nursed to her breast with her golden sleeping cat, the shameful excitement of it and the memory of her boy Johnny, out there somewhere lost too with no one to hunt after him.

CHAPTER SEVEN

Seeing Kate Tranter at Dorchester station in a blue cotton dress, seeing the way she held her head high under her boater, as if she were not afraid though her blue eyes said she was, Lord Liscombe thought: She is not like other girls. There is no false girlishness about her, no little exclamations. This was the first time she had seen a train at close quarters, there was no doubt of that, and she quite frankly stared at the throbbing monster billowing its steam out.

Kate watched Charles Hardy for he would show her what to do. And he, Lord Liscombe of Liscombe Hall, watched Kate Tranter and felt himself lifted from his usual boredom with travel and reluctance to leave Liscombe.

He went so far as to walk down through the second-class carriage from his own first- to the third-class compartment where Charles and Kate sat amongst other servants, sharing the Liscombe food hamper.

He felt foolish then, and looked it, he thought. All the servants' faces turned towards him, shocked to see a gentleman in their own place where they were allowed to take off their hats and be themselves and talk of their masters and mistresses with cynical pride.

'I was wondering whether I might have a glass of brandy, Charles,' he said, and had to repeat it for no one had heard him over the roaring of the train. Kate Tranter did not look up at him so it had not been worth it.

He drank a glass of brandy he did not want, alone in his own carriage, where he then had to pretend to be asleep to avoid Sir Henry Bassett who had caught sight of him passing and would want to bore him again with the problem of his gout.

All through the change of stations in London and getting into the boat at Dover his eyes were on Kate. He had to go to some trouble to manoeuvre himself to see her flush with bewilderment at the London traffic and with wonder at her first sight of the sea. He almost fell overboard leaning from his first-class section to see her walking with Hardy and pointing up at the seagulls, waving goodbye to the cliffs of England.

He told Hardy they would share a cab at the Gare St Lazare and when he was placed opposite Kate, she would not look at him. He asked her, ignoring Hardy fussing over their hand luggage: 'And what did you think of the train and the sea and the boat then, Kate?'

'Oh, marvels, your lordship. Things I have read about but not thought to see yet, not for years. I shall write home and tell them all about the noise of London and the carts and motor cars and the great train and the sea. No one has ever seen the sea, at home. I should like them all to see the sea, just once to see it.'

'Perhaps they will, one day, eh?' He had been right, he thought, she had imagination and enthusiasm, a taste for life.

'I am going to work so that they will, your lordship.'

He laughed out loud for the pleasure of hearing her say such a thing; she had ambition too. He had never known a girl with ambition beyond marriage and its safe haven. He was ashamed of himself then, for she looked down at her gloves, cotton he saw, and grubby from the journey. There were little tufts at the fingers from wear. He felt his heart constrict to see her worn gloves. He could not remember ever feeling so touched and by such a simple matter as the gloves she wore and her boots, polished and repolished by the look of them to something that was hardly still leather. The hem of her dress had been clumsily sewn. He imagined her fingers working at the mending by candlelight; it was probably her only dress while he would like to pile silks upon her and laces and the finest jewels and put pearls about her neck. He wanted to say to her 'Look at me' so that he could show her he knew of her mending, of her worn gloves and that his heart turned over for the pity of it.

He rolled with the jolting cab and saw the curve of her full cheek and straight nose as she looked from the window to the streets of Paris, and not at him. There was a sweet upturn to her mouth and her eyes would melt the heart of a savage. He must stop staring at her for there was a flush about her skin that told him she knew.

Kate, watching the elegance of the Paris streets passing, the trees and the handsome horses, finer than those of London, dancing along with arched necks, could not store up the sights and sounds and the new smell that France had to recount later to her mother and Beth and Letty for his eyes were upon her. She shared the small space of the carriage with his lordship and Charles Hardy, and felt his lordship's eyes upon her and her poor dress, and knew that he was wishing he had brought a better-dressed servant with him, that he was ashamed of his son's nursemaid, in Paris. In the carriage, there was the scent of his cedar cologne that was now familiar to her, and his long legs stretching across in their gleaming boots. He held his hat upon his knees and looked at her. She dared not so much as glance to the seat where he sat for fear that she should meet his glance and feel again the shame of the day on the cart.

*

124

'Charlie, I think I should like to go home.' Kate walked up the servants' back staircase at the Hotel Edouard VII in Paris with the valet. If she had travelled alone with Charles, Paris would not be spoiled for her.

'Don't go all Dorset on me,' he said, 'there's nothing to be afraid of, you'll soon get used to it, and anyway you can't go, his lordship says he wants you here so you're here.' He seemed to be bent double under the weight of his own small suitcase.

'What is it, Charlie?'

'I don't feel too good, that's all. Just keep going.'

At the top, both breathless, Charles gave Kate her key. 'Go and wait for me in there,' he said, 'I'm going down to his lordship and then I'll fetch you for our supper.'

Kate took her key, hardly hearing the words Charlie spoke. 'It does smell different here, doesn't it, Paris? I can smell a kind of cigar smell, and is it coffee do you think?' She gazed unseeing down a long dark corridor with sets of doors leading from it. Since the cab journey, she wanted to find reasons to dislike Paris, to be afraid of Paris.

'And the voices, the way they speak . . . isn't it strange and gabbling? And the people do seem dark and small somehow, and their faces are different. I did not think I should ever live through anything so strange. Charlie, are you all right?' Kate put down her own bag and took his arm. 'I'm sorry, Charlie, I didn't notice, I was so excited.'

Charles Hardy, whose face had taken on a pale sheen, pushed her away.

'I'm all right. Take my bag with you, I'll just get on down.'

Inside the room which held only a high bed with an odd assortment of bedding and a hard bolster for a pillow, Kate gazed from the window until it was quite dark and she could only see, below her, movement from the pools of light beneath each street lamp and from the great sweep of light that beamed from the hotel main entrance. She had watched the carriages come and go and pass each other with clattering wheels, she had watched the ladies' pale hats seem to float along the pavement. Now it was dark and Charlie had not come for her, she did not know what to do. She could not find the courage to leave her room. How could she go about a foreign hotel by herself? Hunger and thirst finally made her ease the strange door lock aside and step into a dim corridor. Charles's room number was 362. She had remembered it. He had simply forgotten her briefly, or was still changing his clothes, for he had clothes to change into. It would be all right. When she found him she would ask him to take her for a cup of tea. Although her mother had told her they drank only coffee in France, she now suddenly longed for tea.

Only one person passed her, a serving person dressed in black and with an oily face; he smiled at her as Albert had used to, but she slipped by him and knocked on door number 362. She knocked twice more and listened, pressing her ear to the door. A kind of groan seemed to be coming through it. She turned the handle because she could not go back to her room to be alone again. Charles was lying amongst that strange billowy bedding with the hard bolster for his head and he had been very sick all over it.

Because she had to, Kate ran all the way along the corridor until she found a door which had no number on it, for that would be a service room, Charles said, and there was a modern brass tap, which she turned and some sandy water spurted out. Kate took up two buckets and a mop and what seemed to be a towel of sorts, there was no one to ask if she might, and ran back to clean up Charles's room. She left a bucket by his bed, for the valet was still moaning and sweating, his pale face paler than ever in the candlelight and his pale wispy hair stuck in tendrils about his ears.

Now she had the worst part to do, for Charles said she must go downstairs to the servants' dining room, or find another English servant, and ask to be directed to his lordship's room on the first floor. His lordship must not be allowed to wonder where his valet was and why his dress shirt had not been laid out properly.

So it was that Kate found herself on the first floor of the Hotel Edouard VII with the soiled hem of her good blue dress trailing into rich red carpet. She had to stand before his lordship and speak to him.

She was startled when he answered her knock though there was no one else to answer when Charles was lying upstairs ill. She had the sense to curtsey and look up into his face where the grey eyes looked back into hers.

He seemed both surprised and amused for his mouth turned up into a smile and his eyes seemed to lighten. She held her breath, waiting to be told to speak.

He leaned forward and back, rocking on his heels, considering her, listening to her tale of Charles and sickness.

'Well now, do you think you could valet for me yourself, Kate? I am sure you could do anything you tried to do.' He was smiling at her. The lamplight behind him made a halo about his head.

'I do think as how I might, your lordship,' she said. Surely she could do anything now she had come this far into the unfamiliar and had faced him, looked up at him and not seen disapproval there but a smile that touched his eyes.

He led her through a sitting room where everything seemed to be white and gold. There were gold curtains caught up with gold tassels and she could see the fuzzy glow outside from the gaslamps. The walls were white with a tracing of gold and on the bed was a white and gold silk spread. Lord David sat at a little white table and said he was writing out her duties.

'You can read, Kate?'

'Of course I can, your lordship. At school they wanted me to be a pupil teacher, I was in the top class for three years.' Remembering Miss Otten, Kate pulled back her shoulders and stood up straight. Miss Otten said you should face the world and never be afraid of it.

'A pupil teacher, eh? And why did that not happen?'

'Because they are paid even less than a maid and Mother would not be able to manage with our two youngest still to bring up.'

'Ah, I see. And would you have liked to become a teacher, Kate?'

Lord David went on writing with a distracted air. Perhaps he was only trying to be polite. Kate felt herself shiver with nervousness.

She was alone with him. The two of them seemed, in this muffled gold and white place, quite alone in the world.

'I think I did, once, but now I think I should like to be a special kind of cook that makes the best kind of things. They have their own sitting room and they earn £50 a year. I should like to send my brother and sister to a proper school where they should learn something so they didn't have to be servants.' Kate twisted her hands behind her back and hesitated. There was silence and, to fill it, she went on: 'Or perhaps, since I am already upstairs, I might work up to be something higher, though I am not sure what, for cooks do earn most of all.' He was drawing out her most private dreams. 'Your lordship,' she added lamely.

128

'You want to be something high up like a cook and you want a good school for your brother and sister,' Lord David repeated. He laid down the gold pen and looked up at her, smiling. Kate gazed at his hands on the desk. He had long thin strong fingers with dark hairs like those at the back of his neck. He rose and came towards her. Kate heard the tiny ticking of a clock. He was there now, before her, with his thin fingers holding out the list and his fine pale face leaning down to her, the grey eyes heavy, looking into hers. She saw the strong square shape of his face and his mouth drawn down. 'We shall always find work to suit you and your family on the estate once you become one of us.'

'Yes, your lordship.' Kate gave a curtsey and took the note.

'As for schooling, Lady Sarah has in the past sent a gifted child to the grammar school. I shall see. Go and have supper now. I'll have some sent up with Hardy's, and some brandy for him. Tell him not to move until he is well, for you will look after me, won't you?' He smiled his sad smile and Kate nodded again. 'Come back after your supper and get my things ready for bed. It's all on the list. I am sure we shall get on splendidly, shan't we?'

So Kate became a gentleman's valet. His male silk shirts and his fine suits, his hats in their boxes, were now briefly hers in the gold and white room. They smelt of his cologne and tobacco and seemed to hold his presence even when he was not there. She was glad to have so much helped her mother with the dairymen's whites for she had learned to fold and care for clothes. She folded and brushed and breathed in the scent of him; she fingered his cedar cologne bottle and the Euchrisma hair dressing he used and his leather box that held the cigars he smoked in the evenings. In his bathroom, she took the top from his bath oil and touched a finger in it. She turned on the brass taps for the pleasure of seeing hot water burst out.

In her letter home, she described the gushing taps to her mother. 'One day, Mother dear, I hope we shall have such a marvellous thing. Imagine, there would be no more buckets of water, no more copper boiler.'

She did not say that she spent most of the day in Lord David's room for she thought her mother might find that not quite proper. Kate herself thought that perhaps it was not, for moving and working amongst his things with the scent of him always there, it was as if she knew him, as if, almost, he was as familiar to her as her brothers for she had his buttons to sew on too and there had been a little tear in the cuff of a shirt. She knew the way his hair grew just as she knew the way all the Tranter men had a tuft of hair sticking up at the crown. She sat in his room, waiting to hear his step in the hallway which would be the signal for her to run his evening bath and it was as if she had some close personal connection with him. She almost said once: 'And has there been any sign of Harry today?' when she knew she must wait for him to speak first.

Harry and Lady Blanche had twice been seen in the city but she knew she must not ask directly anything at all for she was a servant. But she was glad to see him and to wait for him to speak. His were the only English words she heard apart from Charlie's. All the other servants seemed to be foreign and the nights, in the dark attic room, were long and lonely.

On their fifth evening together, Lord David watched Kate move about his bedroom. She had, he thought, such a sweet way of holding herself, with her eyes kept firmly down on her work with his clothes, brushing and folding. Sometimes she would glance over at him as he sat at his desk, pretending to write. He had letters to attend to; the French telephone system was a mockery, but that night he found himself lingering over them, when he might have been out at the Duchesse de Vuillemin's making himself known, so that Blanche would learn he was in Paris. Someone in their circle knew where she was and it would only be a matter of time before one of them gave her away. He had only to be patient, and meanwhile he watched Kate. It seemed to him, in the odd circumstance of their coming together, that he would never want to watch anyone else, no other woman, no Sadie nor any Blanche. The night before he had dreamed of her again; her face and her eyes had been smiling at him and she had lain her cheek against his and, in his dream, he fell soundly asleep with an intense feeling of joy. Suddenly the desire to feel her cheek against his, where the skin, he knew, would be like silk, was so strong that the words blurred before him and his hand stopped on the letter to his land agent.

'Kate.' He put down his pen and turned frankly to watch her fold down his bedlinen and lay out his nightshirt. Such intimacies on the part of a girl were wifely ones; he should never have begun it. He should have seen to his own clothes. He was paying for his folly now. His body was overcome with an ache of desire just to leave his seat and walk over to take her in his arms. And he must never do it.

'So you want to be a special kind of cook, eh?' His voice, to his own ears, seemed strangely far away.

Kate laid his blue silk dressing gown beside the nightshirt and smoothed the bedsheet. 'I don't want to be at the bottom of things, sir. I want to be something more even if I have to work very hard for it. I think I want to be in charge of things. I liked being in charge of Master Harry, I felt I could make things better for him. Cooks are in charge too, and they make things for themselves, that come from their own heads. Cook is willing to teach me how to do that, as I told you, your lordship.' Kate gave an unnecessary pull at the turn of the sheet. His voice seemed different. She turned round to look at him at his desk but he was coming towards her across the carpet where his boots made no sound. In the lamplight, his face seemed filled with shadows, under his eyes and about his mouth which was drawn down as if he were in pain.

'Sir?' she said. She put out a hand towards him. Was he ill? His eyes seemed very bright and they were looking down at her as if he needed help. 'Sir?'

'Kate, of course you shall have a place as cook. I shall see to it, I promise. Come here and tell me what you really want.'

'I think I have told you, sir.'

Suddenly, he took a last step towards her and took her in his arms and held her against him. He thought: I have been waiting so long for this. He said: 'I only want to hear it all again, Kate, for I . . . I . . .'

Kate stood very still. Lord David had put strong warm arms about her and it did not feel wrong although it must be. It was a dream. The warmth of his arms seemed to fill her body. She could smell the lavender scent from his shirt; the silky ruff of it was against her cheek. She felt she would like to lay her head on his shoulder. She felt overcome with the need to lay her head there. Her body trembled and she knew she must not. She lifted her head very slowly; it was hard to make any part of her move. His eyes, that had always seemed so intensely grey, had a black rim about the iris and his eyelashes were long and black. She felt herself sway towards him.

Then he began to kiss her. She could feel the rough skin where he had not shaved and the hardness of his mouth on hers, and though she whimpered he did not stop.

Lord David felt himself flooded with joy. I should stop now, he thought, it is wrong, I am wrong. And it is right, it is what I have searched for without knowing, the feel of this girl's body and knowing she will love me as I love her. That I shall not be alone any more. His fingers were trembling on her lovely lovely skin. He took off her camisole and she stood quietly against him; he could hear her breath. He cupped his hands under sweet little breasts, he could just see them in the dancing light from the gas lamps, and when he leaned down to kiss them, she did not move away.

Kate felt she could not move, that this man and the extraordinary intimacy he had forced upon her was what her life was going to be; she would not be alone any more nor have any fears for he would hold her.

He heard his own breath coming now, panting, rasping for her. He tore down the skirt of the dress and the cotton petticoats and the thick drawers that made her seem so young but still it did not stop him. He carried her to the bed with her black boots still on and unlaced them, tearing at them, all the time wanting to stop, knowing he should stop, and still she said not a word.

Kate could not speak for he had taken charge of her body and she had given it up to him.

She lay back into the pillows and she felt him run trembling hands down her naked body and into her most private places. She waited for them to reach her breasts again and found herself leaning up to meet his fingers and his lips.

He knew that he should release her, even now, that he should stop but the gentle beauty of her face against

133

the pillow with her big dark eyes growing darker and the sweet welcome her body gave him, made him only pause. He did not want to stop but he wanted to speak to her, he wanted Kate to speak to him.

'Kate, Kate dearest.' His breath was coming very fast. 'I love you, I think you are the sweetest girl, I think I cannot not love you.' He cupped a hand about her face and ran a finger over her lips which were swollen from his. 'Could you love me, a little?' He put both arms about her and hugged her silkiness to him and buried his face in her hair.

Kate felt her body would not allow her to answer. She could not speak or move. She wanted only more of him, she wanted him to hold her tighter and put his mouth back into the secret places.

'I cannot stop, forgive me, Kate, I must . . .' It was the way her lips swelled and parted as his hands moved about her and his mouth searched again and again for hers, that made him go on. He tore into her finally until he lay panting and spent with his face pressed into hers and shameful tears coming that he could not stop because she put one silky arm about him and said: 'Do not cry.'

The painful joyful thrusts of his body into hers, each one making her gasp with pain and with pleasure, had stopped. Her body burned. Where he had entered into her, his place now, burned. And he was sobbing. She put her arm into its rightful place, about him.

'Forgive me, forgive me, Kate,' he said. What had he done? And it was too late. He had not cried since he was five and he was sobbing into the arms of a girl because he loved and needed her and had waited so long for this joy. 'I have waited to love you,' he said, 'so long.'

Kate held her arms about him and gave way to the

warmth of her body where nothing now could ever matter but this man and his body so intensely linked with hers.

'We are not alone any more,' she said. There was pain now where he had entered into her. 'I am glad.' The heat of their two bodies wrapped about her. Under her hand there was his skin and the rough feel of the hair on his neck that she had so often watched when he had been at his desk and she had hardly dared move about the room for fear of disturbing him. She need never feel that again. She would never disturb him. This man would always need her and would always comfort her and they would always be together.

Half sleeping now, she murmured: 'I did not know love could be like this.'

Pressing his damp face into the line of her neck, he said: 'It is only just begun for us, darling, and there will be no end to it.'

They awoke together, still entwined as morning began to lighten the uncurtained window. He said, 'Darling!' and caught her up and lifted her from the bed to carry her naked into his bathroom. 'Our first day!'

For him, it was decided. He had slept deeply, healthily, and woken to find that she had not been a dream. He felt twenty years old again, only when he was twenty he had not known Kate.

Kate, as the sleep left her, let him lower her into the bath and turn on hot water. And he put his long legs into the water before her and poured in the cedar-scented liquid that he always used and had always meant to her that he was near. She, who had rarely looked down upon her own nakedness, now saw his. He had long muscular legs with dark hairs like the hair upon his arms. His member, that had entered so fiercely into her, had black hair about it and there was fine dark hair on his chest. She felt herself flush at the heat from the water and this other intimacy.

'Kate, Kate, Kate!' Lord David put out wet hands to her and reached his legs about her hips. 'See how close we are, entwined for ever.' He was laughing and took up his sponge to lift the scented water over her breasts where the nipples rose and hardened. Kate felt the night's warmth begin in her loins and her lips seemed to part of themselves.

'Ah,' he said, 'ah,' and grasped her wet body in firm fingers so that it all began again and they were still lying together, damp and scented on the bed, when the waiter knocked at the door with the breakfast tray.

Outside of the love-making, it became difficult for them both. He made her take coffee with him, sitting by his side on the sofa, she in his nightshirt, and he in his breeches, and when she rose to lay out his clothes, he had to make a joke of it.

'We shall do it together, Kate,' he said, catching at her hands to make her look at him. 'Forgive me for making it so sudden. I should have talked to you first, we should have first become close with talking. Only I was taken over by you, I could not help myself.' He gathered her up to sit on his knees and held her cup so that she could drink again. 'I shall make it right for us, for you, do you understand?'

'I do not know, sir,' she said. 'Oh, what shall I call you? How can it ever be, you and me? What have I done?' She felt suddenly cold although his arms were still around her and she could feel the warmth of his long legs. 'What have I done?' She watched the laughter in his eyes change to concern. 'Oh, I don't want to hurt you.' She pressed her face into his. 'I don't want to see you stop smiling at me. But now it is morning I cannot understand how it will be. I did not think, until I went to put out your clothes as before. What shall I do, now, today, and what shall I call you, and how shall I tell my mother?' She gasped with the thought of having to tell her mother what she had done.

'I know, my darling, and it is all my fault, making it so difficult for you. Of course, your mother never need know, we shall sort it all out, but you are not my servant any more, or at least,' he paused to kiss her face and neck and the curve of her breast, 'only in love.'

Kate saw the love in his eyes, the way that his face turned in to hers said that he loved her, how his mouth and his arms and his body said it.

'I can hardly believe . . .' she began.

'No, it is hard to believe for me too. I can hardly believe I dared to touch your hand even, darling Kate. But I did and here we are and I am enchanted and overjoyed and our lives will never be the same again. I shall work everything out. Today you must just wait for me.' He buried his face in her breasts, opening up the buttons of his shirt that she wore. 'I have an appointment with the police commissioner. He seems to have a scent of Harry and Blanche, and I must leave you for a few hours. You are worth a hundred of her, you know.' He lifted her up and took her to the bed. He found her camisole and petticoats amongst the bedclothes and helped her dress in them. Piece by piece, as she dressed, he saw her take on her old self and her hands seemed to tremble as she reached the blue dress.

'Kate.' He pulled the dress around her and caught at her chin. 'Don't grow away from me, not now that you know my heart and my body. We are to be together. That is all you need think about. And this dress now. I see you look at me touching it. I know it's not what you deserve and I know you feel awkward in it, with me, don't you? Tell me, you do, don't you, Kate? Look at me?' She was fumbling with the neck of the dress and would not look at him.

'Actually, I love this dress.' He was laughing, helping her with the buttons at the back. 'Because I first saw you in it, sitting on the cart, and it was all dusty.' He held her against him. 'I longed to buy you silks even then, I think.'

'I remember the cart and the dress and you looking at me,' Kate said. She sat down on the bed and saw the faded cotton around her and remembered the day on the cart. 'You looked so disapproving and I was ashamed.' She felt suddenly weak, remembering that day and wondering how it was that she had come to this remarkable moment, when he loved her and was helping her to dress. She stared at the rich carpet and remembered her different self, at the bottom of Liscombe Hill. He was kneeling before her now. He was on his knees and his handsome dark face had only laughter in it because he could not understand how it was for her to be taken into his world.

'Ashamed!' he said, kissing her hands and her wrists where the stuff was worn. 'You ashamed before me! I am hardly fit to clean your boots.' He was still laughing. 'But I cannot clean them now, I am late. Just wait for me, dear heart.'

He was gone. Kate fumbled with the neck of the blue dress. She felt cold. Her legs would not move. She could not lift her arms to dress her hair. She was not the same. Only no one need know.

She must make herself pick up his last night's clothes and brush them the way she had perfectly well before and fold his nightshirt. Only now there were two and she had worn one of them.

Whatever should she do now? Kate turned about the room and heard herself give a little whimper like a sick dog. Whatever would her mother say?

Her knees trembled and her body was as weak as if she had been ill. But she had only been wicked enough to let his lordship love her. She saw him now, again, as his lordship, for what else could he be to her? She picked up his suit, the suit he had been wearing when he had first caught her up so joyfully in his arms. She had given him that, a night of joy, with her. Now she must suffer for it. His face, when he had first looked at her, after his first kisses, she would remember all her life. She would always have that memory to hold in her heart and all the days to come would not take it away.

She managed to go upstairs to Charlie's room.

'Charles?' He was still asleep, snoring quietly but looking better, less pale and sickly. He had eaten some bread and taken tea from the breakfast tray.

'Charlie, you must get up today, please.'

'What is it?'

'You must get up. I cannot valet for his lordship the way you do.'

'I thought as how you was doing well, girl.' Charles sat up. 'Did he say as he needed me?'

'Well, he kind of did,' lied Kate, 'but he is going out all day. You've only got to get ready his evening and night things.'

'All right,' groaned Charles, 'I suppose there's no peace for the wicked. And there's me thinking a girl could manage. Should have known, I should, as no girl could.'

He was pleased, Kate could see, to think that his lordship could not manage without him.

'So you'll see to him this evening then, Charlie?'

'I suppose I must.'

'Thank you, Charlie dear.'

But now what should she do?

Kate walked back down the corridor to her own

room and lay down under the coverlet with the hard bolster pressing into her undressed hair. It did not matter, her hair did not matter nor anything else, not now. She would lose her place, even if Master Harry were found, she could not go back to Liscombe Hall nor ever go home.

She felt so cold that once she rose to put over herself her shawl and her mother's black silk dress and the print one too. She could not stop trembling.

Last night, she had not been cold. She had lain in Lord David's arms, and his hands had felt along her body and into her most private places and her skin had burned with pleasure.

She had not wanted him to stop. She had let him. She might have been a puppet. She was wicked. Her nipples warmed with the memory of the way he had kissed them and it had not then been shameful, she had wanted more of it. Now she must pay, she knew. Girls must almost always pay, her mother had told her. She would have to pay first by losing her place and then what would become of her?

Her mind and her body seemed to have become suspended in a kind of half-sleep and she lay in a daze of bewilderment and fear until she heard a knock at the door. She rose stiffly and put stockinged feet to the cold floor. Lord David came in before she had found the strength to move across the room.

'Darling! Whatever are you doing here? I thought to find you ready and waiting for me. I thought . . .'

'Charlie is better, your lordship, he says he will take charge of your clothes.' Kate looked up from her feet to his face, smiling at her, full of joy to see her. His dark maleness seemed to fill the space in the room. She would never get away from him; she could not want to.

'It cannot be, sir,' she said, quickly. 'Oh, how can I

go back to Liscombe? How will my mother manage without me, and shall I never see them again? I am so ashamed!' The tears felt very hot against her face and the floor under feet cold. Her knees were trembling.

'Darling, don't worry, I shall sort everything out. You are in my charge now, you and your family, I shall look after you all.' He took two steps across to her bed and put his arms about her. 'Why are you trembling, my sweet? Don't you see what I can do for you all?'

Kate trembled still and pushed weakly at him. 'But they will know I am a fallen woman, they will know my shame.' She tried to put up her hands to wipe away her tears.

'Shame, darling? There is no shame in loving.'

'You know there is, for you and me, you know.' She fell back on to her bed, sobbing. 'You are a married man. I am a servant. Nothing can change that.'

Lord David wiped her face with his handkerchief and lifted her up, pressing his face against hers. 'I was wrong, my darling, I know, to take you as I did, but I have been so unhappy and lonely, and seeing you there about me, I just . . . loved you and thought – or rather did not think, I suppose. Come, we'll go back to my room and have supper and tomorrow we'll get you some clothes and you can go about with me, we'll see Paris together. You'll love Paris, Kate. It's a place for lovers like you and me.'

In the familiar room where Kate had been happy tending Lord David's clothes, Charles Hardy moved softly about, laying out the evening shirt. The lamps were lit on the gold and white walls and a fire burned in the grate. From the open windows came the sounds of Paris night life beginning, carriage wheels and horses waiting and the calls of the cab men. Hardy looked up at their entrance, showing, Kate saw, no surprise.

'Hardy, go up to the servants' floor and bring down Kate's bag, will you?' Kate felt herself flush from her feet to her hair.

'Certainly, your lordship.' Hardy moved away from the bed and passed before them, silently, across the carpet, his mouth in its habitual tight line.

'Glad to see you up and about, old chap.' Lord David winked at his servant.

'Yes, your lordship.' The door closed behind Hardy.

'Now, darling, it will be difficult, but we'll manage, won't we? You'll have a new life with me.' Lord David put a strong arm around Kate and tried to turn her about to face him.

'Charlie . . . knows?'

'Of course, darling, but he is used to it and is always discreet. Don't mind Hardy, it's part of his job.'

Kate let herself be led to the bathroom and he turned on the taps for her and took off her dress. His long thin fingers felt warm at her neck and his mouth burned her skin where he kissed her breasts and the marks at her waist where her petticoats had been. He kneeled before her, taking off her stockings. Kate could see his thick dark hair and feel the roughness of it as he laid his face into her thighs.

'Don't tremble so, darling, it will be all right, don't you believe me?' He put his arms about her legs and put his face on the silky skin of her belly. Kate took a sharp intake of breath.

'No,' she said weakly, 'it cannot be, whatever will my mother say? And why is Charlie to know? No one must know.'

She protested no more for the strength of him seemed to take her into his charge. She thought, letting him lift scented water over her shoulders as she sat in his bath: It is too late. I cannot fight him.

It was Lord David who took the black silk dress from Hardy and helped Kate into it, laughing at the waistline where the bustle had been.

'You shall have the latest modes, darling, we'll get them here in Paris.'

He left her sitting at his dressing table to take his own bath and Kate used his hair brush to dress up her hair. She looked at her face, it was the same and yet different for her eyes seemed bigger and she could see her mouth open slightly where the breaths she took were coming so quickly. The last time she had seen herself was at Liscombe, with Letty, when they had put up her hair together and Letty had made her see how pretty she looked in the little square of looking glass.

'Letty!' Kate murmured to her reflection. Letty must never know her shame. She would never see Letty again, or home, or Liscombe, or any part of her old life. How would her mother manage without her? Charles Hardy moved about the room behind her, still silent, and Kate sat as silent, waiting for Lord Liscombe to take charge of her again.

He came from the bathroom with only his breeches about his waist and sent Hardy away. 'You shall help me button my shirt, my own darling, come here.'

Kate did not look at herself again but moved across to the bed to the man who must now manage her life, and sat beside him obediently, buttoning his shirt.

'We shall eat here tonight, darling,' he said, 'I've ordered dinner to be sent up to the sitting room.' He kissed her neck as she fumbled with his cuff-links. 'I have ordered the most marvellous things for you to taste, my darling, I shall teach you about so many things.' His mouth travelled across her cheeks and against her mouth and under her eyes. 'You wanted to be special, didn't you. You wanted more than a servant's

143

life. I can give you that. And we shall love each other, shan't we? You do, Kate, don't you, love me just a little already?'

She felt herself forced to look into his eyes, the grey heavy eyes that seemed to draw her to him. 'Yes ... no,' she murmured, 'No, I want ... to go home. Please sir, my mother needs me.'

'Of course you don't want to go, darling, our life is just beginning. You don't need home now, or only for visits. I can do more for your mother than you ever could, believe me.' He wrapped his arms around her black silk dress and Kate felt weakened, helpless. She did not have the strength to fight. Her body would not allow it. She was under his control and another night only confirmed it.

CHAPTER EIGHT

In the department store, Kate stood miserably amongst rows of clothes with Charles tugging at her sleeve. He had been told to see that she was properly dressed, for his lordship.

'Choose something,' he said. 'Go on, choose something and take it into one of them cubicle places. Go on.'

Barely seeing, or caring, Kate put out a hand towards a garment that seemed to be made of grey woollen material; it did not matter for all of this new life of hers was wrong.

'*Non! non!*' A dark little woman in a black dress glided towards Kate and shook her head. '*Ce n'est pas la taille de Madame,*' she cried.

'Us anglaise,' Charles said.

'*Ah!*' The woman began to smile and gesture.

'It's too big, she says, try another.'

Kate smiled and went along with the woman pulling her towards the cubicle. Charles said she must hurry and she would. She did not know how to choose dresses; she had never had any choice before. The woman helped her out of the black silk dress and the black hat with its rose and did not seem to flinch at the sight of Kate's thick petticoats and camiknickers. She insisted that Kate should take a bluebell-coloured silk dress that had a slim straight line.

'*Belle! Belle!*' she cried, and twirled Kate about before the looking glass. Kate saw a beautiful girl looking back at her; the girl had her face but could not be her.

An hour later, Kate found that Charles had paid for

four dresses, two in wool and two in silk, and a two-piece suit in heather tweed. There were hats to be chosen too, it seemed, one for each garment. A dozen or more saleswomen had appeared. Kate sat before a row of looking glasses and allowed them to put upon her hair hats of their choosing. There were hats of all colours and shapes brought from drawers and taken from wire models. Cries of delight came from the women. Kate smiled and nodded and watched her own cheeks grow pinker as, finally, a display of underwear was brought to her and she had to indicate her choice of it. Tearfully, she held up two fingers to indicate two cream silk camisoles, but Charles nudged and held up five. Kate felt her own thick garment hot and itchy against her skin and remembered the repeated mending of it at home by her mother. She longed to be at home where everything had been simple and the same and her dreams were safely in the future.

'This cannot be for me, Charles,' she whispered, for there was no one else to say anything to.

'He says you got to have it so you got to,' Charles sniffed. 'You got stockings? Ladies always have silk ones not them cotton things you got on. Then there's boots. Do you think you can go about with them servant things on your feet?'

At last it was over. Kate, outside the store doors, gratefully breathed in Paris air and watched the horse-drawn cabs clop their way noisily past. A faint smell of horse reached her, a country smell which said home. 'I cannot go back home, can I, Charles?' she said. He was her only link now with her old life.

'What, with everyone knowing your shame? Course you can't! You've done it now, you have.' He held up an arm for a cab. Kate watched him supervise the packing into it of her new wardrobe and felt no resentment against him. She felt she had become an object of shame.

Lord David found her standing before the gilt looking-glass in his bedroom in the dark bluebell-coloured silk dress the sales-lady had so wanted her to buy. She had put up her hair and stood, a slender column wrapped in blue, her eyes startling against her dark golden skin.

'Darling!' He caught her up in his arms. 'I knew you'd be even more beautiful in the right clothes. Look, look at yourself.'

'I think I have looked at myself enough today, sir. Before, I never saw myself at all.' Kate felt his skin cold against her from the evening air outside; it was hot in the room, always too hot for her. She put her arms about his neck and he put his lips to her breasts where the dress revealed them. 'Am I right now, sir?' she said. She slid to the floor and turned herself again to the looking-glass.

'A beauty,' he said, standing behind her. 'A lady, from your glorious hair to the tip of those lady's boots.'

Kate looked down at her feet shod in dark blue leather as soft as gloves. A cold feeling of horror suddenly lodged in her chest. These could not be hers. These were not her feet, in these alien boots. She must have black servants' boots upon her feet because that was what she was born to.

'Kate, what is it?'

She drew in a deep breath. 'I am wondering what my mother would say to see me and my boots,' she said. She could not tell him the truth for he would scoff at her and try to wipe away her fears with loving.

'There'd be no one so proud as your own mother to see you so beautiful, Kate.' He stood beside her, looking at them both in the glass.

147

She looked at his reflection beside hers and knew that nothing he could say would begin to reach across into her world. He could not see, now, that her mother would die of shame to see her daughter dressed in silk by Lord David Liscombe.

'Come on, darling, stop dreaming.' He took off his jacket and let it fall to the floor. 'I'll have my bath and we'll go out on the town. A lady doesn't have to stay at home in Paris.'

Kate picked up the jacket and took it to the wardrobe. She was not a lady, but she was not a servant any more. And after this room, this time, in Paris, what would she become?

As the days and nights passed, Kate struggled to find a balance between her old self, worrying for her future, and her new self who had found love and joy in her own body and his. She could not tell whether she was fearful or happy, whether she blamed or blessed the man who had so changed her life. In her letters home, she spoke of Harry not found, of the streets of Paris, of her walks in the parks with Hardy, and waited for the porter to bring up her mother's to her, recounting Liscombe days and life in Stone Cottage. She could not believe that she would never go home again, nor how it would be if she could.

She asked Lord David again one evening when they dined in the hotel suite, for he wanted to sit closer to her than a public place would allow.

'I want to gaze at you while we eat, sweetheart, and not be interrupted by waiters. Shall we have . . . what shall we have? What would you like?'

Kate chose stuffed quail and raspberry soufflé and put on her blue silk dress to please him and dressed up her hair with the new mother-of-pearl combs he had chosen for her in the rue de Rivoli on one of their walks together, looking for a glimpse of a boy like Harry in a sailor suit and an English maid like Mary. Lifting up the hair, seeing her own flushed face and swollen lips that he had bruised with his kissing, she had a sudden sense of foreboding, a sense that today, or soon, something would happen. Seated before him with her untouched vichyssoise soup, a scented golden pool, she heard herself ask what he hated her to ask and it seemed inevitable that she should again, this very evening.

'What is to become of me after this?' She saw his look of joy in her and love change. He almost took on his old expression, with its angry look about the eyes, but he laughed too and said: 'Dear Kate, don't spoil tonight. Paris is our secret, most joyful time before we meet the world again. After this, we shall go to London together, and ever afterwards we shall be together except when I have to go to Liscombe.'

'And I shall not be able to come to Liscombe with you nor go on my own.' She watched the face she loved and knew better than her own go on smiling. He reached out a hand to touch hers. Kate looked down and saw her own hand beside his on the white cloth. She said: 'Look at our hands.'

'Why?' He laughed and covered hers with his long tanned fingers.

'The difference between us, is all there, in our hands.' Kate heard her own voice come very loud and fast. 'Look at mine, so red and cracked still though I have done no work for days and days. I always had to work, washing and scrubbing with soda. All my life since I was six I have worked, and you take up my hand as if it were just like yours, nice to touch and warm and smooth, when you know it is not. You pretend not to

149

notice because you love me but you should notice, you should, because all the difference between us is there and you do not want to admit it. You want to be blind to it and you want all this to be real when it is only a dream, and even my dreams have always been of work, so I cannot begin to understand yours, you see, and you cannot begin to understand mine nor the fact of my red hands which will not go away.' Her voice seemed to echo around the gold and white room and there was no other sound.

'All my life my hands have been in water and soda, they have scrubbed and cleaned and mended and cooked and they will always be red because all my life there will be work and it will go on and on and for people like me it is always like that, and you cannot begin to understand.' She was crying. The tears were slipping easily down her face and through them she saw his eyes change from laughter to concern and then astonishment. He stood up opposite her and held out his fingers that did not work. 'See your hands,' she said, 'look at them beside mine.' She held out her own hands, though they trembled, and put them beside his. 'Look, that is the difference between us, and all our talk of love is nothing for it can never be possible and I must go home where I belong.' She sat back in her chair and he came to kneel beside her.

'Darling, I cannot tell you how sorry I am. How could I be so clumsy?' His arms reached about her waist. He put his face into her breasts and said again: 'I am so sorry, Kate.'

It was some time before she could speak. He went on holding her and waited. Once the tears were over, he thought, they could talk and reason away the difference between them. He would have to be patient and less clumsy. His love made him carefree; he no longer thought before he spoke and he felt all of himself was open to Kate. Soon it would be the same for her. He loved her enough to make it so.

'I have always hated being poor,' she said, turning towards the window over Paris and the sky which was darkening now into night. 'I thought I could work my way out of it, for myself and for the others, but the highest I can ever be is cook or lady's maid for I cannot stay here with you.'

'You can! You can, Kate. It is enough to love as we do, and everything else will come out right. What does convention matter? Are you really concerned about social differences?'

He hugged her to him though her face remained averted. 'What does the world matter? You'll have no worries. I'll set up your family, the boys will have an education and your sister, school and so on, whatever you want for them. My money can buy that, can't it? And why shouldn't it, eh? Won't it be exciting, Kate? We'll go back soon and start changing their lives. Maybe there's a way of getting you home, say I've got you work as a governess here or in London and then you can go home in your new dress? Eh, darling?'

'But your money can't make it proper nor right between us. There will always be my hands and the way I speak and everything that is wrong and different between us. And everything *is* different.' Kate sat stiffly in the chair and would not soften in his arms.

'When I first saw you,' he said, 'I thought it is not right that such a girl should be so ... well, obliged to sit on a cart like that. I spoke of it to my friends at dinner and they said it was not right either.'

'You spoke of me then? Did you feel sorry for me? Did they laugh?' Kate looked down at his face and the tenderness in it, now so familiar to her, that she could not go on seeing each day of her life. That had only been a dream and she had woken from it. 'Was it because you found me pretty?'

'No, no. I was not just being male. I thought that, of course. I also thought you looked fine and intelligent and pure – unlike Blanche, I suppose. I followed you about and caught glimpses of you, and you know the rest. For ever after I have been obsessed and entranced with everything about you.'

Kate pushed him away and stood up. 'No, it can never be and I had better go home and somehow begin my life again. My mother cannot manage without me. And what about Liscombe? Who must know there? And what about Lady Blanche?'

She felt quite cold. 'You must understand, as I have, that it is all impossible. I cannot become what you want.'

'Kate!' He stood up to grasp her to him and she turned back to look into his face. It was very pale. His mouth was drawn back in its old tight unhappy line. Her heart seemed to turn over. She let him take her in his arms and lift her towards the bed. 'Never the end, not for us,' he cried. 'Other people don't matter, and especially not Blanche!'

They talked through the night. She told him all of her life, from her first memory of her mother in childbirth to the moment they left in the cart for Liscombe and their meeting at the bottom of the hill. He in turn, offering his life up to her, recounted his own past, his pious and gracious mother and his longing to leave his books, Treeves teaching him to clean a gun and the endless Latin lessons when the sun shone on Liscombe Hill and he was not allowed out; his solitariness, his loneliness in his marriage with Blanche. He left out nothing. She sipped champagne and put her hands up to touch the skin around his eyes where his unhappiness had used to show. He had been unhappy, as she had. He had yearned for what he could not have. He had not been much loved. She would love him as he had never been loved. She had the power to fill his face with joy and take away the anger. Could she have been willing to throw it away?

'I could weep, darling, when you touch my face like that. As if it weren't ugly.'

Kate held his head between her hands and looked into his eyes. 'I used to think it almost ugly,' she said, 'with crossness, and then I found I could change it. It changed when you loved me.'

'Nothing else matters, Kate. We will work it out, between us. As long as you don't say it's the end of our being together. I thought my heart should stop then. I think it did stop.'

Their loving, towards dawn, was the most joyful they had known, from the new understanding they had of each other.

The next day, Lord David sent Kate to the English bookshop with a list of books she might consider buying for herself; he had put *Pride and Prejudice* on the list ('Your pride and my prejudice, Kate!'), *The Mill on the Floss* and *Middlemarch* for the strong women described in them, and *Little Dorrit* for her to cry over. He was going to teach her himself about books and music and painting. It was to be part of their growing together.

He was writing to his London bank, asking them to release funds for the purchase of an apartment for her, when he learned he was to receive a visit from his wife. He had just time to put into his pocket the hairpins that Kate had left on the dressing table when Blanche was there, sweeping into the suite in the way she always did.

'If you divorce me, I shall never give up the boy!' were her first words. She threw herself on to the sofa in the sitting room and knocked to the floor the bowl of roses near it.

'Blanche, control yourself!' Lord David watched water seep into the hotel carpet. Whatever happened, he would have no more of the turbulence Blanche liked to arouse. 'You know you have no feeling for the boy. You never noticed what that nanny was.'

'Your precious heir to Liscombe is my son too. I love him. I want him about me. I want to see him grow up.' She arranged the skirt of her rose-coloured dress about her knees and tilted her Leghorn hat. Lord David sighed. He longed to be alone again with Kate. He put his hands into his pockets and turned his back to Blanche. He would let her go on, burn herself out, and then perhaps they could begin a discussion about her settlement.

'Nanny was a niece of my own nanny. She begged for a place for her. What could I do? She seemed all right. Why do people put on me so? The boy seemed all right with her. Your sister Sarah is supposed to see to the children, anyway. I have too much to do already with the entertaining we do.'

'It is you who want to entertain, Blanche,' Lord David said mechanically. They had trailed through this kind of conversation many times. 'And Sarah told me she asked you to dismiss the nanny years ago, and you refused.'

'Of course your sister is more important to you than I am! I've always known it . . . and wretched Liscombe. A house more important than me!'

She went on. Lord David turned again to pace the room. He must get Harry back first. All he had to do now was get the police commissioner on to her next movements.

Blanche saw him smile to himself. 'You won't see the boy again!' She shouted and stood up to pin more firmly her flowery hat with its deep rose flowers beneath the brim. She strode across the room with a dramatic flourish.

Lord David watched from the window his wife's hat descend the hotel steps and disappear into a cab. Within a few seconds he had made his telephone call to the police chief.

Charles Hardy, arriving at the hotel steps with a supply of his lordship's cedar scent, heard a voice calling from a fine carriage waiting there.

'Charlie!' Lady Blanche's maid Mary was leaning from the cab and waving. 'Fancy seeing you in Paris.'

He went to the carriage window. 'You got the boy? I tell you, he ain't pleased about all this.'

'No . . . that is, I'm not saying. Her ladyship's up there now with his lordship. I can't say nothing, you know I can't.' Mary held on to her boater and leaned back into her seat.

Charles slipped up the hotel steps and chose a place in the shadows behind the porters' lodge. He did not think he would have long to wait, and within a few minutes there she was, walking crossly towards the door.

'Your ladyship!' he called and slid from his hiding place. Their conversation was brief and soon Hardy went back up the hotel staircase with his lordship's cedar scent under his arm and a smile upon his face.

It seemed that the police had not been quick enough to trace Lady Blanche when she left the hotel and Hardy chose to tell no one that he knew where they were staying, under false names no doubt. He had decided to bide his time. On her return, Kate, delighted with the purchases made on her own, did not notice the irritability that Lady Blanche had caused in her husband, and demanded that they begin the process of unpacking her books. She had almost decided she should start on the new novel, *Tess of the D'Urbervilles*, because it told of the Dorset she had known all her life. Kate sat beside David on the sofa, fingering the leather and the fine silky pages of the books, breathing in their smell. He sat with *Tess* and flicked through it, his mind preoccupied with the question of whether he should tell Kate that his wife had paid him a visit.

'This is considered rather daring, Kate. I wonder if . . .' He was interrupted by the arrival of a page who passed him an envelope on a silver tray.

'Kate!' he cried, reading it. 'It seems that Harry's been found. This note's from some lady friend of Blanche's. I don't recognize the handwriting but I believe she's been to Liscombe. Margaret Ponsonby. Probably been snubbed some time by Blanche. But, look, he's in Lyons. I must get down there.' He leapt to his feet. 'Help me pack, dearest. I'll be away a day or two.'

She ran into the bedroom for his bags. 'Poor Harry! How sad he must be and wondering what's happened. He will be so pleased to see you.' She took out his grey suit and three white shirts. 'How many suits will you take?'

'Just the grey and I'll wear this one.' He was in the bathroom collecting his shaving kit. He did not think to call Hardy for the task; he too had learned new capabilities, since Kate.

'And what shall I wear for Harry?' Kate stood with his nightshirt in her hands. 'Shall I wear my print dress? Shall I be his nursemaid again?' In the looking-glass of the wardrobe she saw her new self, a girl in silk and lace with hair upswept into glittering combs. She had no apron, no cap, no working boots, no symbol of her old self left. 'Harry will not know me.' She felt a tiny sense of panic returning and took a deep breath.

'Now Kate, my darling, don't you dare start that again. All that matters is that we love each other, we agreed that, remember?' He hugged her and threw his things on the bed. 'Quick, dearest, I think there's a train in an hour. I might make it if we hurry. I'll telephone from Lyons. Tell Hardy what's happened. And you must wait for me and think of me and be ready for me when I come home to you with the boy. I can see the three of us together. We'll keep him with us. We'll be a family, sweetheart.' He kissed her face and her mouth and shook her gently. 'And I don't want to see that sad look coming back. There. Smile, darling, for me, or I shall worry every second I'm away.'

Kate saw the tender concern in the face she loved, and smiled. 'Do not worry,' she said, 'I do not want you to worry for me, nor have anything more than Harry to think of. I shall remember, it will be all right.'

'That's it, Kate, that it *will* be. You promise to remember that?'

She smiled again to promise it and turned away to finish packing his things. He telephoned for a cab and there was no time then for any more but a kiss before he was gone.

Kate was alone in the strange muffled silence of the hotel suite. She sat again on the sofa with her books and picked up *Tess* and began to read. She would have to read so as not to think. But she felt cold. She rose again to put a shawl about her shoulders; she was often cold when he was not there, and in his absence old thoughts returned. Home, and her future, and herself with Harry.

When his lordship was with her, he drove away her doubts and her bewilderment. He made everything seem possible, with their love. But she had two days without him and she had promised not to worry. She looked down resolutely at the page but could not read. She needed something practical to do and walked about the suite, finding nothing to occupy herself. And there was the looking-glass where she saw her new self and the bed where they had lain in joyful intimacy. How his face had twisted with pain when she said it must end! She felt a twist about her heart, remembering.

She had two days to pass and no idea how to do it. She must leave the room and go up the hotel stairs and on to the servants' floor.

There were her old print dress and all the other signs of her old self: Mrs Baker's black bag and her black Sunday cloak, her good blue dress and her prints, her mother's poor black silk dress with the alteration at the back.

Kate closed the door behind her and took it into her arms to hold against her face. It smelt faintly of moth balls and the lavender bags her mother made. She could hear her mother's grumbling voice. The sudden longing to see her again made Kate gasp, but she put the dress aside; she must not stay here either for the memories it held. She must never need her mother again and her mother must not need her.

The knock on the door startled her into sitting backwards on the bed. No one could know she was there but Hardy and he would not knock, for her. His eyes always reminded Kate she had lost her virtue.

'*Entrez*,' she said. It was one of the things he had taught her and she had been delighted to learn. But it was not one of the French porters who opened the door. It was Lady Blanche, dressed in rose pink and with a smile upon her face.

'Good heavens, what a poor sort of place, my dear.' Lady Blanche, a little breathless from her unaccustomed climb to servants' quarters, closed the door behind her.

'I can quite see why you want to get out of this sort of life, but I'm afraid my husband is not going to be the one to set you up. Oh, no.' She smiled still and picked up the stuff of Mrs Tranter's dress between gloved fingers. 'No,' she said again, dropping the silk, 'not my husband. Though I'm sure, with your looks, you'll have no trouble finding yourself someone else. While you're young at least. And you're clever ... you have been clever to get to work so quickly, haven't you?'

Kate did not answer. She turned her head, almost painfully, back to look at the stained wallpaper. She could smell Lady Blanche's scent and hear the rustle of her skirts.

'Now,' her ladyship said, 'let's get down to business. My husband has sent me, my dear.' She opened the reticule at her wrist and drew out banknotes. 'He wants you to have this. It's enough to get you to London and into lodgings. You've only to set yourself up, though I'm sure I don't know how a girl like you can seem so innocent, waiting her time. And, of course, my husband fell for it! He always does, and now he doesn't know how to disentangle himself. Here.' She held out the bundle of notes. Kate stared at her hand in the pink gloves and the fine white paper of the banknotes.

'Whatever will your mother say when I send Mrs Baker down to tell her?' Lady Blanche put the bundle on the washstand.

'Oh, please!' Kate slipped from the bed and stood before Lady Blanche. She had found enough life in her to move. 'Please don't send down to my mother.'

'Why ever not? Do you mean to disappear entirely from her life? Surely the poor woman will want to know what's become of you. I thought you country people were supposed to be close.'

'We are very close.' Kate's face burned with the thumping of her heart. She had to find the courage to answer Lady Blanche, to do as her ladyship wished, so that she should not tell Kate's mother. A feeling of dread seemed to have settled in her chest. 'I do not want my mother . . .'

'Well, look.' Lady Blanche's tone was friendly. 'Look, my dear, Lord David has made a fool of himself. He's gone a little too far this time, he realizes that. And he's sorry, he says.' She gave a little laugh and walked across to the window with a swish of her pink dress. 'Men always are, aren't they! He gets carried away with his girls and then he gets tired of them and I have to sort it all out. He's a bit of a coward, you see.' She laughed again. 'He can't tell you himself but . . . he's sorry if he's led you to believe there's anything serious between you. But then you know there can't be, don't you? You're a sensible girl, really. You'll just take this money, won't you, and . . .'

Kate heard Lady Blanche's voice saying the things she thought she had expected to hear, that she had been waiting for someone to say to her. The voice went on but there was no need to listen any more. The feeling of dread in her chest had become a pain.

'We know how men are, don't we, dear?' Lady Blanche seemed to lean down and touch her lightly on the shoulder. 'He's sent the money for you, he wouldn't want you to be in any difficulties, and he's asked me to see you pack up your things. Then I'll have my carriage take you to the station. My man will buy your ticket and so on.'

'I have nothing to pack. That is, my dresses are not . . . I have nothing.' Kate heard her own voice finding words from somewhere.

'You'll soon find yourself clothes in London, there's enough in what he's given you. He's been generous, you'll find.'

'I shall take my print dresses for my next place,' Kate said. She picked up the black Liscombe bag and folded into it her old things and put over her arm the black Liscombe cloak. She would have liked to take off the heather-coloured fine woollen suit that she wore but did not know how to do so, before Lady Blanche. She had no hat or gloves. She saw her red hands holding the bag and cloak.

'Don't forget to put your money in the sweet little bag,' Lady Blanche said, 'and then we're ready, aren't we?'

'My hat,' whispered Kate, 'and gloves.'

'Ah, yes,' Lady Blanche hesitated by the window. 'You'd better run down and get them. Let me take those things and I'll meet you in the foyer. You've only a minute, though, for I have someone coming to see me in the suite in half an hour. Look, I'm putting your money in the bag. Run along quickly, do.'

Kate held out a stiff arm with the bag and cloak and Lady Blanche took them. They seemed strange against the rose-coloured stuff of her dress. Kate lifted her eyes and looked into Lady Blanche's face under the rose-coloured glow of her hat. Almond-shaped eyes were shining brightly back at her and the mouth was curved up into a generous smile. Kate turned away to the door and though her legs seemed to be trembling, they moved her down the servants' corridor and the black stairs to the first floor and along to the white and gold suite. Inside was the smell of his cedar scent and his cigars and the muffled silence that had once wrapped about them. She looked at nothing but her own new boots crossing the carpet. Inside the wardrobe were his things

beside her own but she looked at nothing save the hat
boxes, a row of three beside their boots. The lilac-
coloured one was in the centre box, beside the matching
gloves. She bent stiffly and took them out, fixing the
hat upon her head and drawing the gloves over fingers
that would now have to begin work again. Her boots
took her back across the white carpet she would not see
again. The skirt of her heather-coloured suit rustled and
swished. He had liked the colour of it; he said it brought
out the violet tint of her eyes that were mostly bluebell
blue but had a wash of something else.

Everything in this room had been a mockery.

Kate closed the door behind her.

At the hotel entrance, she heard Lady Blanche speak to
the coachman and pass him some money.

'He will buy your ticket and show you the right
platform, my dear,' she said. 'I hope you have a lovely
journey. And there'll be no word to Mother, promise.'
Kate saw her wave a gloved hand and smile under the
pink hat. She herself was inside the carriage without
knowing how she had got there. The cold feeling in her
chest seemed to have gone now. She could hear herself
breathing. Turning once at the window towards the
hotel steps, she saw Lady Blanche holding on to her
Leghorn hat and smiling very sweetly at her. Her mouth
seemed to be framing one word with the smile: Whore,
it was saying, whore. The word echoed in Kate's mind
as the fine-sprung carriage transported her through the
Paris streets and on to the Gare St Lazare.

With the word was his face, filled with love for her,
but it had not been love because he had asked Lady
Blanche to send her away. He could not do it himself.
He could not tell her himself. He had seemed to love
her and it had been betrayal and falseness. His love had

not been real but a mockery. And she had earned the shame that would follow her for the rest of her life. She had let her body and her heart love a man who was of the gentry and married to Lady Blanche and it had been a hundred times wrong because he did not love her. She was conscious, suddenly, of her body, moving with the throb of the carriage; every part of it he had kissed and touched. She had given up the whole of her body to him, shameless and weak. This body she must take with her for the rest of her life and it would always carry the memory of her shame.

She took his money from the black bag and pushed it between the carriage seat and its back. Someone would one day have a lucky find.

Blanche did not go back to the hotel. She had been cleverer than her husband imagined. Harry and her maid Mary were waiting for her at the Gare du Nord, whilst Kate was sent to the wrong station to avoid a meeting. Frightened by the foreign bustle, noise and smells, Harry and Mary were holding hands, a little oasis of England, surrounded by the eighteen trunks of Lady Blanche Liscombe. That day, she had said, they would probably continue their travels. Perhaps they would go home. She would have to see.

Harry and Mary, keeping close to each other, saw her arrive at the station. Her Leghorn hat with the deep pink roses came towards them through the crowd. Mama is smiling, thought Harry, but it's not a good smile. It was the hard sort when she would be very bright and brisk.

'I hope we are going home to Liscombe, Mary,' he said, clutching tighter at her hand. Mary was all he had to cling to now.

'So do I, dear,' she said. She had grown fond of the

boy. 'I am sure we are. I expect her ladyship has the tickets this very minute!'

And she had. Blanche Liscombe, followed by her cousin Betty who had married a French count, held a set of tickets to take them through to Liscombe. Betty's manservant carried a hamper of food from Fouquet's. Rage had made Blanche unusually competent.

Rage made her silent throughout that long day and night while Harry and Mary sat quietly side by side, watching her. She hardly spoke or looked at them, gazing out from the trains or at the moving seas from the boats, seeming sometimes to mutter to herself. From past knowledge of her, Harry and Mary kept silent too, hand in hand. At least, they each thought, she was not goading them, laughing at Harry's white face and fearful looks at the ocean, not shouting so at Mary with the eighteen trunks to see to at each changeover that the woman could not think straight.

The two of them finally found themselves following Lady Blanche, exhausted, into a hired carriage at a little port in Ireland. They were, she said, to have a holiday there.

The French police lost their trail at Dover; Blanche had been too efficient.

PART TWO

CHAPTER NINE

The journey from Paris took Kate forty-eight hours, much of it spent miserably on station platforms, but in London she found the courage to take charge of herself. Here she could ask the way. She could go calmly into the catering establishment at Victoria Station and order herself a cup of tea and a sugared bun; it was the first time she had ever entered such a place. After that, it was easy. She asked the way and walked to the house of her Aunt Bessie, number fifteen St John Street, off the Strand. She had often written the address for her mother and very suddenly there it was, a fine house several storeys high with an iron railing in front of it and area steps for servants to get down to the basement. This was her aunt's house, the only home she knew about apart from her own. It had a red door beneath a shaded porch with a red lantern.

No maid answered her knock, only an odd-looking man, very short and somehow almost as wide with a twisted face turned up into a grin. 'Yes?' he said.

Kate wondered if he were the butler, for he was wearing a black suit as misshapen as himself. 'Is this the residence of Mrs Bessie Villiers?'

'It is.' The man grinned at her and looked from her boots up to her hat. 'Turn around,' he said.

'I wish to see my aunt.' Kate felt her voice rise. Aunt Bessie was family and she needed her family, very urgently. 'I am not a servant come for a place.'

The man's twisted mouth turned up higher, and his left eye winked. 'No, not a servant,' he said, 'not now.' A long arm gestured to Kate that she should pass through the door into the hallway.

Everything inside the house seemed to her to be red, from the carpet to the chandeliers which gave a dim red glow to the red drapes which hung about the doorway and which must, she thought, lead to the salons and dining room. Even the walls had red stripes to them and it was warm, the air of the house was warm and scented. It was of a different kind of grandness from Liscombe, but it was grand even so, Kate decided. Aunt Bessie would be able to help her. She breathed in the scent and felt the warmth wrap about her. She had been cold for a long time, since Lady Blanche had burst into her room and she had known it was the end.

She watched the man limp along the red carpet and disappear and suddenly, Aunt Bessie was there. It must be Aunt Bessie for her face was like Mrs Tranter's. She was wearing a red dress, though it was only six in the evening. The woman in the red dress was advancing towards Kate across the red carpet and it must be her Aunt Bessie for she said: 'Kate? Kate Tranter?'

Kate held on to the reticule which had her last two pennies in the world and the figure approaching seemed to sway a little. It could not be her Aunt Bessie, not her mother's sister. This woman had breasts swelling out of a red brocade dress with a cluster of sparkly stones at the neck. She had frizzy hair in an Alexandra fringe which had been dyed a gingery red. There was red on her lips and a patch of something on plump cheeks, reddish powder in the lines of her skin. But her eyes were blue like Kate's mother's, only they had not that vague hopeless look that Susan Tranter's had. They were giving Kate a look of horror that must match her own.

'You had better come into my private quarters though I haven't long to spare you, not this evening.'

The man had not returned. Kate followed the figure

that must be her Aunt Bessie down to a basement area and into a sitting room which was a darker and grander version of their own. There was a table with a green chenille tablecloth on it and a plant in a pot. Brown photographs lined the mantelpiece and china ornaments stood on small tables. It was like their own parlour but more comfortable too for instead of a hard settle there was a pair of low armchairs before the fire.

'We'd better sit down,' the woman said.

Kate sat, hugging her bag to her knees. Everything was not going to be all right, but she would find herself a place somewhere. There must be somewhere for her. If only Aunt Bessie would seem a little more like family; if only the word 'whore' had not suddenly echoed in her head as she watched her aunt, so like her mother. How would she ever be able to face her mother again?

'Mother send you, did she?' Aunt Bessie, in her red brocade dress, picked up a fire iron with a plump hand like Susan Tranter's, but white and smooth and with rings on every finger. With a gesture like hers, she stirred the fire into life and pushed a silver kettle on to boil.

'Shall I make the tea, Aunt Bessie, if you're going to a ball?'

'I'm not going to no ball, my girl.'

Kate heard her sigh and sit back heavily, looking into the flames and not at her niece.

'No, Mother did not send me.' Kate answered the question that seemed to hang in the air. 'I am come to see if you might help me find a place in London.'

'In trouble, are you?'

Suddenly the woman looked sharply across at her. 'That's something I can help you with.'

'Not in trouble,' said Kate quickly, for she was not now, Lady Blanche had forced her out of it. 'I want to get on in the world, like you, Aunt Bessie, and have a grand place for Mother to visit and be able to send her money for the kids.' She thought it must be the first real lie she had ever told; now her whole life would be based on a lie.

Aunt Bessie looked into the fire. Kate saw a smudge of black under her eyes. She had make-up on her face like the stage actresses in her mother's magazines.

'London's no place for a girl like you. I'll give you your train money and you'd best be going back home. There'll be something for your mother too. I've a lot of expenses, a big house to run, staff and all. Things aren't going too well but I can manage it.'

'The house is very grand, Aunt Bessie. I shall write to Mother and tell her about it.'

'You just be careful what you write, my girl.' She was fingering her rings and pulling together her dress where the silky stuff did not quite meet over her breasts. Kate had never seen such a display before, only when she had helped her mother with her corsets.

'Well, you had better stay tonight and I suppose you had better write. She's such a worrier, our Susan. Just say you're well and safe in London, don't say where. Gideon'll put it in the postbox. Then we'll see about things tomorrow,' said Bessie, setting out two pink flowered cups on the chenille cloth. 'We'll sleep on it, things always seem different in the morning. I'll send some linen down with Gideon and you'll make up a bed on my couch next door. You can make up a bed, I suppose?' Aunt Bessie passed Kate strong tea. 'You must see to it yourself, I'm busy tonight.'

'Are you entertaining, Aunt? Shall I help in the kitchen?' Kate left her chair. 'If I could help, I should feel . . . better.' She suddenly felt very tired and longed to be at home and for nothing ever to have happened to her but school and home. She turned about the room with her teacup and sat again at the parlour table. She felt the cup rattle in her trembling hand. 'I could help you, Aunt Bessie, there must be a place for me somewhere.'

'Here, none of them tears.' Her aunt got up and passed her a red silk handkerchief.

Kate wiped wordlessly at the tears she had not known were falling. 'I'm sorry, Aunt Bessie,' she began.

'Here, we'll make up the bed together. You get some sleep. Everything will seem different then. I can see you've been through something, you tell your auntie all about it tomorrow.'

Afterwards, Kate remembered nothing more, only that she slept at the foot of her aunt's bed as if she would never wake up again.

Lord David was delayed longer than he planned in Lyons for the address he had been given as sheltering Harry and the maid was in fact a dwelling of ill-repute. There were girls within it and a house madam. It was, he thought, Blanche's little joke. He had no doubt that the letter was a false one and had probably been written by some friend of hers to her dictation. Standing in the doorway, seeing the madam before him with rouged cheeks and painted lips, he knew with a cold certainty that this was part of Blanche's plan.

He returned, running, to the station and from there began the first of his calls to the Paris hotel. But Hardy was not there, the staff informed him, there was no reply from his suite and the lady with his lordship had been seen leaving the premises in a carriage that had been waiting for her.

There was no return train until the morning.

He spent most of the waiting time on the telephone

and finally someone found Hardy who confirmed that he too had seen Miss Tranter leaving the hotel in a carriage which, he said, seemed to be waiting for her. No, he said, he had not asked her where she was going. No, he had not thought to follow her. Hearing the valet's quiet, familiar, suddenly sinister voice down the telephone line, Lord David knew that the man was implicated in Kate's flight.

'How much did Lady Blanche pay you, Hardy!' Rage flooded through him. If the man had been there, he would have beaten him. 'You're dismissed. Don't let me see you again.' He heard himself shrieking through station noises. But there was still no train until the morning. And then he had to steam up from Lyons in the slowest train he had ever known. The feeling of anguish that he had had to bear all the long hours was confirmed at the hotel. Her things, the dresses and the new hats and the mother-of-pearl combs, lay about like dead matter. She had gone. She had decided to go and Blanche had helped her. She had gone because he had shamed her. She had not been able to bear the loss of her virtue and her place in the world. She had not understood that his love would replace all the rest.

But it did not matter. He took in deep swift breaths to calm himself. He would have her things packed up with his and he would go home to Liscombe for she would be there. And he would very carefully and slowly make everything right for her. He would divorce Blanche, and after a decent interval Kate would marry him and they would live their lives out together, at Liscombe, and the intense joy that they had in each other would develop into deep love and no one would be happier than they.

If only he could hold her that instant and tell her all that! There was an empty space about him where she should be.

He stood before the wardrobe and took out her blue silk dress. He began to fold it, laying it out on the bed. He would pack what was hers himself; no one else should touch what was part of Kate. This silk had been wrapped about her, as his own body had and would soon be again.

When Kate woke, she thought Lord David was there beside her; just for a moment, the eiderdown seemed like his body warm against hers. But it was not he and never would be again. She got up from the couch in the cold room where the fire had burned out. Today, her second new life would begin. She must somehow face it.

In her aunt's nightgown, she walked through to the sitting room. The strange man, Gideon, in shirtsleeves and a baize apron, was raking out the ashes.

'She'll be wanting her tea,' he said by way of greeting. 'Best make it once this fire's heated and take it in. Then you'd better get yourself dressed if you're in for training.'

Kate washed and dressed in her travelling clothes; they were all she had now. Aunt Bessie still snored from the big bed.

With the tea made and her aunt wakened, Kate could only sit by the fire with her own cup and wait. She had twopence in her reticule and nowhere else to go. She could hear a clock ticking gently somewhere and from the street the sounds of carriages passing. There was only that in her head, the clock and the street noises; she must not think of anything else.

'That tea made?' Aunt Bessie appeared dressed in black silk and suddenly, in the doorway just for a moment, seeming very like Kate's mother. Only, when she moved towards the fire, Kate saw how much older she looked. There was patchy red veining on her cheeks, the skin sagged beneath her chin and the gingery red hair which last night had seemed rather grand, this morning looked as if it were perched upon her head like a wig. Kate had to pour two cups of tea before Aunt Bessie seemed willing to speak.

'You had better tell me what it is that has brought you, for if you'd come proper then our Susan would have written to me. She wouldn't let no daughter of hers leave home sudden.'

Kate drank the last of her tea, cold now, and watched Aunt Bessie's hand tremble as she raised her own cup to drink. It was so like her own mother, the way she drank tea as if she had had none for a week, that the story burst from her, from the beginning when they had moved to Liscombe through to the days and nights with Lord Liscombe.

'I don't know how I ever let it begin, only I seemed to be drawn up in it and nothing could make me make him stop. He seemed so to love me, he seemed so to love all of me, and I wasn't alone any more, working and worrying for Mother and having a dream that would never come true because I would never be able even to be a lady's maid and it would take me so long to earn just six shillings a week. I knew I would never have more than one good dress which must last me years, and I knew my hands would always be red and my dreams nothing. And he loved me and I wasn't alone any more. I didn't have that silly dream then because he was going to give me everything. And it was so nice, all of it, you see, and he became so dear. I could make all the anger go away.

'The other day, I told him it could not be between us, that it was all wrong. But he made me love him again. My heart turned over when I saw his face grow sad as it was before. It was all false, I know that now, but then I did not and it was so nice, all of it. I did not want it to stop. If he came to me now, I should run to him, I know. If he said just one word to me that showed he did not mean me to go away, I should go into his arms.'

Tears were running down her face and through them she saw Aunt Bessie fumble for a cigarette.

'If he came to me now, I should let it all begin again. I would not have the strength not to love him. I wish my coming here were a dream now, and his sending me away and Lady Blanche saying I was wicked.'

'Huh!' said Aunt Bessie. She took a taper from a jar by the fire and lit her cigarette. Kate had never before seen a woman with a cigarette. It was only one of the many things which were a wonder to her now. She felt overcome with weakness. She had not meant to say the things she had. She did not know what she thought or felt.

Aunt Bessie drew on the cigarette and blew out smoke. 'You won't begin again, not even if he comes here and begs you,' she said. 'And none of it was love, that's just nature's trick, that is, and we got to fight against it.' She blew out another puff of smoke. 'I got caught the same way and it's not going to happen to any girl of our Susan's. Better to be married to someone real low like your father and settle for that than go the way I went.' She threw her cigarette into the fire.

'Gideon!' The misshapen man arrived from nowhere.

'Got to take the new one upstairs, have I?'

Aunt Bessie stretched herself to her full height and said clearly: 'Miss Tranter is my niece, Gideon, and will be treated like she should. There won't be no upstairs for Miss Tranter. Get us some breakfast brought in. What are you standing about for?'

Kate refilled the kettle from the brass jug on the hearth, and Gideon limped back in with a tray that looked too big for his height though his long arms managed it well enough.

'You be laying up, this girl'll want feeding. First, I'm going to show her upstairs and it'll be the only time she sets foot up there. Come on, Kate, you're going to see what real life's like.'

Aunt Bessie led the way past a dark low kitchen where a woman was at work and up the twisting staircase the way she had come the night before.

'Now I'm going to show you something, my girl, just the once I'm going to show you, and then you'll tell me again what you found nice back in that bedroom, 'cause this is what happens to girls what finds things nice before there's a ring on their finger.'

They were in the hallway that last night had seemed so grand and warm and scented. It was dim and cold and the scent was of old tobacco and, faintly, urine. The red drapes had lost their glow and the red and white wallpaper which had seemed to be of satin had a dull yellow tinge.

'This is after, you see, Kate, after the nice. This is the real part of it all. Now, you come on upstairs.'

A drift of last night's perfume lingered here with something unpleasant underlying it. A number of closed doors led off the landing, each draped with a froth of dingy lace. One open door revealed the shameful lavatory with its rank smell and drip-drip of a leaking cistern.

Aunt Bessie opened a door.

'See this,' she whispered, and pulled at Kate's arm.

A young woman lay sprawled across a bed draped in lace. There was nothing else in the room but a hanging cupboard and washstand. The morning light, dim through a shuttered window, showed the puffed rouged face of the girl who might once have been pretty. She lay in a tangle of red hair and a nightgown torn at the shoulder, revealing heavy breasts with dark nipples. A putrid smell seemed to have its own thick presence in the room.

Kate backed away; this had nothing to do with her, though she had lain as shamelessly in his bed.

'Have a good look at it.' Aunt Bessie pushed her forward again. 'I don't want you ever to forget.' Kate looked about the room, bewildered. Now she could see that an empty wine bottle lay under the bed with broken glasses beside it. On the door of the cupboard hung a transparent gown and on the floor very high-heeled shoes painted gold. There seemed to be a heap of something dirty – garters, flowers, something nasty – by the wash stand together with a number of cigar stubs. The smell of it all made her reel and long to leave, not to see any of it again. Lady Blanche had thought she was a girl like this, or would become one. 'Whore.' She had mouthed the word at Kate.

'Now we'll see the others.'

Aunt Bessie opened each door and from them the smell of alcohol, urine, cigar smoke, sourness, hidden things, made Kate retch. On each bed lay a girl or a woman, abandoned to sleep, and not one of them stirred except the last who muttered: 'What is it, Ma?'

Aunt Bessie closed the last door and led Kate back down the two flights to the parlour which welcomingly seemed so much like her mother's.

'All that, what you've just seen, that's what would happen to you if you let that lord of yours set you up. Say that to you, did he?'

'Well, he said London. I could not go home, Auntie, not ever, not to Liscombe or . . .'

Aunt Bessie sat back heavily in her chair by the fire and poked at it with a fire iron. 'You don't need to tell me, not any of it. I can see it all. We'll get this breakfast eaten.'

Kate sat silently beside her aunt and chewed on toast and butter, grateful for it. She was hungry. Her last breakfast had been in the gold and white room and she must not think of that. 'Whore' Lady Blanche had called her, and how could she not have seen that for herself. Whore, Kate thought. She put down her toast. She could not eat. He could never for a moment really have loved her.

'You see, it happened to me.' Aunt Bessie suddenly spoke through the toast she had no appetite for. 'Oh dear, it do seem to have brought it all back.' She put down the bread and took up her tea cup. 'That Arthur Villiers, he did make me the same offer, you see. I never did marry him.'

'You're not married to Uncle Arthur with a job in a bank, Auntie?'

Aunt Bessie shook her head. 'I ent married,' she said. 'Nobody'd have me, girl, and there's nobody I'd have. Not now.' She threw a piece of toast into the fire. 'Not now,' she said.

Kate saw a tear slide down the worn skin of her cheek. And her mother had been so proud of Aunt Bessie!

'He didn't have no thought of marriage, that Arthur, only all them years ago, though you'd never think it, I was a fine figure of a girl. And he saw I'd fall for it, I suppose. He saw me that day in Dorchester and made up to me and I fell for it. I did think he would marry me once we was in London. I was that much of a fool. He set me up in a little apartment and put me to work, loving other men – friends of his, he said.'

Kate hugged her arms about her and could not believe he would have made her do such a terrible thing.

'Work like them girls upstairs have been working the night through. No doubt they all thought it was nice once too and it was some man as led them into it. I don't ask no questions. I don't like nobody knowing my own shame.'

'It wasn't your fault, Aunt Bessie,' Kate cried out and leaned over to put her hand on her aunt's knee. 'And it wasn't mine, was it?'

'Well, it was. I should have known better, and I'm going to see that you do too.' Bessie took another cigarette from her box and lit it from the fire. 'I got it all worked out these last years. I got plenty of time sitting down here of a morning. You know how I got myself set up here? That Arthur went off with someone else, younger of course, who could earn him more. The funny thing is he has a real passion for her, while she's leading him a dance.

'Now we women, as I see it, aren't at the mercy of our flesh. Or we needn't be, not like them. I started keeping my head a while back, watching and waiting, counting up the shillings, and then it came right for me. He went off and I been keeping my head ever since. One day I shall go back to a little Dorset village with a church and I shall have the vicar to tea and your mother will be proud of me then.'

'Oh, come back now, Aunt Bessie. Let's both go back. I'm not sure as I shall like London and we can be nice and simple like we used to be. No one need know about me if I tell the right story. I'll say it was Charlie who . . . I'll say something, that I had an accident and lost my clothes and you bought me my tweed. I . . .'

She felt a sense of panic; she must live now on lies.

'No,' Aunt Bessie said, 'it'll sound trumped up and lies is always caught out in the end. When you came I thought that was it. I thought Susan'll know now, but she won't, eh, not yet. And one thing's for sure – you're never to go back to that man, not if he comes begging. We'll write again to your mother. We got to be careful. No doubt he'll be writing to her too, or seeing her more like. He was responsible for you, in a foreign country and all. We'll write and say you run away to . . .'

'To make more money for home, to make enough to keep them all, we'll say that, Aunt Bessie. Say I saw the chance in a big city like Paris and decided to come to London and try my chances. I could do it on £50 a year, help them at home, if I became a high-class cook.' She must find her old dreams again and put away the memory of Paris as if it had not been.

'A cook, eh, is that what you want? £50 a year, you say? But it's hard work, girl, and hardly ladylike and it's no fortune.'

'I don't mind hard work, I'm used to that. I hardly knew how to pass the days in the hotel, waiting for him. I'm not used to being free. I'm not right for being a lady, I could not get it right for him.' There were sudden hot tears on her cheeks. 'It was all so wrong, all of it, and I cannot think now how it was, how I could have . . . If only none of it had happened.'

'I told you, my dear, it's a terrible trick of nature and we got to fight against it. And you got to remember, once you're up against it, to start planning for yourself, in a small way, like I did. You can't be going in for grand gestures that no one but you will ever know about.' Bessie poured fresh water into the pot and lit another cigarette. 'What about being some kind of business girl, working in an office? A typewriter they're called.'

'Do they earn well, Auntie?'

'No, perhaps not. Not enough anyway if you're to send back home to your mother.'

Kate pushed aside her plate. 'It has to be enough for that, you see, because I always meant to look after them. I always wanted to and planned to. Mother is always so tired with the miscarriages . . .'

'And that low father of yours taking his pleasure like all of them, I suppose.' Aunt Bessie drew crossly on her cigarette.

Kate shivered and hugged her arms. 'How can I have not thought of Mother? How could I not have thought that I could not go home again.'

Kate and Aunt Bessie talked through the next days, with Gideon joining in around the parlour table. It was he who suggested Kate should become a cook as she wished.

'There's a woman,' he said, 'what started off in the big houses, learning her trade, and now she's in London and has started up catering for others, like she goes into their places and does fine banquets and that. They do say she's cooked for the Prince of Wales many a time, and done more for him besides.' He winked at them over the green chenille cloth. 'And she's making a fortune. There's some people who'd go anywhere for a taste of her stuff. She uses all the best things – gallons of cream and things in layers in pies, surprising things.'

Kate said excitedly: 'The Liscombe cook used to put layered things in pies so that when you cut into them you had a shock. There'd be little birds wrapped in leaves, and inside the birds little balls of stuffing.'

Aunt Bessie and her manservant, for years each the other's only companion, watched the face of the beautiful girl who had come so suddenly into their lives.

'And in Paris,' Kate went on, 'there were cafés and restaurants and people were eating there dressed in the finest clothes. There were men dressed in black like butlers. They were so clever at moving fast round the tables. And the food came on silver platters like at Liscombe, like in a grand house, but ordinary people were there, paying, you did not have to be gentry. He took me,' she finished lamely. 'I went dressed in a blue silk dress and I guessed there was rosemary cooked into the lamb. It was all so busy and exciting. There were glass lamps hanging from the ceiling and velvet and gold on the walls.'

'You want to get set up for one of them places,' Gideon said. 'We'll help. I'll give you my wages, if you like. I got no need for money. I got all I want here.' All his life abused and ridiculed, begging on the street before Aunt Bessie had taken him in, Gideon gave himself up to Kate as he had to her aunt.

'No call for your wages,' Aunt Bessie said quickly, 'I got enough put by, for Dorset. She can have that, she can borrow it. Look, we'll both put something in to get Kate trained and you can pay us back, girl, when you makes a fortune like this woman Gideon's heard of. How's that? And why don't we go the whole way and let you have enough weekly to send a few shillings home to Mother? Then your mind'd be at rest.'

'Oh, if it could be enough for Mother too so that I could worry less, if she could just have what would have been my wages, there would be ham for supper, things from the shop, and boots for Beth! Oh, thank you, thank you. I shall repay every farthing!'

'We'll shake hands on it,' Aunt Bessie said, 'and, Gideon, go and fetch us down a bottle to celebrate.'

Two days later Aunt Bessie, properly accompanied by her manservant, made her way down the Strand and into the back entrance of the Imperial Palace Hotel. She had an appointment with its master chef, Monsieur

André-Pierre Levallois, whose special sexual tastes had made him a client of her establishment.

When later she sailed out again and back up the Strand with her man in black limping and winking beside her, it was all arranged. Next week, Kate was to enter training with Monsieur Levallois for the sum of £50 a year for five years, though that would not be enough time for her to learn all he knew, she must understand that, he had said. And how would she manage to survive in a kitchen full of men?

'She'll survive,' Aunt Bessie said drily, 'and she has my manservant to look after her.'

To Kate, waiting in the parlour, watching at the window to see Gideon limping and her aunt's skirt sweeping past, Bessie cried: 'It's done, Kate, and I don't think it'll take you five years neither.' She looked suddenly younger, with her cheeks flushed and the feather in her hat fluttering. She sat down at the parlour table.

'He weren't willing to take you straight off,' she said. 'Get me a cigarette, Gideon. "A girl!" he said. I soon put him right. There's women doctors now, I said, and dental surgeons. Women can do anything men can, I said straight, anything what don't need physical strength, I said, and that's all men got over us. He stuttered and hummed and hahed a bit and I said women didn't have no special needs either and he got it then. So you starts Monday.' Her cigarette smoke drifted into the fern in the plant pot.

'I start Monday,' repeated Kate dreamily. 'I start cooking on Monday, here in London. It's as if I've been through a long illness and am being given something as a reward. Mother once gave me a little kitten when I had had scarlet fever. It made me get better because I had to look after him.' Tommy . . . when would she see Tommy again? She felt weak with longing for her old life.

'You have saved me, Aunt Bessie and Gideon, what would have become of me, without you? I shall work and work, and one day I'll be able to go home with my head up and all of the rest forgotten!'

Aunt Bessie's cheeks, patchily red from her walk down the Strand, grew redder with excitement and pleasure. 'You'll hold your head up high as long as I've got anything to do with it! Get the paper out and start writing to your mother now, before we forgets. Say you got a good job going and'll be sending a few shillings shortly. Say as how my dear husband passed away quietly. I don't like them lies between my sister and me. We'll get rid of Arthur while we're starting fresh!' She gave a hoot of laughter and pushed away her teacup. 'Get us some champagne down, Gideon. We're making a fresh start too and it'll do us good.'

Gideon hugged his long arms about his twisted chest and agreed, and Kate, leaning both arms on the table for support, echoed: 'A fresh start.' Her fast-beating heart, which sometimes kept her from sleeping on the couch in Aunt Bessie's room, seemed to lurch and set itself to a quicker pace.

A week after Kate had begun work at the Imperial Palace kitchens, Aunt Bessie had a gentleman caller early in the morning. Gideon was about to turn him away, saying with a twisted grin that the establishment did not open until six o'clock, when he passed over his card. Gideon saw the words: Lord David Liscombe, Liscombe Hall, and led him through the red hallway and down into Aunt Bessie's parlour where she was at breakfast.

'Mrs . . .?' Lord David Liscombe held his hat under his arm and tapped a leg with his cane.

'Mrs Villiers,' said Aunt Bessie calmly, offering him the other chair.

184

'My business will not take long, thank you,' he said. Tall, cutting out her parlour light, finely dressed and as handsome as you please, he did not outface Aunt Bessie. She waited. She would let him be the one to start. She was ready.

'Am I right in thinking you keep a – er – bordello here?'

'I do, sir.' She was not going to make any excuses to him.

'And you have your niece, Kate Tranter, with you?'

'I do.' She watched him pace to and fro, or try to with the parlour table in the way. He could not think of what to say next and, she thought, it served him right.

'It seems to me – forgive me, please – that it might not be quite the place for a girl of her kind, Mrs Villiers. Forgive me.'

Fine grey eyes he had looking down at her, so polite. A gentleman, Aunt Bessie saw; they were the worst.

'Kate's the kind of girl who left her mother honest and pure as the day, and when she came to me she wasn't that no more.' Aunt Bessie resisted the desire for a cigarette. She must show no weakness before him. 'And while she's with me, she won't set no foot upstairs.'

'I see. Yes, of course, Mrs Villiers. And your niece came to you upset, I see that, but please understand that in spite of my behaviour, which was,' he bowed, 'unforgivable, I have every desire to do right by Miss Tranter. And indeed I shall see that she is set up well in life. That was always my intention, believe me, and if she had not run off like that . . .'

'She was right to run off. She's got her pride and she won't let herself fall into that kind of life. Not like I did.' Aunt Bessie left her chair and felt her temper rise. 'Do you think I can't see how it would be? You'd play about with her for a bit, as long as the novelty of her pleased you, and then there she'd be, a respectable girl, respectable no more, and no trade behind her, nothing. I shall set her up in a solid business and she won't have no need of the likes of you, sir.'

'I can assure you, Mrs Villiers, I should see to it that Kate was properly provided for in her lifetime, and her family. It would be quite the best thing for her, my protection. She would never work as a servant again.'

'Your protection! And how long would that last, and what's it done for her so far? You've gained her nothing but tears, let me tell you.' Aunt Bessie shook her fist at him and Lord David backed away, his cane knocking against the parlour table.

'Please, Mrs Villiers, control yourself. I cannot say fully what I intend for Kate, not yet, but I assure you . . .'

'Oh, I can control myself, and so can our Kate. It's you what can't – you with your nasty lusting after a lovely young girl. You get out of my sight and don't you never come here no more. I shall look after Kate, it's my protection she'll have, and she won't have to dirty herself for it. And you'd best remember, the girl's a minor. It wouldn't take me long to make a statement to one of my policeman clients. It'd be a fine scandal for Lord Liscombe, that would. She keeps saying over and over how she wished it had never happened, how it was forced on her.'

Gideon, waiting for this stage in the conversation, appeared from nowhere to escort the pale gentleman, Lord Liscombe, back up the stairs, along the red hall and beneath the red lamp, out into the street.

He turned back once towards Gideon and said: 'I think Miss Tranter would like to know that Master Harry has not been found. Please be so kind as to inform her.'

Gideon bowed on his short legs and watched his lordship stride off down the Strand just as so many lordships had from number fifteen only usually they went off at night.

The Viscount Liscombe adjusted his hat and walked towards Shaftesbury Avenue and on across Piccadilly Circus to his club. There he took a whisky with an old friend and retired to the writing room where no one would disturb him. He wrote only one letter.

DEAREST KATE,

I called at your aunt's house this morning and was told by her that she intended to take charge of you for the moment. But, Kate, how can this be? How can you ever have left me? Can you not imagine the pain I felt to find you gone in Paris? To know that you had suffered, being alone and without me, and had an impulse to leave, to go home? It surely was just that. I curse myself for ever leaving you.

I am trying to keep very calm and be reasonable, to think of the future with care and without haste, so that all will be right for you. You are only sixteen as yet. I must not rush you. But I am to divorce my wife and then I want you to consider marrying me. I say consider but I really mean just marry me, Kate.

I do not think, you see, that I can bear life without you. Can you imagine my pain to find you gone? I try and imagine the pain you went through in deciding to leave me – for you cannot have done that lightly.

I suppose we must wait until you are eighteen. I can bear that if I know it is to come. For the moment I find it hard just to get through the days and nights. I cannot rest for the need I have of you.

Your poor mother is distraught and needs you too, though of course I am doing all I can for her and for your family, as I once said I would. I am being very discreet, my darling. You will not be shamed.

Just think, dearest, how happy we were in Paris and how happy we can be again. Can you bear to be without me? If I could just hold you again, if you could just see my pain, you would not leave me ever after. Your aunt says you regret what happened between us, but I think she has persuaded you into that.

Please, please write to me and nothing else will matter from the moment I have your letter in my hands for it will be a part of you and a tiny step towards our future.

Your loving,
DAVID

He did not read it through for he knew he had failed to say what was in his heart. None the less, Kate would understand and would probably fly to him at Liscombe. He sealed the letter and put on his hat to walk out to the porters' lodge for the messenger boy to deliver it.

He would not wait now in London. Kate would write or go to Liscombe and he must be there.

At number fifteen St John Street, the letter bearing a Liscombe seal was received by Gideon and taken down to the basement. He and Aunt Bessie considered it in the gloom of the parlour and fingered the seal it held.

'Put it in the safe,' said Aunt Bessie finally. 'She don't need no letter from him. And anything else he sends can go there with it.'

CHAPTER TEN

DEAR MOTHER,

Yesterday I had another lesson at typewriting at the Haverstock Business Academy. Aunt Bessie thinks it will help me when I am in business for myself. She wants me to be an independent woman, a modern woman, she says, and I hope I am clever enough. Sometimes I feel I could do anything I wanted to do, but sometimes I am afraid. Gideon says there is a lady here who is very rich and very famous. She cooks for the King, Mother! Aunt Bessie says she will not be happy unless I do that one day too. Imagine what the village women will say to that!

Of course, it will be many years before I am a true cook. I am still in the Sauces section and have to practise Basic Béchamel all the time. I have only a tiny corner to myself but the kitchens are huge, all made of steel and worked with gas and charcoal. They have chimneys right up to the ceiling and there are dozens of men and boys working round them. I should like to try something else for a change but the Maître, as we call him, says I must learn to cook without English lumps first. Aunt Bessie says you could cook without lumps at your mother's knee but I do not have your skill yet.

Tell Beth and the boys that London is very strange and very noisy and dirty. There are the new motor cars everywhere making fumes and soot on all the trees and all over the windows and doors. It sticks to your clothes and makes everyone dirty.

Aunt Bessie and me sometimes sit with Gideon in the afternoon and tell him about home, for he does not know the country. We tell him about the hens hatching and there being an egg for Sunday tea and if you were lucky some lovely dry pink ham and an onion. I tell them about Pa coming in in his Sunday cap and having a smoke and you falling asleep and the kids squabbling over the last piece of anything.

Aunt Bessie says she longs for a sight of Dorset sky and a sniff of the air and she wants to come home soon to retire. The sooner I learn my real cooking, Mother, the sooner you and she can retire together and there'll always be ham for Sunday tea. She says she does not know how she managed without me around to keep her young and dreaming of home. She'd grown so dull, she says.

I worry about her spending so much on me but she says I might as well have now what she would have left us in her Will.

I worry about you too, Mother, and the kids, but I hope what I have done is for the best.

Your loving daughter,
KATE

Mrs Tranter, mulling over her daughter's letter, found it hard not to compose in her mind an acid reply to her sister who had no daughter of her own and kept the pleasure of hers. Her first and most frequent pleas to her daughter to return from this extraordinary adventure in London – caused, she thought, by a brainstorm brought on my foreign travel – had not brought Kate back to her. She could explain her daughter's actions to no one for she did not understand them herself, and least of all could she find any reply to Lord David who called so often to inquire after her.

'Have you any news of your daughter, Mrs Tranter?' he asked each time. 'I do rather worry, you know, since she was in my care when she . . . made her decision. Is she in need of anything, do you think?'

Mrs Tranter could find no answer, only kept as non-committal as she could; she was not one to spread family business about, and in any case felt some obscure shame over Kate's leaving home. She did not want to talk about it.

Scrabbling to her feet when he called in the afternoons, she curtseyed and watched him settle himself at her kitchen table as if he were the carter or the farm manager, and talk of young people and their ways, though she would say nothing of Kate, however much he prodded. He had taken Beth and Billy up to the Hall for their daily lessons with Miss Lulu, for she was lonely, he said, without Harry. All gentry children were lonely, Mrs Tranter knew, it was in the order of things.

Most extraordinary of all, he had offered to take them all in his carriage for a trip to the seaside. She had been so bewildered that she had found no words to answer him and the offer had hung in the air until he had taken himself off.

The day he so foolishly offered Mrs Tranter a trip to the seaside, Lord David made the decision to go to London and confront Kate with the fact of his need for her. He had waited too long for a reply to his daily letters. She would not be able to resist him if she saw him, if he stood before her. She would lift her lovely head and he would watch the blue of her eyes soften and darken, when she saw his pain and heard his voice, pleading with her.

In the train, in his walk to Curzon Street, in his room there, bathing and changing, he saw only that scene before him, Kate's face and his voice saying all the things that he had had in his heart and mind, the things he had written to her and she had not answered.

He very deliberately chose the time: six o'clock. If Kate had been put into business by her aunt, she would not be likely to arrive back before that. And he had chosen the place: the corner of the street leading into the Strand, for there was a coffee house there and he would not be conspicuous. He would look, almost, as if he were waiting for one of the girls from that house to pass his way.

He waited four hours at the coffee house before he saw Kate coming along the road towards him. It had not seemed long because he had been sure she would come. He had not contemplated, since first the decision was made, that she would not do so, and there she was. She wore an ensemble which looked to his eyes to be the very one he had bought her in Paris. She had the lilac hat with a feather in it on her dark hair but he knew it was she simply from the way that she held her head. But beside her was the disabled man from her aunt's establishment. Lord David hesitated. Was this, then, the aunt's idea of a chaperone? Well, it was a good one, he thought, but it had made him hesitate instead of run towards her and now he was too late for they were walking together down the basement steps of number fifteen and had disappeared.

It did not matter. He knew that Kate was there. Just to be so near to her made his spirits lift. He too went down the basement steps. He would not risk the front doorway where the red light was already glowing.

'It's the front door.' The disabled man, chaperone to Kate, appeared and seemed to wait for him to apologize for his error.

'It's all right,' David said to the man who each day lived beside Kate, 'I wish to see Miss Tranter, please.'

192

He knew that Gideon had recognized him. He took off his hat and waited, to show the man that he intended to stand there until Kate should come. The man closed the door but it did not matter because soon someone would open it again.

Kate's aunt appeared next. He saw that she knew who he was and had decided not to pretend otherwise, for she said: 'My niece will not be coming to see you, sir. She does not want to see you again.'

'I'll wait,' he said. 'Please tell Miss Tranter that I shall wait here until she is able to see me.' He smiled at her and bowed slightly. 'I shall wait all night if need be.'

Aunt Bessie saw his firm strong face with its narrow grey eyes, looking at her; she saw the set of his chin and his mouth drawn into a smile. But there was pallor and shadow in his face. They stared at each other, waiting for the other to make some move or some remark and neither heard the carriage above them stop and the sound of boots going up the front steps, the ring of the bell. Aunt Bessie saw that he would do as he said; he would wait there all night and in the end Kate would be bound to see him. She would have to give in to him. She said: 'I shall call my niece, sir, and ask her if she will spare you a moment and that will settle the matter.'

'Thank you, Mrs . . .' He bowed to Kate's aunt and his heart sang. He trembled. The moment he had dreamed of had come.

He waited for several minutes but the time was of no import. Aunt Bessie appeared again and asked him into the room. It was like one of the parlours of the cottages at home, like Mrs Tranter's that she had showed him into once. He saw the gloom, with only one lamp alight, and then there was a rustle of a skirt and Kate was there, the man behind her.

She had taken off her hat and jacket and there was a

silky blouse about her breast and neck, he thought afterwards, but then he saw only her face and his heart stopped. It was not quite the face he had known; it was more beautiful. The light in it had quietened. There was sadness, stillness. She had suffered too for leaving him; she had been waiting for him to come.

'Kate,' he said and held out a hand. She made no move towards him, but stood and bowed her head.

'Look at me, Kate, and tell me you don't want to see me.'

Kate shook her head and did not answer. Aunt Bessie said: 'I told you, sir, and I hope I don't have to tell you again, Miss Tranter has no wish to see you, not now or ever. Me and Gideon are looking after her, which is more than you did, and she'll be safe with us. You might say we've taken the place of her mother and father since you made it too awkward for her to go home, and that's how it'll be.'

He said: 'Say that to me yourself, dearest Kate, say that you never wish to see me.' He did not rush to take her in his arms. The words her aunt said meant nothing to him. He hardly heard them. But he needed to see her face, he needed to see that she saw the pain and need that was in him.

'I want to see you alone, Kate, let me have that, just that, please. I want to explain everything.'

'No, sir.' He heard her speak very clearly and slowly but she did not raise her head to look at him. 'Not alone. There is no point in that. Aunt Bessie, my aunt, has said to you what I . . . feel.'

'Kate! You mean it? You cannot mean it. Look at me, just for a moment, look at me and hear me tell you how much I love you and need you. I have nothing without you.'

'You made your decision, back in Paris, and she

made hers,' Aunt Bessie said. 'And now you'd best go, like I said.'

He felt himself unable to go, unable to move. She had said she did not want to see him alone. She could not mean it; he would not accept it. If they were alone, the world would change!

'It is best, sir.' Kate's voice was very low and quiet, a whisper almost. He longed to hear more of it. He must hear more of it.

'Kate, can you stand there before me and say you do not care for me, that you have never cared for me? Kate?'

'I do not care for you, sir.' The words seemed to echo in his head and he shouted at her, but she turned away and silently left the room with the man following. He wanted to run after her but could not move.

He and Aunt Bessie stood together in the parlour. He could hear a clock ticking.

'It's like I said. You'd best go,' her aunt said. 'She won't change her mind. She's suffered too much already and she's only a girl. Whatever have you been thinking of? A gentleman like you. She wants no more of you, I tell you.'

'Suffered?' he said. 'Kate has suffered? She'll never suffer more with me.' He heard his own voice echoing round in his head. 'Can't you see that I mean what I say? I need this girl.'

'Yes, well, them's men's ways and we can do without them. There'd be suffering and more to come if she did what you say. Love don't last,' Aunt Bessie said, 'not your kind, men's kind, for it's based on lust and we all know that, don't we? She don't need your kind, sir. She's only a girl and she's got a loving family around her. That's the right kind.'

Lord David felt himself turn around to face the door

by which he must leave. The pounding of his heart was echoed by the pounding in his head. He was going to leave because Kate had said, 'I do not care for you, sir.' What he had not contemplated had happened. He had seen Kate, she had looked into his face and seen his love and longing there, and she had said, 'I do not care for you, sir.'

He left the room and the house but could not remember the movements he made nor how he had made them nor how he eventually reached Liscombe House in Curzon Street.

Kate, turning away from him, heard herself say, 'I do not care for you, sir,' and the words echoed on through the hours when she lay upon her bed and wept. The sight of his face with the shadows about his eyes looking down into hers the way he always had, twisted her heart. She had been strong; she had not let herself hear all the words he said. She must not. He had loved her before and had sent her away. He had forgotten that he had sent her away.

She hugged her arms about herself and sobbed with longing. If she had taken one step towards him, she might have been in his arms and safe again. Why had he sent her away if he still loved her, had always loved her? He had not explained that.

Kate sat up and brushed damp hair away from her face. 'I should have let him explain. It was a mistake!' She took gulps of air. She should not have rejected him. 'I should have let him explain!' Her own voice seemed to whisper back from the walls, from the looking glass where she could see herself reflected, a dark and solitary figure in the bed.

'Ain't no place for explaining.' Aunt Bessie appeared in the doorway with a steaming glass of toddy in her hand. 'What's there to be explaining, in men's ways?' She sat down beside her niece and held out the glass. 'He had a whim to see you again, have a little play with you again, that's all.'

'But if there was a misunderstanding? The way he sent me from Paris ... he could not have meant it. What if I would not let him explain and all the time he needed me?' She lifted her knees and leaned her arms on them. 'It could be, Aunt Bessie, couldn't it?'

'What would a man like that be doing needing you?' scoffed Aunt Bessie. 'There's plenty more like you he'll find soon enough. It won't take him long to forget there was ever a girl called Kate Tranter, you mark my words.'

Kate took the glass and did not feel its heat upon her fingers. His face, his dear face, looking at her, as it had used to. She could not now put aside Paris as if it had never been, as she had made herself do, for he had come to remind her. She sobbed openly with her aunt beside her and the toddy spilling on to the bedsheet.

Aunt Bessie, knowing the power of tears, let her cry, and thought the matter would very shortly be closed for good so that Kate could get on with her young life.

But Kate, dwelling on the visit, on the image of his face shadowed with pain, became convinced that his sending her away from Paris had somehow been a mistake. Lady Blanche must have misunderstood him. Of course! How could she ever have doubted him? She had been ignoble. She must go and tell him the truth. The words she had said in the basement had been untrue. She loved him and would always love him.

The resolution made, Kate went several times to Curzon Street where she knew his second home, Liscombe House, was one of the line of mansions. For two weeks after his visit, after leaving the Haverstock Academy, she placed herself at the corner of the street and watched for his passing.

On the third Tuesday, Kate saw him. She had just taken a turn about Stanhope Gardens and was walking into Curzon Street. It was he, walking ahead of her. She knew at once, by his firm step and the way he held his head under his hat. And he had on his fine grey suit that ... Kate lifted up her arm and ran, stumbling a little along the pavement behind him. She would have called out: 'David! David!' but in the sudden shock of seeing him, though she knew she would one day, and with the coldness of the air about her face, she could not make her mouth say the words. He stopped at bottom of the steps. He had sensed she was there. Kate felt her heart lift with the joyous certainly that he knew she was there. She stopped, breathless, and waited for him to turn around to her and see her.

The door at the top of Curzon Street steps opened and a butler appeared. Behind him stood a lady. Kate turned a smiling face towards the door. It would be Lady Sarah, staying at the house with her brother. She would be glad that he was to be happy again.

But it was not she. It was a fair lady, walking down the steps, who had not quite Lady Sarah's stateliness. Kate saw in a blur that she had on a blue outfit and a dark blue hat with a mass of flowers about its brim and a veil. She was lifting the veil. She had a very pretty face. She was a girl of eighteen or so and she was not Lady Sarah.

Lord David was running up the steps towards the girl. He called: 'My dear, you look lovely.'

Kate waited to see the girl reach down to take his arm and the pair of them turn to walk together down the steps of Liscombe House.

They walked ahead of her down Curzon Street, arm

in arm. The girl laughed up at him. He turned his head to look down at her.

Kate felt that she would be able to move, in a moment, when her heart had begun to beat again.

She would go around Stanhope Gardens, for she knew the way. Her feet would take her. And then when she could, she would go home.

David Liscombe, walking down Curzon Street with his niece, the daughter of his widowed elder sister Diana, smiled down at the girl. Her eyes were almost as blue as Kate's and she wore some kind of outfit that was a blue as the blue of Kate's poor dress, that day on the cart.

He was taking his niece to the house of Lord and Lady Montague, around the corner in Half Moon Street, there to leave her with a group of other giggling girls whilst he and Lord Montague began some negotiations for the marriage of the Montague heir with Lord Liscombe's niece. The boy would be waiting anxiously in his father's study so that he might that day make a formal application for the hand of Louisa Bicester. Everything, thought Lord David, seeing the glow in Louisa's eyes, was right with that little part of the world, which would go on as it always had. Kate had worn a dress of the exact blue of Louisa's outfit but no marriage would ever be arranged for her that would bring her an income of £20,000 a year and that for fripperies, and she would some day be in the arms of someone else! He swayed slightly, turning into Half Moon Street with Louisa.

Aunt Bessie and Gideon, watching Kate, saw that her tears had ceased. She was healed then, they thought, and thank God for it.

Kate's tears had turned to nightmares.

199

Each night she saw Lord David walking away from her, on the arm of a girl.

Aunt Bessie had been right. He had another girl. It was two weeks since he had come to the basement and asked for her.

Everything about him had been false.

She would not cry for him again.

Only sometimes, her body would betray her and would waken her with longing.

About her heart, she set a seal; she would never love again, nor give any part of herself in innocent and true love. Men's ways, Aunt Bessie had said. Kate nursed bitter knowledge to herself and shame at her foolishness.

She got through the days; she rose and dressed and spoke. Her time at the Imperial Palace assumed an automatic routine. She leaned over saucepans and basins, stirring and mixing and seeing Lord David on the arm of another girl; she could not rid herself of that final image of him.

One day, in spite of herself, she seemed to feel the way the sauce formed itself and when Aunt Bessie said yet again, during the quiet afternoon time: 'What you done today then, girl?' replied: 'Basic Béchamel, Auntie.'

'Ain't it time you did something else?' Aunt Bessie said. 'I wonder if I oughtn't to run up and see that Frenchman. He isn't having us on, is he?'

Kate felt herself make an immense effort to speak, to form words and sentences beyond the essential daily remarks.

'I did think he might be, Auntie.' She heard her own voice sounding very loud. 'Only I didn't dare say, but I think I've got it now and I think I know why he makes me do it. With cooking, you have to understand the way the mixtures work. You got to feel it and you can't until you do one thing over and over and over.' She paused to take a deep breath, watching their faces full of concern and interest, willing her to go on. 'It's funny,' she finished lamely, 'but I seem to understand sauces, somehow, though I don't know how I've done it.' She did not know, either, how she formed the thoughts she had, nor the words, for they were not of Lord David and the girl in Curzon Street.

'Born to it, you are,' cried Gideon, 'like some are to painting or singing.'

'Born to it!' cried Aunt Bessie in joyful agreement, spurring Kate on to further revelation.

'The men,' said Kate, 'in the kitchens, they shout at me, "No English lumps" and then Monsieur Levallois goes past and he shouts it too.' She felt the beginning of a smile on her lips and could not remember when she had last smiled.

'The very idea,' scoffed Aunt Bessie, 'as if your mother and your auntie couldn't cook without lumps before he was thought of. And you won't take no five years to learn nothing he knows. I can't wait for you to get started proper like you wants.'

'Yes,' murmured Kate, forgetting that she had ever wanted anything but rising early from the parlour table to walk back down the Strand for evening service and the mixing of sauces that she was beginning to understand.

Gideon and Aunt Bessie sat on at the table, as they often did, the two of them together, dreaming for her and for themselves, given new life by Kate.

Kate, watching their faces over breakfast and tea, watching them planning for her, knowing they loved her and she them, tried to push aside intrusive thoughts, resolving each day to learn more, for them. If she felt a little sick over her first cup of tea, it was her own weakness, she thought, and if when the first food smells reached out to her across the Imperial kitchens; hotel guests' breakfast, bacon and kidneys and haddock smells, and she felt herself retch over her white stock and arrowroot, she thought it was her turbulent dreams disturbing her. She thought it was fear of her new life and the men's jibing. She thought it was the sense of loss and rejection that still wrapped about her when she could not think of other things.

But in October, when the new autumn class started at the Haverstock Academy and she could not do up the waistband of her heather tweed skirt, then Kate began to worry.

'What you doing in that old black silk of mine?' Aunt Bessie said one afternoon towards the end of the month.

'It fits me better at the waist, Auntie.' Kate stood fixing her hat at the looking glass in the parlour. Her hand shook. The pin stabbed into her forehead. 'Oh!' She felt the tears start and watched one roll down her cheek. Of course, it was because she was eating so well here at Aunt Bessie's where sometimes in the afternoon she would try out a recipe.

They would all taste it, the three of them and the old cook and the girls running down before their evening toilette, snatching a bite of something with their tea, admiring her skill. She was eating too much, putting on weight like her mother. Kate watched a second tear roll down her cheek and a blush spread all about her neck from the heather blouse and up to her eyes.

'Auntie, I think I am going to have a baby.' The hatpin dropped to the hearth and Kate put her face in her hands. It was said. She had said it to herself and Aunt Bessie at the same time. 'Whatever shall we do? All our plans are finished. I am to have a baby!'

'I thought our luck was going too well.' Aunt Bessie helped her into a chair.

'Not your fault,' said Gideon. His winking eye that had once so disconcerted Kate, looked on her with love.

'Of course it wasn't her fault,' snapped Aunt Bessie. 'What chance did she have to see the truth of men's ways?'

'He said there would be no baby yet, he promised me.' Kate stood up and looked into the glass and saw her own face fuller and rounder and her eyes big with fear. 'Whatever shall we do?' She sat down again; there could be no peace for any of them now, no more sitting at tea with their plans. There would be shame now, and hiding, and no work possible for a long time.

'Too late for the doctor, it must be four and a half months,' said Gideon, limping round the parlour table to seat himself in his chair. 'We better have one of our talks.'

'I wouldn't trust Kate with that scoundrel doctor,' said Aunt Bessie, sitting beside Gideon and regarding the girl who had become her own. 'Look what happened to Ethel Brown. Terrible death that was.'

'Death, Auntie? You mean I should try to . . .?' Kate wrapped her arms about her waist, remembering tales of knitting needles and gin.

'Not you, girl, no, we can't trust to that. You'll have to have it.'

'We'll look after it.' Gideon's face twisted into its familiar grin. 'Me and your auntie. Send it to school later.'

That night, in the old wine store beside the kitchen that they had made into a bedroom for her, Kate stood by the washstand with two kettles of hot water and a bottle of gin. She had stolen it from Aunt Bessie's stores. She had somehow to get more hot water from the kitchen without being seen and then drag in the tin bath from under Aunt Bessie's bed. There still remained the knitting needle. No one in this house knitted, she thought.

That would be the hardest thing, finding a knitting needle. The rest would be easy, she decided, for it was not really a baby, not yet, and it would be for the best. She could not, in her circumstances, bring a baby and shame to this house; trouble and expense and an unwanted baby, and no father to give it its rightful name.

She would begin by taking her first glass of gin; there was a lot to get through, and perhaps one bottle would not be enough.

The gin slipped quite easily down, half a bottle was gone before she had managed to pull the bath across the corridor with no one seeing and had refilled the kettles. The problem was that the water in the bath had already cooled before they had boiled.

Kate hoped warm water would be enough; she felt so very hot, she would probably have no need of it. She giggled to herself, refilling the kettles for a third boiling. She had never felt so hot; she was so fiery hot her own body would keep the water boiling and melt away the stain that was in her and must not ever become a baby.

Gideon found her slumped over the sink. A kettle had fallen to the floor and with it a broken bottle of gin.

Kate, waking late the next day, heavy with nausea and self-disgust, saw the blur of her aunt's face leaning over her and tried to form words of regret. She was sorry. She had lost the baby. She had murdered her baby and murder was a sin.

'Auntie?' She lifted a weak hand to show that she was sorry. 'I have killed it,' she said, and began to cry. Weak sobs began to grow somewhere in her but she was too sick to let them out. 'He might have been like Harry,' she said, and let her hand drop. 'I thought of that during the gin, last night. I thought, I am killing a little boy like Harry, but I think it was too late.' Tears slipped into her hair. She had not the strength to wipe them away. 'And now I have done everything that is bad,' she said, 'not only all that before, so shameless I was and so foolish, now I have murdered a baby, my baby, his baby, and no one can ever forgive me, Auntie, can they? And I must go on and try to forget but always in my heart I'll remember. I knew that, drinking the gin. It all seemed funny. I was laughing, and I knew one day I would realize it was for the best.'

'Here.' Aunt Bessie wiped her face with something cool scented with cologne. 'You been silly, that's all, but there's no harm, my lovely girl. Thank God, there's no harm done.'

'The baby is gone, Auntie, and that is for the best, I suppose.'

'Not gone, dear, not so far as I know. It don't always work, you know, and thank God you're too far gone to try any of them other tricks. It would've killed you.'

'You mean, the baby is still there?' Kate struggled to find the force in her limbs to sit up. 'It must not still be there, Auntie, still a burden to us! The shame for us all, never to be forgotten. I can never go home if I have a baby.'

'Lie down,' Aunt Bessie said sharply.

Kate fell back and closed her eyes. 'I can't, Aunt Bessie. I mustn't have a baby, not his baby, always to remind me, always to be there.'

'That's right,' her aunt's voice came more gently, 'and a fine thing to remind you. There's no shame in giving life, no matter there's no ring on your finger, no matter you was taken in and he was just playing. Never mind all that, I tell you, if you'd lost that baby the way you wanted, you'd never more live easy. Never more, I tell you, you'd go on aching and longing to hold that mite in your arms.'

Kate opened her eyes to see her aunt rocking quietly on the bed and on her face wet tears making rivulets down the patchy rouge.

'And ten years on, twelve years, you'd say to yourself, she'd be going to school now, doing well. I made up my mind mine was a girl, always wanted a girl to bring up, but I still did it, still . . . got rid of it. Too much trouble, not convenient what with Arthur and all, he'd have booted me out. But I could have made it on my own, and my girl'd have showed the world what a modern girl can do. There'd have been no shackles on her. She'd have been clever and done something, my girl.'

Her aunt's voice had stopped. There was no sound in the room but the ticking of the clock and outside the London traffic a faint murmur. Kate reached out her arms to her aunt.

A week later, the three of them sat in the parlour for a serious discussion of Kate's future. By the fire, toasting bread, Kate suggested: 'Can't I go on with the Imperial Palace training for the moment, so as not to waste too much time? Then afterwards, when the baby is weaned, just pretend I was married all the time?'

'It ain't just a question of being married, is it?' Aunt Bessie sat heavily at the table. 'A woman can't go about the streets and into the business world if she shows. It ain't respectable, no matter if this is the new century.'

'Why don't she learn herself?' Gideon poured tea. 'She's done some cooking down here, trying out them things she saw at the Palace. She could learn it from a book.'

'Mrs Beeton's book!' cried Kate. 'I read it at Liscombe. Cook lent me it. It tells you *everything* about cooking, all about the herbs and the simple things right up to dinner dishes and proper desserts!' She dropped her fork and stood up.

'Basic Béchamel, I hope,' said Aunt Bessie wryly.

'Basic Béchamel and all of it, Aunt Bessie. I could start at the beginning and go right through, practising the layered things and the soufflés. What could be better?'

'I'll run down the street to that bookshop. What did you say the cooking book was?' Gideon took out a pencil from his pocket.

'*Beeton's Book of Household Management*, edited by Mrs Isabella Beeton,' recited Kate. 'That's all I'll need, Auntie, I think, except for the utensils of course and the food. Oh, the food!' She picked up her fork and resumed toasting. 'Shall we be able to afford it with that big sum paid out to the Palace? We'll have to have the basic ingredients and the best.'

'We'll afford it somehow, and maybe you'll be quicker. I never did see how anyone could take five years over it and months on them damn sauces,' Aunt Bessie muttered.

The three of them laughed at her implacable hatred of Palace sauce training. She fetched her hat to go straight down to see the chef and demand the return of their £50 investment which must now be put to the purchase of utensils. Kate, thinking she felt life move in her belly, felt very nearly happy.

CHAPTER ELEVEN

At Liscombe, Lord David rode about his estate and contemplated the future that remained to him; a life there, alone, as before but changed irrevocably for there had been Kate. He saw his life now as bereft.

The nights alone were the worst times for the longing to hold her again, to tell her again how it could be for them, to spend and renew his passion over and over again with her. He imagined her Lady Liscombe with Blanche gone happily, remarried and in the South of France. He wanted to imagine Blanche happy so that Kate would not have to feel awkward in her place. He saw Lady Kate Liscombe, older and fuller about the face, sitting under the portrait of his mother and in conversation with Daisy and Lulu and Harry, older too. There would be other Liscombe children, theirs, shadowy figures in his mind but all with the look of Kate, in nursery and schoolroom, running to their mama, Kate.

It would be so real that he would rise and go up to the nursery, empty now, with his own and Harry's and Kate's ghosts in it and the bear picture moved to its new place where it could hold no fears. He would take brandy up and sit in the cold fireless room and curse himself for his dreams that only the brandy could dull.

Once, walking back down the stairs before the servants should wake to stare and wonder to see him there, Lord David came upon his sister, woken by his wandering steps. She offered him tea and comfort in her sitting room and they watched the dawn lighten the sky over Rookery Hill. He stretched out his long legs on her fireside rug and leaned back in the chintz chair that was too small for him.

Lady Sarah began: 'You used to sleep well, David dear, didn't you? Is it Harry still that's troubling you?' She passed him tea in a fine porcelain cup and he stirred himself to take it.

'No,' he said vaguely, 'no. That is, of course it does, but Blanche will have to give him up to us sooner or later. She'll tire of him, won't she?' His glance travelled around his sister's room which held their mother's favourite things, a mother-of-pearl fan, the opaline jug, the Chinese lacquered fire screen whose crimson and gold were dull in the morning light. He heard himself begin to speak and it was strange because he had never spoken of Kate to anyone but her mother and that once to the Ramsays.

'It was the girl on the cart. Were you there on Blanche's birthday when I spoke of her?' He could see his sister's gentle face, pale above her nightgown, lean towards him with concern and love.

'No,' she said. 'But tell me now. If you want to. If you are ready to tell me.'

'Blanche mocked me, of course. I saw the face of this beautiful girl sitting on a cart and afterwards I could not forget her. I followed her about, here, when she was nursemaid to Harry and no one saw. In Paris, it all . . . began. I could not help myself.'

Sarah poured tea and passed him another cup with a hand that trembled slightly. She was to learn now what had so troubled her brother for the past weeks. She dared not speak nor make any sound that would disturb him. She sat very still and he talked on and finally said: 'And she stood there before me and said she did not care for me and I could not believe it. It had been a dream. I still cannot believe it. I offered her a safe and happy future and she threw it away and with it my heart. I suppose she cannot forgive me. She's a country

209

girl. I frightened her. What we had together frightened her and once I left her alone –. God, if I hadn't left her! She gathered up her old ways and ran off then. I still imagine her here with me. I still talk to her in my head. I've gone quite mad, you see.'

'She is very young,' Sarah said tentatively. 'A young girl of sixteen cannot know her own mind.'

'She was very mature in many ways.' He sat amongst his sister's chintzes, dark and shadowy about the face and with the old angry look that his sister knew so well, and more there too, deep sad lines drawing down his mouth. He held his tea untouched and gazed out at the pale Liscombe sky. 'She's run the household for her mother since she was about eight, I think. She worked and worried and dreamed of a better life. There was more in her than anyone could imagine and I saw it the first day on the cart. The intelligence in her face. Her realization of her place in the world. And I could have taken her out of all that, Sarah!' He put the teacup down on the arm chair with a rattle of its spoon. 'I would have looked after her family. I am doing that, I hope.'

'I think there has been some notice taken of the fact that the Tranter children have been brought up to the Hall for their lessons.' Sarah tried a smile towards her brother who did not see it. 'I never thought of you . . .'

'Setting foot in a cottage, no.' David gave a wry smile at himself. 'But it won't be the last time. I can do more, Kate showed me that. The unfairness of life can be tackled. I always knew it, of course I did, but we keep to the social order of the life we have known, don't we? What else can we do, I always thought. It's a bottomless pit, as Arthur has always said, as so many say, and so only a few of the brave and sensitive try it.'

'Shall you join the new Labour Party, dear, do

something really daring and shock everyone we know?' Sarah began to collect the untouched teacups. 'It would be exciting to do that, wouldn't it, David?'

'Well, I suppose I could join, yes, but I don't see me doing that. I'm thinking of something more direct. You know, like helping the Tranters, seeing the results, giving personal help. The Labour Party! All those committees! And nothing ever done, and then even the best ones, the most honest and true ones, pushing their way to the top and having the privileges we've always had so there'll still be others left behind. I can't see me getting embroiled in all that. And the boredom of it, Sarah! I just want to help young people like Kate, I think.' He stretched out his legs and stood up stiffly.

'Only I've done nothing yet, but think about it and dream of her and wonder if she knows I'm helping her family. Every time I see that girl, the younger one, she has the same blue eyes . . . I go up to the schoolroom and stand there, miserably aware of myself, and look for Kate in her face. I imagine her writing to her sister: "Lord Liscombe came today and said my French was improving." Can you imagine me so ignoble, Sarah, and reduced to such small things?' He stood by the window and gazed down into the valley. 'Even now I am thinking: her father will be in the dairy by now, her mother will be giving the boy and girl breakfast, and I wish I were down there with them. I do, Sarah. Aren't I quite mad!'

'Well,' she said. She too got to her feet rather stiffly. She stood beside him. 'I suppose I must say it is rather a waste of your time, David. Why don't you do something practical, the way you used to? You didn't use to waste any of your time, especially not at Liscombe. Here at home you used to be always occupied and happy, too, in your way, as long as you were out around Liscombe hills anyway.'

'I don't remember being happy,' he said. 'I suppose I had occupation enough.'

'And you haven't enough occupation now, and if it's that you need why don't you come down to the village today?'

'Helping the poor,' he said. 'Do you remember how Blanche used to mock you?'

'Blanche mocked everyone,' Sarah said sadly. 'She seemed always to take the purity away from one's actions. I am glad to think that Mother did not live to see her here for very long.'

They were silent together, watching the horses being led from home stables along the stream path towards Flush and the beginning of their day's work.

'Mother called them the poor too,' Sarah said suddenly.

'Yes,' he said. 'She would not have understood about Kate, would she?'

'It's patronizing, to call them "the poor". Even for me to say "them" now. Mother saw it as her Christian duty to help "the poor", to give love and charity to "the poor". But what right had she, or anyone, any Blanche or anyone less awful than her, you yourself David, to group them all together? It means they have no individuality, are nothing of any importance in themselves or for themselves. They count for nothing. And they doff their caps and bow to us and know their place.'

'Sarah?' David took her arm and turned her to look at him. 'I had no idea you had such feelings.'

'You have never asked me. You have just seen me as your sister, taking my mother's place here and filling it well. Even when I had grander plans, for extending the village school, for instance, for sending that Beale boy for orthopaedic treatment, you only agreed because I wanted it, not because you felt it was a good thing to do for the young people who will benefit.' She looked wryly up at her brother's face. 'You never saw them as you see Kate Tranter now, as a fine person who deserves more than she was born to, did you?'

'No, to my shame, I never did. It took Kate ... Kate.' He gripped his sister's arm and went on. 'All right, I said I would do something for people like Kate and I will. I will start now, with you, Sarah. I've only been too miserable and self-pitying. I'll come down with you today.'

She smiled at the new light in her brother's face, the old energetic light he had had sometimes, planning for Liscombe Farm or his hunt stables. 'We'll bathe and dress first, David,' she said. 'And we'll breakfast sensibly, then we'll go down to the village and I'll show you what you can do for people like Kate.'

His old energy seemed to carry him through the village school door and into the room where rows of solemn faces looked back at him. He saw a muddle of calico pinafores and white ribbons on the girls' side, on the boys' rough patched jackets and hands that would have drawn water that morning, that would, he knew, work the potato and the hay-fields. There were children there who never had a full year's education. There would be some who did not always have boots for walking to school. And he had had none of it on his conscience.

He sat in the teacher's chair and watched his sister put the children at their ease in a way he could not have done. He tried not to look for a face like Kate's among the row of girls. And he had seen at once there was none there to match her! He set his mind to his task, the task that had been at the edge of his mind in the long time he had spent alone since Kate. He would work

213

with Sarah to make Long Trenthide village into a place
where there was no need nor any stunting of ability or
intelligence. It should be done slowly and carefully;
there would be no hint of charity. Kate had wept at
charity. These children should keep their pride; they
must work and show their worth. He would go that day
into town and begin the setting up of a fund. The
Liscombe Trust Fund he would call it. It would help to
still his pain. It would exist in memory of a girl on a
cart.

Soon after the abrupt finish of her training at the
Imperial Palace, Kate set to work on Aunt Bessie's old
kitchen, where the cook, used only to serving Aunt
Bessie and Gideon and the girls, had grown lax.

'Not one of them have the stomach for good food.'

'They'll enjoy it when I start my real practising,' said
Kate, passing her a bag of stale flour with mites in it
and a packet of suet gone hard with age, to be thrown
away. 'Let's get started on the cleaning up so that we
can stack our things away properly. A good cook always
keeps the shelves in order, then she never has to waste
time looking for things. You can't afford to do that in
the middle of a soufflé. I can see Liscombe kitchens all
laid out and gleaming now, Mrs Hampton, the pots and
the barrels and the rows and rows of food. I'd never
seen anything so startling in all my life.' She passed Mrs
Hampton a dusty jar of preserved plums. 'I think I
wanted to take up cooking the moment I saw Liscombe.
You should have seen the cook at work!'

'I were cooking before you were thought of!' grumbled old Mrs Hampton.

Contrite at her clumsy tongue, Kate hugged the
woman whose sagging figure reminded her of her mother's, and within a week Mrs Hampton had adapted to

her secondary role and Kate's real period of training began. Her precious Mrs Beeton constantly before her, pored over in the evenings, referred to throughout the days, she began on soups and worked through to fish. Moving from table to range, from shelf to sink, with Mrs Beeton, Kate felt her baby grow within her, move and kick and remind her; she had this baby's future to work for. He would never be poor. He must have new boots for school and never wear cast-off clothing. She would work and plan for him just as she had for the ones at home. The baby had become 'he' to her from the first time she felt a definite movement in her belly. There were no more vague thoughts of a baby to come. She had thought: He's kicking, and the image of a little boy had formed in her mind, a little like Harry, dark-haired and with her brother Johnny's jaunty good looks. He seemed to her to be all the more precious for having once been under threat from gin and hot water.

She had started on sauces, pickles, gravies and forcemeats when the size of her burden forced her to stop. She could walk no more across to Covent Garden, Aunt Bessie said. She was not decent and she should keep away from Mrs Beeton or the child would be born with a loathing of food.

So Kate relinquished the kitchen back to Mrs Hampton, who grumbled and hoped for the birth early so Kate should be back. The upstairs girls, learning to like their new regime, grumbled too and helped Kate's last waiting days with cornets of sugared violets and gifts of tiny lacy garments for the baby they would never have.

'No-ooh! Mother! Help me!' Kate, flattened into the twists of wet bed linen by her terrible burden and the pain that rent her, wound her hands about the rope of cloth Aunt Bessie had tied to the bedposts. If only she could press her nails into her own flesh, pierce and bleed it so the other pain would go away. If only she could arch her back. If only the burden she bore would let her arch her back against it. She felt sweat trickle down the mound of it and into her groin.

'Mother! Mother!' she heard herself scream, and the sound seemed very far away.

'Your dear mother can't ever come and know about this, darling. Oh, it'd break her heart.'

Kate saw dimly the shape of Aunt Bessie beside her. 'Aaah!' She was panting. She was like an animal, a great zoo animal panting in the bed with the beat of blood at her temples. If only the baby would come. If only it had never been!

'Read the book to me, Aunt Bessie, read out the recipes,' she whispered.

Aunt Bessie wiped sweat from Kate's face with the corner of a damp sheet. 'No more recipes, darling girl.' She felt her heart would break to see Kate panting and suffering there. 'Push, push, like the doctor said,' she whispered weakly. She could not help the girl now, no one could, and the doctor said it would not be yet. How much longer?

'Gideon!' She went to the door, but she need not have shouted. He was there, waiting.

'Send that messenger boy for the doctor again – any doctor come to that. It can't be much longer. And bring us a bottle of champagne. It'll ease the pain and she can't stand spirits.'

Kate felt the tiny champagne bubbles burst against her cheek but she could not drink. They had had champagne together, in the hotel sitting room. David had laughed at her surprise. He had said: 'You shall always have champagne, darling. You should have been born to it, if beauty and sweetness were the measure of these things.'

If he could see her now he would not say she was beautiful. She was like a gasping thing that was giving up its life on the bed. A wrench of pain made her push away the glass and throw herself back into the pillow.

'Curse him, curse him!' Through her pain she could hear Aunt Bessie's voice.

'No, no!' she whispered. 'Not him, not his fault.' For it was not. She had loved as much as he and this was the fruit of it, this pain. She must thrust through the pain. It would be over soon and she would hold his baby in her arms. She must not die from it for the baby would need her. But she could not breathe or move. Her heart was bursting.

'Curse him!' Aunt Bessie's voice echoed round the room and Kate saw the stain on the ceiling that had seemed to be the shape of Liscombe grow red and spread out until she could not see it any more.

'David!' The redness was filling her body. 'Please come.' She had called out to him at last, had given in to the need to feel him with her, and now he would come.

'What's all this? Nearly our time, is it?' The doctor brought cool ordinary air with him into their hell. He shut the door on Gideon who got on to his bent knees and leaned his head against it, listening for Kate's pain.

'Strangled on its cord,' the doctor said. 'Let it die. It won't take long.'

'Shouldn't we try and save it? She did so want ...' Aunt Bessie saw the bloody shape shrouded in Kate's sheets. The doctor picked it up, putting it in the basin on the floor. Kate's blood mingled with the warm water that had been ready to wash her son. 'Shouldn't I clean it, see to it?' It had given a little whimper, and a tiny arm seemed to wave into the air.

'It would be an idiot. Too late.' The doctor was

217

bending over Kate. 'We must get this girl cleaned up,' he said. 'She'll maybe not live, there will be a fever. She'll have to be watched.'

Aunt Bessie dragged herself away from the sight of the baby that must not be allowed to live, to Kate, her darling, lying still in her own blood and sweat.

'What's happening to our girl?' The weight that had been pinning her to the floor seemed to disappear and she could move. 'Kate!' Was there life in her? 'Kate!' The dear girl's face was cold and wet.

'Get the sheets off her, gently. Get her into something fresh. I'm going to send for a nurse. She mustn't be left, it'll be touch and go. And I want this bed raised at the foot to help stop the bleeding.'

Aunt Bessie barely heard him speak. She touched Kate's skin that seemed to have no life in it. 'Gideon!' she called. He would not be able to bear it either.

Somehow, it had become evening. A nurse was with their Kate and her baby was dead. The nurse had taken it away though Aunt Bessie had asked to see it, just once more. A boy it had been. It was Kate's boy and she had made plans for it, just as Bessie had for her own daughter. Bessie Villiers cried for Kate's dead baby as she had for her own, twenty years before. She sobbed for twenty years of loss and loneliness.

'We was fool enough to think we'd have a child to bring up.' She sat with Gideon in the kitchen when at last there were no more tears. There was gin in the glasses before them but they had no heart for drinking. Aunt Bessie's cigarettes were unsmoked. They had no heart for anything. Mrs Hampton had gone out in the search for ice. Ice, she said, would stop the bleeding. Something must stop Kate bleeding for how could the two of them bear it otherwise?

'Where's my baby?' A thin voice was coming from the bedroom.

'She's round, Gideon, she's come out of it!' They both ran, Gideon all twisted up in his own legs, to the bedside, where the nurse was smiling down at Kate.

'Yes, dear,' she was saying, 'but you keep still now, you must keep still.'

'Aunt Bessie?' Oh, the cold blue face she had still, the slightness of her, lying there. 'Is it a boy?' It was just a whisper now. Her eyes were closing.

'Yes, darling, a fine boy.' Aunt Bessie looked from Kate to Gideon, from Kate to the nurse.

'She's asleep,' the nurse said. She was a stout comforting presence in this room where Kate's baby had torn the life from her. Aunt Bessie whispered. 'I can't tell her the truth, not yet, can I?'

'She may never need to know it,' the woman said. Aunt Bessie heard Gideon give a moan. She put a hand on his shoulder. 'Our girl's country,' she said, 'she'll make it.' But the sight of Kate lying there seemed to swim before her. Kate dying? It couldn't be!

Kate felt that the pain and the blood had gone. She was lying by herself in a cold white place that was not inside a room. She was up high and quite alone. She had lost something very important, but she was very cold and could not find her breath to speak. She wanted to say: 'I have lost my baby.' She realized she had lost her baby but no one could help her for she was too cold to speak.

Aunt Bessie and Gideon sat on together through the night, a strange silent night. Gideon had put up a board: This establishment is closed until further notice. They could not be bothering with business. The baby was dead; perhaps Kate would die too. There would be no more business for them then.

Only the doctor came, and the nurse, into the kitchen for cold compresses made with the help of Mrs Hampton's ice. As a dawn light began to filter into their darkness, Aunt Bessie thought: It's three o'clock. People always die around three if they're going to. She would just sit here and wait for the doctor to come and say Kate was gone and then she'd pack the place up, and she and Gideon would go home to Kate's mother. There would be no life here now, not without Kate.

Afterwards, Gideon said it had been twenty-three minutes past five that the doctor came through to them.

'She might well survive,' he said, 'she's strong, but she's got to be kept still. She's asking for you, you'd better come.'

It was hot in the room, with the fire blazing. The warm light from it seemed to have brought a little life into Kate's face. She lay on her back, her head lowered by the raising of the bed at the foot.

'Aunt Bessie.' It was just a whisper. She seemed to be trying to lift a hand. 'They won't let me see my baby. Just once. The baby. I must see that he's all right, that I didn't kill him.'

Aunt Bessie leaned over her. There was warmth in her skin. 'She feels warm, Gideon!' she whispered. 'Feel.'

Gideon put out his long arm and grasped Kate's hand. 'Warm,' he repeated. 'Life.' Aunt Bessie saw the tears glistening on his twisted loving face. 'Tell her it's in hospital.'

'The baby's in hospital, darling girl, he's not well. It's . . . it's his . . .' Aunt Bessie turned desperately to the doctor.

'It's his lungs,' the doctor cried jovially. 'Yes, he's got weak lungs. They'll see to him there.'

'Take me to him, Auntie.' Kate was trying to touch her hand, but the weakness of her. Would she ever be well enough to move from the bed?

'Soon, dear heart. You just get better.'

In the kitchen, over his coffee the doctor said: 'You'd better keep up the pretence for a while, until she's stronger. She must get stronger. She must not sit up, you understand, it could be fatal if she so much as sits up. I'll be back in a couple of hours. Tell everyone else in the house that the baby's in hospital. No one must let out the truth to her, not yet.'

For two long days Aunt Bessie and Gideon moved about the basement with the upstairs girls, on holiday, whispering and trilling above them, suffering too for Kate, listening for the sound of her voice, her weak voice, crying out for her baby. Mrs Villiers had told them the baby was in hospital but often babies never came out.

Forty-eight hours after the birth, Gideon took Aunt Bessie into the parlour where they had not the heart to sit now, without her, and said: 'I've had a thought that we might, you know, get another.'

'Another what?' Aunt Bessie sank into her fireside chair and lit a cigarette. 'Another what? Is that her calling? Can you hear her calling, Gideon?'

'I can't stand it any more than you can and I thought this morning, what if I get down to Whitechapel and see what's about?'

'Gideon, I'm too tired to work things out. What do you mean?'

'I mean a baby. What if I don't get on down there and see if I can't get her another? There's plenty not wanted down there.'

'Aunt Bessie, where's my baby?' The call came through the door. 'Where has my baby gone? He needs me, he must be crying for me. I didn't kill him, did I? I haven't lost him?'

221

Each word seemed to pierce their hearts.

'Get the safe keys, take what you need. And hurry back. I can't stand hearing her call like that. When will it ever stop?' Aunt Bessie threw away her cigarette and clasped her arms about herself.

'I'll stop it.' Gideon grinned. 'Leave it to me.'

He was gone all day. Aunt Bessie dismissed the nurse though she had rather she'd stayed to tend Kate. But they would not take the risk of letting any stranger know their business. The upstairs girls were sleeping out another night of rest when Gideon came quietly back, down the basement steps in the dark night with no one to see him. In his arms, wrapped in a torn and dirty piece of cloth, was a whimpering baby.

'Dark one, I got,' he said, grinning and holding up the baby to Aunt Bessie. 'Now she'll be happy, won't she? Shall I take him in, say I took him out of the hospital?'

'You'll do no such thing, not yet. Look at the state of him! Filthy he is, and stinking. Let's get him cleaned up. You go and get some milk on to warm. He'll need feeding.'

They worked together in the silent dark kitchen, Aunt Bessie with the little bath they had bought and the clothes they had had ready but had sadly put away.

'There don't seem much life in him, Gideon,' she said, 'though he sucks that teat hard enough.'

'Wouldn't be, would there? Not where he's come from. He would have died, probably, if we hadn't taken him on. The mother had six about her skirts already. No doubt she would have let him die.'

'We done a good turn then,' said Aunt Bessie, wrapping the baby in the shawl Mrs Hampton had knitted. 'But he do seem a mite, well, not like Kate shall we say.'

'She'll be wanting him to look like the father, won't she. That's why I chose a dark one,' said Gideon, adjusting the bottle at the baby's mouth. 'I could have had several fair-headed ones. This one will do nicely, I think.'

Washed and fed, sleeping now, a rather weak and underweight three-day-old baby was taken into Kate where she lay sleeping too. Aunt Bessie laid the bundle gently against her neck.

'There, my girl. Your baby, darling.'

'Aunt Bessie?' Kate stirred. The baby whimpered. 'My baby?'

They watched her turn and feel this living thing beside her.

'Oh, my baby,' they heard her say. She struggled to sit up.

'No, darling, you just lay there keeping him warm, the doctor said. You can sit up tomorrow. Just hold him, do, he's been lonely in that hospital.'

'And I've been lonely, waiting for him.' Kate turned her face to the shawl. A warm, warm baby, limp with sleep. A smell of milk. She must feed him, now. He would feed from her breasts, she would give him life. It seemed to be a dream and yet she could feel him, her baby, his flesh against hers.

The night that Kate screamed out her pain in giving birth to Lord David's baby, Lady Blanche, her son and maid took a hired carriage at Dorchester station, leaving twenty-two trunks for collection later by Flanagan. No one knew they were to return; Blanche's last letter to her husband through their solicitors demanded reconciliation, and his last to her refused it.

Treeves and Mrs Baker ran out to them, fussing, apologetic, down the front steps to help her ladyship in, followed by Lady Sarah, calm and unfussed, welcoming Blanche politely. She said: 'David is away shooting in Scotland, Blanche.' She had better not say he had gone away again in search of her and Harry.

Mary watched her mistress not snap at Lady Sarah and thought: I shall get it tonight. This quiet can't last.

But it seemed to. Blanche brushed aside butler and housekeeper and accepted a cold supper without complaint.

'Will you keep me company, Sarah?' she said in the hallway. 'I do so hate to eat alone, don't you?' Sarah, hearing her sister-in-law's bright voice and friendly, treacherous tone, thought: What barb will she choose to throw at me tonight? And: Why did she not just send back Harry?

Mary, unusually free from a burden of instructions, took Harry up to his old room at the top of East Tower. His sisters left their schoolroom and fussed about him, ordering his supper from Frank. Without a nursery maid, things were not going to be easy.

'Where have you been staying, Mary?'

Daisy was trying to be grown-up, asking a casual question. She must not let the servants know family matters, though how could they not know of them?

Mary, confused, lost without a solid wall of demands from Lady Blanche and wanting a good gossip, did not know what to say.

'And did Mama buy us some new dresses?'

'Shush, Lulu. What a thing to be thinking of.'

'Well, I thought . . .'

'Mama did seem to be buying a lot of things.' Harry sat up at his old nursery table and drank his milk. If only Kate were here it would be so good to be back. He felt tears begin and drew down his mouth to stop them. 'She was out and about a deal, wasn't she, Mary?'

The sky outside darkened and conversation in the nursery tower slowed to nothing. The girls put their brother to bed and left him the lamp. There would be nightmares tonight.

'Perhaps we should take him down with us, Daisy?' Lulu folded Harry's clothes at the bottom of his bed and saw her brother's grey eyes grow darker in his pale face on the pillow.

'Better not. Mama might come up.' Who could say what Mama might do next?

Mary went down the back stairs and along to her mistress's room. Surely she would be shouting for her by now.

Daisy and Lulu crept, whispering still, down to their schoolroom floor. There they could gossip all night if they liked, only they had talked it all over so many times.

They went to bed and did not hear their mother go up their schoolroom stairs and on to the nursery floor where Harry lay sleepless, watching the moonlight throw strange shadows across the patch where the bear picture had been.

He heard the footsteps and felt his heart leap about painfully. Frank! It must be the nursery footman coming up to frighten him.

'Harry dear.' It was Mama's voice but she never called him 'dear'. 'I've just seen that maid of yours you liked so much. Kate, is that her name?' Harry sat up. Kate had come back.

'Yes, dear, imagine! Now –' Blanche Liscombe leaned over her son's bed for the first time in his life. '– she's just downstairs and she said to me, "Tell Master Harry to wait in bed for me. He mustn't move, tell him, and I shall be up to tuck him in very shortly."'

Harry gazed back at the shape of his mother. Her

face seemed different in the lamplight. Her eyes were so big and dark. He held his breath. He would be all right. Kate was coming.

'Yes, Mama,' he said. His voice sounded small and squeaky. Let Kate come soon!

'It does seem rather chilly in here, Harry.' He saw his mother give a little shiver. 'I think I shall light you a fire in the nursery room. Then you can have some nice warm milk together and you can tell Kate all about your trip, darling. You just lie there quietly.'

She disappeared and shut the door behind her. Harry lay stiffly with the bedclothes clutched about his shoulders. It was cold, very cold. Everything was cold and wrong. He heard himself whimper. But Kate would come! She would have been waiting for him ever since they had been in Ireland.

He must have been dozing when he smelt the smoke. What a big fire his mother had made. But then, she had probably never made a fire before. Harry lay still. He coughed. There was rather a lot of smoke. Perhaps he had better go and see if she had put the fireguard up. Kate was very strict about that. He padded across the room and opened the nursery door. A wall of black smoke met him.

Daisy and Lulu smelt the smoke at the very same moment that Frank shouted them awake. Afterwards, they realized he had Harry slung across his shoulders like a sack, but he wouldn't let them speak or run about uselessly in their room, trying to save something.

'Get out, just get down them stairs!' He was pushing at them, rudely pushing them in their nightgowns. They were not even allowed to put on their wraps, nor slip their feet into slippers. Confused, hearts beating frantically, they found themselves within seconds barefoot in the damp grass of Liscombe Hill beyond the beeches and the laundry place. Servants in nightclothes ran about them, shouting. There were a lot of buckets clattering, thrown about then hurled back down the hill where the water was. And there was Frank, panting, laying Harry on the grass beside them.

Black smoke swirled about making the night darker than before, but they could see Harry, lying there, choking. He was alive. Daisy and Lulu knelt beside their brother. His head nestled into Daisy's arms, he too gazed up at East Tower until he screamed, very suddenly: 'Rats! A rat over my foot, Daisy!'

But a lick of flame was playing over East Tower and the fat black shapes running into the blackness by the trees did not matter, not now. Frank was calling out: 'That mad mother of yours have gone back in!' Unbelieving, they all looked up. Their mother had gone back.

'She said as how it weren't burning fast enough. She went back in,' Frank said again. Behind them, down in the valley, Home Farm stables' lamps were all lit and the horses harnessed to bring up the water. They could hear the shouts of the men as they unwound the long twist of piping that had stood so long unused down by the stream at what their father had called the fire station post.

And then their mother was there, at the nursery window, screaming. A white hand showed through the blackness and a tiny lick of flame seemed to float over her head.

'Why isn't Harry burning?' The terrible cry seemed to hang in the smoke.

'I'll have to try and get back in. Don't you move.' They saw Frank look back at the tower once more and run towards it, towards the tower where other licks of flame were playing ominously over the golden stone.

227

'He's gone for Mama.' The girls knelt beside Harry and watched, unbelieving, as the footman, the one they had never liked, ran back across the basement steps and into the kitchens. Shouts followed.

'Get that man out.' Mr Treeves in shirt sleeves was running after him.

Afterwards, they said the scene had been played out before their eyes as if it were a nightmare, but they did not remember much of it. Only Frank dragging the body of their mother, they remembered that, and then she got up, for she was not dead. She got up, screaming, and her dress, the pink one she had arrived in, was on fire. Their mother was on fire.

A lick of fire was creeping up the pink dress and it seemed to be in her hair. The burning figure, their mother, burning, went past them with the repeated cry: 'Why isn't Harry burning?' And they all held out their hands to her but she did not stop. They got to their feet, somehow, to watch their mother run and roll, burning alive, down the hill to the stream where they could not see her any more for the dark night and the dark smoke and the people running. And then Mr Treeves brought out Aunt Sarah lying dead and blackened in his arms.

Mrs Tranter, in her nightgown, watching from the window of Stone Cottage saw, amongst the billows of smoke and the stumbling shrieking servants, the form of Lady Blanche Liscombe, burning, come running and rolling down their hill to fling itself in their stream.

She fetched one of her best sheets to cover the woman when the men had dragged her out. She could not see whether she had drowned or burned to death.

CHAPTER TWELVE

There was not a sound up at the top of Rookery Hill. Johnny Tranter, two weeks after the fire, arrived at the place where the rooks had always shrieked and dipped over his head but only sat now, rocking on their branches. Other things were different too, for although the March sun shone full out of a pure spring sky, there was a kind of deadness in the air. He could feel it.

He sat down on the grass with his back eased against one of the familiar elms. He had better give himself time for a look about. He unlaced his boots which were now hardly more than uppers, so worn were the soles, and pulled a bit of knitted stuff that was the rest of his socks around his ankles. He would have to look respectable if he were to risk a sortie down there.

He could smell his own feet. They were as black as his socks. There had been no one to tell him to wash them, nor any place to wash nor water to wash with but the streams, and he had grown lax over it. His mother would have something to say, if he were to risk going down.

Johnny felt in his keeper's pocket. A dozen or more cold rats' tails, only a little bloody, and each one from Liscombe land. They should give him a penny for them. It would keep him in bread for a few days. He felt better, somehow, being in familiar territory. Only was he going to dare to make himself known? And what was wrong with the place?

The cottage was down there. No sign of his mother. He might have given her a shout. No sign of anyone. He felt a sudden welling of misery, thinking of his mother. He would like just a sight of her, really. He would do anything for a taste of her apple pudding. Maybe there was an apple pudding on today?

Through his misery and the sweet-remembered smell of apple and clove pudding, Johnny saw it, the farther East Tower along the ridge. It was not there. What he had taken for shadow in the sunlight was smoke stain. Johnny caught his breath. He was losing his touch. He had not noticed a whole tower gone. He felt a sob rise in his throat. He was having hallucinations; you had them from starvation and thirst in the desert, and now he was starving. He had roamed the whole of Dorset and no one would give him a job. He had scavenged and begged and sold tails for a penny until his clothes became so grimed and worn and his boots so holed, everyone turned him away on sight. And now Liscombe had changed and he had not seen it and he could scavenge no more, for his strength and courage were gone.

'Johnny! Johnny!' A faint distant cry reached up to him and there was his sister Beth running, panting, up the hill towards him and he was so glad to see the mass of her hair and her shawl and skirts flying up he might have kissed her. He let her throw her arms about him and kiss him with cold eager lips upon his dirty face.

'All right, all right, our babe, leave off,' he said, but his heart sang out for the sight of her because he was home and could not now slink off again unseen. Behind her Billy stood scowling with a black armband around his jacket and then there were the two Liscombe girls, watching him with horror, and they were dressed in black.

'Where have you been, Johnny? You'll be in such trouble, but Mother will be so happy she'll cry for a week.' Beth brushed away her dark curls and stood grinning and weeping at him.

Johnny replaced his half-boots and stood up. 'Maybe there's been trouble here,' he said. He did not care about their stares; his own state was surely nothing compared to what had happened here.

He gestured towards the lost tower in a silent question, and saw Daisy turn towards him defiantly as if to say, Don't you dare look, it's our private trouble. Plump Lulu began to weep, holding Beth's hand.

'Here, for heaven's sake,' he said, 'let's sit down and you can tell me all about it.'

They sat round in a circle, only Daisy slightly apart and not joining in with the telling. Johnny thought: My luck's in, they'll forget all about my little lot with this going on. But the mother setting fire to it! He had always known the gentry were mad.

At the end of the story, Daisy said haughtily, looking at no one: 'We must be getting back. The piano teacher is to come this afternoon and there's tea and so on.' Johnny understood she was ashamed.

'I am learning music, Johnny, and so is Billy.' Beth tried to hold her brother's dirty hand. 'So many things are different now. Since Kate went to London, we have all our lessons up at the Hall with Lulu and Harry. His lordship said they were lonely and we were too. Only everything's spoiled, since . . . the accident.'

Johnny stood up and thought: Kate in London? He had some catching up to do. He hoped the changes would turn out to be to his advantage. And as long as he did not have to kowtow to anyone, he might stay for a while.

Susan Tranter, sleepless and worn out, standing at the stove with her fourth or fifth cup of tea that morning, looked out through the doorway of her cottage to see again the sooted grass where Lady Blanche had rolled, burning, to throw herself into their stream. She would never get over it, seeing it as she had and Lady Sarah dead and the boy gone mad, screaming at the rats running all over the grass. She sighed and picked up her golden cat who had watched it all, round-eyed, from the privy roof.

'Whatever shall we do, Tommy?'

He was suddenly out of her arms and running through the door. He had heard something, and so had Floss.

'Tom!' Johnny's voice! Was it Johnny's voice? Her heart turned over because there he was, her lost boy, his head up, whistling along by the stream with his clothes worn from his back and looking like a tramp. The cat was in his arms and the boy was grinning at her, all charm and devil-may-care, but you could not fool a mother. Her boy was in trouble.

'Got any grub going, Ma?'

He stuffed himself with cold porridge and yesterday's bread whilst she cooked up the last of his father's bacon and set the copper boiler on to heat. Cold water would not get the dirt from him.

'What'll Father say, Ma?' Johnny jammed a piece of bread and butter into his mouth. Tommy lay purring about his shoulders. Floss's adoring head was on his knee.

'We won't think about that.' Susan Tranter was full of energy now. 'We'll get the dirt off you and some proper clothes on your back first.' She looked him up and down from the tip of his half-boots to the top of his head where the hair stood up from the dirt grimed in it.

'Then perhaps you'd best hide out upstairs, at least until he's had his supper. Our Billy won't tell on you.'

'He'd better not,' Johnny put in, but his heart was not in it. He would not be bothering with Billy any more.

He groaned through his mother's scrubbing. She used

up all her precious toilet soap and had to resort to the Sunlight. There would be no clothes washed now until she sent out for more. His clothes would stand no washing anyway, nor his boots cleaning. Floss and Tommy watched entranced from the doorway until the gritty water washed along the floor to their paws, and at last Johnny stood pink and naked, revealed to his mother in all his young manhood for the first time since he was eight and had insisted on washing himself.

And then he was in bed and at home and began a sleep which was to last a full twenty hours. There was no need to hide him from his father that day. It would be a problem for tomorrow.

And the morrow brought Lord David Liscombe to their cottage. Susan Tranter fussed over the range fire for something to do with her hands whilst his lordship filled her whole kitchen with his dark maleness.

'I understand your son Johnny has been seen at the top of Rookery Hill, Mrs Tranter?'

Flustered, she almost sat down opposite his lordship as if he was just anybody.

'He is home, your lordship, yes,' she said, 'and no doubt his father'll be seeing to him later. He weren't too pleased at him going off like that, leaving a good place that don't come two a penny.'

'I think we shall forget that little escapade, Mrs Tranter. He has a lot of spirit in him, like your Kate, running off, eh? The truth is I may have another place for him. It's my son, you see. The doctors say he must be free from all worries now. There must be no learning, nothing but fresh air and exercise. I thought your boy might be just the companion. I shall want Johnny to take him out on his pony, teach him to fish, that kind of thing. I hear your boy's very good at getting my

233

pike.' He almost smiled then, standing up and looking down at her. He did not mind about the fish. He was a man who made everything seem all right. And so handsome. Susan Tranter watched him leave her kitchen. The room seemed suddenly chilled without him there. And he had never given her a word of reproach over Kate running away as she had.

'Will you send Johnny up to the Hall on Monday then, Mrs Tranter? It'll be six shillings a week. And a bit of freedom for him, for a year or so. It'll suit his high spirits. He'll only have me to answer to.'

She watched him cross their stream and walk up through the sooty grass where his wife had died. It made her heart turn over to see his shoulders so bowed.

David Liscombe, seeing the soot powder his polished boots, wondered if this was where Blanche had rolled herself down to die in the stream. Had she known it was the end? That it was too late?

On he went to the line of beeches where Daisy said they had brought Harry, choking, and he had begun to scream when he saw the rats and his mother run past burning alive. They had lain Sarah there too, Daisy said, beside Harry, and all her hair and most of her face was gone. Now she was dead and Harry lay silent and sleepless staring up at the ceiling, all pictures in his new bedroom removed, together with all trace of his old life. Who could tell what would bring him more nightmares now? There would be nightmares enough, and for them all, and the long perfect line that had been Liscombe had been destroyed for ever. He would not have the tower rebuilt. What would be the point of it? There was space and enough for all of them; there would never be any more guests, no one else but Kate should come, if she ever would, if one day she might.

Often Harry moaned for Kate in his first terrors after the fire. David too found that in half-sleep he called out aloud for her and Treeves came with brandy that he did not drink, always, for sometimes he did not want the release that alcohol would give him. He wanted to cry out for her when no one could hear him. He wanted to pretend that she was there beside him when he woke, he wanted his arms to feel her slender silky body against his and his fingers to pretend they brushed against the peach skin of her face and he was watching the sweet light in her eyes come and go as their loving grew and deepened.

His boots went up the hill taking him on past the basement steps where the earth and grass had soot ground in but the burned stones had been removed. She had made up her mind in that stubborn way she had not to love him any more. She must have made up her mind to it for it could not have just happened.

He glanced up to where the workmen were already building a new roof over the first floor. He had decided to let the odd unbalanced look of Liscombe always be a reminder of Blanche's madness. He would not rebuild the tower although everyone expected him to, from the builder to the Ramsays and Treeves. He had lost everything that had real meaning; his sister dead and mourned by him and the estate and village people, his life at Liscombe as it had been, his only love. Even for the Liscombe Trust Fund now, he was alone. Had he not counted on Sarah to manage it all?

He found himself staring down at his muddy boots and muttering to himself. The builder called down from a ladder: 'Does your lordship want these stones saved?'

He realized the man had been staring at him for some minutes. All of Liscombe stared at him and he did not care. 'No. Yes,' he said. 'All right, save them.' He would have them saved, for if Kate were to come back to him she might like to see the tower rebuilt. Would Sarah have liked it rebuilt? he wondered. She had so cared for Liscombe, although the people mattered more to her than the house. And what shall I do about Daisy, Sarah? He imagined her gentle face considering the problem, and stared down at his boots still. If Sarah were not dead, the problem of Daisy would not be his. Sarah would have seen to Daisy. He made himself move away round past the basement and right up to the front of Liscombe and his sight of the downs that were nothing to him now.

He would have had the heart and the courage to face any of it if only Kate were there.

Treeves watched Lord David make his slow way along past the ground floor windows and up to the oak door with its brass ring he had himself shined that morning. Liscombe life must go on. Treeves bowed his usual bow, but there was nothing cheerful for him to say, no word that could be said that was cheerful at Liscombe now. Up Lord David went, past the long mullioned window where the weak sun lighted his way to the centre alcove, and left towards the old guests' rooms. They were all there now, he and the girls and the boy and the schoolroom. Everything had been turned out to make new rooms for the children now the tower was gone and the East Wing could not be used.

'Where is Mrs Baker, Treeves?' he called down as he turned at the top of the stairs.

'I believe Miss Daisy sent for her, your lordship.'

In the Yellow Room where once Liscombe guests had slept, Daisy sat with her brother and sister and Beth and Billy Tranter around the tea table. Mademoiselle and their new tutor had gone to have tea with Lady

Blanche's secretary whose last task at Liscombe would be to pack up and distribute her clothes to some deserving charity.

Mrs Baker stood with her notebook in her new position, by the side of Miss Daisy, awaiting her orders. But Daisy had no orders to give.

'Then shall I go and visit old Mrs Fisher, Mrs Baker? Would Aunt Sarah have gone?' Daisy crumbled Madeira cake on her plate, watched by her sister and the Tranters. They always had cake now, but Daisy was wasting it.

'And must I go down to the school? Is there no one else to go?' Daisy asked helplessly, looking up at the woman she had known all her life and seemed now to be, with the other servants, the only secure part of their days.

'I think it would be much appreciated, Miss Daisy. The village people will like to know that life at Liscombe is to go on as before.'

'But it won't go on as before, not with Aunt Sarah gone, will it?' Daisy stretched out a hand for another sandwich.

'You started on cake, Daisy, you can't have sandwiches now.' Lulu began to cry again. 'I wish everything was the same, I wish we were back in the real schoolroom.'

'Well, you can't be,' snapped Daisy. 'Don't be silly.'

'Please may I be excused?' Billy Tranter blinked from Daisy to Mrs Baker. He wanted to know who was in charge now.

'Oh, don't say that stupid thing,' said Daisy, 'I've told you, we don't say that. We wait for everyone to finish then we all leave the table.'

Beth reached out to squeeze Billy's hand under the table. Billy looked down at his plate, blushing.

Mrs Baker said gently: 'Why don't you leave the table now and get out your games? Except perhaps Miss Daisy. Would you like to come with me, Miss Daisy? I've some ordering to do, and then we could go along and see if the painters have finished in your new bedroom. Would you like that?'

Daisy jumped to her feet and ran from the room. 'I cannot bear any of it, I don't understand any of it. Aunt Sarah hadn't showed me yet, I can't bear it.'

Beth, watching her go with sympathetic tears, said: 'Shall I help you with your reading, Lulu?'

'I shan't stay here.' Billy stood up, a patch of red still showing on each cheek. 'I don't want lessons here, I want to go back to school.'

'Don't, Billy, please. We need you here – I need you. I can't bear it if you leave us alone, not now.' Lulu slipped from her seat and pulled Beth from hers. 'Let's play a game, let's get the games out. Oh, please, don't *you* go away. Don't mind Daisy. She's upset because Papa says she must have Mary as her maid and she cannot think of what to make her do. She has so few clothes, you see, for a maid.' Lulu stood still with a hand reaching out to her friends. 'If only Aunt Sarah were here!'

Beth hugged Lulu and cried with her. Billy wrapped his arms about himself and muttered: 'I wish we could just have lessons, like we used to. I wish Liscombe was the same.'

Lord David called both Mrs Baker and Daisy to see him in his study.

'Sit down, both of you,' he said. 'Changes, at Liscombe, eh? And I am sure we shall cope with them between us, shan't we?'

Daisy held Aunt Sarah's old household notebook in

her hand and looked nervously at her father, frowning into the light of his desk lamp. 'I'm not sure, Papa, you see Aunt Sarah . . .'

'Yes, Aunt Sarah coped with everything, with Mrs Baker's help. Now she is dead and you, Daisy my dear, are going to have to take her place. Isn't she, Mrs Baker?' He looked from one to the other under his heavy lids, dark shadows beneath his eyes. Daisy thought: He does not care about me, he just wants not to be troubled, but I cannot do what Aunt Sarah did. She felt herself flush with panic.

'I am not even out, Papa. Mama did not let me have any grown-up dresses and she said I must keep my hair down, and I look so foolish going about the village in the dogcart without my hair up! I do not know what to say to people like Aunt Sarah did, though she was teaching me, and now I must do it. But I'm afraid, Papa, and I need to look different.' She felt herself begin to cry though she had hardly cried for her mother and her aunt.

'Yes, yes, darling, of course. Aunt Sarah will . . . that is, your Aunt Diana is to come down, she will see to your clothes, and Mary will help you and you must put your hair up, of course you must.' He was looking at Daisy and perhaps he was listening.

'Aunt Diana will come down and I will have new clothes and my hair up?'

'Of course, darling, and in two years you will be presented at Court. I shall do my duty there. You will marry. Think what good experience you will have of running a household by then.'

'Yes, Papa.' Daisy took up he pencil and held it poised over her notebook. She would try, she must try. 'Perhaps Mama should have taught me things?' It burst out. She had not meant to say it.

239

'Perhaps, darling, she would have. Now, Mrs Baker, I want you to take stock of all that is at Liscombe, with Daisy. I want all the East Wing shut up, and Lady Sarah's rooms kept as they always were. Then we shall see what is to be done with the Hall. I am afraid that nothing will ever be quite the same at Liscombe. No guests, no shooting parties, no Hunt. I am going to reduce Hall ways considerably. I am thinking that we all need a simpler way of life, simpler food and work that is healthy.'

'Yes, your lordship.' Mrs Baker stood up. There was a pain about her heart to hear his lordship confirm what other servants were already saying: Lord David had become eccentric, mourning the loss of his wife and beloved sister.

Whilst Daisy Liscombe went fearfully about Liscombe Hall, following Mrs Baker and her elder aunt, Diana, Duchess of Bicester in the hope of learning what they said she must know, Kate Tranter at fifteen St John Street, nursed her growing baby, Peter, and followed Mrs Beeton to the end. She could turn out each dish from it with one hand and was now at the point of developing her own versions. The upstairs girls, tired of day-long feasts, begged for bread and butter. Peter was passed between the loving arms of everyone in the household, and in the waiting time they had until he should be weaned and Kate could work through the day, the three partners began to plan seriously for their future restaurant. Gideon had discovered that restaurant mark-up profit should be one hundred per cent, and showed Kate how this should be worked out.

'Say you take enough steak and kidney to serve a pudding to ten people. You work out the cost of it, you divide by ten, add your hundred per cent, and there you have the price of your dish per person.'

'I don't know that we shall ever serve steak and kidney pudding,' laughed Kate, but she understood. She sat many hours with Gideon in the parlour discussing the menu.

'I want to serve fine meats in rich sauces, and little birds wrapped and stuffed in surprising things, and I want creamy soups and desserts that disappear in your mouth so that only the taste is left and you wonder where it came from.'

She wandered about Covent Garden and Smithfield meat market planning dishes of elegance and refinement. She got to know the porters on the top of the hill at Billingsgate fish market and even the horses slipping ungracefully on the fish-scaled cobbles. Gideon followed on behind her and took down the prices, getting himself known so that he should be in a position to strike a bargain when the time came for their buying. He was to be their accountant.

Kate had the idea that they should study their potential rivals and Gideon agreed.

'What we want,' he said, 'is to know what the London public wants. They're fickle, they are, city people. One day something's the rage, next there's bankruptcy for some poor fool.'

Kate said: 'But I know what I want. I want to serve fine French food the way it was done at Liscombe and at that hotel . . . in Paris, you know.'

They went together, leaving Peter for a few hours, and sat in the red plush and gilt interiors of the fashionable places of London. They tasted *Soufflé de Caille* and turned up their noses at someone's else *Gooseberry Fool*, growing used to the nudges and stares they occasioned, the tall slender girl and her limping twisted manservant.

At the Café Royal in Regent Street, Kate gazed

241

about her with more than her usual interest. Here there was rich blue and gilt on the pillars and walls and an echoing blue on the ceiling. There were French waiters in their aprons bustling about without hurry or clumsiness, and beyond the main area a domino room where a tiny clatter of pieces on marble table tops sounded through the hum of conversation.

'Gideon,' she said, 'this is what I want. This is like the café-restaurant ... you know, in Paris ... this is special.'

They were shown to a corner table and Gideon looked about him. 'Them's anarchists, Ruskies and French,' he said, 'them groups playing dominoes, plotting to overthrow governments. All talk! Then there's poets and that, artists, them wild-looking young chaps, writers and all. They stick to each other and some of them's dying of drink and some of consumption and sometimes the police comes to take one away.' Gideon knew most of London life.

Kate breathed in the sweet smell of wine and tobacco and a drift of vanilla and brandy and said: 'Imagine if we could have something like this, Gideon, somewhere where the same people came every day and we'd be known.'

'We got to get it right if we want that. We got to get it right for one or two people who'll talk about us and then take us for granted. The man what started this place, he's a Frenchman who tried to make a bit of Paris here in London. He succeeded and now there's no one hasn't heard of the Café Royal.'

'I hadn't heard of it, Gideon, back in Dorset. Such things have happened to me from the day I left there, I can still hardly believe them. I wanted, you know, to be a lady's maid or a nursery maid, or perhaps I thought in my very wildest dreams that I might somehow study and become a governess. I used to dream that I should be called Miss Tranter the governess, and the grand people would call me downstairs to sing with the children the songs I had taught them.'

Gideon watched with love the face of the girl who had put purpose into his life and, better, into the life of Bessie, his employer and companion for twenty years. 'You done better than Miss Tranter, governess,' he said, 'you done something different and special, on your own. You learned real fancy cooking. There's no one with a better hand at cooking than you. That book I've been reading up about cooking by that French bloke, I forget his name, he says you need imagination. Well, you got it and that's what makes a cook special. And you got the right mind for planning and you're artistic.' He took a mouthful of his shrimp sauce and tasted it, his head on one side, considering, as he had learned to do in their basement kitchen table over Kate's dishes. 'There's a bit too much salt in this,' he said, 'you could do better.'

Kate felt sudden tears in her eyes. 'Oh, Gideon,' she said, putting down the piece of lobster on her fork, 'you and Aunt Bessie, you do so much for me. It's not just money – setting me and Peter up, supporting me for so long – it's the way you think everything I do is right. You believe in me so. What would I have become without you? What would have happened to Peter? The workhouse for us both!' She reached out a hand to take his. Gideon turned his heavy twisted face back to his plate. Kate saw his eyes blink back tears and her heart swelled with affection for him.

'We will do it, Gideon,' she said, 'we will, and we'll have a place like this, better than this, though it'll perhaps take a long time. We'll do it and it'll be the best thing in the world to do, the three of us working together, achieving something. And with our backgrounds, our start in life!'

'A bawdy-house keeper,' he said, 'a beggar from the streets . . .'

'And a peasant girl who got into trouble. That's how the world sees us, Gideon.'

'The world'll see us different when we makes good,' he said wryly. 'The world always does. You're not looked down on if you're rich and successful. The world only looks down on you when it'll lose nothing by it.'

For Gideon, for Aunt Bessie who had so supported and loved her, and for Peter, Kate was spurred on. She rose each morning early to develop a finer, lighter cheese soufflé, a creamier sauce, learning all the time from the magic alchemy of mixtures and heating what she could do with food. She pored over her growing menu list which had on it six soups, six fish dishes, six main courses and a confusion of desserts which she had not yet been able to choose between. In this work, she dreamed less of the love she had lost, and Gideon and Aunt Bessie saw in her what she did not; they saw her stand straighter and taller, her figure now without its girlish slenderness and a womanly set to her chin.

When she had been able to wean Peter gently from her breast milk to warmed cow's milk, it was decided they were ready and Gideon began seriously to search for premises. It was he who saw the auction notice in the window of the run-down chophouse off the Strand. Aunt Bessie opened the safe and took out the box that lived behind the upstairs takings box. She produced the necessary sovereigns for a five-year lease. It was quickly signed in a solicitors' office and they walked together, the three of them, down the street to stand in the doorway of the Steak Chophouse, which was now theirs.

It had a dining room to seat thirty-five, with dark brown walls filmed with grease and tobacco smoke. Dirt was grained into the furniture and the floor-length window was dark with it. In the kitchen beyond the copper pans were dull from years of poor cleaning and the gas stoves had a layer of grime. Kate, holding the lease tightly to her, breathed in the smell of stale food and tobacco and beer, and said: 'It does not matter. I shall be glad to begin real work again. I feel strong enough to clean a castle.'

Aunt Bessie put a finger down the grime on the walls and sniffed. 'No wonder it didn't go,' she said, 'we shall do better than this.'

The next day, Kate scripted a notice for the doorway. 'This establishment will soon be re-opening for business: French Cuisine.' Then they all began work: Gideon in his baize apron, Kate in her cooking whites, Aunt Bessie in an ancient print dress, the nursemaid with Peter in his bassinet beside her, and some of the upstairs girls too. They all washed and scrubbed with soda and Sunlight soap until the dirt was gone.

They celebrated with a private luncheon for themselves. Kate bought in her first ingredients and began work in her own kitchen where the long line of stoves reminded her of the Imperial Palace Hotel but where she was now in charge. A little breathless, flushed and rather clumsy at first, she prepared six dishes from her planned menu list and Gideon, her washer-up and odd boy, wrote out, in English so as not to embarrass the girls:

CELEBRATION LUNCHEON
SERVED AT THE STEAK CHOPHOUSE 1906
Creamy Asparagus Soup
Cold Salmon with Hollandaise Sauce

Stuffed Quail Pudding
Almond Delight
Petits Fours

Aunt Bessie came dressed in her best red silk, the upstairs girls came giggling in their finest laces, looking perhaps a little jaded in the unaccustomed morning air, Lily the nursemaid came without her apron and fixed a flower into Peter's bassinet. She sat beside Aunt Bessie at the centre table so that Peter could have a place of honour and Gideon slipped into his evening jacket so that he could serve them, limping but skilful with his long arms.

At the quail pudding, where the birds lay wrapped and stuffed, everyone cheered and Gideon called for the chef to give a speech. Kate, standing in the doorway, trembling a little, saw her first guests eating in her restaurant and beyond the shining window with its lettering 'Steak Chophouse'. It was hers. The brown-painted walls glowed with the wall lamps lit and the smell was of good food. She put hot hands up to her damp face. 'Oh,' she said, 'if it can only be like this, like we planned, and one day when we are prosperous a kind of Café Royal. If only it can be!' She ran to hold Peter up to see the restaurant that would be his and everyone clapped.

They opened the next Monday with a notice emblazoned across the doorway: Under New Management. French Cuisine.

By midday, Kate stood in the kitchen, her face burning from heat and excitement. There were six hot soups on the stoves, the salmon lay ready, chicken and quail and cream sauces were being kept hot over steam. The kitchen maid stood at the table shakily beating up eggs, and in the dining room the boy they had taken on to wait at table stood by Gideon who was issuing his orders.

'Move round the tables quick as you can, but don't seem to be hurrying,' he said.

Kate called out: 'And no stains anywhere. If you or a customer spills anything, you must change the cloths as soon as they move. And I won't have any stains on your apron, it does look so low-class.' Her own whites changed, for she intended to be seen by her customers, Kate stood beside the boy and Gideon and waited too for the first customer to come walking through the door.

'He'll have a free glass of something,' Gideon said, straightening a napkin on the centre table.

'And a free dessert,' added Kate, adjusting the set of salt and pepper. 'We'll take his name and ask him back to celebrate next year.'

But no one came. The clerks and the lawyers and the typewriter workers went past the Steak Chophouse and seemed not even to glance in at the window.

At one o'clock, Gideon said: 'We got to give it a chance, don't you worry.'

Kate felt the maid's and the waiter's sympathetic eyes upon her but it did not help. Somehow she salvaged what food she could for the evening service and gave the rest to them to take home. She had not the heart to take it back to number fifteen.

In the evening, no one came, and no one came the next day or the next. On Thursday, two gentlemen lawyers suddenly appeared and the boy leapt to take their order. They asked for steak and steak and kidney pie and Kate did not have them. Everyone watched from the kitchen as the two ate trout in cream sauce without much enthusiasm, seeming not much to notice it, and left without placing a tip under the bill.

Three weeks elapsed and they had sold thirty-two meals, most of them to upstairs girls who came in to give their support. The little glovemaker from the shop next door came once for a glass of beer and said that steak and kidney pies and rice puddings were what Strand people wanted. But Kate, tearful and impatient, decided that it was the décor of the place that was wrong.

'It's so dreary when they look in,' she said to Aunt Bessie and Gideon over their night-time drink at the parlour table. 'I see lots of people stop – they look around and glance down the menu and look back in again and then they go on.'

'We agreed we couldn't afford the paintwork yet.' Aunt Bessie drew crossly on a cigarette. 'And I don't see as how the paintwork could stop anyone coming in.'

'I think it does. I'm sure, really, because when I went about with Gideon, the best places always seemed the ones with gilt and rich colours about. Never mind what the food was like, they had atmosphere. Like the Café Royal.'

'I don't see that we can copy the Café Royal at this stage, our premises are nowhere near big enough.'

'What if we change the name, call it Café ... Café something ... and put in a domino table or chess, then men would come in to play and meet each other and stay to eat.'

'If we put in a game table then that's four less covers to make our money from,' Gideon said.

'Do you think we might perhaps let one table go, if it brought us in customers enough for the rest?' asked Kate.

'I don't know.' Aunt Bessie rubbed a hand over her face. 'I just don't and that's a fact. Maybe we've taken off more than we can chew.'

'I say we sleep on it,' said Gideon. 'There's many a problem solved in sleep.'

But Kate could not sleep. Peter was fretful and feverish. She sat up in her bed, rocking him to comfort them both. He was soothed, nestling his head into her breasts, a tiny hand curled about her fingers.

Kate felt that night the same kind of trembling panic she had felt on her arrival in London, when only necessity and Aunt Bessie had kept her functioning.

She owed so much to her aunt and Gideon and was this how she was to repay them, in failure? She rocked Peter and traced the days back to her first practising in the basement kitchen. How she had dreamed, then. She had not thought of failure, not real failure, not once. She had been arrogant and proud of herself and her cooking skills, her thirst for learning. Even that, she had felt proud of, remembering other girls who had let things happen to them, passive and indifferent to the course their lives might take. Pride comes before a fall, her mother would have said, and here was her fall. Only she had let Aunt Bessie and Gideon get wrapped up in her dream and lose their money because she was not capable of living up to it.

She rose the next morning with heavy but determined spirits; she must somehow make her partners see that her idea should be given its chance. If she were wrong, then the restaurant must be sold and she would get work and keep Peter and herself from her earnings.

Aunt Bessie and Gideon were already in the parlour.

'It's decided,' Aunt Bessie said by way of greeting. 'It's to be done, what you wanted.'

Kate pulled back her chair and sank into it. A wave of relief made her feel weak. And yet what if she were wrong? 'If I am wrong,' she said, 'I shall get a job and we'll give it all up.'

'We'll just give it a try, a grander place.' Gideon

poured tea. 'I'm the accountant, I say how far we'll go. Ain't that my job? There's maybe too many chophouses about anyway and the food we serve don't fit a chophouse, maybe that's what's been wrong.'

'Well,' Kate said, drinking tea, 'the food's been my fault. I wanted to be too showy, didn't I? I was so pleased with myself.' She felt better even as she spoke, and when they said, together, 'Not your fault!' they could all laugh. Kate went on, but with a lighter heart, 'I don't think you'll ever blame me, you two, not even for those dishes I chose and chose wrongly.'

'We all chose 'em,' Aunt Bessie said. 'We all wanted to be grand and now we've been knocked down a bit. That's life. We'll get up and start again.'

'We got to make it match,' said Gideon, 'food and décor, waiters and everything. It's all got to match.'

'How much will it cost?' said Kate. She felt very weak, almost too weak to hold her tea, but she was glad of it. She could not leap up in her usual way and begin work in a rush. 'Oh, dear,' she said and put her cup clumsily into its saucer. 'I've hardly slept for worrying at all my foolishness. I'm going to leave it to you two now and not rush into anything at all.'

'We've just got to start again, but we're halfway there, we got the premises, we just got to change them a bit. You get some breakfast down you, you'll soon feel up to it. Soon as Peter's fed, you'll be fetching that notebook of yours.'

'But how much will it cost, Auntie? I feel I cannot spend any more of your money. How many years it has taken you to earn it!'

'Yes, and I sometimes wonder now what I was doing it for. It seems to me we was doing it for no reason at all. We just went on, didn't we Gideon?' Aunt Bessie lit her first cigarette of the day.

'Just living, we was,' he agreed. 'I'll go and fetch the boy. He's whimpering for us.'

'Well,' Kate said. Her voice shook a little with fatigue and relief. 'We'd better get a start going then. Where's my notebook, Aunt Bessie?'

So the Steak Chophouse was closed once more and Aunt Bessie found the money from the back box for the dining room to be repainted in blue and gilt; the painters charged twenty guineas extra for the gilt leaves that Kate wanted in a frieze below the cornice. A sign-writer took the Steak Chophouse lettering from the door and after some hesitation, Kate chose Café des Princes as its new name. It was one she remembered seeing in a Paris street. They bought a chess set and a domino set and boards in heavy leather cases and set up a newspaper stand which each day would hold the London papers.

'Now,' said Kate, on the day she was finally able to put the white cloths back on to the tables, 'I think we have a Café Royal of our very own. At last! Our customers will pour in, won't they?'

'It do seem a mite small for a Café Royal.' Aunt Bessie, gazed about her at the blue and gold room with its domino and chess corner and the newspaper stand rather crammed against the window. She puffed smoke into the smell of paint.

'Oh, tonight, when the lights are low and the atmosphere's right, with people talking and laughing and arguing over their drinks, it'll seem cosy, Aunt Bessie. Don't you think so, Gideon?' Kate leaned across a table to straighten the perfect white cone of a napkin.

'It'll have atmosphere,' he agreed, 'though I wonder if them chandeliers isn't a little low in the room.'

'Oh, it won't matter when all the people are in. In a few days, a few evenings, it will be full to bursting.'

Kate clasped her hands together and remembered the bustle of Paris and the Café Royal. 'I cannot wait to start our real work,' she said, 'and see the sovereigns tipping into the till.'

Gideon had had a new sign printed in gold lettering on a blue background. It stood now on the pavement outside. The new Café des Princes, it said. Come and enjoy a game of dominoes, take a cup of coffee, stay for luncheon. We never close. French Cuisine. Dinner à la Carte.

But no customer ventured in for a week, not even to read the newspaper. Kate was in such despair that Gideon went along the street into the offices and shops and offered the local people a special luncheon, three courses for only four shillings.

Within a few months, they had begun to build up some custom, though hardly anyone used the domino table. A few lawyers came regularly, and the owner of an import business, some men from the publishing houses. But they lost money each day. And each day Kate had to give away food, often to the tramps who had learned there was a restaurant not doing very well and stood discreetly at the doorway around eleven o'clock at night, waiting.

She became so tired and dispirited that she lost her usual energy. It was an effort now to get up so early to do her buying for meat and fish that perhaps no one would eat. Sometimes she asked Gideon to go and he hardly went to bed then for there was the upstairs business to manage too. It was only that which enabled them to put money into the Café des Princes and to send a little home each week to Kate's mother.

Kate took Peter and his nursemaid with her to the Café each day now for the maid could wash up whilst Peter slept and they could dispense with the kitchen maid. Aunt Bessie sometimes waited at table and sometimes Kate served herself for she had time enough between customers to cook and serve.

The three of them grew daily more exhausted and Kate, seeing the money come daily from Aunt Bessie's box and almost none be put in each night, said once again: 'Shall we just sell the lease? I could get work and have enough to keep myself and Peter with enough for Mother.'

'Not us,' said Aunt Bessie. 'We're not giving up our dream so easy, are we, Gideon?'

'Not us,' he repeated.

'I want,' Aunt Bessie said, 'to be respectable. I'm tired of living the way I do. I want that restaurant going, our Kate, so that I can get me off home to Dorset.'

'Why don't we do well?' Kate cried. 'My food is good, I know it is. People just don't seem to want to try it.'

'I think we'll have to start to cut down a bit,' Gideon said. 'Maybe offer a smaller menu so's we'd have less waste.'

Kate reduced the number of dishes she offered and went on haggling with her traders over the price of a piece of beef because it did not look too fresh, and taking the last fish of the morning at Billingsgate because the price went down, and wondered where her dreams of fine food had gone. Around her the noise of London carriage wheels and the new motor cars and the smell of soot and horse dung and petrol sometimes made her feel excited and full of strength. Perhaps today she would see their first full house. She would dress briskly and swing a laughing Peter around her. She had Peter and Aunt Bessie and Gideon and home and perhaps today she would see their first full house. But when the customers only came in ones and twos and there was more food left to waste, her spirits would drop and she felt more disheartened than ever.

Afterwards, she could remember nothing of the time they found her lying on the kitchen floor at the Café des Princes. She had been preparing her Béchamel Sauce for the day and something had happened. The doctor said she was suffering from nervous exhaustion and must rest. Gideon found a cook from an agency and began to spend all day and evening there in Kate's place and she lay in bed. She had not the strength to move. She thought of nothing, only dreamed the same dream of being chased along the streets of Paris by a mad Lady Blanche screaming 'Whore!' She played with Peter, able now to walk a few steps on his own. They dozed away the afternoon together, he resting in her arms, and one day Aunt Bessie brought her a train ticket.

'You're getting on home for a few days,' she said. 'Gideon and me have decided it's only Dorset air'll do you any good. I've written to our Susan to tell her.'

Kate held out a hand and dreamily took the piece of paper which said Dorchester on it. 'Home, Aunt Bessie? I can go home?'

'It won't be quite right, there's one or two matters you'll have to keep quiet on.' Aunt Bessie straightened the eiderdown and stroked Peter's sleeping head with the dark hair that grew so thinly still. 'You can't tell what we're up to here. Nothing'll make your mother take in the idea of a bawdy-house, no matter it pays her five shillings a week. She'd rather take her last breath than accept it if she knew. You'll have to just say my Arthur left me a bit, we've got this café place and it's going . . . all right, say.'

Kate held up the ticket and stared at it. 'I can't go home. I must not see him.'

'You just stay out of his way. There's that hill you keep talking about between you, so you stay down in the cottage.'

CHAPTER THIRTEEN

When, from the train, Kate saw the first water meadows of Dorset stretching out to the river and the manor house Thomas Hardy had written about, she thought she could smell Dorset air through the smoke and the steam. Dorset and home! Three long years without it. Her weakened mind and body could hardly contain her muddle of emotion; relief, joy, sadness at time past and the change in her, at the change there must be at home. Her blood seemed to pound at her temples with the throbbing of the engine. She could not keep her hands still and felt unwanted tears at the sight of her white kid gloves. Once her only pair of gloves had seemed so important; she had washed them until they were worn and frayed at the tips. She had wept with disappointment because Lord David had seen her on the cart without them, with dust around her skirts. He had claimed to have loved her from that moment but he had been playing with her. Sometimes it came to her quite suddenly, like a fresh and new event, the pain of his betrayal and the immense effort it had taken her to seal up her heart and cure herself by working.

Kate leaned her head against the seat and let Dorset pass. At home, everything would be all right.

Seeing her brother Johnny at the station, taller and with his dark handsome man's face so like their father's, Kate leapt from the carriage and flew to meet him.

'Here,' he said, by way of greeting, 'I promised you this one day.' He pushed a blue silk scarf, prettily tied up with a ribbon, into her hand, and accepted her hug with a grin.

'The best present I ever had, Johnny,' Kate allowed herself to lean her head into his shoulder, 'except for seeing you again.'

'Come on then, they're waiting.'

Johnny swept her through the station and into a Liscombe dogcart. 'I got the use of any Liscombe horse or vehicle now,' he said. Kate saw that he was proud and noticed for the first time, out in the clear sunlight of Dorchester, that Johnny was as smartly dressed as Lord Liscombe had been, riding Liscombe hills. His hard hat was brushed to a sheen of black, he wore a worsted tan jacket which seemed to fit him as well as the pigskin gloves that covered his hands, skilled now, she could see, with reins and whip. And the horse in his charge gleamed like the horses David Liscombe had ridden.

'You look like a gentleman, Johnny,' she said, arranging the skirts of her new blue woollen suit that Aunt Bessie had bought for her from one of the department stores. Kate had been too ill to leave her bed. She felt as weak and tearful still; she wished she were already lying in the feather bed at Stone Cottage and it were night and they had had rabbit for supper and all her future still lay before her. 'Let's get home,' she said and shaded her eyes from the too-bright sun. The sun never shone so bright in London; there was too much soot.

She barely saw the fields rolling by. There seemed to be no thought in her head, only the wish to be at home, but arriving at Liscombe Hill, at the turn where she had first seen David Liscombe, she said: 'Do you remember, Johnny? Our first climb, with so many hopes?'

He did not remember. 'You'll have to get out, sis. I'm not straining this girl, not today.'

Kate was glad that Johnny seemed to need little in the way of conversation. Leading the horse by the reins, all his talk was of Liscombe and how he would soon be head stableman. 'I've had to take Harry about everywhere, keep him out in the open air,' he said. 'I've taught him all the sports, hunting and trapping, and he holds a good seat now.'

'I remember Harry did not much care for killing animals, Johnny.' Her heart was saying: His lordship. How would she feel to see him? But she must not see him. She would not have come if she had to see him. 'Johnny,' she said, 'I don't want to go past the Hall. Let's go the old cow path way like we used to.' Soft September air was bringing out the remembered scent of hedgerow. Kate lifted up her head to see the seagulls and rooks still diving over the fields. She felt dizzy with the lightness of the air and the sweetness. She had breathed soot and smoke for three long years. This air would give her back her energy.

'We can go straight up,' said Johnny airily, 'there's no one at the Hall. His lordship's taken the girls and Harry for a tour of Europe. I'm in charge of one or two things about here now. He's practically given me one of his best horses – Leila. You should see her, Kate, the most beautiful Arab there ever was. We were made for each other, Leila and me. And I can't be stopping with you, I got to get back to her.'

He was not there. Relief and disappointment made her flush. 'Good,' she said. 'If they are not here, I shall be able to see the burned tower from this side.'

And there it was. She stood breathless beside Johnny at the top of their climb and Liscombe stood, a hard cold line with one end cut off and the beauty of it gone.

'Oh, quick, Johnny, I want to get down the hill.' She would be well again, here at home.

'You go on, I got Leila to see to in the hunt stables.'

Kate ran down past the gardens and the exotic tree

walk and the flowered walk and stood finally to see before her in the valley the blue door open to the sun and the last of the sweet peas and roses spilling over and into the marigolds.

'Mother! Billy! Beth!' She felt herself call out though they could not hear her. But they were there too, running from the door, waving.

'Kate! Kate!' Thin high voices reached her and they had jumped the stream and were running up to her as she ran down to them.

Through her tears, Kate saw Billy first. Fourteen years old and already with a grown face showing through the child's one. He had thin drawn cheeks and a little frown between his eyes behind their spectacles. Beth's hair was no longer about her shoulders but swept back into combs and she was wearing a beige velvet dress that must have been Miss Lulu's. She would have no need then of the blue one Kate had carried with her from London and her mother would have no need of the grey silk Aunt Bessie had chosen for she was in mushroom-coloured silk that the maids of Liscombe had sewn for her.

But there were so many tears, so much to say, that they could barely begin to speak. Kate, older, stronger, a woman now, and her family grown and changed, each without the other. Johnny was in charge of his life; Beth and Billy had a new way of speaking with the Dorset nearly gone from it; and there was shop food in the cupboard and on the table to welcome Kate home.

Kate watched the three tall strangers that were her brothers and sister put white teeth into ham and cheese and take it for granted. She saw her father, as strong and silent as ever, stir three spoonfuls of sugar into his tea and her dear tired mother allow herself a spread of raspberry jam.

Susan Tranter, seeing her daughter's older, pale face, her London face, shooed away the younger children to go and gather wild flowers to put beside Kate's bed. 'And there'll be no more chatter from you until she's rested,' she said. 'Can't you see London have wore her out? And no wonder at it, teashop work and all.'

Kate sat comfortably drowsy and at peace in her father's chair opposite her mother and let her gossip.

'There's been changes up at the Hall,' she began, 'and I don't understand none of it. His lordship have taken to the fields like a labourer. Seems there's some story he wants the simple life, wants to live like us cottagers. He's had all Lady Sarah's rooms shut off and left just like when she was there. That ent natural, and nor's his working like one of us. The folly of it! A man in his position have got responsibilities. But he goes about helping in the fields like he wasn't aristocracy. There's many a tenant as is complaining. They don't want a pair of hands, they say, they wants their roofs repaired. And as for that Fund, some say as he should put the good money into the land.'

Kate watched her mother's face that she had so missed; she saw again his lordship's long thin strong fingers and thought of them ingrained with dirt and dark from the sun like her father's. Her mother's letters had complained of this before, and of his lordship's milking the land of money for a fund. Susan Tranter stirred the fire and in the growing dusk talked gently on. 'His eldest sister, Diana – a duchess she is – did see to Miss Daisy's London Season but it seems she didn't get herself no husband, and was back here as haughty and awkward as she always was.'

'Was Miss Daisy haughty, Mother?' Kate asked dreamily. 'I don't remember. I remember her as rather shy and lovely to look at.'

'Oh, she's still a beauty, there's no denying that, lovely eyes and hair and all, but she don't hardly speak to us estate people. There's a lot of talk about it in the village but that Mrs Baker says, or lets it be understood, that she's torn up with shyness. Now, as I see it, gentry ent got no right to be any such thing. Not with all their advantages.' Mrs Tranter put her boots comfortably on to the fender. 'She can't manage things here, not like her Aunt Sarah, that's the truth of it, and it's her mother's bad blood in her.'

'Perhaps she was just too young, Mother, when Lady Sarah died, to be able to cope with it all.' Once she had envied Daisy.

'She weren't no younger than you up in London on your own,' said Mrs Tranter sharply. 'And I shan't never understand why you went off like that. No, I never shall.' Suddenly she was weeping and Kate felt herself begin to cry as if she would never stop.

'You don't know ... you're not a mother,' Mrs Tranter began, through her sobs. 'You can't know what it was like for me.'

Kate bent to the floor to draw Tommy the cat into her arms, feeling him warm there like Peter. 'But I am a mother, you see. I am.'

And so it was told and Susan Tranter clumsily hugged her daughter and muttered over the treachery of Lord Liscombe.

'I shan't never dare tell Father, my girl, not that it was his lordship and you so young and all. Whatever shall we do, living here, knowing, and them kids up there at the Hall sharing lessons? He's told me he shall see they're educated as far as they want to go, and Billy shall be a lawyer and our Beth a teacher and all. Whatever shall we do now?'

Kate said, heart and mind suddenly light with relief, for a burden now shared: 'Nothing must be changed, Mother. It does not matter now. I have almost forgotten the pain of it. And Aunt Bessie and Gideon were so good. It was quite like having you near me. Only sometimes I felt I could not bear the lie between us, and I worried so about leaving you, not helping you any more. I was better when we – when I – could afford the five shillings to send you.'

'You stop them five shillings,' Mrs Tranter said. 'We got enough with Johnny's money, though it's extra, I see that now, because of what he did to you and no doubt Father's extra's for the same reason. The gall of the man! As if he could pay us off like that. And that must be why he didn't dismiss your father after a disagreement over them blasted cows last year.'

'Mother, I know he has done these things for me, because I told him of wanting us to get out from the bottom of things. I think he has done it as a kind of payment, and I think he did feel . . . something for me, just for a while. But it is all past now.' Kate sat up and wiped her face. 'And I have Peter from it. Wait till you see him, darling. He is so sweet and laughing and spoiled by everyone.'

Then Beth and Billy came in with flowers and they could talk no more, and it was time for Kate to sleep.

She slept the sleep of a child each long summer night, with Beth and the window open to sweet air. She stood beside her mother at the copper boiler as once she had done; they were happy and at peace with each other, she turning the handle of the mangle, the hardest part of the wash. There was time to talk of village gossip and London life and Aunt Bessie's basement parlour and of the dream she had one day to come home to Dorset. If her mother persisted in calling their café-restaurant a teashop, Kate did not mind, for such things were outside Mrs Tranter's experience.

One day she felt strong enough to walk with Billy and Beth up past Rookery Hill, they gossiping willingly about Lord David who had so changed their own lives. He had, it seemed, built a village hall and had put in books and newspapers. He arranged lectures. He wanted his people to have informed opinions on matters that concerned them. But the villagers who had known Lord Liscombe all his life, who had never lived anywhere but on Liscombe land, wondered at the changes and did not want them.

Kate's tired mind learned these things and could not judge. She let herself drift into a vague review of her past years when she had lived through so much. She walked the Liscombe paths, watched the September days ripen the blackberries and at last her body grew stronger. She slept well and ate her mother's good food and spent long hours dozing with her before the range and sitting with Tommy by the stream. The strange crooked line that was Liscombe now was the only physical sign of change to the land and she did not look at it. Years before she had been a girl who dreamed that Liscombe would be the start of her life. It had sat on the hill as a symbol of golden perfection. That was gone, and her dream of it, and she could never again dream like that. Reality was work and worry and Peter to raise and the restaurant to run. She could not think of the restaurant, not yet, though she knew that must come too.

Letters from Gideon said that their temporary cook had complained at the long menu they offered and at the time it took to prepare so many sauces. Somewhere, in her planning, she had taken the wrong path and now must find the right one. She felt herself trembling when a London letter lay before her on the table, brought from the Post Office by Billy. Her mother would say: 'You leave it alone, you're not well enough to be bothering with it.'

Kate would take it up and read out the parts that her mother would understand. The rest she would read to herself and read again and feel that there was an answer to their problems, if only she could find it.

One morning, when she woke to the smell of rabbit and herbs and bacon which her mother was preparing, she ran down the stairs and asked: 'What is it that you put in your rabbit stew, Mother?' It was not a clear idea that she had, but with the sleep still in her eyes she sat at the kitchen table and watched her mother as she had so often before she had become a cook herself.

'All my usual things, child, what do you think?'

'Is rabbit stew always made the way you make it, Mother? You know, all through the past, has it always been the same?' She was searching for an idea that lay somewhere at the back of her mind.

'You get on up them stairs and get dressed. Father'll be back for his dinner with you still in your nightgown.' Susan Tranter threw a handful of shallots into her mixture and stirred it with the wooden spoon that was worn to a point.

Obediently washing at the washstand by the window, looking up to Liscombe, Kate made the mechanical movements that she made each morning. She struggled to formulate the idea she had, which was to do with country food, with her mother's food. She found that she was muttering aloud as she sat on the bed to pull on her stockings and lace up her boots. There was no time spent on sauces by her mother. There was neither time nor money for the making of heavy pastries that encased the dishes of the wealthier, from the grandest to the

clerks that strolled up and down the Strand at lunch-
time. Gideon had said their menu was too long. He had
said it many times. And that it was too grand. But she
had persisted in what she saw as the pursuit of the best.
Perhaps it was not the best and there was another,
simpler way to cook.

Kate did not see before her the bedroom she shared
with her sister, nor the sunlight making harsh shadows
along the floor. She did not see Liscombe, for she was
in London and in her mind was saying to Gideon and
Aunt Bessie: 'Shall we change the menu completely?
Shall we start all over again?'

She brushed and pinned without knowing it the chestnut hair that was growing glossy as she rested and slept
like the girl she had been. She felt within her the old
flutter of excitement she had had when first the three of
them set out to open the Strand Chophouse. Since those
early days, there had been work and worry and disappointment and the pile of sovereigns that Aunt Bessie
had so long worked for had grown smaller each day.

Could she ask them to start all over again?

Kate glanced into the square of looking glass which
was all that she and Beth had ever possessed in which to
see themselves. The poor did not usually spend time
upon their own images. She felt a tear fall, and watched
it run down the curve of her cheek. She was still poor!
She had changed nothing for her family, done little to
ease her mother's work. Another tear fell. But it was
not pity, not self-pity! Kate wiped it away. It was a tear
of rage. She would find the strength and the spirits to
convince Aunt Bessie and Gideon. It would be for them
and for her family and for Peter. Had she not sworn he
would never be poor? Kate pushed angrily at the square
of glass. She had been wasting time. The next visit she
made there would be an oval mirror in a gilt frame with

her so that her sister would be able to see herself dressed for her first dance, and Beth would be in ivory satin with pearls about her neck.

She spent the next ten days entirely with her mother. Mrs Tranter, bewildered at Kate's sudden health and strength, turned out her cupboards for her, picked and breathed with her the scent of the herbs she had always grown, as her own mother had before her, and sighed with exasperation at her daughter's prying into such matters.

'I would have thought you'd be eating fancy things up there,' she said, 'with them motor cars and all.' Mrs Tranter had a confused view of London, compounded of her reading of romantic novels and the articles in *Home* which advised on motoring veils and the use of cosmetics for the modern woman of 1908.

'It is fancy food, Mother,' Kate said. 'Too fancy, and we've been offering food that's fancier, if you see what I mean. I began to learn about food up at the Hall, didn't I, and I thought it was the finest thing to do, cook such marvels – soufflés and stuffed birds. I was only a girl!'

She could laugh now at her younger self. She felt suddenly light-hearted, talking to her mother, though her plans were not clear nor could she be certain that Aunt Bessie and Gideon would be generous enough even to listen to her. 'Then in London, you see, the food is rich too, and the ordinary people of London like it like that. They expect rice pudding to be put in pastry, and even custard pudding to be put in pastry.'

'Rice pudding in pastry? Why, that's two puddings, that is. Whatever next? The extravagance!' Mrs Tranter stared across the table at her daughter. 'And my grandson's eating his rice in pastry? Whatever will that do to his stomach? You'd better bring him down here.'

266

'Yes, it is extravagant,' Kate said, gazing dreamily into the peas they were taking from their pods. She found herself stopping often in such tasks as if some part of her mind was occupied elsewhere. 'I can't quite get hold of the idea I want, Mother, but it's something to do with your food – Dorset food, the way it's always been served to poor people, using simple things like these peas and not messing them about.'

Her mother did not understand but she talked willingly on about food as it had long been cooked in Dorset. She herself had never used scales or measuring jug. She cooked from taste and touch and habit, and through the days now she talked to her daughter, remembering with pleasure the old ways.

Kate became restless with the ideas that were forming within her from her mother's talk and decided she must go back to London to put them into action. There was money enough being lost there and Peter would be needing her.

She had her last look at her family, standing grouped together at the station. She would return to see them as a loving visitor, and very soon. It would not be years before she saw them again. But their world was no longer hers. Leaning from the train window, Kate felt clearly that a new phase of her life was beginning.

And she had lain the ghost of Liscombe; she had come back home and that troubled time and the shame she had felt seemed part of another life.

She held on to her hat and smelled the soot from the engine which was working up its power. London smelled of soot; she could not wait to get back home, to London, and Peter, Aunt Bessie and Gideon, and work.

'Dorset food, Aunt Bessie, Mother's food. Don't you see? It would be different, we could be known for it, it would be special!' Kate turned about excitedly in the parlour, throwing down her hat. 'Gideon!' she cried. 'Come down for tea. Oh, I've got such ideas, Aunt Bessie. We're not going to have a French café-restaurant any more. That's been all wrong.'

Hugging Peter to her, and with the tea laid out, she began: 'It was Mother's rabbit stew that started me off.'

'Rabbit stew?' said Aunt Bessie. 'That's country food, that is.'

'Yes, but it's the idea of it you see. It's . . .' Kate searched for the word she wanted. 'It's the way it's so simple.'

'Couldn't be nothing more simple than rabbit stew,' said Aunt Bessie, smiling. It was so good to see Kate home again that she could have any idea she liked.

'I mean, what we do to food is so unsimple, like. We mess it about and put sauces on it and add things and put it all in heavy pastry and weigh ourselves down with it. And I've done it 'specially by wanting to serve grand French food when people don't all want it.'

'That's what this chef I took on has begun to say,' put in Gideon. 'We've been too ambitious for such a small place, he says.'

'Yes, that's it, Gideon. I want food, that's . . . that's like Mother's rabbit stew, simple!' Kate struggled on, seeing them smiling, Gideon's chin on his long arm. 'I know it's a lot to ask, letting me start all over again . . .'

'People are used to that sort of food. I don't know as how they'd take kindly to you dishing them up rabbit stew for their dinner.' Aunt Bessie took a cigarette. 'But I agree, we have been too ambitious.'

'A simple stew could be part of it, you see,' said Kate. 'And other simple things, all like Mother makes them, smelling so good and not heavy at all.'

'Your mother makes good simple food because she

ent got no choice, girl. Doesn't mean others wants it, especially not if they isn't home.'

'Needs some thinking through,' said Gideon, and they talked through to the evening when the other two had to go to work and Kate sat on by herself, with Peter asleep. She got out the old notebook she had used for her first restaurant plans; she sharpened her old pencils and then she began thinking Dorset and rabbit stew.

The next morning, Kate crept from her bed earlier than usual, dressed in her cotton cooking dress and took up the clean folded aprons. She kissed sleeping Peter goodbye and set off through the sounds of London on waking, in the familiar smell of soot and smoke, and unlocked the door of her restaurant with a pleasure she had not felt for months.

To the temporary cook, she said: 'You get on as before, Albert. I got some planning to do. I'll keep out of your way in the corner.'

Kate went through the larder and found nothing that she needed. Soon she had left again by the front door and had taken a cab to Smithfields first, for rabbit, and next to Covent Garden for certain herbs, and then on to Jacksons for the finest bacon they stocked.

Albert saw her return with a consignment of stores with which she disappeared into her corner. A sweet scent of herbs soon began to drift about the kitchen, a smell of bacon lightly fried, of shallots. Her idea was to develop her mother's Dorset dishes, suitably presented for a restaurant, and she thought to put the two together in the first dish: simple rabbit stew with bacon, but with the bacon wrapped about the rabbit. The whole should be in a light sauce of beer as in the old recipe her mother casually followed. Cottagers usually had beer in past times; they could not afford tea. The finished effort

269

was going to be, she thought, both homely and professionally arranged.

After days of testing, Kate produced a dish she wanted Aunt Bessie and Gideon to taste, and ran with it from the restaurant to their parlour table.

'Well, you've made up your mind, have you?' Aunt Bessie, dragged to sit down, did not pick up her fork.

'Light sauce,' said Gideon to cover the awkward moment.

'What's this bacon parcel stuff?' Aunt Bessie, in spite of herself, took the fork and poked it into the food.

'Well,' said Gideon, his plate empty, 'it's different all right, what you been looking for, and though I suppose it's country, being mainly rabbit, it do look like a restaurant dish.'

Aunt Bessie, leaving some at the side of her plate, for the show of it, nevertheless added: 'Put it on the menu then, if that's what you want, but if you want to go country, you'll have to have more than this to offer or nobody'll notice.'

Rabbit stew was added to the menu as *Lapin Campagnard* but it did not go well at first. Kate, making it up each day, would peep from the door and watch the faces of her customers. More than one raised their eyes in appreciation and surprise, she thought. She was encouraged to go on and develop a version of her mother's casserole of lamb.

It was lying sleepless over this one night that it occurred to her that the Dorset dishes were not appropriate to a French café-restaurant. She got up in her nightgown to wait for Aunt Bessie and Gideon coming off upstairs duty.

'We got to change the name,' she said, over their glass of whisky.

'What name's it to be now then?' Aunt Bessie was

270

tired. Kate realized she should have left the matter to the morning, but it was too late to stop for Gideon said: 'What name you got in mind?'

'I was thinking of something on the lines of Country something, or Kitchen something.' Kate accepted a tot of whisky, rare for her.

'Why don't you make the blasted place into a kitchen? Put a range in, why not, then they can really feel they're round their mother's skirts!' Aunt Bessie drank her whisky in one gulp and put out her glass for more.

Kate leapt to her feet. 'Auntie, do you realize what you've said! You've just had the most clever idea I ever heard. We make the décor match the food. We go entirely Dorset – food, drink, décor. We put in a range, we go totally country!'

She reached across to hug her aunt but Aunt Bessie shouted: 'No! And no and no! I'm not having that place touched again. If we fail we fail and that's the end of it. There ent no point in changing the damn décor, I tell you, it's the food what counts.'

'It's the whole thing, Aunt Bessie.' Kate, rebuffed and startled by her aunt's flash of temper, sat quickly back in her chair. 'Aunt Bessie . . .'

'Don't go Aunt Bessie-ing me. There's no point in it, I tell you, and I'm going to bed.'

Gideon put out an arm to stop Kate following her aunt. 'She'll come round,' he said. 'Leave it to me.'

'I know she's tired, Gideon, it's time she went home for a holiday, but we must do something drastic and I feel this could be it. Don't you see? Aunt Bessie's had a marvellous idea. To think of décor exactly matching the food, a real kitchen! Can't you see how charming and right that could be?'

'I can, Kate, quickly like, without putting any thought into it. I can see it looking very pretty but I still say we

271

don't rush headlong. It's one thing changing a few dishes, all the dishes if you like, but trying to put across something really new, that's maybe too much for us.'

'Why for us, Gideon? Haven't you said I could do anything I tried? Well, I must try this. I *know* it is right.'

'You don't know, sweetheart, you can't. Let's sleep on it, eh?'

Kate took out her marble-covered notebooks and began to make a sketch of her mother's kitchen: pine dresser with Willow Pattern plates and an old pottery mug or two, an earthenware pot with dried flowers and bullrushes, a plain scrubbed deal table with a jamjar of simple flowers – primroses, marigolds, whatever was in season – a plate of red apples, a black-leaded range with an old blackened kettle swinging over it. She hesitated over the range; to put one in the restaurant with their present finances would be too costly. She must wait for the range. Aunt Bessie would see that the rest could be done cheaply.

She felt saddened, writing her list of requirements. It was the first time she felt she must go against her aunt. Always before she had deferred to her, and rightly. Only her aunt's money and support had kept her and Peter from the workhouse or the streets.

This idea was right and she must bring her aunt round to see it. She hoped it would be the only time there should be any word of disagreement between them.

But Kate could not persuade Aunt Bessie. They had a heated discussion and spent two sorrowful days without speaking, even passing Peter between them without their usual words of affection.

It was Gideon who had to act as mediator and did so, finally coming to Kate to say that Aunt Bessie would agree to the changes. 'But it's to be for the last time, Kate,' he said.

Kate hugged her aunt and once more the safe was opened up and the box taken from the back. It was the very last time, they all agreed, trying to make it a humorous moment to heal the rift between them. Albert was thanked for his services and the Café des Princes was closed. The signwriter was engaged to replace Café on the window with: Tranter's Dorset Country Kitchen, the name itself coming from Aunt Bessie's own lips. 'Might as well use the name that father of yours gave you. If there's a name that's country, it's Tranter.'

Painters were taken on to strip off the blue and gilt paint that had never looked right and replace it with plain whitewash. The newspaper stand and the chess and draught sets Kate put sadly away in the basement at number fifteen; how wrong she had been to put in those and lose a table into the bargain. London was not Paris. London life could never be made to seem Parisian. She had been very wrong, arrogant even. Gideon and Aunt Bessie had not reproached her for it. Aunt Bessie was right, now, to hesitate over a new scheme. Somehow, she must make this one work.

To have the room kitchen-like she and Gideon purchased deal benches and square deal tables, two pine dressers and a set of Willow Pattern china. Aunt Bessie lost her green chenille cloths. They found jamjars to put on the tables to be filled every day with the simplest old-fashioned flowers, and an old earthenware pot which Kate stuffed with grasses.

When, finally, it was all done and Kate and Aunt Bessie watched Gideon fix up the last little water-colour print of Woolbridge Manor he had found at a booksellers, Kate knew it was right. She breathed out a sigh of pleasure at the sight of this cottage kitchen of the kind she had known all her life.

'Why didn't we think of this before? Why didn't I? I was so silly, trying to do French things! This is special, this is individual, this is our very own and like no other.' She hugged Aunt Bessie. Gideon, climbing down from the crate he had used to reach the right place on the wall, muttered: 'It's our last gamble. Let's hope it's the right one.'

'How you two have found such patience with me as you have!' Kate kissed Gideon and held her arm tightly about Aunt Bessie's waist.

'Patience,' Aunt Bessie said, 'I won't deny it, we've gone along with you right enough, but I was just saying to Gideon last night – the fun we've had with it!' She turned a tearful smiling face to her niece's beautiful flushed one. She had seen it mature and bloom from girl to woman. She had seen her despair and tire and that had twisted her own heart about as if Kate had been her own daughter. 'We were saying, weren't we, Gideon,' she said, 'what a trial it's been with the work and the worry, but how it's lifted us out of our mouldering old ways with that upstairs work and all.'

Gideon considered the position of the picture he had placed, with his head on one side. 'It's been worth it,' he said. 'I'd never have thought there was such pleasure to be had in working.'

'And searching the shops 'till you found the right perfect picture,' Kate said. 'Even that's right. Everything's right. We'll build up a clientèle and have them streaming in until the safe money is all paid back and there'll be enough to send Peter to school before we can look round.'

Even with the whirlwind of excitement and preparation for the day of the new restaurant's opening, Kate

274

was able to sleep at night. Peter slept soundly too beside her in his own bed, content to have her home with him and sensing her new peace of mind. He learned to add to his chatter the words 'Tranter's Dorset Country Kitchen off the Strand'. Kate slept because her mind and body were in accord. Awake and sleeping, she prayed that their work and care would now bring them the success they needed.

She dreamed often of a fine parsley sauce for her Broad Beans with Dorset Ham, of a dish of perfect red raspberries with the merest sprinkling of Demerara sugar, of an as yet unperfected dish of gooseberries without cream. But the dreams did not waken her with a sense of nightmare. She was sure of success this time. She had to be.

The success was not immediate, but the name Tranter's Dorset Country Kitchen made people stop and look in at the window. And the sight of the tables and chairs, the simple whitewashed walls, and country flowers, made them exclaim. Gideon, stationing himself along the pavement to watch, saw them glance in and held his breath until they passed through the door. Standing at the service hatch, Kate would see them too, doing that marvellous essential thing, sitting down at one of the tables. There would be smiles and murmurs of recognition: a kitchen like home, a kitchen many had known in the villages around London. They sat down at the tables and exclaimed again at the Rabbit Stew boldly listed on the menu with no French name to soften it.

Soon Kate and Gideon could talk of their regulars. Kate would leave the kitchen area to speak to the groups of clerks and lawyers who came day after day. They grew familiar with her as time went on and called her Miss Tranter, teasing her for her flushed Dorset cheeks and asking for more of her Dorset food cooked with her own hands for it was the sweetest they had ever tasted. Gideon rejoiced for it was what he had once, long ago, pointed out to Kate that they needed: a regular clientèle who would soon bring in others, and make their name, but neither Kate nor Gideon knew quite when it was that a different kind of person began to call at Tranter's. First Kate noticed some girls coming in groups. They giggled together and daringly smoked cigarettes in full view of everyone. Gideon said they were bohemians, with no chaperones and a shocking apartment on their own. Kate was glad to have them and add them to the list of regulars, and the dancing girls too who suddenly tried Tranter's, just out of bed after their late nights at Drury Lane.

They came humming Hitchykoo together and squealing over food like their mothers had made.

In the evenings, Tranter's was all at once the vogue amongst the smarter set, slipping out from their balls and parties to meet again everyone they knew at Tranter's, because Tranter's was different and they yearned for change in their self-indulgent lives.

Tranter's daily losses became small profits and the partners could use that to pay for a commis chef to help Kate in the kitchen. One celebratory week, they put £1 15s 4d back into the upstairs box. It was a Saturday, the day Gideon worked out the week's accounts which had always before shown a loss. Kate, holding Peter on her knees at the parlour table, helped his small fingers count out the money and put it safely away.

'Before we know it,' she said, 'we'll have enough to put aside for his schooling. Once we could not have really thought of that, or only as a dream. Back in those dark days of French cooking. All those sauces! It seems such a long time ago.' She kissed the top of Peter's head.

'We'll not take it for granted,' said Aunt Bessie, taking a farthing from Peter's fingers. 'If we think we're doing well, someone up there'll give us a kick in the backside again.'

'Backside,' crowed Peter with delight. 'Backside!'

But it seemed that Fate had decided Tranter's Dorset Country Kitchen should be allowed to flourish. Kate went on cooking and developing versions of her mother's recipes and the customers flooded in. They were then in a position to consider taking on a second restaurant. The day that Gideon, over the accounts book, pronounced that fact they opened a bottle of champagne to help in the planning of it and Peter had his first taste.

Kate never lost the thrill of pleasure she felt each day seeing Tranter's Dorset Country Kitchen splashed across the door. Success had given her confidence and a new energy. Though she slept the sleep of exhaustion at night, mind and body worn out, the days flew by in a whirl of activity, buying and cooking and planning towards greater success. One day there would be Tranter's Country Kitchen, Regent Street, and a Country Kitchen, Oxford Street; there need never be an end to it.

And none of it was a dream.

Her only dreams now, which sometimes for a moment woke her in the darkness, were of a tall dark man standing far away and looking at her silently. For a moment the same old sense of loss made her open her eyes and feel like a hurt girl again. But Peter would murmur in his sleep and she would remember it had been a long time ago.

And if she occasionally saw a figure like his walking down the Strand, a dark frowning face like his, then she would turn away and go back to her work which was her life now.

It was not sudden, the change from Kate Tranter, cook, to Miss Tranter of Tranter's. Aunt Bessie and Gideon saw it, watching with proprietorial pride as she grew in confidence. They had learned and worked, suffered and rejoiced with Kate, and they saw the new direct look in her eye and the manner of her walking with her head high and the firm way she had of dealing with their staff.

Kate herself discarded her working boots in the evenings and bought shoes, her first, and two blue silk evening dresses. The planning and buying, the organization of the staff done, she became hostess, sensing the added cachet she gave the establishment in the projection of herself as a new woman for the modern age.

The day they were able to open a second restaurant in Piccadilly and increase their staff to twelve cooks and waiters, she thought to telephone the *Daily Mail* and invite a reporter to its opening.

An article duly appeared headed: 'Miss Tranter opens a second restaurant to make us feel at home', and Kate, pinning it to the frame of her dressing table, recognized her achievement, there in black and white, and wondered if Treeves would pick up the newspaper from the servants' hall and take it into his lordship, carefully ironed and on a silver tray. David would know, then, how far she had come, far far beyond the nursemaid he knew, free and independent too from the plans he had made for her. She was aware of the ways of the world now, as her new adult self, and had an adult's recognition of the shame and precarious life of the kept woman. Even her shame then had been innocent and simple, a girl's shame. She would not feel that again.

She had earned with honour her new name of Miss Tranter of Tranter's Country Kitchens, grander, finer, more astonishing than that of Miss Tranter, governess.

The day the article appeared in the newspaper, Aunt Bessie took the decision to make number fifteen a little more discreet. What, she said, if a reporter were to discover that Miss Kate Tranter lived in a bawdy-house? She had her old red lamp taken down and the hallway stripped out and redecorated. It was too soon, yet, to give up the solid security of that trade, but the day would not be long coming.

CHAPTER FOURTEEN

In the years while Kate developed and matured and became Miss Tranter of Tranter's, Lord David Liscombe went rarely to London. Since his abortive visit to her aunt's house, he felt he had no reason to do so.

Kate had made it plain enough that she had no wish to see him, that he was no more to her than an interlude in her youth. She had answered no letter of his, had never, probably, read his pleading words nor his avowals of love. She could not, he thought, have gone on reading them without some move towards him, however small, even if only from pity. She had it seemed become prosperous, having with her aunt some kind of teashop. He often imagined her in a long spotless white apron, a little bob cap on glossy hair. She would move with slender grace amongst the tables, flushed with the heat of work, and the boiling urns, and her shyness. There would be a little notebook about her wrist and men would make regular visits just to gaze upon her.

It did not matter whether he was in London or abroad or at Liscombe. The background to what he was about was always Kate, especially at Liscombe working as he did upon the training and education of its young (hoping for a glimpse of some girl like Kate, one day), or in the fields or barns or stables with its men, amongst people as untainted by the world as she had been. Until he had spoiled her, with his love, and she was displaced to dirty and dishonest London.

Today, because he was in town, his mind pictured her in the teashop. He watched his polished boots stride along pavements where she might have trodden, where she might be stepping at this very moment. He would have to look up and around him and sometimes he thought he saw a girl like her in the turn of the head or the way she walked. But that girl would always have a coarse face or a vulgar giggle that could never be Kate's.

Today, he was walking back to Liscombe House from his bank. At Curzon Street his elder sister, Diana, was waiting for him to continue their discussions on the future of Daisy and Lulu but there was time yet for Diana to finish her breakfast and get into good enough humour to talk to him. Diana did not approve of his behaviour since Kate, though she knew nothing of her, and thought of the change in him as being caused by the fire at Liscombe.

For Lord David, nothing good had happened since Kate. He was going to allow himself a moment of his own today, a moment that was not for his daughters or his sister or his bank managers. He was going to walk casually past number fifteen St John Street where Kate had found refuge with her aunt, that harridan of an aunt who must have had much to do with her decision to turn him away. He did not know if he would go up the steps and ring the doorbell today as he had before. He had planned only to get this far, to the pavement before the house.

Number fifteen. He stopped. The red lamp was gone. A maid-servant was coming down the steps with a plump boy dressed in blue.

'I want to go to the park, Lily. I want to, I want to!'

'What wants, doesn't get,' the girl said, dragging at his hand.

There were new tenants there obviously; workmen were at the window, waving at the girl. White painters' cloths trailed through the doorway. The bawdy-house was gone. Kate was gone.

He set off again down the street behind the nursemaid, the boy still piping: 'I want to go to the park, Lily.' He was a lucky boy, to want, thought David. He wanted nothing now, himself. He was not even to be permitted a glimpse of Kate. He would never find her now unless he asked her family outright for her new address, and how could he do that? Her mother would hardly answer him when he tried to speak of her. He had been mad to have dreamed of this one glimpse of her. Where could he go to find her for the one look he had hoped for and could not now do without?

The name Tranter's struck at him suddenly from the corner of his eye. It was emblazoned in round green lettering on one of the double-fronted restaurants that proliferated thereabouts. Underneath, in smaller lettering, it said: Dorset Country Kitchen. He peered inside at deal tables and kitchen pine dressers and a mass of the Willow Pattern china such as village women favoured. There were countryside sketches on the walls and a big stone cider flagon set over a bar. It was an original idea, to set a part of Dorset in London; the Arcadian dream was fashionable again. The new motor cars moved too fast, the world too to some people and they thought of the countryside as a place of sweet tranquillity and peace, while its reality was work and damp cottages and beasts of burden used until they dropped and living things slaughtered to feed the very same people who lived in the city. Still, someone here had been enterprising. It was a time of enterprise now. There was no limit to what a man with ideas and energy could achieve, and he admired that. Where had his own gone?

Of course, this couldn't be . . .? A sign on the window said: Tranter's has opened another establishment in Piccadilly.

A thin London boy answered his knock. 'Master's at the Piccadilly place,' he said, 'and mistress. Don't know when they'll be back here, but we'll be serving as usual come eleven o'clock.'

'I don't want to eat, thank you.' Lord David automatically slipped him tuppence.

It was run by a married couple then, master and mistress, and of course it could not have been Kate. She could not have got so far as a business needing capital and real knowledge of food.

But not to see her today! Finding the bawdy house gone. He was a fool. He must simply go back to Liscombe at the end of the season with Lulu safely out, and ask the mother, casually, what her eldest daughter was up to these days. It would be a perfectly natural thing to do. He had supported the other Tranter children, done what Kate wanted, given them a good education.

Kate could have anything else she wanted, if only she would change her mind and come to him. If only her mother would not clam up the moment he broached the subject of Kate, and Johnny Tranter too. He sometimes thought they must know, that Kate must have told them, the reason for his shameful impetuosity. If he could ask to be forgiven, ask to start all over again! He would stay in that kitchen until he had a proper answer to a perfectly normal question.

Head hanging down, he none the less caught sight of his old friend Henry Bessington, passing within inches by Pall Mall. David pretended he had not seen him and amused himself imagining Henry's thoughts. Poor Liscombe! A mad wife, and three children still to marry off. Who would marry them now?

Turning down into St James's Street, he wondered if he might be so daring as to invite Kate's sister Beth to spend the season with Lulu. She was a charming girl, with quiet delicate good manners. Why shouldn't she enjoy what Lulu did, when she was brighter, gentler, prettier – like her sister – than so many girls of their circle who even now would be riding up and down The Row to show a fine figure on a horse to their admirers and would spend the rest of the unearned day clothing their persons in silks and lace to exhaust themselves later in partying.

All undeserved pleasures too. The world was not right. The world had never seemed right since Kate had left him.

Arriving in Curzon Street, indifferent to the hustle of the London Season, the carriages, the gleaming horses carrying their gleaming society ladies, the delivery cabs depositing dress boxes, heaps of summer flowers, scented fruits and cases of wine at basements, Lord David ran up the stone steps of Liscombe House, his eighteenth-century mansion. He ran through its open door, throwing hat and cane to the butler. He would have the sister brought to London, then Kate would call and see her and he would see Kate!

'Diana!' His sister would take some persuading. She had never entertained any modern thoughts of egalitarianism.

Diana, Duchess of Bicester, was breakfasting in the morning room. Early London sun shone harshly upon the gold flock wallpaper and the gold velvet chairs, faded now. Family portraits and the dark photographs of an earlier age lined wall and shelf and table. Himself on horseback aged eleven, Diana wide-eyed in flounced silk at three, Sarah, gravely beautiful even then, by her mother's knee aged eight. Sarah, beautiful once and now dead.

Before her at the central table the Duchess had a pile

of gold-edged cards and scented pink notes with messages scribbled across them: 'Darling Daisy, your party was delightful. You looked too deevie for words. See you at the Framptons'. Vi.'

'All this.' She pushed at the pile, disdaining it. 'It's all very well, but it's leading us nowhere, David.'

He threw himself into a low chair by the fireplace, where his mother's firescreen, the one she had spent her last year on when the cancer was making her too weak to move from her room, made him suddenly see her working at it, red and gold thread showing against the thin white skin of her fingers.

'What is, Diana?' He had longed to see Kate; he would never see her. Suddenly, he knew he would never see her again.

'All these invitations.' Diana poked a ringed finger at them again, and pushed back the hair that once had been gloriously blonde and was now faded patchily to white. Her mouth turned down with what her servants called her Duchess look. 'They don't mind inviting the girls, they go everywhere just as if they were part of the set as they should be. But they aren't, David. Thank goodness I have no more daughters to come out and can soon go back to Scotland and peace.'

'Of course they're part of the set, darling, the Liscombe name is too old for anything else. And look at me, there have been enough of the set after me. It's been indecent.'

'You've got the whole of Liscombe to offer, but the girls will have only the small dowry Mother left them in her will. Greed will overcome a lot of other disadvantages, as we well know, dear, but the girls do not appear to have enough to offer to overcome the legacy their own mother left them. Insanity, David, and before that the affairs and the drinking. Tainted blood, that's how they see it, and nobody will propose.'

285

'Of course they will! There'll be some dowry – there'll be an impoverished line somewhere that'll need it. Look at me, marrying Blanche to save Liscombe.'

'The girls won't have as much money as their mother did, and anyway that should be enough to go against our choosing one of that sort,' said Diana. She took a sip of her China tea.

'Daisy's been out three years and heaven knows, she's a beauty. Can't you see there's something wrong? Our only chance, I tell you, is to accept the Berwick boy.'

'But the line's spent out, Diana. The father was syphilitic, the boy's a weakling – they say there's epilepsy there. Can we let Daisy fall into that?' He got up and lit his first cigar of the day, forgetting to ask his sister's permission.

'I'm over twenty-one, Papa.' His eldest daughter, his pride and his present problem, brought her glorious slender height into the room.

'Don't stride, dear,' said her aunt automatically. 'You're late going to the Row. Is Lulu lying in? Have some of this breakfast first, and a cup of coffee, do.'

'A good breakfast will set you up for the day – I know, Auntie.' Daisy sighed and swished her riding habit to one side to seat herself in one of Grandmother's gold chairs which were not made for someone of her height. Setting her riding hat beside the coffee pot, she began to spread butter thickly upon the toast that was now cold. Daisy never took the cooked breakfast that would lie almost untouched on the sideboard here as it did at Liscombe Hall.

'I'm over twenty-one, Papa,' she said again, only slight defiance in her tone. 'Can you manage my dowry? I think I must accept Hadley Berwick. What choice have I? There doesn't seem to be anyone else and I've been out three years now.'

'And she's amongst the most beautiful, David, every-one knows that. Just look at her.' Diana gazed fondly, and crossly, at her niece. A mass of chestnut hair, growing thick and strong, smooth dark golden skin, hazel-coloured eyes that now looked at the world with less enthusiasm than they once had. Soon those looks would fade and then where would they be?

David crossed the room and patted awkwardly at his daughter's shoulder. 'The most beautiful, darling, if I'm any judge. But you can't take that Berwick boy, it's a weak line, not unless you feel love for him. I do not want you to marry without love, Daisy.' He wanted to add: As I married your mother. He wanted to shout at her, Look at me and your mother, but hesitated and the moment was gone for Daisy went on:

'Our line is weak too, Papa, so I think it's for the best. Of course I love Hadley ... well, anyway, he's sweet, really.' Daisy had grown cynical and he had not seen it happen. 'He likes to please me. He's willing for me to have anything I want.'

She left the table with another swish of her riding skirts. 'And you needn't worry, I shall be all right. A house in Devon, one in London, the one in Scotland. His mother and those maiden aunts of his can go on managing them. You know I'm no good at that sort of thing. Hadley says we can go to the South of France. I can do anything I like, he says. I think that's one of the stipulations, isn't it, Auntie? My freedom to move about, to travel a bit. I can't be stuck in one of those houses. I want to see a bit of life.'

Daisy looked back wryly at her aunt. They under-stood one another and Lord David was out of it; he had no say in the matter. There was too much of her mother in Daisy and Sarah's influence must have faded now. 'I want you to have what is best for you, Daisy,' he said. 'I want you to consider this marriage very carefully but of course I shall not stand in your way.'

She went to the door. 'Well, this will be the best for me,' she said, 'unless you would like to see me one of those suffragettes or something? Or one of those spinsters doing good works?'

Her aunt took a sudden intake of breath as Daisy knew she would. Daisy closed the door quietly behind her. She had learned to accept her fate. So must they.

'How much is there put aside for her?' Diana rose and moved to pull the bellcord by the fireplace. 'I need another pot of tea. My nervous system is too old for all this.'

David drew on his cigar and frowned. He would need to ring the bank trustees; if Daisy were really set on this marriage, he must make her dowry available.

'Now,' Diana sat back at the table, 'Lady Berwick tells me the estate needs at least a hundred and fifty thousand.'

'A hundred and fifty thousand!' David exclaimed and turned to face his sister. 'I could only manage that by selling this place. Of course I had thought of that, but when it comes to the point I don't know if I should care to lose it.'

'You have no choice, David darling, you must see the two girls right. There'll only be enough of Liscombe in Dorset for you and Harry. You never liked this house anyway. And I know old Lady Berwick says that's what the estate needs.'

'I suppose there's enough of Liscombe left for us, Diana, yes.' There was certainly enough for him for he wanted so little, unless Kate would ever return to him. And if that should happen, there would be no wanting either. 'I suppose Daisy is really set on this. What's the boy like?'

'Oh, the usual sort,' Diana said vaguely. 'He gets out and about a lot, is seen by everyone. Impeccable manners, I will say that, none of today's brashness. Seems fond of Daisy.' She fanned herself with a pink invitation card.

'Then I suppose we must consider it.' Lord David threw away his cigar stub with distaste.

Kate was obliged to remain all that day at the Piccadilly restaurant, her crêpe morning dress swathed in whites. Their newly appointed chef had cut his hand badly at the crease between thumb and forefinger. It had to be kept clean and away from the kitchen. Kate was not sorry; there were one or two things she had not been happy about in his work: the way the sauces were kept hot, for instance. She suspected reheating from the day before and that she would not permit. A suspicion, no more, had also formed at the back of her mind that the new man was a little too friendly with the supplier of meat, and that the wholesaler was not anxious to leave his day's load when Kate was to be seen about the premises.

It was a hard day, therefore, and a depressing one for the meat man who, faced with her suggestion that their stocks did not match his bills, admitted his guilt in a barrage of scorn. It was well known in the trade, he said, that no supplier expected to give a full and proper order, it was in the manner of things. Between tackling dishes, Kate found another meat supplier. Now the next day lay in wait with a dismissal to be got through, a new chef to be found, and a further round of cooking for her until he was.

Walking back down the Strand, Kate remembered the man's mocking look when she had sent him away: You don't know the ways of the world, it said. Everyone takes a little gift. It is because you are a woman, it said, you do not understand. You will fail, it said, because you are naive.

But I have not, and I will not, Kate thought, holding her head high under her blue hat. Honest work also succeeds, and honest dealings. It was not the first time she had come across such matters. Some chefs in London had no salary but worked entirely on commission from suppliers. She wanted none of that.

It was a hot night and all of London seemed to be around her on the streets. The last of the revellers were making their way home. Kate thought: We have fed some of those, and fed them well and honestly. She felt a lift to her spirits, reminded of her achievements. They had that day served hundreds of meals, sold dozens of bottles of cider and pints of apple brandy, and they would do more, open another Kitchen, there would be no end to it.

Before her, turning the corner of the Strand into St John Street, a couple with arms linked had stopped under the lamplight. Kate saw the young man tenderly bend and kiss his girl. Only a tiny twist of pain seemed to touch at her heart, as it sometimes did still, seeing others happy and together. It was not that she envied them, that she knew such brief happiness might have been hers; she might have courted and married, as others did. Tonight she did not have to remind herself that their happiness together might be short while she herself was not made for love but for work. Pausing there, with other couples moving round her she thought only: All these people . . . London never sleeps. We could give them breakfast – English breakfast, country breakfast. Tranter's need never close . . .

Running past the couple under the lamppost, Kate flew down the basement steps at number fifteen, checked that Peter slept peacefully in his bed beside her own, took out her marble-covered notebook and her pencils from the drawer in the kitchen and began to write, peering through the flickering candlelight: porridge with syrup, fresh-baked bread and yellow butter, creamy milk in blue jugs with muslin covers weighted by blue beads, bowls of plum and raspberry jam. Breakfast at Liscombe, and breakfast at home when there was money to spare.

At first light, Aunt Bessie, still full of sleep, her first cigarette as yet unlit, listened to Kate's joyful recitation of country breakfast tables and muttered: 'You can't expect people to wait for their breakfasts 'till they gets out and about. People want their tea and their first bite safely at home, like I do. Where's that tea, Gideon?' Aunt Bessie grumbled on, sipping at tea that was too hot, but Gideon sat opposite Kate at the parlour table with his chin on one long arm and his cup forgotten.

'It'd be a full exploitation of our premises,' he said. 'We hardly need to bother to close, but there would have to be some shift work for the staff. Staff costs would go up, and heating and so on, but there'd be no rent extra.'

Kate saw him gaze up at the dark parlour window and held her breath. Gideon could see profit to be had; there was more than a chance that he would support her. She felt as excited as she had when first she had the idea of country food. She could not sit still but ran into the kitchen and returned with a bread board and yesterday's loaf and the little blue jug that had been her grandmother's, kept for thirty years by Aunt Bessie. 'Look,' she said, 'imagine this sort of thing on our tables with those muslin covers and brown teapots – not silver! Nothing grand at all, you see, no silver trays or anything. Real Tranter's Country Kitchen style all the way through.'

'People won't want to go out for breakfast, I say,' Aunt Bessie muttered again, 'no matter it's not grand.'

Gideon threw hmself back in his chair and grinned up at the ceiling. 'People won't want to go out for it perhaps, but what's to stop us providing their bed too?'

Kate looked up from her enthusiastic slicing of the unwanted bread. 'You mean we get a lodging house, Gideon, a place where people can stay? A Tranter Inn? Like the King's Arms in Dorchester?'

'Better than that. We get a hotel, a proper respectable place where people come to London to stay for their holidays and their shopping and the London Season – toffs and all we could cater for.' Gideon grinned round the table.

Aunt Bessie forgot to draw on her cigarette and Kate said breathlessly: 'What sort of place could we afford, Gideon? You don't mean we could manage a proper hotel? Us with a hotel?' Beyond the basement window, Londoners scurried past. There were so many people out there.

'Why stop at offering breakfast? We need never stop.'

'It's all decided then, you two,' Aunt Bessie said. 'And I ain't got no say in the matter? What about our retirement savings? When are we going to stop all this work?'

Kate put out a hand to her aunt. 'I am sorry Auntie, I did not think. I think you should stop, I do, and go home to Dorset. I can earn enough here at Tranter's to keep us all without you being so worn out and always working. We could sell this place and I'll keep Tranter's going and . . .'

'Sell this place?' asked Aunt Bessie irritably. 'Throw our security away? We own this. The other places is only rented, remember.'

'We don't need to sell it.' Gideon got up and began to limp around the parlour table. 'All we got to do is change it. We got a hotel over our heads, we got one! Our bawdy house could go respectable.'

'Tranter's Country Hotel here!' Kate heard herself almost scream. 'A sort of Liscombe Hall, grand and with a butler at the door.' She dropped the bread knife and put out a hand to Gideon. 'A real hotel, Gideon, a grand one with the porter like a butler to welcome people.'

'No, no, not grand, not grand at all.' Gideon looked up at Kate and grinned. 'Tranter's,' he said, 'country cottage not country house. Or country inn, say. Never mind the damp walls and the earth floor you told me about and the outside lavatories with the spiders and the ivy growing in so you can't shut the door and the double seats you're supposed to share. People don't want that, they want the dream of it, or they will do by the time we've finished.' He sat down beside Aunt Bessie and rocked to and fro on his chair. 'By the time we've finished, they'll want it though they didn't know it before. And we got our premises here – Tranter's Hotel off the Strand.'

Kate sat opposite and hugged her arms about herself. 'Not grand bedrooms either,' she said, 'but country cottage bedrooms with feather mattresses and rag rugs and chamber pots and a bowl of dried flowers and a chipped washbowl and jug that's generations old.'

'All that,' Gideon said, 'but no damp nor sacking pillows nor rusty old nail behind the door for your only spare jacket. We'll have them heavy old wardrobes that nobody wants any more, and we'll have the chamber pots but water cisterns too, in the corridors. We'll still be modern underneath it all, like.'

'So, I'm to retire then?' Aunt Bessie said suddenly,

pouring cold tea. 'I'm to retire and get out of your way and let you take over this place, our only safe livelihood we can be sure of. Fashions in food may change but men's ways never do. We can always be sure of this business, you know we can. I don't know as I want to give it up.'

Contrite, Kate ran to her aunt's chair and hugged her, pressing her cheek into the rough hennaed hair and breathing in the familiar smell of smoke that was part of her. 'Auntie, how could we ever have been so thoughtless? This is your house. We'll find another way, won't we, Gideon? We'll make fresh tea . . . what am I thinking of? I have to meet Albert at Covent Garden. We'll talk later.'

When they met again in the quiet of the afternoon between restaurant services, it was Aunt Bessie who broached the subject first. She accepted a madeleine finger Kate had bought from the corner bakehouse.

'I went up there this morning. I've been neglecting it a bit, with the Kitchens and all. It's got grubby,' she said. 'That sluttish maid I never bothered to dismiss hasn't scrubbed them lavatory floors in a month nor cleaned under any of them beds. Elsie's in one of her drinking bouts again, she's been fighting with Dora, given her a black eye so she hasn't worked two nights. That doctor skipped his visit again.' She bit on the sponge and dipped a piece into her tea. 'I told 'em all we're closing. It's done. I been thinking for ages now we couldn't have Miss Tranter going on living in a bawdy-house, no matter we stopped advertising it. What if someone found out?'

'Aunt Bessie, are you sure?' Kate, watching her aunt's tired face shadowed in the afternoon light and the way her hand trembled slightly, holding her cake, felt her heart twist with pity. Her aunt had worked thirty long years in that house, had earned her living from it, had bought the premises after years of struggle and before she had Gideon to help, on her own. Kate had never been ashamed to live there herself, only sometimes she had thought she wanted no one amongst her staff to know of it. Mostly the business was a background part of her life, not much thought of except with gratitude for the start it had given them.

She said: 'I've been thinking, we've easily enough to rent premises. Why don't we put a manager in here and you can retire properly, Aunt Bessie, with no worry about money for the rest of your life.'

'Retire?' Aunt Bessie blinked back tears. 'I ain't ready for no retirement. I want to see them breakfasts served, Tranter breakfasts,' she said. 'I've no mind for retirement. What would I do with myself back in Dorset even with Susan for company? I'm too young, I am.' She put out her cup to Gideon for more tea. 'And don't you be sending me off nowhere. If Tranter's goes on, so do I.'

Gideon grinned and passed her an almond tart. 'That's what I thought,' he said.

'I've been meaning to close down this year past.' Aunt Bessie bit into the pastry. 'Just haven't had time to see to it. Better get them girls sorted out, Gideon. Give them a little sum each. We don't want them to go into the streets. See if the Williams woman will take them.'

Gideon gave a mock salute and chose a macaroon. 'She won't take Elsie.'

'See if Elsie can go to one of them homes by the seaside or one of them reform places you know. We don't want her dying in the gutter with a bottle of gin in her hand.' Aunt Bessie sniffed. 'We'll pay something towards it.'

'You are sure, Aunt Bessie?' Kate said again. 'You've been here thirty years and it's been your life. We could rent, you could still see Tranter breakfasts. I feel we were so clumsy just saying we'd use this place when it's yours. Gideon, we should have thought.' She put out a hand to her aunt's arm, feeling the familiar cool silkiness of her black bombazine. 'But I do think you should give it up anyway. There's no need for you to do it any more.'

Gideon grinned and winked at Kate. 'Best this way,' he said. 'Now she's forced to give it up.'

'You been plotting it, I shouldn't wonder,' Aunt Bessie said. 'Light me a cigarette, and I think we'll have some champagne. I feel like celebrating. How soon can you get the girls placed? How soon can we start?'

'We'll start now, today,' laughed Kate. She sat down opposite her aunt and took up a pencil. 'Now, what about an open hearth in the entrance hall, with a dog around to lie in front of it, and a couple of old guns fixed over, like Pa's that he went poaching with when he could get away with it. A poor man's guns they must be. Have you two any good ideas? A sort of country inn, remember, nothing grand.'

'Very fat feather mattresses in the bedrooms,' said Aunt Bessie.

'Them wooden doors with rusty latches,' added Gideon, from the doorway, going to fetch champagne.

'Them stairboards with like a worn dip in the middle from generations of boots, and no *plumbing*, of course, at least not on show, but washstands and copper jugs for the hot water.' Aunt Bessie sat back for a comfortable search of her memories and Kate kept writing.

Lord David did not see the posters announcing the opening of Tranter's Country Hotel in the Heart of

London that next spring for although in town he was much occupied with the arrangements for the marriage of his daughter, Daisy. It would be the last grand occasion at Liscombe House in Curzon Street. He had sold the premises to the life peer Lord Toptree of Hartlepool who planned to rename it Toptree House.

Daisy had chosen a deep oyster-coloured satin for her wedding dress and a bouquet of palest pink roses. The two colours suited her dark skin and chestnut hair which that day was arranged with combs of mother-of-pearl. In her old bedroom at Liscombe House, her last time in that room, she adjusted her bodice with trembling fingers and wondered: Shall I look right? But it was not for her husband to be, Hadley Berwick, waiting for her at the Abbey. Daisy took no note of Hadley's opinion. She merely wanted to look good for the part of London society who would be there to see her commit herself for a lifetime into the arms of the weak Berwick heir. Daisy thought only: Thank heavens, I have managed it. No more worries ever again. His female relatives to see to things, and for me Hadley says the South of France and Italy and whatever I like, and only sometimes the family houses to keep his mother happy. And she thought: Once I have given him an heir, that will be over too.

'You do look lovely, Daisy.' Her sister, Lulu, plump and prettily blonde and blue-eyed, clapped her hands and regarded her sister. How many times had Lulu made the same exclamation? She would hear it again. They would meet often still; one did, usually. Daisy held out her arms to her sister.

'You too, darling. One day soon, you'll see.'

Lulu embraced her sister clumsily; a comb slipped from her hair and fell amongst the pins on the carpet. The Liscombe maids too stood back from their handiwork and gazed at Miss Daisy with pride; this they had achieved, sending Miss Daisy out the most beautiful bride of the season.

'Are you children ready?' Diana, Duchess of Berwick strode into the room and turned to each girl, adjusting the pearls at Daisy's neck and tutting over the combs in Lulu's hair, already slipping again.

Daisy looked once more into the set of mirrors at her dressing table; she saw herself repeated four times, only the slightly long nose she had from her mother marring the perfection of her beauty. It has only brought me Hadley, she thought, and felt herself take in a little panicky breath. They said he'd had fits as a child and sometimes he had strange moods and would not speak to her. They had had silent carriage trips together going to balls. But he would not bother her much afterwards. Daisy straightened her shoulders and put up her slender neck where Aunt Diana's pearls lay glowing in a reflection of oyster satin.

'We'll put on a good show, Auntie,' she said.

'The best, darling.' Diana and her niece understood each other.

Lord David, waiting at the bottom of the staircase for his eldest daughter to be taken on his arm to her wedding, saw her make her way down to him, a little shakily, in a glory of satin which brought out the bloom of her skin and the hazel eyes which had the shape of Blanche's.

'Darling,' he said, 'you look . . . lovely, so lovely.' He stepped across the hallway with the servants grouped behind him and took her hand. He could feel her trembling.

'Not too late, darling, if you want to change your mind,' he whispered.

Daisy freed her hand to place it on his arm. 'I shan't

change my mind, Papa,' she said. Just for a moment, he thought he saw a flicker of something in her face – fear, panic? Wedding-day nerves, he thought. At least I hope that's all it is.

At the reception in their ballroom at Liscombe House, the last time they would ever use it, he watched Daisy, impeccably correct, greeting her guests, thanking them and showing them the long line of gifts which lay in the next room. And he thought: I have not known how to make her independent enough not to care about all this. I have not known how to make her different from her mother.

In a new age, a new century, when some women were looking beyond the bounds of marriage, Daisy had never had a thought that was not of her own caste and circle.

But if it had not been for Kate, he might never have thought of women as people rather than as adornments, with their own rights to fulfilment as much as men. There were Liscombe village girls learning to think for themselves now, but not Daisy. He had failed with her.

Daisy moved about the room and he watched her. All she has is her beauty and her impeccable manners, he thought. Her cheeks grew more flushed; she drank the glasses of champagne the waiters held out to her and did not once look at her new husband as his small fund of conversation dried up and he grew morose behind his glasses of whisky.

Rather too early for his sister's liking, Lord David left his daughter's reception and went down to his study. How could it have been different? If he had married again? If Sarah had lived to guide them? He must think of other matters. There was to be the coronation of the new King, George V, in a few weeks. He must telephone Treeves to bring down his robes and get out the coronet. He could at least play his part as a viscount at the Abbey. Let him not fail in that.

On Coronation Day, 11 June 1911, Lord Liscombe, smiling faintly, vaguely, feeling rather foolish and smelling of camphor, stood in the hallway of his sister's London house. He let Treeves adjust the crimson and miniver cloak about his shoulders and Mrs Baker, up from Liscombe for this special day, give a final smoothing to the crimson velvet of his coronet.

Mrs Baker, standing at her place beside Treeves, regarding with him the figure their master made in his viscount's finery, saw how he had changed since old King Edward was crowned and he had last worn his regalia. She and Treeves had stood then together to see him go, nine years before, and Lady Blanche had been with him then.

Mrs Baker held the coronet on a silver tray and watched the way the master's shoulders drooped and the way his mouth was drawn down in sad lines and his grey eyes that once had sparkled and flashed with temper were now dull. Sometimes, he had a faint vague smile as if he were laughing, mocking something, she did not know what. There was a touch of white above his ears now and the brows that had once been thick and black showed grey. He was not the man he was and all at Liscombe knew it. Lady Blanche had had the last laugh. By dying, she had dragged him down into a kind of living death, so Cook said, and it was true.

Mrs Baker held out the silver tray, hands shaking a little. She could hardly see him now for her tears.

'Oh, I'll put it on in the coach.' Lord Liscombe put the coronet under his arm. He did not wish to look any more foolish going into the street.

The whole of London, it seemed, was out and about in the morning drizzle to see their aristocracy, their betters, gather about the new monarch and watch him crowned. There were their carriages going past, the ladies' hats and fine robes showing, the crimson and the ermine and the coronets wobbling on their heads. It was a pity the sun was not to shine upon them that day.

The Liscombe carriage, that had rumbled in the same way to take his grandfather to the coronation of Queen Victoria, trembling and shaking then on its iron wheels, made its slow way amongst the others, they too dragged from the back of country coach-houses for the crowning of a new monarch in Westminster Abbey.

David Liscombe, breathing in the remembered smell of old leather and, slightly, mould – though Johnny Tranter had worked so hard to rid it of damp – wondered if he would live to see another king crowned or if it would be Harry who would be sitting there in his place on another day such as this. He felt the weight, against his knee, of the packet of sandwiches Treeves had packed into the hem of his robes together with the flask of whisky. He remembered the exact feel against his leg the last time. No doubt there would be cold ham in them and a touch of Gentleman's Relish. If Treeves were to see another king crowned, he would pack the same set of sandwiches even if it were to be for Harry Liscombe, and Harry too would suffer the long, long day standing for the King.

The last time, Blanche had been with him. Feeling still slightly ridiculous and uncomfortable, tightly buttoned in by Treeves, he remembered turning the same corner in Curzon Street, with Blanche beside him, waving to the crowds when it was quite inappropriate to do so. Who was she to wave to them? And who was he to be dressed up like a puppet? He had even today, so many years since Kate, only dabbled in his personal charity. If he had been serious enough about it, he should have given over the whole estate to a co-operative.

He sighed impatiently at himself, tugging at the stiff old window catch. Harry wanted it all kept as it had been before the turn of the century. He claimed people wanted the old ways. But in the old ways, the fine qualities of someone like Kate were lost in a life of drudgery and childbirth. He could not speak to his own son any more; they had nothing in common. But he had the power now to take away the boy's birthright, if he wished. He would probably do nothing and let the days and weeks slip away into years.

And then he saw her, the girl. Only she was not a girl now, but a woman. She was standing with a boy of about five or six at the corner of Westminster Bridge, watching the carriages pass. The boy was waving and she was holding his other hand. Kate! He pushed at the window. Let him get his head out. Let him call out, 'Kate! Miss Tranter! Here, look here, over here!'

The carriage rumbled and swayed round the corner. Let it stop, let him get out. 'Kate!' He shouted it out and she turned towards him and he saw it was her from the pile of dark hair under her hat and the glow of her Dorset skin. She turned towards him, looking about vaguely, and he called again, 'Kate!' through the noise of the wheels and the horses' livery jangling and the muffled sound of the crowds. He wanted to get up and jump out but the noise and the weight of his cloak seemed to push him into his seat but he heard, quite distinctly, like the sound of a bird carried by the wind, a high little voice call: 'Mamma, I want to go to peepee,' and the people about laughed, indulgent, understanding. He saw Kate smile down at the boy and tug at his hand.

The boy's mother. Kate was his mother. Kate was married.

David Liscombe found the strength to close the window. He was a fool. Of course she would be married. It was just that he had not dared think of her lovely silky body in the arms of some tradesman.

Miss Kate Tranter, standing with Peter at the corner of Westminster Bridge to see the Coronation carriages pass, so rarely out with her son but having promised him this day, thought she heard a voice, calling her, a long forgotten, well-remembered voice calling: 'Kate! Kate!'

Lord David was back at Liscombe before ten o'clock the next morning; he had not gone to bed after the ceremony for he would not have slept. He had taken his sister's car and driven down to Dorset through the night.

He had to make sure that it was so, that Kate was married. How had he dreamed so long that she might one day come back to him? How could it not have occurred to him that someone else, a tradesman, a cook, would not have found her beautiful as he had, and had loved her at once, as he had?

What would he do if it were true and he could not live on dreams any more?

At the cottage, he found Mrs Tranter sitting in her doorway, shelling peas with the marmalade cat and her old dog dozing beside her in the sun. He knew them both, because they had been Kate's, and he knew her mother's stout and tired body, sitting so heavily always, with her boots unlaced and her grey hair untidy about her face. He knew it all, by heart, because she had known it, and had worried for and loved her mother. His extra shillings must have eased her life, though they were little enough. Even he could not shower gifts upon the dairyman's wife.

Not one of them moved when he approached across the stream; it was too hot and they were too old and were used to him passing. Mrs Tranter did not scramble to her feet as once she had; he wondered vaguely when she had stopped doing that.

'Fine day, Mrs Tranter!' he called.

'It is, sir,' she said, blinking up at him through the sun.

'Not too good yesterday in London for the King's coronation.'

'Ah?'

'No, misty, drizzling sort of day.'

'Shame for all them out in the streets to watch.' She split a pea pod into the colander in the folds of her apron. 'Cook'll be sending the newspaper down, no doubt, for me to read about it.'

'Yes.' He leaned his shoulder into the warm foliage around the doorway that Kate had known and looked down into the lap of Kate's mother. Swollen red fingers worked amongst the pea pods; the peas made a tiny sound, a little plop against the metal colander. Sun burned against his neck and upon his head. Sun burned on the heads of Mrs Tranter, hatless too, and on the golden cat and the dog, grey now around the muzzle. Kate would not see this any more for she was married and would never come home again, and he would never see her, would only see what she had once known, and the memory of her would get more and more distant and unreal and soon her cat would die and her dog and her mother too and nothing more exist of what she had known and what he wanted to grasp to him, for want of her.

'Funny thing,' he said. He could smell roses and Mrs

304

Tranter's lavender and warm animal fur. Her fingers split another pea pod.

'Maggoted,' she muttered and threw it down into the rose root.

'I saw your daughter, Kate. Yes. Very like your daughter, if not her. A girl standing in the street with a child, a small boy, and I thought at once, Why, it's Kate Tranter – but of course your daughter has no child, has she?' He waited and she spoke no word, only seemed to bury her chin further into the mound of her bosom. His head was throbbing painfully, from the sun.

He had to begin again for he had had no answer. 'I thought to myself, Why, that is so like . . . but of course it could not be your daughter, Mrs Tranter? Although you once told me she had stayed on in London with her aunt after that little youthful adventure of hers.' He found himself leaning down, with his head throbbing, to touch the hot fur on the head of the marmalade cat who lifted it slowly to give him a look of disdain, blinked through the sunlight.

'Tommy don't want stroking, this weather.'

He got himself up again. His hand touched hot stone and a rose thorn scratched across his thumb. A little bubble of blood formed and seemed to set in the heat. He said: 'Of course, she is no doubt married and quite settled by now, only I thought it could not be Kate, with a child. Though time does so fly, doesn't it? I can hardly believe Daisy's a married woman. Married this year. I walked her down the aisle and wondered where the years had gone, Mrs Tranter.' He saw Daisy's sad and lovely face, suddenly, in memory and wanted to talk to this woman about her. He wanted to ask for a chair so that he could sit there beside her, it did not matter about the sun, and she and the cat and the dog would listen to him talk about Daisy and the fire and Sarah. And Kate.

'Our Kate, she's married too,' Mrs Tranter said, and he saw her as if in dream get heavily up from the chair. He saw himself put out his hand with the scratch on it to help her. She clutched at the colander of peas and brushed empty pea pods into the roses and he felt that the sun had gone in, that something terrible and drastic had happened in the world. She said, brushing at her apron: 'Yes, a married woman, our Kate, although of course I couldn't go up and nor could Father, but my sister saw to everything and gave her ... what was right. Gideon's his name, sir. Yes, Gideon. A strange London name I thought, but there's no accounting for the young, is there?'

'No,' he said, 'no accounting at all, Mrs Tranter.' He watched her cross the sunny patch on her kitchen floor and disappear into shadow by her range.

'If there's anything, Mrs Tranter ...' he heard himself say, and stared up the hill to Liscombe, an awful black line, wondering how he was going to get himself up there.

Mrs Tranter rattled the peas for her husband's dinner into their saucepan, threw a pinch of salt on to them and wondered what she must do next. She had forgotten how to cook peas. She had forgotten whether she had bacon roly-poly or cold ham for her husband's dinner.

She did not know how the lie had slipped from her, but he deserved lies, a man like that.

She would not turn around to see him go off up the hill all alone with his shoulders bowed down.

PART THREE

CHAPTER FIFTEEN

August 1914

Johnny Tranter, twenty-two years old and dashingly handsome, able to raise a blush on the cheek of any girl in Dorset, let his horse Leila have her head round Flush Hill and down through the flowered walk beneath the beech trees. 'Gently, girl, gently does it,' he called and his voice echoed up into the hot still air with the sound of his Leila thudding through the daisies. Dust scattered about her hooves. It had been such a parched summer.

'Steady now.' She was lathering. He slowed her to a walk towards the stream and along to Stone Cottage. This was happiness, him and Leila, the two of them one together, Johnny thought, lifting off his hat to let the air cool his head. He had always known he was made to live with horses. And this horse! This black sinewy creature that was his Leila. Love for her was both burden and joy. Now he had to leave her for a few days, trusting no one with her care. He waved to his mother, from his side of the stream.

'You mind how you go on that journey and tell Kate I wants her home for a visit soon, and she can send that boy down here if there's to be a war.' Mrs Tranter stood framed in the blue cottage doorway, as she stood every day to see her son pass, hoping for a word or a smile from him.

'Yes, Ma!' grinned Johnny. 'Tell Pa to go up and have a look at Leila tonight, do. I'll see you in a few days.' He gave another wave to his mother and walked Leila back up Liscombe Hill and into her stables where he recited once again the stableboy's list of instructions.

Whistling the latest song to reach Dorset, he dressed in his rooms above the stables in new flannel trousers with turn-ups, a Fair Isle jumper and yellow socks. Johnny Tranter no longer wore boots except for riding. Boots were old hat. Smoothing a touch of Euchrisma hair oil on to the obstinate tuft of hair at the back of his head and grabbing his weekend bag, he danced down the stairs to meet Harry, his childhood friend. 'Hitchy-koo, Hitchykoo!' he whistled, sending the echo across the yard to Harry Liscombe waiting on the Hall steps.

'Yellow socks, Johnny!' Harry pointed, laughing. 'Not a gentleman, then, old boy.'

'Dark socks are old hat,' Johnny grinned, lifting one long leg into the runabout Lord Liscombe had in-structed his agent to buy for Harry. Johnny was to give him a few driving lessons in it on the way up to London, taking the lanes where they had ridden on horseback as boys. He threw his bag into the back, pulled on his trilby and eased himself gracefully into the driver's seat.

'What if war's declared today, Johnny?' Harry got in beside him, knocking knees and elbows. He had none of Johnny's ease, and remained as thin and pale as he had been as a child.

'We won't go to war,' Johnny scoffed, revving up. 'They'll all draw back at the last minute. They're just threatening each other like a lot of fighting dogs.'

Beth Tranter stood at the bottom of Liscombe Hill on her way to the village stores for her mother's weekly shop. Here was the car roaring down the hill. Do go carefully, Johnny, Beth sent up a silent prayer and stood in the dust waiting for a glimpse of them in a flash of red Austin.

Johnny gave a loud toot to his sister. She must think he was blind, and Harry too, if they thought he had noticed nothing.

'Oh, look, it's your sister Beth.' Harry waved politely, earnestly, at Beth Tranter, so sweetly charming, standing dust-covered at the bottom of Liscombe Hill as he had told her, in her blue summer dress and wide straw hat that cast blue shadows on her lovely face.

Oh, look, it's your sister, mocked Johnny silently. As soon as Lord Liscombe came home from France for the war period, he would put a stop to that little matter, he thought.

Going towards London at twenty miles an hour, Johnny Tranter drove Harry up the Dorset lanes, scattering hens and toddlers, raising a dust fit to choke on, sending horses cantering away across their fields and meadows, stopping the cows in their chewing, raising a thirst so they had to pause for lovely ginger beer, threepence a glass.

The little motor was running a treat; there was no rattling cough in her today, no heart-lurching thud to mean they would have to stand by the roadside, ignominiously begging for a lift to a garage.

And it was such a fine day; the sky was so clear. There could be no war coming.

'I don't see how England can withdraw with honour,' Harry shouted over the engine noise along the Dorchester road. 'We must support our allies. Belgium and now France have been attacked with no declaration of war from Germany. Won't we be next anyway?'

'France and Belgium should be able to look after themselves, I say,' said Johnny. 'And if our lot are mad enough not to declare our neutrality in all the mess, then I for one shan't join in. I'm not going off to get myself killed for the Frenchies.' He roared the motor along towards Bere Regis. 'And don't think you'll want to if the time should come. Why, you can't kill a fly, never have been able to. And didn't you sob over the fox hunts? You couldn't stand vermin being killed, you couldn't, and the Germans may be vermin for all I know, but you couldn't hunt 'em down and kill 'em off.' Chivvying, affectionate, Johnny Tranter glanced across to see his friend's face, with the dust in his eyebrows and coating his hair under his cap, sticking to the sweat on his forehead. Oh Lord, he thought, Harry was going to do something heroic, and would be the first to be killed.

At Kate's hotel, they separated to put on their evening clothes and each go to a different theatre, Harry to sit entranced before Chekhov's revelation of the human soul and Johnny to sing along with Miss Elsie Janis at the Passing Show revue.

'Florrie was a flapper, she was dainty, she was dapper . . .'

A Players Navy Cut burning at his bottom lip, Johnny clapped and sang and cheered with the other men about town and whistled 'Florrie was a Flapper' all the way along to the St John Street hotel, or almost, for he was hampered before he got to Westminster Bridge. There were crowds, more than the usual London summer crowds, going, someone said, to Buckingham Palace to show their support for England. Patchily, through the mass of people and along the street, bursts of song began to reach Johnny.

'Land of Hope and Glor-r-r-y . . .'

Johnny began to run. War! Well, he was not going to fight. He had to push his way through. People were laughing as if it were a carnival. At open tavern doors cheers floated out: 'Stop the Kaiser! War! War!'

He reached St John Street where Kate and Harry stood amongst others on the front steps of Tranter's. A faint echo of the singing and cheering charged the night air around them, and the murmur of voices mingled into the one word: 'War.'

'I think we must go, Johnny,' Harry said, taking his friend's arm.

'Not me,' he replied, throwing his cigarette stub down the steps. 'You're not going either, is he, Kate? He's only eighteen. It'll be over by Christmas.'

'Over by Christmas,' she echoed. She took Johnny's hand and Harry's and led them into the foyer of Tranter's Hotel. 'But can it be true, after so much talk? And where's the sense of it?'

'*Never* any sense in war,' Kate heard Johnny say through gritted teeth. 'Can't be any sense in anyone killing each other, sis.'

'No, but neither of you will go – you're too young. The Army will sort it out. And Harry hasn't seen my hotel yet, Johnny, so you go and order your drinks in the bar and sit down quietly and have yours. You stop letting that rage of yours build up, and I'll show Harry round and then we'll join you.' She pushed her brother towards the bar.

'I wish he would not get so wound up, Harry,' she said, leading the young man she had once nursed through nightmares across the foyer. 'Look,' she whispered, 'see how I have tried to make this like a country cottage. See the rag rugs – remember my mother having them? – and look at the porter in his Dorset funeral and Sunday suit like my pa's. And we've drawn the beams down, look, and have scrubbed deal tables and bowls of simple flowers . . .'

Kate stopped by the reception desk, still holding Harry's hand as if he were a boy of nine. 'Just like home, Harry, isn't it? But if there is a war, it will all be gone. A proper war takes everything, not just the soldiers.' She was a little breathless from nervous excitement at the day's announcements.

'This is very like your home, Kate dear, yes, not mine

alas. I wish it had been. I wish . . . I wish a lot of things, Kate.'

She turned to look up into his face. He was taller than her now, but there was the same dark hair, grey eyes that were so often afraid, that had in them now perhaps fear still but also sympathy for her because she was about to cry and he felt always for all suffering. Hers was nothing if there was to be a war, but Harry would find time for it.

'I hope you do not lose this nice place and your restaurants, Kate, if there is a war. You have worked so hard, and Beth is so proud of you.'

'And how do you always manage to bring Beth into the few conversations we have when you come to London, Harry?'

Kate smiled up at him and he burst out: 'When I look at you, I remember all the love I felt for you. You were the first person I ever loved, the only one for a long time although you went away. You were so sweet and loving to me, Kate, and suddenly I loved Beth, your sister, because she has so much of you although she is marvellously herself too.'

Around them a few guests moved and chattered. The porter answered the telephone. No one noticed them, standing by the reception lamp.

Kate saw the boy's sweet sad smile and the tears that threatened because he had told her, he had been able to speak of Beth, probably for the first time. Johnny had hinted at it, and she had not wanted to believe such a terrible echo of herself and Harry's father could be possible.

'Harry dear,' she said, 'I don't think his lordship would care . . .'

'My father wouldn't care one way or the other, Kate.' Harry rubbed a red patch into his cheek and bit at a finger. 'If you mean I should marry someone . . .'

314

'Just that you're too young perhaps,' she finished. 'How is your father?' Each time she saw Harry, she found herself asking the question although the answer was always the same and in any event she had no reason to ask it, their past together was long gone and finished with.

'All right, I suppose, for all I know,' Harry said on cue. 'I think he's leaving the French house to come home because of the war. I suppose he'll have to, patriotism and all that.' Kate heard the bitter note that mention of his father always produced. She wished she could talk to him about the bad feeling that had grown up between them but could not think she was in a position to act as independent listener. And what did she know of Lord David? Only that he had seduced a girl, her own past self, and falsely claimed to love her. She did not want to think of that time, to have it all brought back to her. Harry would never hurt Beth, not deliberately, only the impossible situation could hurt her. She must somehow find time to talk to her sister.

She took Harry's arm again and said: 'Come on, let's not be gloomy. Come and see the rest of the place and tell me how Beth is. Does my mother know about you?' She led him up the wooden stairs which had the worn look of cottage stairs although polished to a dark shine. Her mother would not want it, not Beth and Harry.

'No one knows,' he said fiercely, 'no one but you now, Kate, and you must not tell, for people will make a fuss. They'll say I'm only eighteen, you know. But if I am to go to war, I want you to promise me that she shall have everything that is mine, all my books and my personal things and anything that is in my bank account. Do you promise me, Kate? Everything that is mine Beth is to have.' They stood outside a bedroom and Kate promised.

315

'I do, Harry,' she said, 'but I want no more talk of it. There won't be a real war. It'll soon be over, only the Army will go. Now, Harry, look at this, and tell me what you think of it.'

She opened a door and in the dim light of the room pointed out the fat feather mattress and pillows plumped up, the fresh floral curtains, pink flowered china wash jug and bowl on a pine washstand with a marble top. 'Isn't it nice and homely? You can't imagine how much people like it. We hardly have a room empty some nights.'

'It's just like your cottage at home,' Harry said, smiling from the doorway. 'I used so to envy you all. There was always a smell of something, apple or herbs, something cooking on that range, and I used to go up with Billy to his bedroom after Johnny went to live over the stables, and we used to talk about the Labour Party and how we'd join it and work to help the poor, he with the law and me with the estate. And then your mother would call us down for huge stews and dumplings, and puddings with treacle poured over them, all steaming and hot, and I think I was never so happy until Beth. Maybe I loved her even then. She was always so calm and untroubled and thoughtful. I used to long to go down to your cottage.'

Kate saw tears in his eyes and felt her own throat tighten. Past times, lost for ever, never to be redeemed. 'I used to look up to Liscombe Hall from that damp bare place and long to be near the rich like you – not one of them, that would have been too far to go – just near them, a lady's maid or something, with a lady's hands that were never in soda, and perhaps a silk dress for best.'

'What a dreadful sad irony, Kate, we should each have had something in the middle and not wasted so much time grieving for what we could not have.'

The light from the corridor made shadows on his boy's face and Kate saw another, a little like his, only without his softness, shadowed too, reaching out to her. She cried: 'I do not know why things were so bad for you, Harry. I could never understand it, nor your . . . nor all of Liscombe, I suppose.' She moved to put her arms about him. 'I hope there is no war and no more class system so that you and Beth can marry and have a home of your own choosing, with steaming puddings for supper and simple things and a tranquil heart.' She had never hoped for so much for herself and Harry's father. Let it be possible for Beth and Harry then!

She felt him draw his arms about her and lay his head upon her hair. 'If my father does not manage to stop me. He may, you see. You cannot tell with him. No matter how much he has put into that Fund for the deserving poor, I am afraid that when it comes to me and Beth . . .'

'You say he hardly comes home to England now, Harry, and will probably make the estate over to you. He will not mind then what you do.' His arms dropped from her shoulders. 'I cannot trust him, Kate. He is a stranger, so much abroad. His agent has seen to my school fees and my allowance. I've hardly seen my father since the coronation in 1910 so how can I . . .?'

A sudden cry interrupted and startled him.

'What's that?'

'Go away, dwarfie! I want my mummy!' Peter's high voice reached the top of the staircase where Kate paused, unbelieving.

'Harry,' she said quickly, 'go down to join Johnny. My son must be having a nightmare. I'll come down shortly.'

'Peter!' She ran to his room and saw Gideon go limping past her. 'Gideon?' Gideon did not stop.

'Peter!' she cried again. 'How could you, to dear Gideon, when you love him so much?'

'I don't love him, he's a dwarf!' Kate saw her son sitting up in his nightshirt amongst a tumble of sheets. The glow of the lamp showed up the plump sulkiness of his eight-year-old face. Kate felt a twist about her heart. Why was Peter so often hurtful when they had given him so much love? Gideon was father, brother, guardian all in one to him. 'Darling.' She stood helplessly in the doorway; she wanted to turn back to comfort Gideon. She wanted her son never to have cried such a thing to such a dear man.

'You haven't kissed me goodnight, Mama,' Peter began to whimper.

Kate stood still. She must not kiss him, to punish him, but she wanted to gather him in her arms and make him understand about Gideon. She wanted Gideon not to suffer; she wanted Peter to be wise enough to see the worth of him. She had failed them both. She gave too much of herself to her work.

Kate sighed at herself and crossed the room. 'There'll be no kiss for you tonight. Lie down at once and go to sleep. I shall have a talk with you in the morning. You will apologize to Gideon then. Gideon, Peter! You've always loved him. What can it matter if he is small?'

Peter opened his mouth in a howl. 'Kiss me goodnight, Mama, kiss me!'

Kate stood hesitating by his bed, waiting for him to choke himself into silence. He often had such tantrums at night. She put a hand upon his head where the dark hair grew thin, so unlike his father's. 'Peter,' she said gently, 'I shall not kiss you for you do not deserve it. And I shall not give in. I cannot bear to think of my son hurting a friend so. Now, lie down and go to sleep and in the morning we shall both go to Gideon together.'

She eased away the damp pillows behind him and turned them to their cool dry side. 'There, my boy, lie down now. I shall not kiss you but I'll stay ... But what's this, Peter?' Under the second pillow there was something pink. Kate drew out a pink shawl and a grubby white garter.

'A garter, darling, and a shawl? Whatever are you doing with these?' She held the shawl and the garter in her hand and could not believe that such unlikely items lay there, that she had drawn them from Peter's bed. Had one of the maids gone mad?

'They're mine, Mama, mine. Give them to me, I can't sleep without them!' He set up another wail, with his mouth open wide. Panicky choking breaths let out the words: 'I sleep with them.'

'Sleep with them!' Kate let the things slip to the floor and sat to take her son in her arms. 'What nonsense,' she said, stroking the wet hair from his face. 'What nonsense.'

She stayed holding him until he finally slept and wondered in that rare quiet moment, in the muffled silence of a hotel bedroom that was only Peter's because it held a few of his toys and books, how it was that she had been so busy, always too busy, to know her son had needed women's things in his bed. He would have to go to school, to be with other children, instead of being petted and pandered to in an adult world.

She went slowly down the corridors, mechanically running a finger along the picture frames for dust, and down the banisters that maids were forbidden to neglect. All this was hers, her achievement, but suddenly there was Harry to remind her, and Peter, of all the past sorrows she did not want to remember. She was made to work, had to work, for her partners and for Peter and for home, and here were things to jolt her equilibrium. And the war.

In the bar, Johnny and Harry had been joined by Lulu Liscombe, excitedly recounting the very last London party of the peace. It seemed that in the mansions of the golden mile, the sons of the aristocracy had sent their servants to bring round their motors and they had all roared about the streets of that part of London which was aristocratic territory. 'They were shouting, "We'll see off Kaiser Bill!"' cried Lulu, a glass of champagne in her hand, basking in the attention of the crowd at the bar. 'They've been waiting for it. No one was going up for the grouse this year, and now it's come!'

Kate saw Harry silently usher her out of the room to collect her key. She too was to stay at Kate's that night so the three of them could make an early start for Liscombe and the beginning of their new war lives.

In the parlour, with her two partners, Kate kept her hand in her pocket on the soiled garter to remind herself she had matters that needed urgent attention. They talked quietly about the war. Now that it had come, what could it do to Tranter's? The tight band of unease about her chest did not relax; she felt that everything was slipping away from her.

At Liscombe the next morning, still dusty from the drive, Lulu Liscombe paused only to throw off her motoring scarves before rushing downstairs to Mrs Baker, to discuss with her the forming of a group within the Hall servants to knit woollen socks and gloves for the soldiers already mobilized. It would be something to help, Lulu had repeatedly called to her companions on the journey from London. Lulu, as plump and as prettily blonde as she had always been, yearned to help someone, something weaker than herself, so that she could feel she had a place in the world. For young animals and the starving poor, for the flowers destined daily to die and the cows destined for slaughter, Lulu's heart had bled; for herself, overweight, clumsy and slow at learning, Lulu's young heart had wept. Now at last there was a definite and permissible focus for all that; everyone's heart would bleed for the young men, dying on the battlefields.

Lulu turned and paused at the bottom of the Hall staircase, a trail of chiffon at her feet, one plump hand on the warm bronze of the pillar. She gave a rapturous glance across to her brother standing hesitantly in the hallway. Light from the long mullioned window gave a sheen to the dark silkiness of his hair and cast shadows beneath the grey eyes that were so like their father's. 'Harry!' she breathed. 'You will have to go, soon.'

'If I can, Lulu dear.' Harry gave her a slow sad smile.

'And if you are injured, I shall come and nurse you, the way I did when we were young. I shan't let anyone stop me coming, not any of those Generals, and I shall bring you home here, to get well. I can bandage and dress wounds already and . . .'

'You'd better go and see Mrs Baker, before the wounded start coming in, Lulu.'

Harry watched his sister's full calves in their silk stockings carry her up the stairs before him and smiled again, wryly, to think that she would probably see war in terms of the young men she knew lying gracefully on the field of battle, moaning bravely over wounds no bigger than a fencing cut.

He stood very still. The warmth of the Liscombe sunshine wrapped about him. Light played on the pillars and across the oak floor where he had run as a child. Warm wood and light. It always seemed warm in the Liscombe hall. He could not say to Lulu: 'Battle is limbs torn away. Battle is dying, shrieking, in a mess of

321

your own flesh with your beloved horse thrashing in its death agony beside you.' Harry stood in Liscombe sunlight and remembered sitting on his old iron bedstead in the nursery and sobbing over tales from the Crimean and the Boer Wars. Homes laid waste, children and girls butchered. Terror, flight, pursuit. He remembered his boy's heart stopping over the cry of the hunted fox. The very sound of the bugle and the hounds baying had pierced his heart. He had hugged his arms about him and imagined the fox's dread, the fearful animal crouched, panting and spent, waiting for death.

Harry shivered in the warm sunlight and remembered his vow never to hunt down beast or man; he had said he would never go to war but now he must: for Lulu, for Liscombe, for Beth, waiting for his return down in the valley. Beth! He imagined her trailing across the countryside, as the poor Belgian women had – to what safe haven? Would any part of England be safe before the Germans?

He found that his legs would move and strode up the stairs, knocked at his father's study door and boldly stated to the man who had once briefly seemed to love him, but had just spent four or five years abroad: 'I intend not to go up to Oxford, Father, but to join up immediately.'

'Nonsense, my boy, of course you won't go.' Lord Liscombe sat before the telephone in his study and glanced up at his son. 'You'll go up to Oxford for Michaelmas term. The war'll be over by Christmas.'

Harry watched the tic come and go at the corner of his father's mouth which never smiled at him now. There had once been affection, long ago it seemed now, after the fire. His father had seemed pleased to have him alive and back at Liscombe. Then the old distant look had come into his face. Harry had been sent to

Eton, and to Europe; he had been sent to do the things everyone of their circle did and his father seemed hardly to notice he had become a man.

'I think I must go, Father, for England. I cannot . . .' It sounded foolish, even as he said it.

Lord Liscombe snorted. 'No need for you to die for England, old chap. The Army's been on already.' He nodded towards the telephone. 'I'm to persuade rural minds of German wickedness and drive them off to be slaughtered with the love of England in their breasts. But there's plenty of them – more of them anyway. Aren't you always on about the estate needing management, the people needing their livelihood? Well, you'd better stay here then and help me see there's a place for them to come home to. Or at least that their families will continue to be looked after. By us. That's our responsibility; you've always said it. Don't think I haven't heard you talking to Tranter out in the stables.'

Harry saw his father move papers about on his desk and his mouth twist up into a wry smile. 'You'll have your chance one day, Harry. Now, I'll need your help with the harvest. Some of the men will enlist even if I don't persuade them. Food . . . we'll all need food. The Army as well, remember.' He stood up and rolled back his sleeves as if he were ready to hold a scythe in his own hands that very moment.

'Anyway, it'll all be over by Christmas. Here, old chap.' He went towards his son and put a hand on his shoulder. There was a kind, sad look in the grey eyes that had so often frightened Harry. 'Look at it sensibly. You're not eighteen yet. I know how you feel. I'd be the same, if I had your energy. Your idealism. It's fine to be an idealist, son. But you couldn't fight, not you. You wouldn't hold a gun, remember? And the hunt. Kate said . . . Anyway, you're not a fighter, are you? I am, I suppose. I'd go if I were younger. I'd go willingly. But I think this estate needs us more than the Army does.'

Harry fought back foolish tears, feeling the weight of his father's hand upon him. How rarely he had felt it. How rarely had his father lifted him in his arms or put a comforting hand upon him. 'I think I must fight, now, Father. For . . .' He could not say England, not again. England was an idea. 'For the King,' he said. 'For all of us, for Liscombe and the people on it.'

'Yes, yes.' Lord Liscombe patted his shoulder again and looked down at the floor between them. 'But I can't let you go, son. You're the Liscombe heir. Liscombe'll need you after the war. When the Hun's been vanquished. It'll all be over by Christmas. We'll see then, if it isn't, eh? I don't want to lose you, Harry. You're all I have. Lulu will be gone soon, be married. What will I have kept Liscombe for, if not for you?'

The silence then, with only the old clock ticking and the distant clatter of horses from the stables, seemed to Harry to hold in it many things unsaid by his father who had always seemed sad, even before the fire and the loss. Harry felt with a sudden shock of remembered revulsion the scurry of the rats over his legs. 'All right, Father,' he said, for the strength and determination he had felt, coming up the stairs, was gone now, as it always was when he stood before this man. 'We'll see again at Christmas, if the war is not over.'

He looked into his father's face and saw the old sadness, the shadowed eyes, the greying of his hair at the temples. They were physically so alike. One day, he would look like this man, only there would be no sadness in him, with Beth.

He and his father never spoke of the burning of Liscombe tower and the death of his mother and Aunt Sarah. He supposed they never would now. And yet he would have liked to hear his father say something of it. Perhaps: 'Your mother was mad, Harry,' for that would have excused it, or 'It was not your fault, Harry,' for it had always seemed to him that it was. Only Beth had ever made him feel worthy of love. He wanted to tell his father about her, wanted to tell him that he was to fight for her, to earn his place at her side for the rest of his life.

'Right then, cut along and get changed, eh? The harvest can't wait for any war, not even one that will be over by Christmas.'

Harry turned away with the words unsaid and felt his spirits lighten. He would allow himself these few weeks. It would be easier, afterwards, to say that he was going. He could quite openly be near Beth and watch her face and her smile and her look that was just for him, their secret.

All of Liscombe, as always, joined in the bringing in of the harvest: Will Tranter and his dairymen, the stable hands, all the villagers, men and women and children. Working with them, Harry allowed himself to be happy. He stood on the haycart in the top fields and took the heavy dusty sheaves from Will Tranter's hands, tossing them up the way generations before him had. What use had Will for the learning of the alphabet and the reading of newspapers? His father was wrong: country people did not need to move away from the life they had always known. Under his management, Liscombe ways would go on.

Sweat stung at Harry's eyes; dust dried the blood on his arms and face where the hay scratched. He lifted up the sheaves that Will Tranter threw him and through the dust watched the lovely distant sunhazy figure of his Beth, dressed in blue with a pink straw hat. If, as his father said he intended to, the estate was passed to him after Oxford or the war then one day soon he and Beth would stand together, master amd mistress of Liscombe and its people. The Carters, the Williams, the Beales, all the families he had grown to respect and love since the fire, since Johnny's teaching him about country life, would all stay and prosper with him and Beth on Liscombe land. There would be fifty Liscombe harvests for him and Beth, fifty golden summers until it was their own grandchildren who joined in with harvest work.

Beth Tranter, watching her father and her beloved work at the same cart, each as hot and dusty and sweating under their caps, thought that Harry was too young to go to war and her father too old. She thanked God for it, and at noon poured them cold tea and cider under the shading oak trees.

Beside her sat Johnny, impatiently swallowing dust and cider. He did not want to harvest this year, Beth knew; he wanted to spend all his time with Leila, the light and joy of his life. He must know the Army would not take a thoroughbred horse for the war effort, but he seemed to find it hard to sit with them under the trees, to work at the harvest as he had all his life.

Beth watched her brother, so oddly not joking, so unusually not the one to start the singing at the day's end, and once touched his arm to whisper: 'They will not take Leila, Johnny.' He shook his head and stared into the oak leaves above their heads and did not answer.

Each day her mother took her heavy legs up across Liscombe Hill and down into the lane to climb again to the fields being worked, and join her family for the noon break. She lowered herself heavily beside Beth under the oak tree and watched her boys eat with sweat and dust-grimed faces, Johnny brooding and gentle Billy dreaming behind his dusty round glasses that he did not need but only wore for protection. Beth knew that her mother's bread and cheese would form a lump under her heart and she would soon mutter over indigestion and ask Beth again to speak to his lordship for confirmation that Dorset boys, needed on the land to feed the Army, would not be taken yet.

But his lordship would be powerless! Beth left her own lunch untouched and watched anxiously, greedily, the familiar faces about her: Harry, her brother, Jim Williams, Joe Carter, all the others, sunburned and sweating. Dirty hands reached out for more white Liscombe bread and yellow cheese, healthy white teeth bit into strong onion flesh. Let it all go on, let there be other Liscombe harvests, and all these men and boys sit here again under this oak tree. She asked only that.

Three weeks later, the last cart stood half-filled in the field beyond the water meadows and was brought in by the Carter boys. Only the children were left to run about, playing at gleaning, following the gossiping women.

That afternoon all the male Liscombe workers turned to carrying down from the Liscombe kitchens the food that had been in preparation. Under the orders of Treeves, the men took down to the big barn beside Home Farm stables trays of glazed hams, shoulders of mutton, a whole side of beef and six suckling pigs. Cook sweated in her kitchen, dreaming of the dancing and the music, turning already to a tune in her head. She sent down bowls of yellow custard, red fruit jellies, heaps of late raspberries, mounds of the exotic fruit from Liscombe glasshouses, now once a year for Liscombe workers since there were no great house parties as in the old days. For the rest of the year, the fruit was sold for income for the Trust Fund and Cook did not know which she disapproved of most: she wanted the old days back, the gentle supervision of Lady Sarah, and the poor in their place and the rich in theirs.

Treeves sweated in the barn in his baize apron and shouted his orders: 'Put the cider flagons to one side of the stage, put the beer on the other and lay out those tankards. Fetch down another table. Freddie, get some straw brought in to keep the dust down underfoot.'

At six o'clock, hundredweights of food lay waiting and gallons of drink. The barn and the valley were silent. The evening sun slanted down behind Liscombe Hill, lighting up the last motes of dust about the barn door and the midges dancing over the stream.

All the Liscombe people were in hot silent bedrooms, feeling sleepy, reluctant to pick up their Sunday best, too tired from the weeks of work and heat to make the effort. Billy Tranter went on reading in the room which was now his, scanning yesterday's *Times* for war news, feeling his heart beat in the silence with fresh rage. The ruling class made war; the poor fought it. Billy burned with the injustices of human life, and turned the pages carefully so as not to waken his nephew Peter, sleeping in Johnny's old bed.

Beth, in her bedroom, pulling on the blue linen dress which daringly showed her ankles, called to her mother: 'Have you seen my blue beads?' It was too hot for beads, but Harry said they reflected the blue of her eyes; she only ever thought to please Harry and he her.

'They're where you last put them,' Mrs Tranter shouted back, a mechanical reply to each of her children all through their lives.

Will Tranter, outside in the last of the sun, bathed his chest and arms in the stream, running cool water past where the sun line showed dark up to the elbows. He had yet to shave but the music was already starting up in the barn. 'You women get on down,' he shouted, 'get us our places.'

Freddie, the kitchen boy, who had played the accordion at the Liscombe harvest for the past forty years, flexed his fingers over the buttons and sent the notes of a nameless Dorset jig, centuries old, floating over the stream and down the valley and up the hill.

Hearing Freddie's music begin, the music she had heard at harvest all the years they had been at Liscombe, since she was ten, Beth stood dreaming, warm from the day's sun. Heat was still wrapped about her in the room, though the sun had dropped behind Liscombe Hill and the Hall showed a dark uneven line in the shadow. Beth stood still in silk-stockinged feet and lifted heavy lazy arms to fix the beads about her neck. Soon Harry would kiss her there where the fastening was and into the line of her hair which she had so carefully pinned into a knot; it would fall about her face but no one would guess that Harry had kissed for no one knew they were together. Though they might not long be so, with the war begun.

Beth felt her heart constrict. Harry, her secret love, to go to war and she to be left to imagine him somewhere, dying, without her.

'Beth!' Her sister Kate's voice interrupted her thoughts. 'I think Peter's dropped off, but I shan't leave him until I'm sure – he gets such nightmares sometimes. Billy's keeping very quiet with his newspaper so as not to disturb him.'

'He'll be safe with us, Kate, until the war's over.' Beth leaned her arms on the warm window-sill. 'Look up to the Hall, see the third window to the right. Harry's there, bathing and putting on his best silk shirt

329

that he looks so handsome in, and his light worsted suit and light shoes for dancing.'

Kate too leaned on the warm wood and looked up to the Hall, remembering other times when she had leaned and watched. Why should it seem so different now, to know that Beth too loved a Liscombe? Why was their love just sweet innocence while hers, even long past, was shameful and to be hidden? She felt her sister's warmth beside her and there was no bitterness in her heart, only gladness that Beth should have Harry's love and hope she would not be too hurt by its ending.

'And imagine all the maids getting ready, Kate. All their boxes will be out on their beds, they've been sewing silk flowers everywhere for weeks, and everything will smell of lavender and Soir de Paris. Priss has got a white dress she looks really huge in and the hem's crooked. She wouldn't let me sew it up for her, she couldn't see how it was. And dear Cook'll be waddling about the corridors in her violet outfit, telling everyone off. Poor Ada's got bright pink – can you imagine? – although we all advised her against it. Mrs Baker will be in purple, of course. Nothing ever but black and purple for Mrs Baker.'

Kate breathed in the scent of her mother's roses and listened to her sister's sweet low voice that never had any malice or spite in it, only goodness and affection for the people she had known most of her life.

'Beth! Kate! Father says to get on down.'

'Coming, Mother. Come on, Kate!' Beth, full of sudden joy and strength, with all her tiredness gone, pulled her sister's arm. 'Tonight you must dance with Harry too, if I can spare him for one dance. Tonight we do not have to hide, you see, dear Kate. We can dance and dance and be together, and no one will notice. We shall have this time and not think of the war nor anything else, not our future which can never be – oh, I know it can't, Kate, no matter what you try and tell me – but I do not mind for no happiness endures for long, does it?'

'No, darling, not for long, but do not be too ... too happy, I was going to say, for then the fall afterwards will be all the greater. But I am silly. Everything is going to be all right for you, Beth.' She saw the glow of love in her sister, her bright eyes and flushed skin. Nothing would stop her suffering one day. She felt her throat tighten. 'You're so young,' she said.

'Not as young as you when you had Peter.'

Between them, in the quiet hot room, a fly buzzed. Kate saw in her sister's face only love and pity, neither blame nor judgement. She wanted to sit down upon the bed and forget about the special evening and the dancing and recount to her sister from the very beginning how it had been from the moment she had dreamed Liscombe would be the start of a new life, and how she had let herself love Harry's father. She put out a hand. 'I want ...'

'No, dear Kate, there is no need. I know that you loved someone and marriage was not possible, and then there was Peter. I always knew it was all right though Mother would never tell me and said we must always pretend you were married. I did not see why we had to be ashamed. I am proud of you for not hiding Peter but it is better I suppose, for him, that we should let people think you are married. I just wish you had been able to tell me, Kate, so I could comfort you.'

Kate saw her sister's calm and lovely adult face looking at her with love. 'I wish so too, dear Beth. I thought you would be ashamed of me, and then some-how time passed and Mother had let people here think it was all right. Perhaps I should have stopped her pretending? I wish you could have told me about Harry – sooner, I mean. There has been so little time for us to be sisters, hasn't there?'

'Now we are both grown up,' Beth said.

'Yes.'

'Shall we go on down, Kate?'

'You go, darling, you've someone waiting for you. I'll just see how Peter is before I leave.'

Kate followed her sister down the stairs and watched her fly along the stream path towards the barn where her Harry waited. She stood in their blue doorway, in the very last light from the sun, waiting to see off her mother too, for Susan was not yet ready. Letty was running down the hill, nice little Letty in a black and white dress Kate had sent her and a pair of worn court shoes she had bought herself from the jumble sale at the summer fête. Behind Letty was poor pale Eric, trying to stride, to look tall for Letty, trying to keep up with the girl who did not want him, Beth had said. Kate smiled. Another young love. She hoped for a kiss for Eric and a dance for Letty with someone handsome, perhaps Jim Williams from the village. Behind them walked the other Liscombe servants, Mrs Baker and Treeves sedately last with Cook, puffing a little under the wide expanse of her violet silk chest.

Kate watched them all hurry along with the pace of the music floating from the barn; all would be happy, just for a few hours tonight. But she could not go to the supper herself and face Lord David amongst his staff as she had promised herself she would. She could not go now for Beth had shown her what she had never wanted to acknowledge to herself: her mother's pretence of her marriage had become established. At Liscombe she lived a lie. If she went to the supper, there might be questions asked. 'And how is your husband?' people might say.

He, Lord David, would hold out his hand to shake hers and pat his son's head, all unknowing, looking at him absent-mindedly, his own son.

Kate felt herself give a gasp of pain. She could not stay here with Freddie's music and the sound of the people laughing and Lord David there about to look at his own son. She turned away and climbed the stairs to sit with sad angry Billy and Peter. Tomorrow, early, she would leave Liscombe. The pretence must go on, for her mother's and Peter's sake, but she could not stand before Lord David with his own son and mouth words that were a lie.

Beth, waving to her sister from the distant barn door, waited for Letty so as not to go in alone to blush at the sight of Harry waiting there too. Hearts quickening a little from the rhythm of Freddie's music, the girls went together into the dark scented barn where all the food was laid out under dusty sunbeams from the skylight. Beth saw Freddie behind great plaited loaves of bread given pride of place in the display, and beside him her handsome Harry, his eyes fixed on the door, for the first glimpse of her.

Soon the village people had filed in, with their shiny well-scrubbed faces, they too in their summer best and a little stiff, a little shy. They and Liscombe servants always began their harvest supper very politely until the food and the drink loosened their tongues and they became themselves. They raised their tankards in salute to each other and laid waste to the meat they had reared and cooked between them until it was reduced to bone and slivers of fat and the harvest plaited bread lay in crumbs about their plates.

Separated by an expanse of table, Beth and Harry ate and gazed across at each other, eyes transfixed in a wordless message ever repeated. At the top table by the stage where soon the singing would begin, Lord Liscombe sat smiling down at his workers, known now, since the traumatic evening which had cost him his wife and sister, each one. His workers at the lower tables spoke of his loss and the change in him and raised their tankards in silent salute to a man they did not understand but who was so much part of their lives they discussed him and his affairs as if he were in their immediate family. It was unusual, they decided, to see him smile, but then it was eight years now since the fire; most of them had forgotten he rarely smiled before that, that it was Lady Sarah they saw amongst them then, in the school and with the sick.

They watched him dance the first dance with Mrs Baker, when Jim Williams got up to help Freddie on to the stage. Jim Williams called for dancers and tapped his heavy boot along with the music, clapping together strong hands that had lifted the most sheaves at harvesting. Cook agreed with Mrs Tranter sitting beside her that Jim Williams would be taken by the Army if they ever saw him, so big and wide was his chest, and his thighs in their new shiny corduroys as strong as oak trees. They kept their eyes away from Jim and enviously watched stiff Mrs Baker turn about the floor by the stage in the arms of Lord Liscombe.

Mrs Tranter had to remind herself that this was the man who had ruined her daughter and hardened her heart against the lift it had from the waltz tune. When Miss Lulu rose to Treeves's bow and set off to have the first dance with the butler in what would have been her mother's place, Mrs Tranter kept her eyes on that pair and was able to scoff at the awkward step of Treeves as he led the pretty girl, smiling up at him, so anxious to please, past and around his lordship and Mrs Baker.

The waltz over, they all sang 'For He's a Jolly Good Fellow' to Lord Liscombe to thank him for their evening, and he left, as was proper, as he always did, so that they could really enjoy themselves. Mrs Tranter hardened her heart again at the lonely sight of him slipping through the barn door and jumping the stream to go and sit by himself in an empty Hall, and rose from her seat to dance a jig with her husband, the only one he would allow her, for the sake of their distant youth when they had danced at other harvest suppers and love had been on their minds.

Will Tranter began his serious drinking then with the other men, stopping only to sing his song 'Two Little Girls in Blue' to false sobs from the audience, and Mrs Tranter sat back on the benches in her dove-grey silk dress, to gossip with Cook of the war and who would go, who would be lost.

Billy Tranter whirled in front of them, dragged by Miss Lulu in a scandalous new dance they knew she must have learned in London – the tango. It was shocking, they agreed, to see two young people so close and not married. 'And Billy's always had two left feet,' Mrs Tranter muttered crossly, ashamed before Cook that her son should let himself take part in such a display. The couple went round and round the tables, tutted over, and out into the dark summer night, Billy frowning through steaming glasses.

Mrs Tranter thought: They'll never take Billy, for his suffering from eyestrain and too much book-learning. She wanted to say to Cook: 'They won't take our Billy, will they?' but she had said it twice already and Cook would not understand. She was not a mother. She had not carried the boy in her belly, or nursed him through croup and the whooping cough or seen him go off with paper cuffs under a black jacket to work in a lawyer's office, knowing he was free of labour on the land.

Cook, longing for Frampton to ask her for a dance, her feet tapping impatiently, watched the shiny red faces of the Rose twins, two of the seven boys, all below thirty, dancing with the post office girls. All that evening, in spite of her humming, of her tapping feet, of her heart lifting with the sound of the music, there had been a strange cold feeling about her chest. The Carter woman would suffer for some of her sons lost at the war; Jim Williams's mother and grandmother would live out the rest of their lives dressed in black if he were to be killed. The little Beale girl, just married to her childhood sweetheart Samuel Sweatman, and no doubt with her first-born already within her, would for ever after be the poor widow with a fatherless boy to raise, if she should lose her Sam. If only she Hannah Fellowes sat there with the fear of loss filling her life with purpose, if only she too would one day have the pity of all about her for that loss!

Cook felt envy and sorrow and longed for the days of Lady Blanche when there had been no talk of war and she had a proper place in the world and no time for regrets.

'Oh, oh, Antonio, He's gone away . . .'

The sound of the latest London song rang cheerfully up into the rafters and Mrs Tranter, swaying gently in her chair to the music, did not see her youngest daughter slip from the barn. Harry, dancing his duty dance with Letty, was watching only Beth. Seeing her, he took his cue. He slipped out through the breathless couples, back on the benches, hands waving in exaggerated fanning of hot faces.

Eric would not get his kiss from Letty, for how could she, fresh from the arms of his young lordship, demean herself by going round the back of the barn with the oddboy? Her heart would not stop for Eric going off to

336

war now, though she knew that Master Harry belonged to Beth, the nicest girl in the world.

Freddie drank a tankard of the sweetest Dorset cider straight down and picked up his accordion to play faster and faster. All the couples had to dance; Treeves danced with Mrs Baker, the farmhands and the gardeners took a maid each, and Mrs Tranter went round and round the floor led by the head carter.

The dancing became so fierce that the youngest amongst them whirled out of the barn and ended up shrieking with laughter, their boots in the stream. Even Mrs Baker, Cook and Mrs Tranter, watching, did not mutter over the ways of the young for war was coming and only the young would go.

Beth took the familiar path round behind the barn and along the stream, the one she often took to see Harry. Suddenly, dancing, she had felt such a pain about her heart. Would Harry go now the harvest was in? There were thousands killed already; her Harry might one day lie pierced with a German bayonet and she not be there to hold him. She felt she would know, if he were to die in battle. She would know and stop living at the same moment.

She climbed on up the path through Flush woods where their special place was, a long seat among the birches. Before her, dipping down, was the flowered walk where they had played as children and where he would come now, in a moment. Harry never kept her waiting. In the dark summer night she could just see the paleness where the daisies and buttercups grew. And here he was, striding up to her, her dear Harry who loved her.

She spread out her shawl and his jacket and they sat entwined, the way they always did. Faint sounds from the dancing reached up to them.

337

'Lulu is making Billy dance the tango!'

'Did you see him? Afraid to hold her, afraid to tread on her toes!'

Poor grave Billy who could not take his final studies in law in London with the war on. The war would change all their lives.

Beth said: 'You shan't go, shall you, darling? Not yet, not until they make you?' She held his hand to her breast. Better to say it, better to plead than just see him walk off as if he were going to school.

'I think I must, Beth. I am eighteen, a man. How can I justify going to Oxford when so many who should be there now have died? Chaps I knew at Eton dead; chaps from Dorset dead. I must go, Beth. I must, can you not see? Look what the Germans have done to Belgium and France – all those women attacked, their homes pillaged, refugees now. Should I let it happen here, darling? Shall I just let them come here and take our land, turn your mother out and . . . I must go for Liscombe people, so it won't happen. It's my responsibility.'

Beth thought: Mother turned from the cottage, walking the roads on her poor swollen legs! Of course he must go. All the men must go that could fight.

'I know you must go, darling,' she said, 'only I cannot bear it.'

'I shall go down to Dorchester tomorrow probably,' he said, holding her. She had known he would say it, tonight; she had been waiting for the words all the last long hot weeks.

In the end, hardly any more words were said, for they could not speak. They lay in their secret place and he unbuttoned her dress at the front to put his lips on her heart and it was she who gave herself to him, guiding him, for that was all she had. She lay beneath him and he cried out for the joy of it, fumbling into her. This was love!

Only the rooks saw, and the wild things, waiting for their night.

Afterwards, he dressed her and put his arms tight around her as they sat back against the log. All was changed, their whole lives changed now.

A quarter moon was out in the navy-blue sky. The wood and the valley were silent; the roisterers, exhausted, had stumbled off to bed. Freddie's accordion would be put away till Christmas. What would Christmas bring? The Germans?

Only tonight, they had had tonight. Beth breathed in the night air and pressed her face into Harry's shoulder. Her love. Her lover. Soon to go to war.

'Are you hurt, Beth?'

'No, darling, only a little and I am glad of it.'

'When the war is over, I shall come back to you.'

'No, no, darling, it will never be allowed, you and me.'

'Oh, yes, we shall one day be Lord and Lady Liscombe, just think darling.'

Beth smiled into the darkness. Let him think it, let her love think it would all be possible. They had had this time together. She knew what love was. She had given hers to him, and would ask no more of life.

He cut a little of her hair with his penknife and gave her a piece of his own. Each folded a lock solemnly between sheets from Harry's diary. That they would always have, and the memory of this night.

They went back, walking together, no eyes to see them now, but Beth had begun to tremble with the chilled air and the thought of his going. Stronger than Harry she might be, more grown in mind and body, but she was a girl still and hadn't she ... hadn't she ... Beth trembled and was still glad of it. She had nothing else to give him. Harry trembled with her, walking back down the hill. What had he done?

339

'But you'll be my wife, darling, it will not be wrong.'

'Yes, Harry, one day soon.' Beth let him hold her as they walked.

She kissed him at the cottage door and took off her shoes and crept with a candle up the wooden stairs. Her mother must not hear her. She would know what she had done, she would guess it and would not understand.

Harry watched the candle flicker away and appear again at Beth's window. He would watch over her that night, his last here perhaps; he would watch the window as he had so many times before from Liscombe tower. Only now he was watching over his wife. And the feel of her against him and her gift to him. In the morning, he would go and see her brother. Johnny must look after her in his absence; it would be as if they were married and he would make her an allowance from his own account.

He sat beyond the stream with her golden cat, a part of her, in his arms. The cat's eyes were wide with the stillness of the dawn coming, watching for the wild things. He was off before Harry; he had work to do.

Harry glanced once more up at the cottage window. There she would be, her dark hair spread upon the pillow, the lovely glow of her skin flushed with sleep. One day he would lie with his face pressed against hers or in her hair, his arms holding her safe.

First, he too had work to do. Up through the debris of a night's rollicking, up to the top of the hill, he went home through the kitchens where the scullery maid, still dreaming of the dance, was turning round and round in her unlaced boots, her arms held up to an imaginary partner.

'Brew me some tea, Letty.' She jumped. 'I'm going to pack a bag then I'll be back for it, and you're to tell no one you saw me. Swear?'

340

'Cross me heart, Master Harry.' Letty could be trusted with a secret; she would never tell a soul, not even if the Germans came to drag it from her.

Bathed and changed, having honoured Letty enough to drink his tea with her – how she would dream over that! – Harry crept round the back of Liscombe Hall and across to Johnny's flat over the stables.

Through the straw and up past the horse smell he must go to Johnny's bedroom. How long before he should see all this again? All this background to his childhood and youth, the old golden stone and the great door and the sweep of the lawns going down to the downs that his mother so much hated. He loved it, all of it, though he had often feared one day to be master of it. It was for this that he had to leave for war, and though battle might be like the hounds after the fox, let there not be any bugles nor strong against the weak. Let it be a fair fight. He asked, he thought, only that and he was ready.

In his pocket was a note he had typed in his father's study two days before on paper headed The Viscount Liscombe, Liscombe Hall.

To Whom It May Concern
    I hereby authorize my son and heir, Harry David Lonsdale Liscombe, to apply for enlistment in the regiment of his choice.

Harry had thought of everything.

Johnny was not in his riding clothes but wearing his best suit and the yellow socks, on a working day.

'Didn't you hear the silence?' Johnny shouted.

'What silence?' Harry said blankly.

'The silence. There's no sound of horses or feed being got ready, is there?'

Johnny seemed to space out his words.

341

'No. I suppose I thought I was too early.'

'Well, you thought wrong and they've gone.'

'Who's gone, Johnny?'

'The horses, my horses!' Johnny was shouting and turning blindly about his room with the clothes strewn about. 'They've taken my Leila and Nell and the other mares and the pony.' He seemed to be screaming. 'The requisitioning blokes came and they took them. Your father let them go, he let them go! Oh, God.' Johnny sat on his bed and put his face in his hands. 'They took them last night. You didn't see me at the harvest supper, did you? Fifty pounds Leila was sold for.'

'No I . . .' How could he tell Johnny to look after Beth? He would not listen, and how he would suffer for the loss of his beloved beasts. Harry watched, anguished, as his friend turned about the room.

'Well, I'm going now, I'm off to enlist. Maybe they'll put me in the horse section or whatever it is. I'll ask for that. I've got to be with my Leila, she needs me, there's no one can understand an Arab just like that.'

'You're enlisting, Johnny? Let's go down together. We'll join up together, now, today. We'll go to war together and find Leila and . . .'

'You'll be an officer, won't you?' Johnny stood and put on his jacket. 'They won't take me for an officer, though to see Leila I'd even try that. Betray my class, as Billy would say.'

'I can't be an officer just like that, and anyway I'm going under plain Mister. I'll go for a private. They're taking anybody in the first rush. I'll be gone before my father finds out.' He wanted Johnny to approve of him, to say it would be worthwhile to enlist, necessary even to leave Liscombe in order to save it.

Johnny had hardly heard him. He propped an envelope on his bed. 'Do they look after mothers?'

'I should think your money will go to her,' said Harry. 'I'll have mine sent here too if you like. I shan't need anything.' His would be for Beth. He must somehow see that she had money; with the war coming perhaps so far as Dorset she might have need of it. Beth was his wife and his responsibility now. He felt a thrill of pride. He wanted to tell Johnny but could not. He would not, perhaps, understand. He had flirted with girls enough but had surely never felt love for anyone but his horses.

The two long-time friends, Johnny the strong one, near to sobbing for his Leila, and Harry the one in need of support, filled with pride to know that he was fighting for his Beth, went off to war together.

At Dorchester Barracks they were sworn in as privates in the Dorsetshire Regiment. Within hours they had passed before a medical officer and been pronounced fit. Their Oath of Allegiance was given to the King, and their clothes taken from them. By evening they had been issued with vests, Army shirts, tunic, trousers and heavy boots; there would be no flannel turn-ups nor any yellow socks for them now, but that was, they agreed, the least of it all.

They had not imagined what it would be like to be imprisoned within an Army barracks. Each of them, outside of the restrictions of day-to-day life, Johnny at the stables, Harry at school, had known adult freedoms; they had decided upon their own activities, governed their own leisure time and their own money. Now their lives were to be ruled by ugly shouted commands and useless routine tasks that had to be done over and over again. There were barrack room duties, latrine duties, kit duties, parade duties. There were foul-smelling messes to be eaten in the canteen, hunks of bread and margarine, warm soapy tea; there were sleep and rest times to order in narrow bunks in damp huts smelling of sweat and urine and men's feet. They had to wash in cold water standing with a row of others who smelt, Johnny said, as if they had never washed before.

Harry said it was like the worst kind of boarding school and Johnny remembered the brief days as lamp boy at Liscombe Hall. But there would be no fighting his way out of this, no running away to freedom for the Army always found its own.

Johnny admired Harry for not flinching over latrine duties. Beside him, he longed for good healthy horse manure and cursed himself and his folly for joining up.

'It's not as if we're in the bloody war,' he would mutter, bending his back to dig in the stuff. 'Not even any bloody war glory.'

Harry, too proud to flinch at the task, poured another bucket into the mess, said: 'I think this is supposed to make you tough enough for it, somehow. Or just ready to do anything the Army says you must.'

'Yeah, to lower you to nothing.'

Around them other recruits joked and jostled each other and seemed to enjoy the pain of it, the endless duties and blistered feet and rough clothing that rubbed their skin sore.

Considering the other boys, Harry said once: 'I think it's something to do with a kind of male camaraderie – they're together against the Army. They spend all their time complaining about it but all the time a kind of spirit is growing up, like it does in schools. You'll see, there'll be prefects appearing soon – they'll be corporals, I suppose – then there'll be the bullies and the toadies, and the weakest will be picked out, and it will all be part of it. Afterwards they'll remember it as a good time.'

'If they survive,' Johnny reminded him. But there was hardly any talk of war.

The two friends, always together and therefore apart from the others, watched and waited, Harry for his letters from Beth and for the day he would know he was to be allowed to go and fight for her and for Liscombe and for England, Johnny for the day when the request for a posting as groom might bring him nearer to Leila.

CHAPTER SIXTEEN

'I suppose you could say the war's done us a bit of good!' Aunt Bessie sat with Kate and Gideon over tea in their parlour with the cash-box between them on the green chenille cloth.

'Awful to say it, but you're right, Auntie.' Kate picked up her pencil. 'By your reckoning, Gideon, what should we offer for number nineteen?'

'We'll offer £950,' he said, continuing to scrutinize his tiny figures along the margin of the accounts books. 'That'll give us fifty-eight letting rooms if we use all the attics, less if we have all the maids living in.'

'We can use the attics for clients. They'll take anything with the war on.' Kate eased her back with one hand and stretched. At the basement window, the dark November day showed little light. 'It'll be a real peasouper tonight,' she said, 'that'll mean extra cleaning if it lasts days. We'll leave the curtains on the first floor 'till it's dispersed.'

'It'll be a problem finding men to decorate the rooms.' Aunt Bessie poured herself a third cup of tea. 'With so many gone.'

'Some chaps are coming out of retirement, Auntie, with such good rates being offered. Maybe we'll offer double. It'll be worth it to get the extension opened and revenue coming in. We'll offer double to war-wounded, even if they are slower.'

'You're too ready to offer double,' grumbled Aunt Bessie, 'your heart can't bleed for everyone, our Kate. And you didn't cause the damn war.'

'Yes, yes, I know,' she sighed, 'but I feel we'd be

doing a little to make up for what they have suffered. You know, just something. I feel guilty sometimes. We live here in such comfort, lacking for nothing, and moreover profit from the war. The kitchens are busy, the hotel's full with soldiers on leave, we've hardly an empty bed. Now we're to open next door. Sometimes I feel ... guilty, that's all.' She smiled at her aunt and yawned. 'I suppose I'm just tired.'

'And you worry over that brother of yours,' Aunt Bessie said crossly. 'Let me tell you, that boy has the luck of all the charmers of this world *and* the luck of the Tranters. Didn't you tell me he was always lucky?'

'As a lad he was,' Kate said. 'He even survived months of living rough and practically starving, and when he was a boy he poached and stole from the land and never was caught, and did it all with such a grin and a devil-may-care spirit in him. But out there! And so many are lost, thousands they say, and the men coming back say the reports never tell the whole truth. There's more lost and in worse ways than anyone can ever say. Don't you see the look they have standing at the bar and going back next day? Not even able to drink themselves into forgetting.'

Watching her face sadden, as it so often had in the long war months when there seemed there was never going to be any news of her brother, nor of the Liscombe boy she had once been nursemaid to, Gideon tried to put her mind to practical matters. 'Ham's up a penny a pound and the best beef twopence. Either we take out Dorset beef from the menu or we put it up fourpence. What do you think, Kate?'

'I think we had better keep it on. It's popular, and no one can seem to get enough food down them once they've been at the Front. They've money enough to spare on leave anyway. There's nothing to spend it on

347

out there.' Kate drew a sketch of a Dorset valley with a cow grazing under an oak. In the grate, the fire hissed and a little puff of sooty smoke drifted from the chimney.

'The fog's settling in already,' grumbled Aunt Bessie, 'our hair'll be ruined going out tonight. Better leave off that new crêpe-de-chine of yours, Kate. The fog'll be in it and you'll never feel it's new again.'

'Yes, Auntie,' said Kate automatically, shading in the oak tree. 'There's never any fog in Dorset, not real fog.'

'There's fog, but there ain't no soot to sit in it and make a soup of it.' Aunt Bessie prodded at the notepad where Kate's country scene was almost complete. 'An oak spreads wider than that,' she said.

'You can't remember,' Kate laughed, 'what an oak looks like, you've been too long up here.'

'Too long,' agreed Aunt Bessie.

Warm stale air and gloom settled over the group at the table until Kate suddenly said: 'If they've nothing to spend it on out there and they can't get enough food, what's to stop us going into hampers like some of the stores – only better?

'Fresh Home Food for the Troops,' she said dreamily and wrote it under the stream in her valley. 'It sounds good, it looks good. They've certainly money enough – Captain Waddington was telling me last night. They've awful Army rations that the cooks try to make into something, but the meat is so bad no one can tell if it is beef or mutton or pork and the poor men sometimes go off to fight and die on a tot of rum and a mug of watery tea. Poor Johnny will miss Ma's pudding and her roast rabbit and stew and that suet roly-poly of hers.'

'Suet roly-poly? We don't serve that!' Gideon sat up. 'We've missed something. Isn't it cheap? Doesn't it use bacon ends? It'd be easy to pack and it'd keep long enough.'

348

Kate stirred herself and turned to a clean page. 'Suet roly-poly,' she wrote. 'Roast rabbit legs. I'd love to see Johnny bite into a rabbit leg! Oh, let's cost it, Gideon. I feel better. We can make it really cheap, just cover costs say. I'd feel each hamper was for Johnny. It will be our very own contribution to the war effort. If we hurry, I might be able to get something started up before I go down home to fetch Peter back. I think he's too much for Mother now and there doesn't seem to be any danger here in spite of all the scare stories. He'll be as safe in London as in Dorset.'

She had decided to go to Liscombe and not let her own pride, her own shame at her past, prevent her. What could such useless emotions matter with a war on and thousands of men dying each day in agony and squalor?

In his Aunt Beth's bedroom, Peter Tranter reached into her wardrobe. Fingers in his mouth, hot with fear for his Granny must not see him, he reached in to touch the cool, cool silk of a nightgown she had left behind. Oh, the sweet scent of it! Peter pressed his flushed face into the cloth and breathed in. The lovely stuff made his skin shiver. He put out a hand to the pink Indian shawl that held the scent of his mother still, for it had been hers. She had worn it at harvest time. Trembling, he drew out the long silky skein of it and wrapped it about his neck. There! If he turned just a little he could catch a glimpse of himself in his aunt's looking glass. How pink his cheeks looked, how pretty he was!

But he must not stay with the sweet forbidden thing around him; his grandmother would come and grumble and shout as she always did and ask what he was about with women's things. Breathless, flushed with fear and pleasure, Peter gazed at himself draped in Indian silk.

The delicious shiver of his skin! Soon his mother would be here, bustling about, and there would be no more time. He put the silk up to his burning face. Just one more minute, here in the silent room with the sweet shiver in his back . . .

'Peter! Come on down. I can hear that noisy motor of your mother's!' Mrs Tranter, in the doorway, watched her smart daughter run down the path by the stream, her arms full of London packages.

'Ent no reason for you to be bringing all that down here, our Kate,' she called. 'We got all we need, and enough for Johnny too.'

Kate dropped her parcels on the kitchen table. 'Mother,' she said, 'we're going to send Johnny one of our hampers, all the nice things that a man likes. You'll see.' She kissed her mother's plump cheeks and called for Peter.

'I got here what our Johnny likes,' Mrs Tranter said, pushing aside Kate's offerings and showing her. 'Forty Players Navy Cut, his favourite, shortbread biscuits from the shop, and the bar of Cadbury's.'

'Oh, Ma, I remember Johnny bought a penny bar of Cadbury's from his first sale of rats' tails and he cut it into pieces for us all to share.' Standing by the range, Kate hugged her silent and sulky son, who would not speak until he could find something to say that would make her feel guilty about sending him to the country. 'It had the same purple wrapping paper, Ma, do you remember? And Billy cut his into even smaller squares and saved one for you. You had to eat it whilst he blinked up at you so earnestly and lovingly. Do you remember, Ma?'

'I do.' Mrs Tranter peered into a steaming pot by the range and prodded its contents with a fork. 'Ham's done,' she said. 'It's for Johnny. Put that boy down and give me a hand to get the danged thing out to cool. I got to get his parcel off today.'

Kate saw a tear roll down her mother's cheek. 'Peter,' she said, 'go and pick Aunt Bessie some nice flowers. You know how she likes them.' She must not mention his silence or it would last the day. She watched him run down to the stream. He was looking very flushed but healthy from the good country air.

Together, she and her mother lifted the steaming ham into a dish and carried it to the window-sill. 'I remember Johnny swallowing his chocolate whole, all at one go, for the pleasure of it,' she said. 'And Billy saving those bits as if they were gold.'

'They're as different as chalk and cheese, my two boys,' Mrs Tranter said. 'As different as the rabbit and the fox. And Billy's not gone.' She carried a bowl to the range for the ham stock to be saved for soup. 'Hold this for me. Mind it don't spill.'

Kate held the bowl as she had so many dozens of times before, in her childhood, and her mother said again: 'Billy's not gone to war,' as if Kate were not aware of that fact.

'We must be glad at least about that, Mother,' she said. 'Billy couldn't fight, he couldn't kill a spider. They'd have to make him a stretcher-bearer or a clerk or a groom.'

'Grooms go,' said Mrs Tranter sharply. 'Johnny's put down as groom but they only let him tend them horses when there's no fighting going on.' She took the bowl of stock across to the window-sill for the fat to settle on cooling. 'Read his last,' she said, 'on the table.'

Kate sat at the table where Mrs Tranter had laid out brown paper and string beside the cigarettes for Johnny and his chocolate, and picked up the letter.

DEAR MA.

I am as well as can be expected, and so is Harry.
Leila and Neil seem well but I am nervous for
them. We're going up soon.

'That must be up to the Front, Mother, where the
fighting is.'

'I know where up is,' Mrs Tranter said crossly, but
she had not known, thinking it to be farther up into
northern France.

Kate read on:

We try and keep cheerful though it's not easy with
the wet and all and the noise. France must have
been a nice country once though it isn't now. The
Fritzes have seen to that. Can you get Navy Cut
and any eatables from home? But don't go walking
up that hill and wearing yourself out.

Kate paused. 'No, Mother, we'll send his parcels from
London. Hampers, rather. I've got something here,
don't you . . .'

'You think I can't manage to feed my own boy out
there, with his wet boots and the noise and all and no
food in his belly?' Mrs Tranter sat down at the table
opposite her daughter and Kate felt a twist of pity for
her, tired still, always tired, and now burdened with
worry for Johnny so far away and perhaps wounded
in some hospital, even as they read this letter written
weeks before. He might be killed but the Army would
take a month before they sent a telegram to tell
you. She put out a hand to hold her mother's. 'At least
Billy is not gone,' she said. 'We've only Johnny to
worry for.'

'Read what he says about Billy.'

Of course Billy must go on with the law. There's got to be law and order and Billy wouldn't be any good out here with his eyestrain and not being able to kill anything, let alone a German.

'He's right, Mother,' Kate said. 'Remember him coming racing down the back hill with a rabbit under his jacket, and Billy following white to the gills because Johnny had made him carry the bloody corpse of a hare under his?'

'They'd make him learn to use a gun, and when the Germans were coming at him, he'd drop it,' Mrs Tranter burst out and Kate saw her begin to sob. She got up and moved round the table to put her arms around her mother.

'He would, Ma, he'd drop it, Billy would. He was always so clumsy. What a good thing he's not going.' She tried to laugh.

'But all the village boys have gone, our Kate, every one of them have gone.' Between sobs, Mrs Tranter rocked on her chair.

Kate held her and turned to look towards her own boy, playing by the stream with mud up to his knees and the flowers for Aunt Bessie forgotten. 'Are those village women whispering things to you, Mother? They had better not! Johnny's out there in the thick of it and that's enough. We can't let Billy go. You must talk to him, make him understand he's right and there's nothing to be ashamed of, in refusing to fight. I'd make Peter do the same if he were old enough to be sent for.'

'That boy of yours'll never fight, not even in boys' games.' Mrs Tranter stopped crying. 'And when you gets him back to London, you see as he goes to school instead of being round your skirts. It ent healthy.'

'Yes, Mother, I've been thinking that too, but let's

get these things sorted out for Johnny. We'll make up the best parcel he's ever had. He'll be able to share it out with his friends. The war'll be over perhaps before we can even get the next letter from him, and it'll certainly be over before they send for Billy.'

'He's had a letter.' Mrs Tranter stood up and began to move Kate's London parcels about on the table. 'The postman brought it Saturday up to the Hall and Cook ran down with it. There was one from Harry Liscombe for her too, and while she were reading that out to me, our Billy sat there, at the table, and he opened his letter and his face went as white as my sheets. He sat there with the letter and out of it fell a white feather, Kate. A white feather floated out and Cook saw it and she went on reading and ever since I can't hardly stop crying – his face was so white, white as that feather. Tommy ran off with it. Now I know Billy must go, and maybe he ought to, Kate? Maybe our Johnny's dying out there and Billy ought to go and kill some of them Germans too or how will it ever stop?'

Lying in a trench in some part of northern France, Johnny Tranter had not removed his boots for a week and no longer knew whether they were wet or dry. They had formed a crust and were part of the covering he had now, mud and sweat-soaked clothing and unthinkable things from the earth and the sky that battle had thrown up at him.

He was listening. He was trying to get breath enough to force himself up and over the parapet again, to help Harry bring in one of the wounded from the desolate stretch of earth that was all there was between them and the Germans.

Only this bloke was a German.

Johnny lay panting and listening for the low careful

sound of Harry crawling through the mud, dragging the German, the muffled dragging sounds and the tiny grunts Harry would have to give because he would not be able to help it. It cost so much effort to bring in one of the wounded when you dare not rise nor show even an arm above the level of the mess of dead out there. The enemy never let up or failed to have a sniper ready on their side, not even if they had lost hundreds.

There, a lull now, for the counting of the dead, and Harry had gone out twice to drag in two who were not quite dead and he had crawled a third time after a voice that cried 'Help me!' in a German accent. Harry said he must have been there all night, had been caught by one of our snipers on a recce, and lain through all of it, caught near the British line. No one would risk going out to him, for the voice was German and he would die before dawn, one German less.

Only Harry had not been able to stand it, nor the rats scurrying over for fresh dead; they had been running over their boots and Harry had screamed because he could not stand rats.

Everyone in the trench was sleeping now, propped up in mud dug-outs, even the Sergeant. The sentry was as still as the dead. Johnny saw his helmet against the ridge of the parapet and decided to risk putting his head over.

He could hear Harry panting now. There was a sense of some movement out there. He made an effort, lifting heavy arms in their covering to drag himself over and crawl towards the movement.

'Harry?' he whispered. A watery moon showed his friend lifting his head.

'Take his shoulders,' he said.

Johnny dragged himself on his elbows towards the shape that lay beside Harry. He saw a white face with blood showing dark against it. 'It's too late,' he said, 'he's finished. And he's a Fritz, Harry.'

'There's some life there,' Harry said. 'Take him in. Just roll him over into the trench. There's another one still breathing, I'm going back.'

'Not for a Fritz, Harry.' Despair gave Johnny the strength to drag at the German soldier's arm, pulling him towards the edge of their parapet. 'But if we save this one, will you stop?'

'I can't.' Harry lay with his face in the mud. 'His eyes looked at me, begging. Very blue eyes, even in the moonlight. He managed to pull out a photo of a girl for me to take. He's all mixed up with some of the dead.' He gave a stifled cough into the mud and turned his head slowly towards the German line. 'I've got to do it, to make some good of it, you see, Johnny.'

Johnny watched him drag himself painfully round in the mud to face the other way. He wanted to shout something, anything, to make him stop. He lifted his own head. It was so hard to move any part of you, in the mud, but he had managed to pull the German right to the edge of their trench when the bullet rang out; he heard it and he knew it was for Harry, because they had seen him move. He had moved too quickly across towards the German soldier he was going to save and now it was too late for both of them.

The sniper's fire had stopped. Johnny kept his head down and began the weary journey towards Harry; he was about fifty yards away, perhaps less, but it would take half an hour.

Johnny saw him amongst the others because he made a movement with his hand and in it was the rope he had used to drag in the wounded.

'Harry,' he whispered, and reached out his own hand

356

to touch his friend's. There was life in it still, a little warmth that said life. Johnny made a supreme effort and dragged himself to lie beside his friend, feeling along his body for signs of the gunshot wound. It was on his left side; a mass of warm blood was seeping through his tunic. But he was alive.

'Harry!' he breathed. 'I'm taking you in.' He took his rope and wound it carefully, painfully, under Harry's shoulders. No sound came in the cold still night. Did the sniper sleep too? With infinite care and slowness, Johnny wound the rope the way he had wound it in the cold stream water at home, catching pike. He was cold now but there was warmth still in Harry and he was taking him in; he would see to him, the way he always had.

It was near dawn when he had sight of their own parapet; he had dragged Harry in inch by careful inch and now he heard their Sergeant's voice, an urgent whisper across the yards that remained of their journey.

'Tranter, if you draw the gunfire this way, I'll shoot you both.'

'Which is best, Harry,' he asked. 'Shall I let him shoot us and have done with it?'

Harry did not answer. Johnny put an arm about his shoulders and lay there. The mud felt cool against his face.

'I think I shall stay here with you, Harry, and we'll take our chance.'

He suddenly felt so weary that it did not seem to matter. Afterwards he could not imagine how it was that he had slept. But sleep he did, beside Harry, who was dying. They both slept.

That was how they brought him in, because he was asleep. Sergeant Tomkins had himself crept over the parapet and reached out for him with a pickaxe, catching at his tunic to drag him in.

Johnny came to as he was pulled over the sandbags.

'Harry, now, Sergeant,' he stuttered, still full of sleep. He wanted still to be asleep so that he could not remember Harry was dying.

'Liscombe is dead, Tranter, and it'll be lucky for you if I don't have you court-martialled.'

The other men were sleeping. Johnny saw the lines of boots in the mud. Sergeant Tomkins had left him in the dugout he had shared with Harry, a tot of rum in his tin mug and his knees drawn up to his chest. It might have been the rum which made his head swim, and confused him, but he was sure that he heard it again, Harry's voice calling out.

'Stop Mother burning,' the voice was crying, and who but Harry had had a mother burn?

He got up quite calmly, because he could not sit and hear Harry call, even if he was dying. He would let himself be shot by the Sergeant; it did not matter.

When Johnny reached him, the blood was flowing freely from Harry's mouth.

'Go away, Johnny.' His voice seemed to bubble as if he were talking through water. 'Let them finish me off. I can't stand dying, it's so long, so long. I knew it would be awful. Do you remember the foxes? Half-killed, waiting for the end, for the hounds to get them. Like me.' Dark blood formed a stain around his mouth.

Johnny took his hand. It seemed cold now through the mud. He knew then there was nothing for him to do but wait, wait for the cold to creep into Harry's chest where the blood was leaving it. Then he knew what he would do.

'I shan't leave you for the rats, Harry,' he whispered. His friend could no longer hear him, probably, but he must say it. And when the last rattling breath came, Johnny picked him up in his arms and ran back across the wasteland in the dawn light and did not care if a

German sniper saw him. Perhaps they too were asleep now for no bullet came shrieking over his head. Johnny fell to his knees at the parapet and passed Harry to the sentry.

He did not care what Sergeant Tomkins had to say to him; he did not listen. He sat down in the dugout they had shared and began to collect Harry's personal things, taking particular care of the letter for Beth which was folded in his wallet. That he put into his own.

'The rats won't get Harry, not even now, Sergeant,' he muttered.

'They'll take the boy away and have him properly buried, lad. There's no more you can do for him, and you're lucky I'm torn between having you court-martialled and recommending you for bravery. Let's just see what I decide, eh?'

'I shan't be leaving him, Sergeant,' said Johnny, 'not 'till I see him buried in a proper place. He can't abide rats, you see, and there's rats about here, there's rats everywhere here, and I shall have to tell his – his wife I saw him buried decently, you see. She'll want to know, his wife.'

Beth Tranter, in London, lodging at the flat in Albermarle Street bought by Lord Liscombe for his daughter, sat at the table in the sitting room writing a letter to Harry.

DEAREST LOVE,
It is afternoon here in London and I am waiting for Lulu to come back from day shift at the hospital. It is comfortable and warm, waiting, though outside the April wind is blowing all the dust of London about. The maid has gone and soon I shall get up and put on the kettle for our tea. We are very cosy in this room. The chairs and carpet and

paintings are all from Liscombe Hall, so can you imagine it, darling, all gold and dark?

I am to go to the hospital this week, Harry, but do not worry. It is nothing, only I am a little overtired from a month's night shift. One never quite gets to sleep properly. All the London streets are busy now, night and day; there are troops everywhere, enjoying their freedom. If only you could have leave soon! I long just to see you, just to hold you.

But here is Lulu's key in the door. Darling, I shall write again tomorrow.

Beth pushed aside her writing case and got heavily to her feet.

He moved, her baby moved! It made her heart leap. Dear God, she prayed, let Harry be home soon to know he is a father. Let him not die out there, not even knowing. She could not tell him by letter. She wanted to see his face when he knew she was with child, his child. He must come home soon. He would not mind what the world said. She knew that, just as she knew that their love would endure for ever though they could never marry.

'A personal telephone call for you, Miss Tranter.'

'Don't go, Miss Tranter – Kate – let the porter say you're out.'

'I must go, Philip, it might be important.' Kate did not let him touch her arm in his sweet tentative way. She felt herself blush. Philip Waddington was becoming something of a problem. Work problems were something she could deal with; Philip Waddington was not. He had stayed six weeks in the hotel, recuperating from his war wounds. He seemed to have no home to go to and chose to spend his time waiting for a glance from her.

'I've just been reading the article about you in the *Daily Mail*.' Philip folded the paper on the bar and pointed. 'The Queen of the London Restaurant world!' he said. 'A woman of achievement!' There was no hint of male mockery in his voice, only admiration; she did not want it, having long before sealed up her heart.

Standing beside her barman, Kate did not raise her eyes to Philip's face. 'They want me to say how it feels to have brought about my own emancipation,' she said, 'as if I ever had time to think about it.'

'Too little time for anything else,' Philip said. Kate felt him urging her to allow him one glance. 'Might you not one day consider . . . giving it up?'

Kate thought: I do not know how to respond to him. I do not know how to let him admire me. I am still young, but I do not know how to.

This was not the first time he had tried to broach the possibility of her leaving her business. 'Never!' she said, and moved quickly away. 'And the telephone is waiting,' she reminded him. 'Goodnight, Captain.'

With a swish of her navy blue crêpe-de-chine dress, Kate walked across the reception hall, noting with familiar pleasure everything in its place, low-lit and glowing, from the brass bowls of dried flowers on the deal tables to the pink and cream rag rugs on the polished floor and Buster, the dark gold boxer dog, before the hearth. Everything was right with her world; if she were ever to let her vigilance slip, she would no longer be queen of anywhere. But she wished Philip would not make her heart quicken, that she would not let herself allow him to make it beat a little too fast. He need do no more than stand near her, watch her with eyes that were so very blue, so very concerned and attentive. He loved her. She knew it also from the way he looked after Peter, trying always to occupy the boy, find some pleasure to amuse him. He accepted Peter. He must have known from London gossip that he had no father.

Kate reached the telephone at the reception desk. She cared no longer if the world knew Peter was illegitimate. She had vaguely realized, with some shame, that the fact gave her a certain cachet, a certain mystery. 'Hello, Kate Tranter speaking,' she said. She expected to hear Gideon's voice with a report on the new chef at the Strand Kitchen. The girl's voice made her straighten up and listen more carefully.

'Kate, it's Lulu Liscombe here. I'm at Charing Cross Hospital.'

A cold feeling of dread began to spread from Kate's toes to her chest. She knew what the next words must be.

'Your sister's in the emergency room.'

'Yes,' Kate said. She felt, now, that she had been expecting it, that the summons had been only a matter of time. 'I'll be there in a few minutes. Get me a cab, Brown.'

'What is it, my dear? Can I help? You look quite ashen.' Philip stood by her shoulder.

'No. No, thank you. It's just a family matter.' She had been expecting it, but the cold dread was as fresh as if she had not. 'Will you send a maid up for my hat and gloves? The blue ones, tell her, please, on the dressing table.' The words came out by themselves. She thought: Beth. Beth running down the hill in too-big boots and a too-big shawl tangled up in her skirts, the young girl with a quiet and sweet nature steadfastly loving Harry though it was impossible.

In the cab, Kate remembered the February night

when she had screamed out her own agony in childbirth. She had never been able to bear the thought that Beth should so suffer, not even if there should be a boy like Peter at the end of it. She wanted no bastard son for her sister, none of that uncertain position she would always have, a disgraced woman. Beth disgraced, as she had been!

'Hurry! Hurry, driver,' she called uselessly over the sound of the motor. All of London seemed to be out that night, hindering her passage. The baby had seemed small, and Beth not burdened down by it as she had been, but there had been an air about her these past weeks, a grey shadow about her eyes and a distant look. She carried herself in a slow and dreamy way, as if she were not quite with them in bustling London. Kate had often thought, watching her sister change, calling to see her on most of her busy days, that she was not with them but in some strange world of her own mind where she met Harry and talked with him.

Inside the hospital, the cold smell of it joined the feeling of cold in her chest and she held her breath until she reached the room where they said Beth lay.

Her face was as white as the sheet that covered her. There was a doctor in a black coat, and nurses in long rustling dresses with a flow of white starched cloth about their heads. Kate reached out to touch Beth's hand on the sheet. It was cold. 'Beth!' She shouted it. The hand was cold. 'Speak to me, darling.' Her lips were blue and stiff and her hair had been brushed out on to the pillow as if . . . 'She mustn't die!' Her hair had been neatly brushed as if for the laying-out. Kate held Beth's cold hand. 'She cannot die. Beth?' She leaned down to touch her own cold lips against her sister's and knew they held the chill of death in them.

'It will kill our mother,' she said. She put her cheek against Beth's cold one.

'I'm sorry, Mrs . . . er,' the doctor said, 'we did our best . . . she must have had some shock, a fall or something. The baby's a fine boy.'

'A fine boy,' Kate whispered. 'We don't want another fine boy. We want Beth. Save my sister!' Her words were useless and she knew they were. They could only postpone the final moment when she knew that Beth was dead.

She and Lulu Liscombe cried the night out in the Liscombe flat. Beth could not be dead, could no longer move gently about these dark Liscombe things with her quiet sweet voice soothing their daily cares, but it was so. Lulu repeated the day's event over and over.

'It started just after I came off day shift,' she said. 'She was sitting in the gold brocade chair in her nurse's uniform still. And it hardly showed yet, the baby. She called out to me as I came in. I ran. Oh, I did run, Kate, I knew it was something. You see, I heard this morning before I left that my brother Harry had been killed.'

She sobbed, 'Harry and Beth both dead, Kate. I knew she'd take it hard, of course, they loved each other so much, and no matter what everyone else might say, she was proud of the baby coming. Though the last few weeks she's spoken less about it. She began to worry more about Harry, sense that he was in danger, I suppose. I promised to tell no one about the baby and I never have. As far as I know only you and me and the doctor ever knew about it. I went off on day shift because we are so short of staff at the hospital and I knew Harry would die, I knew he would, so it didn't shock me as much as it did her. She just lived for the day he'd come though she so feared he never would.'

Lulu Liscombe's pretty face had lost its freshness, Kate thought absently. The war had touched her too.

She rubbed swollen eyes and let the tears fall for the only friend she had ever known.

'Beth wailed so this morning, when the letter came, to think that she had never told him about the baby, in case he worried about her, not being married yet and so on, and she screamed: "It's too late, it's too late," and I cannot see how I persuaded myself she might be better left alone to grieve and I'd better get on shift. I blame myself. If I'd been here!'

'I don't think it would have made much difference,' Kate said, leaning back in the gold brocade chair. She felt too heavy with fatigue and sorrow ever to leave it. And Beth seemed to be here still; she had moved about these rooms and sat in this chair. Here she had read the letter and let herself die. 'I always thought she would not survive childbirth. She never seemed quite to fill out as she should, and the look in her face . . .'

'Harry,' said Lulu, 'she feared so for him. I knew he'd never come home. All the best boys are dying out there, aren't they?'

'All the best boys,' echoed Kate and refused to think of Johnny. 'I want everyone at home to remember Beth as she was. I don't want them to know about the baby because they'll make it into something dirty, people always do, and it was only love. What does a ring matter really? It's only nasty tongues. I don't want nasty tongues around the memory of Beth.'

'Harry would have married her, Kate. He had no worldy pretensions at all and cared nothing for public opinion. Anyway, I shall tell no one how darling Beth died. I'm being sent to France next week, thank God, I shan't be able to live here any more, without her. I shall miss her so.'

Lulu took a gulp of brandy and permitted herself a weak smile. 'I needed her far more than she needed me, to protect her here with the flat and so on. Since I was a child, she helped me when she came up for lessons. Do you remember, Kate? She was never showy about it, no one ever knew how much she helped me to learn to read properly without making me feel silly.'

'Yes, she was special.' Kate drank her own brandy and let the warmth of it spread into her chest. 'I never did enough for her, all that I promised to do. I never did buy her a proper oval mirror for her bedroom nor her first evening dress.'

'She never needed any of that. She could have had anything she wanted of mine but she only wanted to be with Harry.'

'Unworldly, she was, I suppose, quite unlike the rest of us. How shall I tell our mother?' Kate poured more brandy into their glasses. 'How shall I ever tell her?'

'I have such a lovely surprise for you, Mother.' Kate stood in the sunlight by the doorway. 'I'll put the kettle on. How's Bessie?' Mrs Tranter dragged herself to the range. She felt she cared nothing for Bessie nor for any tea neither but something made her go through the motions.

'You sit down, Mother. I'll see to everything. Aunt Bessie's fine and says why don't you come up on the train to see us? And Beth's . . . Beth's grave, Mother dear. I should so like you to see. It's a lovely place under a tree by an old stone wall.'

'I wanted her here to bury decent. I wanted her here.' Mrs Tranter sank back into her chair and put her hands to her face.

'You know it wasn't possible, dear. The authorities say the infection . . . Anyway, I did not think you could bear it, that's really why.'

'I can't bear any of it, not her dying, nor dying so far

off. She'd never have got diphtheria if she'd stayed here.'

'Mother, listen, it wasn't diphtheria, but I want you to go on letting people believe it was.'

'What, not diphtheria? What was it then?' Mrs Tranter looked up sharply. 'It was some other war thing?'

'In a way it was, yes.' Kate took a deep breath and threw off her hat, taking Tommy up in her arms for comfort. Rocking him, putting her face into his fur, thin now with age – Tommy would die soon – she said what she had come to say. 'She died from the baby.' Her voice was muffled but Mrs Tranter heard it.

'Yes, a baby, Mother. Beth had a baby and died from it and I have him outside and I want you to care for him and love him as you did Beth. It's her baby and he needs you to love him, Mother, and never, never be ashamed.'

Mrs Tranter moaned but could not speak.

'It was Harry Liscombe, you must have known they loved each other?' Kate put Tommy into the sun on the window-sill and gazed up towards the Hall, a dark shadow against the sunlight. It was nothing to her now; only he remained up there, and all alone they said, eccentric and long past remembering her and the love that had been between them. 'Harry loved her so much. He would have married her, Mother. It was not like the other time.'

'To think of it, another Liscombe child! Liscombe and Tranter . . . bad, I tell you, not right, Kate. And my Beth dead through it, and you shamed. How shall we ever bear it?' Mrs Tranter let her tears fall and the sound of her sobbing go on through Kate talking, explaining, speaking of love and babies. 'Oh, oh,' she sobbed, 'what do it matter? My Beth's dead, and all through a Liscombe, and how shall I ever go on?'

'You will, dear, because Beth's baby needs you.' Kate put an arm around her mother's plump shoulders and leaned her cheek into the faded grey hair. 'Only you can care for Beth's baby as it should be cared for, as she would care for it.'

She watched the sunlight edge its way across the room and waited for her mother's sobs to ease. This was the only way she knew to soften the pain of Beth's death, the only way she knew to give her mother the will to live on. And if Johnny should not come home either, when all the best boys were dying, then the baby would be the only strand holding her to life. Kate stood beside her mother until the sunlight reached the table and her sobs had become sniffs, and knew she could not bear her mother not to be there any more, and her last real connection with her childhood gone.

'He's out there, Mother,' she said, loosening her hold and moving away to at last make their tea. 'A grandson for you and Pa, and he's lovely.'

'Better bring him in then,' said Mrs Tranter. 'You can't leave him out there in the sun. I must see him, Beth's boy. Is he very like?' She walked to the doorway, blinking in the light.

'Oh, the pretty dear. Come to Granny.' Beth's baby lay amongst lace shawls with a healthy round face very like hers had been as a baby. She lifted him from the cradle Kate had bought and rocked him in the old way she had not forgotten. 'Whatever will Father say, Kate? He is like, he is. Long lashes already, like hers.'

'Pa'll accept it as he always does if it doesn't affect him and it's not to do with cows. I've opened a bank account for you and here's your book. Each week I want you to go into Dorchester for your shop and never stint for yourself or Pa or the baby. I can afford it. And you're to get a cab back, Mother.'

Kate whirled about the cottage at her busiest but Mrs Tranter sat back by the range showing the baby that he had at least a grandmother, though he was half Tranter and half Liscombe and that mixture was all wrong.

Kate, running down the stairs with a bag of Beth's belongings, called: 'Mother, listen, I'm going up to Mrs Baker to see if she could release Letty as nursemaid. I don't want to bring a stranger in to know our affairs. They can't need her up there with life so much reduced. There can't be much in the way of pots and pans for her to clean. Not like the old days.' Kate paused in the doorway. Nothing was like the old days, for any of them. 'I'll take these clothes up to her. She can sleep in . . . upstairs with the baby . . . then you need not be wakened at night. He's not up there, I suppose, dear?' Kate spoke casually and wondered if she minded what the answer would be.

'His lordship's in some training camp, they say, organizing something for the war effort,' Mrs Tranter said vaguely. She put a hand under the baby's head and wept silent tears for the familiar feel of it, the warm skin. 'I never had much time for sitting, then,' she muttered.

'You'll have time now, Mother, plenty of time, and no chores to do. Letty will help with everything.' Kate glanced sideways at her mother bending over the baby. This would give her will enough. 'I know you don't need a nursemaid, you'll say.' She smiled as her mother pretended not to listen to her. 'We'll give Letty a trial and see what she can do. If she's any good to you.'

'No harm in that,' Mrs Tranter sniffed. 'But what about them village women?'

'You tell them the baby's the son of some friends of mine who died in an outbreak of diphtheria, and I thought the country air . . . you say something like that, then later you and Pa can quietly adopt him. I have had

369

to register him as the son of Elizabeth Tranter, father unknown, for we don't want anyone else to know anything about Harry. It's safer like that. I want him here, with you, to be brought up the way we were. It wasn't easy, I know, but we were happier than the Liscombes, Mother.'

'You mean his lordship might lay claim to him, with his own boy gone?' Mrs Tranter looked up at her daughter and held tightly on to the bundle in its shawls. 'No Liscombe is going to take Beth's boy away. All that misery they lived in, that mother, them odd daughters! This boy'll be Tranter!'

Alone in Beth's room, Kate began her last task, clearing out her sister's belongings that their mother could not bear to touch. Dust lay on the bedstead she and Beth had shared. The sunlight beaming down from behind Liscombe Hill showed dust on the pink water jug and bowl and all along the floor to a worn pair of black boots Beth had left behind when she said goodbye to Liscombe for the first and last time. When Kate had met her at the station, there had been sorrow in her face then, as if she had known. Kate wrote 'Beth' in the dust on the washstand. How was it possible that a living person could be quite gone, never to be seen or heard again, never to have any presence again, to leave behind them a pair of boots with the print of their feet still in them and this amber-coloured silk scarf on the bedrail?

Kate lifted up the scarf and pressed her face to it. It smelt faintly of the lavender scent Beth had always worn. There had hardly been any talk between them, not since Harvest Supper 1914, of anything important. Beth had calmly announced the awaited birth without shame or fear and Kate had helped her with the practicalities of the matter, and they never even, looking at

Peter, approached the fact that they had both loved a Liscombe, that the child Beth expected was also a Tranter and Liscombe bastard.

Kate went to the window and looked up the hill. Beth had stood here too and dreamed of sweet love, whilst she, before the restaurants, before the hotels, before Peter, had had ambitions. Lady's maid in made-down dresses and passed-on gloves! She could never have those innocent aspirations again, and Beth and Harry would never love again.

She laid her face into the scarf that Beth had worn and began to weep, and through her tears saw Lord David. He was thundering down the cow path on a dark heavy horse and it was just the same as it had been when she was sixteen. There was the same crouching set of his shoulders, and, in a blur, his pale frowning face. He wore no hat and the black of his hair was flattened by the speed of the beast. Cantering down the hill, he let the horse jump the stream and it seemed then to hesitate by her parked car.

Kate's heart stopped. He is coming, she thought. He will knock on the door and say he has heard from the kitchens I am home, and I will go to the doorway and shake his hand and we will talk of the war and Harry's death, and Johnny and Beth and Lulu. Her heart stopped as she stood and waited and the beast suddenly turned, pulled by its reins.

Lord Liscombe and his horse turned away and were gone behind Home Farm barn while Kate stood, waiting for him, thinking: He is come home early and it is meant to be, that we shall meet again, now, at last, and shake hands like old acquaintances.

She was waiting and ready but he had turned away and gone past Home Farm barn away from her.

*

Lord David, released from his war committee work and taking his first furious ride of freedom down Liscombe Hill, had to rein in his horse, startled by the reflection of sunlight on a London car parked by the stream. He scoffed at himself and his foolish heart which at once thought: Kate is here, from London. Because a girl like Kate would be unlikely to travel by motor and anyway her husband would have to be privileged or rich to have petrol enough. He was not free of Kate yet!

Angrily, he turned his horse away to take the path along to Flush. If it had been she, they could have talked, quite innocently, he of Harry, she of her sister, and there would have been a little comfort in it.

Two weeks later, Mrs Tranter left her grandson, Joe, in the care of Letty and walked along the stream to go up Liscombe Hill by the cowpath. She wore a new poplin suit that Kate had sent her, the latest mode with a shorter skirt. She wanted to look her best for her appearance in the courtroom to show that her son Billy came from a good home no matter what ideas were in his head, all come from his reading and tutoring at the Hall.

Liscombe Hall! She would not so much as glance up in sympathy at the burned tower any more for the trouble that place had brought upon her family. Two daughters shamed and one dead from it, and now Billy in court because of it. It had given him fine ideas the other village boys never had. All of them had gone to war. There were seven of them dead and one blinded, and Jim Williams who had sung at Harvest Supper had had his legs blown off, legs as strong as the oaks along the vale. And her Billy refused to go.

Her heart almost failed her when she saw him standing in court as if he were a criminal. They said he was and that he would have to go to prison if he would not go to war. She saw Billy standing there, as pale as a sheet, blinking through his reading glasses that he did not need and used for hiding, blinking at the judge so earnestly, meaning so well. That was the worst part of his standing there; Billy had always meant well, he had never hurt the smallest creature and that was why he did not want to fight though the country and the law said he must.

'And what would you do, Tranter, if a German came and raped your sister? Would you stand by and allow it, your very own sister?'

Susan Tranter wanted to stand up and cry: 'What a thing to put in the boy's head,' but did not.

Billy stood trembling. She knew he would not give in, he would not say he would kill a German. But he would for Kate, and he would have for his sister Beth, whatever he said. Mrs Tranter did not doubt that. She did not want to doubt that.

Lord David came up from the back of the court to speak for Billy. Susan Tranter sat heavily on the bench and watched this man who had so harmed her daughter and yet had done such good for them all since. She could not reconcile her feelings for him, not her in-grained respect for his position and her mother's anger. She heard him speak and watched the brooding familiar face that so rarely smiled, that since the Liscombe fire and the deaths, since the curse on Liscombe, had grown yearly more distant and drawn. And he was the father of her grandson. His son was the father of baby Joe. How could it be that they were so linked?

'William Tranter has been a beneficiary of the Lis-combe Trust Fund and has proved himself worthy of it since he was a lad of thirteen or so. He's a fine intelligent boy with sincerely held convictions about the wrongness of killing.' Lord David put out one hand to grip the witness box and with the other held his hat. His dark profile, turned towards the judge, was as firm as it always had been but Susan Tranter knew that he had changed, that his heart had been touched with grief and regret. Perhaps his treatment of Kate was part of that. Now his son had died and she could not be glad of it, no matter what he had done.

'I believe he eats no meat and has never followed the usual country pursuits of killing animals. He believes we have no right to kill just because we have physical power over other beings. He has believed this since childhood though he was no doubt mocked for it. As a child, he showed a rare independence of mind and I fully support him now. I support that independence. My son, my heir, was as a boy filled with the same belief as Billy Tranter. He hated killing. And today he lies dead on the battlefield. Must they all go? Can none be saved, even those unsuited for battle like my son and this boy here?'

There was a murmur round the court. Lord Liscombe bowed to the judge and left the witness box.

Billy seemed to sway. Susan Tranter felt she could not bear to see him standing there and all the people except his lordship against him. They did not understand. They would make him go to war as Harry and Johnny had. And perhaps he should go. She willed her son to look across at her, but he did not. He looked down at his hands holding on to the front of the box. He was holding on, she thought, so that no one would see him shaking. But perhaps he should go, because all the boys had to go.

She saw him taken away. A policeman held his arm and he did not look back at her. She saw him disappear down the dark steps, with the tuft of hair sticking up at the back just like his father's and Johnny's. What would his father say to know his son was a criminal?

Outside the courtroom she could hear the crowd shouting: 'Conshie! Conshie!' She could not go out now to hear them shouting that. Her son would have to walk back through the crowds without his mother to see him go.

'Conshie! Conshie!'

Lord David Liscombe pushed his way through the faces and the waving arms. It was a sad sight to him, mob emotion. The whole of England wanted to see its boys slaughtered and jeered them on to go, safe in their own lives. He waited at the edge of them. Mrs Tranter should not be long. They had not noticed him. Usually the local people would whisper: 'There goes his lordship,' when he appeared in town. He knew it was rumoured he had gone as mad as his wife, spreading his money around amongst their young for education and apprenticeships. Suddenly Mrs Tranter was before him, dressed, he saw, in her Sunday best for the court. 'Mrs Tranter,' he called.

'It's his lordship.' The crowd parted for him to go to her and take her arm. She was shaking with emotion. Helping her gently into the Austin, he could see the feather in her hat trembling. She would not cry with him beside her; she would be too proud. There was always a reserve between them and she would never speak freely of her family, however much he tried to prompt her. There was so little she had ever told him of Kate; he had had to drag it out of her that she was married.

He started the Austin and set off along the Dorchester road, turning left into their lanes, and home towards Liscombe. His heart still lightened for Liscombe. He still had that; it was all he had now, since the war. In spite of the terrible silence of the place with Johnny and the horses gone, all the men gone, Harry gone. If he had not spent so much time abroad, escaping himself, he would have got to know his son. His own son would have had some comfort from his father before going off to die.

He said to Kate's mother: 'You heard about my boy?' and she began to cry, thinking of her own, no doubt, fearing for them. She wept so that they could speak no more, and he had to leave her down by the stream.

Up at the Hall, he went across to the courtyard where once he had seen his beasts parade after morning grooming. Johnny Tranter had been there with his stableboys each morning, showing the animals off, and each morning he had gone there to see them and Johnny, for he had something of Kate about him, a way of standing, a fine direct look from dark blue eyes. Johnny, as honest and true as his sister for all his scampish ways. He had gone there just to see Kate's brother; it had been a ritual though the boy would never speak of his sister, or only in the most vague way. 'She is doing very well, thank you, sir, in London,' and then he would talk of horses. If Kate were there now, there would not be such deep desolation in David's heart. He paused in the chill empty stable where the Arab, Leila, had been. Her name was still carved in the wood by Johnny's own hand. LEILA. He had given the mare to Johnny because it was the next best thing to giving Kate a present.

And then he had let the horse go!

He had known the requisition men were coming; they had telephoned. He had not hidden Leila, though he might have, perhaps, for Johnny's sake, for Kate's brother, but he had not because his damn conscience had told him, walking down the stairs from his study, that he had no right to do it. All fit horses must go for the war effort.

He could have saved her, hidden her down in the valley, had a word with the officer. It could have been done. And he had not done it, from vacillation and weakness, and the boy had gone after his horses and Harry with him.

His own fault, the silence now.

All that kept him from despair was the same hopeless dream, that Kate might, one day, come to be at his side, for her husband could die, in the war. He had the shameful hope, often.

His other hope was that Johnny Tranter would survive, and the horse Leila, so that the burden of his guilt would not submerge him.

Somewhere near the Somme, part of Johnny's battalion was sent up to the line for a noon attack. He did not go with them; a back injury from shrapnel after he had buried Harry had kept him on groom's duties ever since. He stood in the street in what had once been a French village and watched the walking wounded begin to trail back around two o'clock, spectre-like, covered from head to toe in mud, oozing into their wounds and dripping down their limbs. It had rained all that October and November. Everything had been wet, the ground sodden until frost had hardened it all; for weeks Johnny had feared for Leila, clattering on ice on her sorties with Captain Carr.

Now there had been a thaw and everything had turned to mud, a new danger for horses, mud brought disease to them, but Johnny had not thought he would have to harness his beloved horse and her mate, Nell, for ambulance duties. It was because the motor ambulance wheels could not turn, in the mud, and the stretcher bearers needed transport for the non-walking wounded, and the dead.

So Johnny had to harness his horses and lead them into the line of fire. He had to do it, because he was ordered to. He harnessed them and led them through the village, coaxing them, down the street that had once belonged to a village and out into what might have been field and pasture but was now a sea of mud with the walking wounded struggling on past them and the mess of useless transport stuck in mud. Johnny felt mud seeping into his own breeches. Through the whistling wind that carried the shriek of battle, he kept his head down and watched mud suck past the fetlocks of his lovely horse Leila and up to the belly of faithful, sturdy Nell.

'Come on, girls,' he heard himself urge, 'you can do it.' But they had no choice but to go on, lathering sweat mixed with mud, up to the place where motors were stranded and the cooks' limbers lay just behind the line of fire, but only just. He had time to feel pride in them and they went along with him, trusting him, into it, the mud sucking at them and the high wail of the shells and the bursts of machine-gun fire rat-tatting out into the wind.

He was given a cart and told to hitch Leila and Nell to it. Then he had to turn them back into the road and help load their cargo. Ten stretchers and six more wounded were helped in for their escape. He never knew how they made the journey back, nor how horses so long unused even to field work, should have the strength to pull such a load through such mud. He gave them water before they started back again and still they did not shy nor stumble nor refuse him. He turned them and the cart back and off they went again to bring back more men who had fallen under the most intense German bombardment Johnny had ever heard.

Johnny, Leila and Nell worked all that day and the next. Sometimes it was the dead they carried, for those awaiting their help had waited too long. Doctors had gone up and set to work in field tents but many wounded lay untreated and still covered in mud in shallow dug-outs. Sometimes it was a dead horse they pulled out of the way; a beast caught in a spray of flying shrapnel. Johnny never looked ahead up to the trenches where the opposing lines spat out their fire. He had heard that the trenches were falling in with the weight of the thawed mud and men were marooned in them as if on desert islands on a plain of mud. It was said that three companies of the Manchesters had disappeared, believed drowned, in mud. An entire horse transport of six fine beasts had gone down with their leader in a mine crater fifteen feet deep in mud, while appalled troops had watched, helpless.

But Johnny did not, and would not, let his mind imagine such a scene for then it would have seemed possible.

Suddenly, it came, Nell's turn. She wavered, stumbled, and fell with a piece of shrapnel in her neck, hopelessly caught in the churning mud that was all about them. There was no firm place for her to tread and no steady place for the other horses and men. She fell and took Leila with her and he heard himself scream out. They were both there, fallen. Their legs churned together in the mud and then it seemed that Nell's head was down, she couldn't keep it up, and she seemed to roll over into the earth as he knelt down, still screaming. He could hear himself. It was because she rolled like that that Leila was able to get a kind of hold on her back and she pulled herself up, wildly heaving against the back of her friend, and Nell's head went down. Johnny could see her, looking at him, desperate, her eyes pleading, her mouth open to scream too.

He pushed at Leila, his hands heavy with the mud that covered them all. 'Hey!' he shrieked. 'Take my horse out of it.' A cook, someone, saw them there, struggling, and ran over to take Leila away. Johnny threw himself back into it by Nell's head and harness. It was too late; he was too late; anyone would have been too late. Shrapnel had torn open the vital artery at her neck. Her last breath choked out through mud and blood and Nell was gone.

'Nell! Nell!' His voice echoed out thinly across the waste, through the sound of other men suffering and other horses bellowing.

'She's gone, Leila old girl. Nell's gone.' He had turned back towards the cook's place where the bloke had taken Leila – but Leila was not there.

'Where's my horse, the Arab?' he shrieked. But he knew.

'She's gone, mate. Sorry, I couldn't hold her.'

Johnny went back into it, the jungle of men and horses churning their way from the other horror, back there where Leila had gone. One man raised his head long enough to say he had seen a horse cantering back into it so Johnny went too, his head raised into the icy wind that had in it the sound of those guns going on and on. Terror had taken her that way!

Johnny ran with the mud clutching at his boots, back past the carts and the other horses stumbling to safety, holding on to whatever came under his hands – a cartwheel, someone's great coat – and the muddy faces watched him, not understanding, not caring why he was running back into it.

And then he found her.

She'd fallen into a crater. It was filled with water and only her head showed, but it was Leila. She couldn't call to him. She had not the strength left. Her eyes, when she heard him shrieking: 'Leila! Leila!' turned a little, in the mud, towards him, but she could do no more.

Johnny knelt and drew her lovely head in its coating of mud into his arms. Mud joined them together. He put his head down beside her. Cold her head was, in the mud.

'Leila! Leila!' he shouted, coaxing, urgent, into her ear. 'Don't die, don't give in!' Her eyes, frantic, resigned, looked back at him. Johnny laid his face against hers.

Lulu Liscombe, at a Casualty Clearing Station somewhere near the Ypres salient, folded the damp blankets of her bed in the tent she shared with two other VADs. At first, when she had pushed her tired body between the rough grey stuff at night to sleep, she had thought of the linen sheets at Liscombe. But wasn't this what she had come for, to suffer too with the boys out there? Now, after eleven months of nursing service, Lulu Liscombe hardly ever thought of Liscombe comforts. It was best not to.

Night shift awaited her and a big push was on, the one to end the war they said, but they'd said that before. For the nurses, a big push simply meant more of it all.

She put her little black bag with her letters in it, her photographs of Harry and Daisy and Aunt Sarah before the fire, all her private things, into the metal locker that was too small. It was the only place away from the seeping rain on the ground. How it had rained that terrible winter. How it rained now, tonight, and there was a big push on. How could God send so much rain to hinder them?

Lulu Liscombe sometimes prayed, vaguely, to her childhood God for the men out there, that they should at least be free of rain and mud. Anything else – an end to the fighting, to the pain and the loss – would be too much to ask for, she thought.

Her gumboots were on now, still damp from this morning's return. Once she had worn a pair of red court shoes to a ball in London. Suddenly, she remembered the thrill of them, all silky and light on her feet. She was grown up, like Daisy, with shoes on and balls to go to. A faint memory of a tango tune sang in the back of her mind. Daisy was still dancing, back home in London. Daisy danced and drank though there was a war on; she did not even pretend to be knitting blankets. There was something very honest about Daisy.

On with her cape now, white with a red cross proudly stitched on to it. Or almost white. Madame Bassas in the town charged fifty centimes a cape. Most of their money went on washing. You could not trust the Army to return anything, let alone return it clean.

She fixed her damp limp cap to her limp hair, bending to the square of glass they had fixed to the tent pole. She must not complain. Had she not wanted to come out, begged to come out, begged to have a chance to do something useful? But it would be nice to be dry all over and to feel the sun on her skin or the warmth of a log fire.

Lulu shivered. She must not think of it, she must not let the low selfish thoughts like that creep in or she would never get through the night. Marjorie and Vi would be back soon off day shift. She would leave them a lamp lit.

Carrying the other hurricane lamp, Lulu walked in her gumboots across the duckboards that served to help them over the mud that oozed and swirled about the camp. Bending her head, holding one hand to her cap – Matron would not accept a muddy cap and once hers had blown off in the wind – Lulu stumbled across the wooden slats and on through the nasty little gusts that always took her on the last lap, past the sleeping quarters of the night reception tent. The whistle of the wind with the rain in it sounded high above the dull boom of the guns out there in the dark. It had rained for most of her service. For two years nearly German and Allies had faced each other around the Ypres salient, in a stalemate. Sometimes, they would have a good month, the Allies, and only lose a few thousand men. But a big push meant tens of thousands would be lost.

And all for nothing. Lulu Liscombe did not read newspapers; she knew she was not clever, but it seemed to her those men would die for nothing and dozens of them she would see die, screaming out for their mother sometimes. That was the hardest part to bear. Each night Lulu Liscombe saw dozens of men die, and now with the push on there'd be more. Someone, somewhere, must see the sense of it.

Tonight, Matron was not in her best mood.

'Your cap is crooked, Liscombe,' she said. 'Get to the ante room. They're coming in now.'

Lulu had heard the rumbling of the motor ambulances grinding their way across the field but she had not wanted to hear it, nor the shrieks that had started up before she even left the tent. She could always hear them through the wind and the guns. They were what went to her heart. And always there was so little they could do but give morphine, and soothe and clean mud from the torn flesh and the torn limbs.

Then she couldn't think any more that night for the stream of stretcher bearers that began stumbling in with their soldier burdens, some dying even as they were lifted on to the rubber sheets that covered the beds. There could be no bed linen here in the reception centre for the men brought with them, folded neatly into their tunics, spilling from their pockets, caked into their eyes and mouths and their wounds, mounds of Flanders mud to hinder and infect.

Her most useful piece of equipment that night was her scissors. All the men had to have their clothes cut from them before they could be treated. Heaps of Army clothing covered in mud soon lay about the floor until, needing the space, they simply threw it outside for the rain to wash.

The men and the boys came, whimpering, screaming, clutching at her hand as she cut and bathed and cut and soothed. No clumsy fingers for Lulu Liscombe now. Here, she gently wiped and washed with skill, holding a leg torn at its hip for the doctor to see, folding back, unflinching, jagged muscle and flesh, into its place, for it might heal, if they could get him away in time, if he was strong, if he was healthy. Gangrene did not always set in.

Here, at night, Lulu Liscombe could run a practised eye over the men who came and know if they would live. Here was one who would not. Part of his mouth and half his face was quite gone under the mud. Another wound showed at his neck where his collar had been. He was trying to speak; he clutched at her hand. Blood trickled down the little part of his chin that remained.

'Letter.' He pressed her hand to his chest where under the mud was his tunic, and breathed again: 'Letter. Tell newspapers. Pity of it.'

'Yes, darling, I'll see to your letter, don't worry. I'll see to your letter. Rest now.'

She held tight to his hand with both of hers. The feel of her hands would be his last feeling on this earth. 'Pity of it.'

'Sleep now. I'll get your letter sent. I'll take it myself.

Here. Here's my scissors. I'm cutting your tunic right away. You'll have to have a new one, won't you? I'm cutting it and I've got your letter. Look, here it is.'

His chest was not wounded, there was a little life there yet.

'Feel, here's your letter. It's to *The Times*, isn't it? I'm going to put it right in my pocket and then it'll be safe.' She gathered both his hands back into hers. They were fine hands, with long fingers. Someone else might have held them, once, with love.

'Rest, rest now.' Better that it should be quick. There was no hope for him.

'Liscombe, get that man moved. We can do nothing for him.' The doctor, his white gown covered with blood and mud, was shouting.

'Liscombe.' The torn mouth said, hardly a whisper, just a faint breath of her name repeated.

'Me Tranter, tell Ma.' A Tranter boy? Lulu bent further over his body, held tighter on his hands. Johnny? Billy? Oh, she could not tell, his face was half gone. Blood spurted from it. It was Billy Tranter. Billy Tranter was dead.

Mrs Tranter stood at the window of Stone Cottage. 'Dratted rain,' she said to Letty, cooing over the baby paddling towards her on the hearth rug. 'Has there ever been such a winter for rain? I did think I might walk into the village to see if that post office is holding any letters of ours.'

'Postman'll bring them.' Letty held out her skinny arms to the toddling baby Joe. 'Two years, four months and walking, sweet little chap!'

'He's here, that Arthur Meadows, and about time.' The postman came wobbling on his bicycle by the stream path. Mrs Tranter held her breath.

'You go, Letty,' she said.

'What a coincidence,' Letty cried, running to the door, 'just as you was saying . . .'

'There's an envelope, Mrs Tranter, one of them tele . . . things.'

Arthur Meadows did not stop for a cup of tea. He turned away, his boots slipping on wet pedals. Too many of those envelopes he had delivered the past three years and he would not wait to see it all again.

'Johnny!' Mrs Tranter cried out and set the baby whimpering. She held a hand to her heart. 'You open it, Lett. It's more than I can bear.'

Letty picked clumsily at the paper. But she could not read.

'Give it to me.' Mrs Tranter had waited three years for this envelope and here it was, in her hand. She sat heavily into her chair and rocked silently. If she did not open it, it might not be true. The words swam before her eyes 'To Mr and Mrs William Tranter, Stone Cottage, Liscombe, Dorset,' she read. Had Johnny suffered? They never told you. He would have died laughing, her boy, to defy them all, mocking the world, he would. 'We regret to inform you that your son, William John Tranter was killed in . . .' Billy!

'It's Billy dead, Letty,' she said. 'And him not out there three weeks.'

'Billy dead!' cried Letty. 'I always liked Billy, he was so quiet and gentle.'

'Make us a cup of tea, Letty.' Susan Tranter could not believe it. Each day she waited to hear that Johnny was dead and never once thought that Billy would die. She had seen him walk down the stream path the day they had let him out of prison. His skin was white. He was blinking behind the glasses that were broken down one side where someone had put their fist into his face.

Conshie! He had sat up in his room four days, as if he were still in prison, then he had to go. They had taken him because he had given in and said he would. The look on his face when he went off up the hill had broken her heart.

'I'm off then, Mother,' he had said, 'I don't know how long I'll be in training camp.' It had not been long enough, evidently. They could not have trained him properly in so short a time – Billy with a gun to kill with, to be trained for killing! It was their fault.

'It's their fault, Letty,' she said faintly, 'they sent him off too soon. He was no fighter. I'll write to one of them Generals and tell them so.' But it would not bring him back. His face had been so white when he came out of prison and his eyes dead as if he could not bear life any more. 'And he'd had such dreams, Lett, of doing good.'

No tears came for she had none left.

Three weeks later, Mrs Tranter received a letter from the Front and it was not Johnny's writing on the envelope.

'No doubt it's that General making some excuse for our Billy dying untrained like that,' she said to Letty.

Letty agreed, peering at the envelope as if she could read it properly. Soon she would be able to. Each afternoon before Mr Tranter came in for his early supper, she and Mrs Tranter would bend their heads over Beth's old learning books. She could read A is for Apple and P is for Pig well enough to point them out to baby Joe.

They both breathed over the letter, considering. They were never in a hurry in the long days they spent together. Indeed, Mrs Tranter often thought she had with her one of her own children, so much part of her life had Letty become. She only occasionally remembered that Letty was a servant girl, and an orphan.

'Shall I open it and see, Letty?'

'Do, Mrs Tranter, read it aloud.'

'Casualty Clearing Station No 15,' she read slowly, holding it close to her eyes. She was short-sighted now. 'Who do we know at a Clearing Station, Lett?'

DEAR MRS TRANTER,

Please accept my sincere condolences for the loss of your son, Billy. I do so remember him when we were children together and he helped me with my reading and my sums and was never impatient. He was kind, even as a boy, wasn't he?

'Well, whose writing is this then?' Mrs Tranter did not turn over the page. That would be like reading the last page of a novel first, cheating.

'He was kind,' she muttered, 'he was, wasn't he, Lett?'

'The kindest boy I ever knew,' breathed Letty. 'He never looked down on me when Kate asked me to tea.'

Mrs Tranter read on.

You will no doubt be wondering how I know about his tragic death when I am so far away. It is like this, Mrs Tranter. I was working as a nurse when Billy was brought in to us seriously injured. I had the privilege of tending his wounds. I am sure it was a comfort to him that someone who knew him should care for him at those last moments.

Mrs Tranter stopped here. She could not see for her tears, as if she had not grieved enough for the boy; they began now, slipping easily down as if she had not grieved enough.

388

'His last moments!' Letty began to sob as Mrs Tranter went on.

> I must tell you that although he was so gravely wounded, he did die very peacefully. We were able to give him morphine so he did not suffer at all. There was a letter in his tunic but the rain has made it so damaged that I have not sent it on to you. I am sure it was a last message of love for you and his family.

Mrs Tranter and Letty sobbed together. Billy had died in the rain. The rain had fallen on him as he lay dying. Mrs Tranter read to the end.

> I shall call and see you when next I have leave, dear Mrs Tranter, I shall always remember Billy with affection and gratitude.

'Lulu Liscombe always were a kind-hearted girl, Letty. But never to read them last words to me, Lett. How shall I ever bear it?'

She wiped her eyes with her apron and she and Letty wept through their tea. Baby Joe, unattended, sobbed too, and the rain fell relentlessly against the window-pane as it had fallen on Billy Tranter dying in Flanders mud with his face gone.

CHAPTER SEVENTEEN

At number fifteen to nineteen St John Street, Gideon was as always first with war news. The day the blocking of shipping lanes by German submarines was rumoured, Gideon heard it first. He called an emergency board meeting of the three of them one afternoon before evening service in their restaurants began and they dispersed for supervisory and other duties.

'As I see it,' he began, 'there's going to be a serious problem with food supplies and we got to decide how to deal with it.'

Kate poured tea and asked: 'Is it serious, Gideon? I mean, can it really affect us? They say the war'll be over soon, and with what's already in the country, the warehouses and so on . . .'

'It could go on years yet. There's stalemate over there. They just go on fighting for a bit of land, then they lose it then capture it back and thousands is lost, and there's no end to it as far as I can see. Or anyone else either,' he conceded. 'Now, what are we going to do about it?'

'I can't imagine, Gideon.' Kate looked about their familiar dark room. 'I am at a loss to think anything at all. I've just finished interviewing two girls for the Strand Kitchen and neither seemed to have the sense they were born with. They couldn't carry a soup plate empty let alone six full. I haven't another thought in my head apart from wishing good waitresses would drop from the sky like one of those Zeppelins, or the war would stop taking all the able men.' And it seemed that she had not her old energy, since the death of her sister.

'We leave all the war stuff to you, you know we do,' said Aunt Bessie crossly. 'You tell us what you've decided to do about it because I can see you have decided.'

'I have.' Gideon grinned and leaned across the table as if the matter was one of the utmost secrecy, like battle plans. 'I've decided we got to go Dorset.'

'We already are Dorset,' laughed Kate. 'We couldn't be more Dorset, could we?'

'Well, we could. We could buy Dorset and only Dorset produce, and be patriotic at the same time.' Gideon lost his grin and began to itemize. 'Dorset rabbits,' he said. 'Dorset ducks. No beef or lamb or pork that can be salted down and sent out to the troops – nothing that the troops might need, you see – only stuff country-produced and fresh. We'll beat the shipping blockade for we shan't need anything foreign, not from America nor Europe nor India. We'll be self-sufficient.'

'And patriotic too?' Kate was still amused at Gideon's idea and was slightly ashamed of herself. If Gideon said it was a serious matter then she should treat it as such. Only, for the moment, it seemed difficult to accept that England should ever be cut-off from her Empire, let alone the rest of the world. She pushed her hair distractedly back into its bun – she had not time now for piled-up hair, the war had made Tranter's far too busy – and waited for Gideon to continue.

'Patriotic,' repeated Gideon, 'people want to be patriotic without giving up anything. We'll have a slogan. "Don't take food from the mouths of the boys out there," something like that, and we'll . . .'

A knock sounded at the parlour door, interrupting him. 'Excuse me, Miss Tranter,' the hotel porter said. 'There's a personal telegram for you.'

They all froze into silence. The porter held out the silver tray which held the yellow paper and no one moved. A telegram was lying there, Kate could see the faint line of it, but she could not move. It would tell her that Johnny was dead, killed in action, and she would not be able to bear it, not Johnny dead too, after Beth.

'I cannot bear it.' She turned a striken face to Aunt Bessie who stared back at her with the same horror. A telegram always meant death, in wartime. 'Gideon,' she said.

Gideon limped across to the porter who turned back up the stairs.

The yellow paper seemed to gleam in Gideon's hand. Kate saw it there and waited. Gideon would open it and read out the news that Johnny was dead and she would wait to hear the words that had stopped her heart already.

'It's from Mrs Susan Tranter.' Gideon read out the address, 'Stone Cottage, Liscombe, Dorset,' to put back the time when the words of death must be said. He coughed. '"Billy killed in the fighting, Mother."'

'I'll send for your ticket.' It seemed a long time before Aunt Bessie spoke. 'And get your bag packed. Susan'll be needing you.'

Kate went home and sat with her mother, and stood in the empty bedroom where she must pack up Billy's clothes.

They were few: white shirts and stiff collars, and his pepper and salt trousers with black jackets for his law work. Amongst them lay a pair of reading glasses, broken. Her mother had said Billy had arrived home from prison with them cracked. He had been attacked because he did not want to go to war. He was supposed to need them only for reading all those books piled up against the walls of his room. They were stacked too in packing cases under his bed and the one he had been last immersed in, *The World Set Free* by H.G. Wells, lay dust-covered on the wooden crate beside his bed. He had not taken his glasses with him to war for there they lay in her hand. What if he could not really see? If he only pretended they were for eyestrain? What if the officer had shouted 'Over the top!' and Billy had not been able to see where to run? Perhaps he had run straight into a German with his bayonet raised ready to strike him down. Kate wrapped the glasses into a shirt, leaning her cheek into the cool damp cloth that still held the scent of Billy. She took up his last book. These she resolved to keep with her in London in memory of the brother she had not had time to see or comfort when he was sent off to war with the prison-white pallor in his face.

'Can I help you, Kate?' Letty sidled into the room, a thin and scrawny girl looking still only sixteen although she was twenty-four. Kate's old crêpe dress, cut down by Mrs Tranter, hung crookedly about the waist and hem, and her ginger hair had been pulled back into a clumsy bun in imitation of Kate's.

'No, dear,' Kate said absently, 'I'll just have Pa ask one of the men to take the books away. I suppose they must be taken away. There's no point in their sitting up here to get damp.'

'All that reading, Kate,' breathed Letty.

'I suppose they must go,' Kate said. 'Such a waste!' She felt tears of anger come to her eyes very suddenly. 'Such a waste, Billy dying when he had all those plans. He was to help the poor go to law to claim their rights. Billy knew the poor had rights. He was obsessed with the poor.'

Letty sat on the bed that had been Billy's and swung

her scuffed shoes. 'He was, Kate. He said to me I had the right to a proper living and respect and I should not wait on the rich, Kate, but I did not understand it.' She smoothed down her skirt and considered the hole in her black stockings which revealed a white shin. 'And his lordship did, too. He kept on about how I should go to one of them places to learn things, like in Dorchester, Kate, and not be a servant any more, but I were that frightened of going on me own, and Cook said I needn't go, and Mrs Baker, so he stopped keeping on at me and frightening me with his talk. Billy said it was pa . . . pat . . . something.'

'Patronage,' said Kate mechanically. 'Billy so fiercely wanted not to be patronized because he and Beth were, as children, and he thought it wrong that anyone should have to be. That the patronage of the rich to the poor was morally wrong. Even with me, his own sister. I gave him a guinea once and he stared at it in his hand and I thought I should never have earned it.'

'Will you take me up to London when baby Joe goes to school, Kate? I'd work, I would. I'd work as hard as I used when we was young.'

'You'd have to,' Kate said, 'I never have time for anything but work.' She began to heap Billy's books uselessly from one pile to another.

'But you is rich, Kate! If I was rich . . .' She jumped from the bed and tried to see her own reflection in the windowpane. 'If I was rich!'

'I am not sure, Letty, that I have my dream. You know, living on a hilltop, do you remember?' She gazed at the cover of a copy of Marx's *Das Kapital*. 'I work a lot in basement kitchens just as we used to do, as you still do, and though I have money, what pleasure is there in it if your brother thinks you have exploited your staff to earn it? He said I should give them more money and a shorter working week and see that they were properly housed. As if I could do all that unless I trebled my prices and then I'd have no business to employ them in. It's difficult, Lett. Perhaps you have been happier, staying at Liscombe and walking out with Cyril Cousins.' She threw down the Marx and moved restlessly about the room, hampered by Letty's presence. She wanted to think of Billy, to feel how Billy had been. She owed him that, for the years he had kept about her skirts and looked to her for love and understanding.

'Huh, Cyril Cousins! He's so short the Army wouldn't have him.' Letty twirled before the window and danced a clumsy tango step in front of the washstand. 'No, Kate, that Ted Burrows have asked . . .'

Kate picked up Billy's broken glasses and held the cool glass in her hand. She let Letty chatter on. She wanted to feel Billy here in this room. She wanted to send Letty away. She must feel how it had been for Billy here amongst his useless books the four days he had sat there before they took him for the war and no one had been able to comfort him.

'And perhaps he'll ask for my hand in marriage,' Letty was saying dreamily, holding out a thin left hand, coarse and reddened by soda and cold water. 'I'll have me own little place and me own front door and he'll bring home ten shilling a week.'

'And it'll hardly keep you two, much less the gaggle of kids you'll soon have about your skirts.' Kate smiled absently at her friend.

'You never did want kids, Kate,' Letty said, 'Wouldn't it be nice to have a baby Joe of our own to cuddle?'

'There's more to it than cuddling, Lett. If you had sons now maybe they'd be old enough for the next war, and then how would you feel?'

Letty was not in the habit of giving thought to such matters. 'But you never did want anyone, Kate,' she said wistfully, 'not like me, wanting someone of my own. You used to say your life would be over if you got married.'

'And so it would have been,' Kate said sharply. 'You should realize, Letty, that marriage is a trap for a woman in your position. You would have nothing to look forward to, no change ever, just endless days of cooking without money enough to feed your brood, which would keep on growing. There'd be boots to find the money for, and you'd see them go to school in near rags, and just have time to cook up another meal from scrag ends before they were back to help you with the latest baby. There would be no end to your skivvying, Lett, if you married that Ted Burrows, so just you think twice about it.'

'But there's no end to my skivvying up at the Hall,' Letty said in a small voice, her eyes round with surprise at Kate's barrage of words.

'No, no, Letty, I'm sorry. There's no end to my skivvying either, every day of my life, though I suppose it seems grander than yours. I wonder sometimes if I am not in the same kind of trap that so horrified me when I was a girl.' She went to the window and gazed up over Rookery Hill where the black swooping shapes were patterned against the grey sky.

'And you're rich, Kate, you don't feed on scrag ends,' Letty reminded her.

'Rich, yes, in the business, but all our profits have to be ploughed back in replacement equipment or new drains or some such problem. We'll only be really rich if we sell. Perhaps if we sold I could come back home, Letty.' Her breath made a steamy patch against the window pane; she wrote in it HOME with one finger.

'But it won't be home any more without Beth and Billy.'

'Isn't it thrilling, Kate, to go into one of them teashops of yours and say "Get that pan cleaned out" or "Scrub that floor, girl"? Ooh, I'd love that, I would.'

'I try and treat them with respect, dear Letty, as you and I wanted to be treated, I don't forget all that, you know.' She turned away from the window and added, for she wanted to be truthful to her old friend, 'But it is thrilling to go in there and know that I have been instrumental in making it the way it is. It is something I have made, and I try and remember I am proud of it and not always worry about small details and not appreciate the whole of it. It is easy in business to get caught up in the rush of the day's routine and not stand back and feel what it is really like. For me to have come so far, Letty . . .' She looked at her old friend's blank face, clearly not understanding, and stopped. It was not fair to burden Letty with thoughts that she herself did not comprehend. 'Anyway,' she muttered, speaking for herself, 'nothing is the same since Beth died. Losing her took something away from my life, and now Billy is gone and the war has changed everything, it has tainted everything, I never spend a day now without the memory of them seeping into me. I feel I owe them something but will never now be able to give it. I feel I must do something special for them, in their memory. They were somehow nobler than me. They had better dreams, Letty.'

'How can dreams be better, Kate?'

'Well, they are sometimes, or they seem so now to me because my brother and sister are dead. They were not afraid to love. Look how Beth loved her Harry, and Billy loved everyone who was poor or not privileged in any way. If he had lived . . . They both had open hearts, you see, big hearts if you like. They wanted to do grand things for other people, loving things, while I wanted everything for myself.'

'But you're the one who's grand, Kate.' Letty jumped from the bed to put her thin arms around her friend and benefactor. 'Or maybe I got it all wrong again?' She looked up into Kate's face, so rarely pale and tired as it was now. 'You're the one who does things for other people. You're always giving your money and everything away.'

'It's all I've had time for, Letty, and perhaps it hasn't been enough. Perhaps I've been afraid of loving.'

Returning home to London, Kate had little time for such thoughts. She set herself to redesigning their menus, basing the new dishes entirely on fresh Dorset produce which could not be sent out to the troops. Their restaurants then sported little notices: Tranter's use only produce which cannot be sent out to our boys. Be patriotic. Help our boys. Eat at Tranter's.

This, combined with their judicious use of their own cellar space, seemed to make them the most prosperous restaurant in London, for other restaurant owners had been less canny when fear of air raids had begun to empty London streets. Kate had had the idea of clearing out the Kitchens' basements and cellars and having them made safe by shoring up with sandbags. Gideon had small tables put in amongst the racks of wine and cider. When their new menu cards were printed, they added a note: You are safe at Tranter's.

They did not want to suggest that any customer was unsafe anywhere, but people soon understood that this meant they could run down into Tranter's as the Red warnings were put up. Many had eaten three courses by the time the All Clear bugles sounded.

After Billy's death, and by the end of 1917, Tranter's had taken over three more restaurants, one in Albemarle Street, one hidden in a little alley-way off Regent Street, and the third a three-roomed business near Victoria Station, offering an all-night service and breakfasts to the soldiers returning from the Front. Each had a safe cellar offering haven from German air raids, and a reduced menu entirely made up of fresh Dorset produce which could not be sent out to the troops.

Kate and Aunt Bessie and Gideon watched their clients stream into their restaurants and saw them eating there each day, confident that Tranter's cellars were safe, and making Tranter's daily more prosperous where other restaurants were bankrupt from lack of trade.

They themselves rose at dawn and worked on through the day. Sometimes they did not gather together for tea since each would be in different parts of London. They had to divide responsibility between them; Kate supervised food, Aunt Bessie their staff, and Gideon concentrated on their accounts and considered the purchase of other leases from restaurant proprietors less enterprising than they. He was to be found late each evening scribbling his tiny figures on sheets of paper, surrounded by bags of coin and paper notes.

Kate suggested one evening: 'Let Peter help you, Gideon, with all that counting. He is big enough now, and it will all be his one day. He must begin to learn the trade.'

When Billy had died, she had worked out how many years remained to her before she could pass the business to Peter. She was tired. They were all tired, the three of them, and had to find the strength to be ever vigilant for Tranter's prosperity, and Peter's future, and the future of Beth's boy Joe too.

That day, Kate led her sulky and reluctant son to sit opposite Gideon at the parlour table.

'It will all be yours, darling,' she said, ruffling his thin dark hair and fixing cotton cuffs over his shirtsleeves. 'You must begin sometime.'

'I don't want to begin.' Peter, a big boy now, looking fourteen, pushed out a fretful lower lip and squirmed in the chair. 'I've got a pain in my head, Mother.'

'What sort of pain, dear?' Kate felt his brow anxiously. She was so busy and Peter had been ill?

'He's got no pain.' Gideon did not look up from his figures. 'Unless it's called laziness.'

'It's Christmas, anyway,' grumbled Peter.

'We work, Peter. We always work, you know that. You'll have to get used to it.'

'You leave him with me,' Gideon said, 'I'll start him nice and easy.' He looked up behind the spectacles he needed to wear now, and smiled at Kate. 'Go on, Kate.'

'I don't . . .'

She hesitated, but left the room. Peter was twelve now, she must not molly-coddle him, and he did have the business to learn. He had no taste for school, though he was clever; she might perhaps take him away when he was sixteen and set him to learn the business properly. It was to be his one day, and he would be prosperous. She smiled to herself, going up the basement stairs, that she had achieved security for Peter. He would be grateful for it when he was old enough to understand. And one day his cousin Joe would join him; the business would remain a family concern.

'Put them bills there all together under each "Kitchen",' Gideon was saying. 'Then sub-divide them into dry goods, fresh produce, drink and so on.'

Peter pushed at the papers on the green chenille cloth and mixed and muddled them so that Gideon swiftly took them across to his own side of the table.

'All right, then,' he said. 'You empty these bags and

put the coins together, halfpennies, pennies, farthings and so on, each making a pound.'

Peter emptied bags noisily into a pile and slipped himself a shilling. He would go out to the Haymarket tonight.

'You leaves that.' Gideon's sharp eyes never missed anything.

'Oh, do it yourself then.' Peter left the parlour, slamming the door behind him. He climbed the two flights up to their own quarters. If Gideon did not watch him he would go into town every evening. He needed to hurry now, sitting at that table had wasted time and the maids would have finished evening service if he were not quick.

His heart thumping, Peter climbed on up one more flight to the maids' rooms and put his plump fingers into their trunks and cupboards, rummaging amongst their Sunday best and day-off finery, breathing in female scents. It was better than listening to Gideon ramble on about profit margins. As if he cared!

No one came up the stairs to catch him that evening, but the thought that they might heightened the shivering at his back and made his skin flush from his hair to his toes. He pressed his face into a nightgown, shivering, waiting, hoping for someone to find him, fearing for someone to find him and cry: 'Dirty Peter!'

Suddenly, the war was over. Kate and Aunt Bessie and Gideon joined with the rest of London, of Britain and of Europe, in celebrating the end of the killing. The crowds came out into the city streets and jostled and cheered their way to the railings of Buckingham Palace, there to call for the King and rejoice for the end of the war that would end all wars. They had suffered. Half their young men were gone, and the best, the flower of their youth, but it would be worth it. They would not have died in vain for there would never be another war. They cried 'Peace! Peace!' just as four years before they had cried 'War!' and the cry echoed all along the streets and up into the November sky.

At Tranter's Hotel, fifteen to nineteen St John Street, the three took a glass of champagne together in quiet celebration of the historical moment.

'No more boys lost,' said Kate, staring at the mantelpiece where Billy's face, ever young, stared solemnly back at her, beside Beth's, smiling charmingly in a faded sepia brown photograph. 'And Johnny home more or less whole.'

'I'll think about that retirement of mine,' said Aunt Bessie, pouring a second glass.

'We got some replanning to do,' Gideon said, leaving his glass untouched. 'Stocks will not be back to normal yet.'

'But that slogan'll have to go. We can hardly go on with "Be patriotic, Eat at Tranter's", or "Be safe at Tranter's".'

'Think up a new one, Kate, get us a new idea.' Gideon leaned his head on a crooked arm.

'I haven't the strength.' She eased off a shoe under the table. 'It all feels very flat suddenly. Different. I feel we've stopped. I feel nothing is ever going to be the same for any of us. The war somehow suspended real life. We've been working in a state of high excitement with abnormal prosperity, and now it's got to end.'

'We're all tired, I tell you. The war may have made us comfortable but it's worn us out. Haven't I earned my retirement, Gideon?'

They watched Aunt Bessie's cigarette smoke drift upwards to the parlour lamp. Gideon poured a third glass of champagne. 'It'll take some reckoning, but let's say none of us need work for a while if we feel so inclined.'

'I say we let things ride,' said Kate, 'until we see how London life changes.'

In London, things were slow to change. The streets began to fill with soldiers returning to the new life they had been promised, to the new peaceful world they had fought for. On some days they seemed to be lining the very streets. They began to ask for work and there was none for them, for the ones left behind had managed very well without them.

Even Tranter's, continuing to do well enough, could not employ the thousands who began to beg for work and a living. Kate would see them shuffling along the streets, young men in their poor blue demobilization suits carrying their cardboard suitcases. Some would linger around the restaurants, hoping for a meal, and she quietly set up her own small soup-kitchens at each one, detailing a waiter to serve all that was left and more besides. She went so far as to order a gallon of rabbit stew be made up daily, in spite of Gideon's protests.

'You're doing it out of our profits, Kate.'

'It's the least we can do, Gideon. Haven't we benefited from the war, from these men's suffering? How can we stand by and see them starve?' It was the first argument they had had and she would not look at him. She saw Johnny's altered face, she saw Billy's prison-pallor face behind his broken glasses, the face her mother had described, in all the faces under the demob hats around their restaurants and would not change her mind.

'It's the government should see to them,' Gideon said. 'Private charity can only touch the surface, and anyway it lets the authorities evade their responsibilities.'

'I don't care about them, I want to do something myself, me, I want to say I have warmed fifty bellies today, I have helped fifty poor devils who might have been Johnny or Billy. Or if it comes to that any one of the soldiers who spent freely in our bars when they had money to spend before they went off to die.' She was standing in the Albemarle Street Kitchen and did not care that two commis cooks had heard every word she had said. She pushed two dirty saucepans towards the sink boy. 'See this, this waste, there's two servings left in the bottom here. If we were more vigilant, we could afford to give even more, and I don't care if it's patronage like Billy would say or if the government *should* do it, *I want* to do it.'

'There shouldn't be any wastage in this kitchen,' Gideon said, putting out a hand for the pans. 'I checked out the service the other day.'

The sink boy opened a full tap quickly on to the pans before Gideon could take them. 'It's burned, sir,' he muttered.

Gideon dropped his arm. 'Never mind,' he said. 'Our profit's going down the drain but never mind.'

Kate stared stubbornly at the back of the boy's head and would not turn to look at Gideon though she felt his softening and saw from the corner of her eye his hand held out towards her.

'We'll go to Smithfield,' he was saying, 'see what they can supply us with in the cheap meat line. We'll get something cooked up special. That suit you?'

'Yes, Gideon, thank you,' Kate muttered. 'I feel I must do something no matter who *ought* to do it. Even Billy would stop reading and writing pamphlets if he could see these men needing food today, this very moment, wouldn't he?'

'Your Billy would be over in Hyde Park, protesting about the government turning a blind eye.' Gideon grinned. 'Come on, let's get on to Smithfield and do it properly. You're a doer, Kate, and your Billy was a dreamer. It's doers what gets things done.'

Soon Tranter's Kitchens had another reputation and tramps joined the soldiers lining the streets behind the restaurants. Kate's principal interest became the forgotten returning soldiers. She kept Peter away from school so that he should stand beside her serving rabbit stew and see what war did to a nation's manhood; so that he would never go to war.

She was so preoccupied when Captain Waddington limped back from Dorchester and put himself up again at Tranter's Hotel, she hardly noticed him.

More tired and sad than ever amongst all those returning soldiers, he took up his old room and his old habits, standing in the bar waiting for a glimpse of Kate. The men in the streets and in the back courtyard of Tranter's Hotel reminded him of the day he had, carelessly, lost thirty-seven of his company. One night, he very quietly cut his wrists in his old room, number twenty-four, where he had written his sweet notes begging for a little of Kate's time. She sent for his only relation and fitted the funeral arrangements around her work at the back of Tranter's Kitchens. She did not allow herself to feel the pain around her heart for what might have been between them. Her heart, she told herself, had been too long sealed, and it was all too late.

When the bell of Liscombe Church rang out the Armistice that November day and the single note reached down to Stone Cottage, Johnny Tranter got up from the fireside and ran out of the room without a word of goodbye to his mother. Taking up Billy's old bicycle from the shed, he pedalled off on legs that were not healed from frostbite.

He thought: It is all over.

He rode on round Flush Hill and through the orchards and back up to the old hunt stables where he and Leila had once lived. Cold, her stable now in the November air, a lingering faint smell of her in the dust, an echo of clattering hooves. He threw aside the bicycle and laid a hand on the smooth old wood of her stall where he had carved her name: Leila. He should have shot her that first day in Dorchester barracks when he found out where she was. Her suffering, her toil in the mud, her terror were all his fault. He had held her head and she had screamed and he could not hold her any more. He would have drowned with her if someone had not dragged him away.

They were celebrating now, in the streets, tolling bells, while a million horses were dead, millions of men, and all for nothing, no good anywhere in it but useless gestures like Harry's. And the German had died too.

They would be laughing in the streets, celebrating as if the whole world had not gone.

Lord David Liscombe found Johnny sobbing in the old stables. 'Come on now, old chap, let's have a glass of something together.' He led him up the Liscombe Hall steps where Treeves, as always, bent to open the door and stand as stiff and formal as if he had forty guests to welcome, like the old days.

Mr Treeves bowed gravely to Mr Tranter whom he had first seen as a lad in torn breeches come for a place as lamp boy. There were no lamp boys at Liscombe now, nor any other kind of boy. Master Harry was dead, Eric, the odd boy, missing believed killed, the two gardener's boys gone, and three stable-boys, blown to pieces on the Somme together with half the village boys.

They went up the stairs together, viscount and stable-boy, reduced to the same misery: Liscombe Hall dead and empty, Liscombe stables too. In his study, Lord David offered Johnny a chair. 'Let's have a whisky,' he said. 'To celebrate, eh?'

'Is there something to celebrate, sir?' Johnny held his glass and did not drink.

'No.' Lord David turned away from him and left his own glass untouched. 'There is nothing. Only perhaps that no more will die.' He stared from the window over Rookery Hill and there was only the ticking of the clock in the room and their silence. He had spent long lonely years listening to that clock. 'I think I have heard enough years tick by, old chap,' he said. He had not known he was going to say that, but did not know how he was going to begin to say, to Johnny Tranter, what he must. 'I wonder,' he began, 'if you might be able to tell me . . .'

'How Harry died,' Johnny finished. Lord David saw him place his glass with great care upon the desk. 'He died because he was good,' he said. 'Because he was a fool.'

'Yes, I see.' Lord David allowed his glance to drop down to the valley where, with his eternal watching, he knew the maid Letty would be walking the little boy by the stream. 'I see. Because he was good.' He took a gulp of whisky that he did not want. 'As a boy, he wanted to save the world. Do you remember?'

'He died because he went out into No Man's Land, by himself, to save a Fritz. A sniper got him with one bullet. I heard it. I knew they'd got him and I knew his life was wasted, but he did it because he couldn't stand the bloody uselessness of it. I asked for a medal for him but they wouldn't give him one. No one had seen it but me and a sergeant, and a sentry who died too. The same day. So I couldn't get a medal for Harry. Anyway, only officers can put in for a medal, as you know. Only officers can witness an act of bravery. One of us might make it all up, I suppose.'

Lord David heard his voice far away, as if from the other side of the cold window glass. Harry had died for nothing. A hero. Uselessly. It did not make anything easier to bear.

'Anyway, after I'd buried him, I had to lie low, really, even though everyone who knew I'd gone absent was dead. The whole trench was blown up. Funny, really. Luck of the Tranters, Harry would have said. I could have been shot for burying him, but all the witnesses were blown up.'

'You buried Harry, old chap, by yourself?' The cold from the window seemed to seep into him and stay about his heart. This boy, this childhood friend of Harry's, had picked up his body and . . . 'How, Johnny?' he heard himself say. 'In the trench, you mean?'

'I couldn't leave him in the trench. There were rats everywhere. Harry couldn't abide rats.'

Lord David sensed that Johnny had picked up his glass to drink but could not move himself. 'He couldn't abide rats?'

'His mother . . . the fire!' Johnny almost shouted. 'And in the trenches rats were everywhere. They grew fat feeding off the dead. Don't you understand? I had to take him away. I couldn't leave him there.'

Lord David turned painfully around to face Harry's friend, and the facts of his son's death in squalor and misery. 'So you took him away?' It was hard to get out the words. The whisky would warm him but he could not seem to lift his hand to his mouth.

'I carried him, on my back, running down the trenches most of the way though they shouted at me. He was heavy. Taller than me, Harry. I had to keep stopping but I didn't let go of him 'till I reached base because there had been a village there and I thought there must be a church. I found it and got a spade from some blokes on burial duty out in the fields. I chose a spot near the wall, by the door, so he might have a bit of protection if the village should blow. It was hard ground but I dug down five feet and six feet long, and I laid him down and said the Lord's Prayer all the way through. No one heard me. No one there to hear me. Then I filled it in and made my way back for my court martial. Only everyone was dead by then, as I said, and I got a bit of shrapnel in my back and so on. But the rats haven't got Harry.'

Lord David saw him lift the glass to his mouth and drink down the liquid that he did not want. He found that his legs could move across the room towards Johnny's chair. He wanted to put a hand on his shoulder but could not. 'Shall we bring him home, old chap?' he said. 'If you could remember where. Then we could be sure . . . he'd be safe, here at home.'

Bringing Harry to his rightful place seemed to free part of Johnny's mind. Afterwards he rode about on his bicycle, getting his physical strength back, and went so far as to buy wood and make a wagon for his nephew Joe for Christmas. By February, he was finally able to let his mother fold away the worn and faded army tunic, and his breeches and puttees, and the secret box that held Harry's letter to Beth, wrapped around a lock of her hair, that would be for Joe when he was old enough.

One day, his lordship bought for him one of the horses returned from the war, having heard of one for sale the other side of Dorset. She was a nice creature, a bay with a shell wound healed on her neck. Her head hung so low when she was led into Liscombe stables it was as if she would never trust life again nor find any pleasure in it. Johnny could not bring himself to ride her at first, and when he eventually did it was very tentatively, walking across the stable-yard and round the Hall and down the hill the way he had gone with Leila.

Lord Liscombe, watching Johnny lift his head into the wind and seat himself on the back of a horse the way he so often had, saw the beginnings of pleasure in him and rejoiced for it. If the gift should help him from his depression it would be little enough recompense for the risk he had taken in burying Harry safely. There had been a body left to bring home to Liscombe. Pitifully small, Harry had seemed, in the new coffin. His father had wept.

He could weep now, he thought, seeing Johnny Tranter lift that stubborn head of his and set his shoulders to go off on the broken mare. Inside, Johnny was like her, full of fear and tortured memory. But he would never show it again. All the Tranters were like that, even Billy, who had forced himself to go to war. Where had Harry found the strength to go out into that desolation, for the enemy? It was the two sensitive boys who had died. Johnny would survive; Lord David could see that now in the way he held himself on the horse. She would help him.

He watched Johnny disappear down into the valley and wished he had something similar to help him through. If Kate had been widowed by the war ... if there had been some chance ... He had asked Johnny outright. He had said, on the boat going over to France, 'Your sister still safely looked after by her Mr Gideon?' And Johnny had said she was, and had changed the subject. He would never be drawn on the subject of Kate.

There was no sound of life in Liscombe as he leaned from his window to watch Johnny Tranter; no sign of life down in the valley, no horses in Home Farm stables now, nor any forge work. He had no need to build it up again, the whole estate, because Harry was no more and that duty, that purpose, had been wiped away too.

He leaned into the wind of Liscombe and heard only its faint haunting whistle, that Blanche had always hated. Once the air of the valley had been filled with the sound of men and animals at work, stable-boys, horses, gardeners, carters. He had had a kind of contentment in it, in spite of Blanche. And then there had been Kate and he had dreamed of it with her there beside him; Liscombe would have been paradise.

He must not think of Kate nor any part of his past life. He must somehow set back his shoulders like Johnny Tranter. If he could get some more horses purchased, then perhaps he could start the farm stables again and get rid of the noisy steam and motor machinery they had begun to use since the war. Perhaps they should buy war horses; there had been thousands returned from France and sold by the Army.

He drew back his head into the silence of his study and shut out the wind. Today he would begin. He would draw up a plan for the re-starting of horse work at Liscombe. Johnny could get on with the buying of them.

They would both have an occupation. Liscombe would have some life in it.

Johnny, taking the broken mare back up to the old stables, raged at the sight of her war wounds and the feel of her neck where the bones showed through. Lifting the saddle from her back – he had mounted her too soon! – he groomed her gently, crooning, and was rewarded with a sideways look, a mere glance. It was enough. He laid his face against familiar warm horse flesh and knew this was where he should be, with horses.

When his lordship ran into the stables, startling the mare with a flutter of papers and a shout, very little discussion between them was needed.

Johnny would get down to Kent the next morning; most of the war horses would be there. He would buy as many as was practical to begin with, and it would be as if each one of them were Leila.

In the months when Johnny began to heal in body and spirit, Kate found it harder to continue with the work she had taken upon herself. The groups of men around Tranter's Kitchens grew; their customers became embarrassed by the presence of want and suffering. Tranter's began to lose business.

The day that Gideon dragged Kate from one of the Kitchens and took her outside into the street she saw what everyone else saw, a group of tramps shuffling in laceless boots and several overcoats and, on their fringes, a few returned soldiers in demob suits, shabbier than ever now.

'Kate,' said Gideon, pointing, 'think back before the war and all this misery. Remember, for most people there's no war on now. There you are walking along the street with your escort and you think you'll call in for luncheon at your usual place, and then in front of it there's this dirty smelly noisy crowd reminding you there's some as can't afford the shilling for a meal. Now . . .'

'I never walked along here with an escort,' said Kate sulkily. 'And, anyway, women hardly ever went to restaurants in those days.' She did not want to listen to Gideon, did not want to see how things were.

'All right,' he said patiently, 'remember then me and you looking out from the first place, hoping for a bit of trade. How would we have thought then to see a crowd of tramps? We'd have called the police, that's what, for we'd have had no trade with them there.'

'Yes, yes, Gideon, you are right.' Her head swam. She felt very tired, weak enough to stand there on the pavement for the rest of the day.

'We'll finish today,' Gideon said. 'And then I'll put the notices up that I've had printed. I've been in touch with the Salvation Army. They're willing to take over your work. We'll donate enough to them. We can do that, Kate, if we get our business back.'

'All right,' she said, 'you must do that, Gideon. I am too tired to fight you.'

'Not fight, Kate, never fight,' he said gently, taking her arm. 'We must not fight, not you and me. We never have 'till now. Come on, I'll help you finish off serving today. You see, the more business we do in the normal way, the more we can give. And give we will, never fear. Aunt Bessie and me, we'll never stop you giving, only it's better for you too this way. No one person can do what you've been trying to do. The problem's too big.'

'All right, Gideon.' She had not the strength to say any more, but she knew that he was right.

And she must get on now with keeping their business prosperous, for Peter's future and for baby Joe's. They were her first responsibility. She burst out: 'I sometimes think my spirit is all gone, Gideon, and the dreams I once had are gone, and my heart . . .' She was crying in the street, and did not care who saw her.

'Never, dear girl, not you. You've got heart and spirit for a hundred, you have. This war have just lost you too much, that's all, your brother and sister gone and Johnny only half what he was. You need rest and you

need time. Aunt Bessie and me have booked you a
holiday, a real one, and you're not going home neither.
You're going to New York, on a ship.'

'I can't go to New York, Gideon!' Kate found she
was laughing through her tears.

'You can. It's booked up, and while you're there you
can look at how them Americans do hotels. You can
work while you're there and come back your old self or
we'll want to know why.'

PART FOUR

CHAPTER EIGHTEEN

'Blow it out in one puff for luck, Kate!' cried Aunt Bessie.

She blew on the solitary candle of her birthday cake. 'How kind they were not to arrange a huge one with thirty-four candles,' she said.

The three partners and Peter sat in their still-favourite place, the first Dorset Country Kitchen off the Strand, for Kate's birthday dinner. The staff had concocted a cake made from fruit, a feat which had prompted her to clap her hands in appreciation. It was a pressed jelly made with layer upon layer of summer berries and bearing in a paper flower one discreet candle.

Kate tasted the portion Gideon had cut and smiled across to the chef, watching from the service hatch. 'It's perfect, Tom,' she called, 'just perfect. And original. I wonder if we might put it on the menu for special occasions?'

'Aren't you tired of tasting food, Mother?' Peter, sitting beside her, pushed restlessly at his plate. 'I am. God, I'm bored with food.'

'You young donkey!' Aunt Bessie tapped the back of his hand with her spoon. 'You sit there as pampered as a cat, like you've been all your life, and your mother's worked for it, worn herself to the bone for your future. And that's the appreciation she gets.'

Peter turned his sulky face towards his mother. Kate saw his pale blue eyes which had never seemed to have the light in them that his father's had, and the pouting look of his full mouth. The thin dark hair lay flat and too long about his ears. There was so little of herself or his father in him. She once thought he would change; she had always hoped he would mature and respond to the love she felt for him, but he was eighteen now, almost a man. She said: 'Aunt Bessie is right, Peter, you're in no position to be bored with food or the life we lead. We've offered to put you in some other kind of business which would please you, you've no obligation to carry on Tranter's, but you can't make up your mind to anything. You spend half the day in bed and all your nights about London. It's no life for someone who'll have to earn a living.'

'We haven't made enough for you to be a man of pleasure, Peter.' Gideon helped himself to the last of the raspberries in their liquid jelly. 'You'll have to do something with yourself.'

'Oh, we've been over all this endlessly.' Peter took one of his aunt's cigarettes. 'Haven't you any Turkish, Auntie? These kill a fellow.'

'No, I haven't,' she said crossly, 'and I'll thank you to leave those alone. Your allowance should cover your cigarettes.'

'It doesn't cover much else.' Peter searched in the pocket of his evening jacket and drew out a silver case. 'And it doesn't last me the month. I don't know how you expect it to.'

'Those quick fingers of yours make up the rest,' Gideon said.

'Peter, I really think you should stop helping yourself to the tills.' Kate pushed aside her own plate. It had been an effort to finish the dish the chef had so carefully worked on. She had done it only to please him. Problems with Peter always made her lose her appetite. She so wished him to be comfortable, never to want as she had, as her family had, but he was not sensible about it and always seemed to stimulate trouble at the table, probably because he rarely spent time with them outside meals. 'It was a penny when you were a boy but you're taking pounds now, Gideon says, and it will have to stop. The staff might see you and think they can do the same. And anyway, you must be more adult. You're eighteen and must understand money is to be worked for.'

'If you let us look at your expenses,' Gideon said, 'see where your money goes, your mother might see her way to increasing it. If there's reason enough.'

'And if you'd put your back into a bit of work now, like you should, like we all do,' Aunt Bessie said. Her face, looking at her nephew, bore its most irritated expression. Kate, seeing it, felt her own disappointment in her son, and her shame. She had failed her aunt in the support she and Gideon had given Peter. They had loved him almost as much as she had. They had all three perhaps loved him too much, centring all the time that was not for work on him, spoiling him with gifts and amusements because that time was not enough. Always he had been capricious with his nursemaids, always there had been tantrums and strange little ways like the hiding of silk garters under his pillow. And she, his mother, had not known how to organize her work so that he would see more of her and less of his maids.

'I do work,' Peter was saying, but Kate hardly listened. They had had the same discussions before and they led to nothing. But he went on: 'I don't know how a fellow can go into catering. Isn't it trade, but smellier and harder? You sent me to school, I worked damned hard at Latin and Greek because you wanted it, all for nothing. I met fellows with fathers who were in the City or who had estates, fine fellows, and I never fitted in because my mother was Miss Tranter and everybody knew it and some said you'd never been married at all.'

They were silent. Around them talk at other tables seemed to have ceased too. Kate waited for Peter to say more, to hurt her again. She felt, looking about the room, that their customers had heard her son say that he was ashamed of his own mother. She said, quickly, so that he could say no more: 'Perhaps we were wrong, Peter, to send you to that particular school, where you met such boys, but what else could we do? You are clever, your masters have always said that, and we should have been pleased if you had chosen university instead of business if that was what you wanted. We only want you to be happy.'

'I don't want more books.' Peter puffed irritably on his cigarette and glanced disparagingly around the restaurant.

'What do you want then?' Aunt Bessie said. 'Go on, say what you want without no moaning about what you've had.'

Peter did not reply. He frowned and blinked through the cigarette smoke. Kate saw the lamplight catch on the puffiness of his cheeks. There was no Tranter good health in Peter. How could that be?

'What about nightclubs?' she said. 'They were becoming very popular when I was in America.'

'I say, nightclubs. Now that might be something. They're the coming thing, Mother, nightclubs.' Peter sat up.

'They are, I think,' Kate said. 'Look how our customers are beginning to leave though it's only half-past nine. There was a time they would have stayed on here drinking, but now they go off to one of those basements and drink and dance. They want more than restaurants. Aren't there some places in the Tottenham Court Road, Gideon? Let's go now and have an inspection. It is my birthday. What's to stop us having one in the cellar here, if that's what Peter wants?'

Within half an hour Kate, not unaware of the publicity value of being seen about town with her twisted limping colleague and her grown-up son, was stepping out of their cab to a lighted basement door where the sounds of a trombone floated into the night air. She let Gideon conduct the negotiations for entrance. They would allow in Miss Tranter. A bottle of champagne was ready on the table they were shown to. Kate saw they were in a small room where the sound of the trombone sang out from a three-man band in a corner and on a tiny square of floor couples danced, shockingly entwined and gloveless.

'American music,' she said. 'American ways. American glamour. I should have guessed it would come here. Well, I suppose I knew it had, I just did not think it had anything to do with us.'

'This is more like it, Mother,' Peter said, tapping his foot. 'Bit different from your rustic stuff, what?'

'It's jazz, the music, Peter.' Kate saw her son's face, eager for once and open to pleasure. 'I first heard it in my hotel in New York.'

'Jazz,' he said. 'We could have jazz. Jazz is the coming thing. American music, everything American's the coming thing, Mother.'

'We can't make Tranter's American, can we, Gideon? It would change it so absolutely. I can't imagine Tranter's not being Dorset.' Kate laughed. 'But there's no glamour in Dorset.'

'Oh, we get rid of all that.' The very lift of Peter's head seemed different. He tapped his foot and smiled around the room.

'We compromise,' said Gideon. 'We can work something out if Peter's prepared to put his back into it. And there's money to be made, I think, and with less overheads in wages than in food preparation. The mark-up on alcohol can be anything we like. I've heard there's five hunded per cent put on champagne in some of these places, and still it sells.'

'Five hundred per cent,' Peter repeated, leaning across the table eagerly, 'that's more like it. And none of the slog you three go through.'

From the corner, the music changed. A sudden urgent beat, a hectic rhythm, was started up by the band and the couples on the floor broke apart to stamp their feet and throw themselves about.

'It's hardly decent, Gideon.' Kate watched as girls' legs showed shiny stockings up to the thigh. 'It never really occurred to me that the English would take to this sort of thing. Peter, will you promise to work hard with us at the planning of it all? It'll take a lot of planning. We can't just go into it tomorrow.' Through the dim and changing light, raising her voice through the noise of the new music, Kate watched her son tap his fingers and his feet and felt hope for the first time in many months that Peter might one day be happy. The waiter came to pour their champagne and Peter tossed back his first glass.

'Champers, Mother,' he said. 'We'll serve champagne at five hundred per cent mark-up and we'll make our fortune within a year.'

'You'll have to work at it,' repeated Gideon. 'We're too old for starting over again. We'll help you, that's all, if we decide to go into it, and then you'll be on your own. Your mother and your aunt have had enough of work. They're dreaming of retirement, back home in Dorset. That's what they've worked for and I'll be going with them.'

'I thought you said you did it all for me.' Peter grinned and leaned back in his chair, putting out long legs in fine black worsted trousers and feet in shiny patent leather shoes. He fixed the monocle he affected into one eye and watched the girls at the bar. Kate saw they were dressed in swirls of chiffon skirts which came to their knees, with the shiny stockings they so daringly allowed themselves to reveal in dancing. They had on cloche hats and no gloves. Their arms were bare and they leaned against the bar as if they were, she thought, no better than upstairs girls. This was Peter's world, she knew. They must give him his chance. He had never talked of mark-ups before, nor shown any interest in figures apart from his allowance. If only he would work at it; he would find contentment and satisfaction in work, just as she had, and lose his restless boredom. 'We'll think it over carefully, Peter,' she said, 'with you, and then we'll see if it's possible.'

He went on tapping his foot. 'Of course it's possible, Mater,' he said, 'everybody's going into nightclubs. I wonder I hadn't had the idea before.'

It was Gideon who investigated the nightclub world. It seemed that the smart set of London, now called Bright Young Things, threw their money willingly away on entrances and cloakroom fees and seemed not to notice the prices of the new American cocktails nor any mark-up on the champagne which was the other obligatory drink. It seemed too that each club had to have a three-man band, preferably with a black American trombonist, and that tea dances were also the coming thing, for everyone wanted to dance everywhere, all day and all night. Across London clubs were opening with bands playing to a frantic new beat. Kate sent Peter on a study of the staff employed, of the new cocktails, of the kind of clients they drew in, but he would return less than coherent in his findings. He had met a girl or an old friend or some fellows he knew. Kate began to dread the mornings when he should give up his reports, and did not want to acknowledge to herself that Peter had not learned what work was in spite of their attempts to teach him.

Aunt Bessie wanted to reject the idea of nightclubs altogether. 'The boy'll never be up to it. We've never managed to make him realize he'll have to work, for all he's seen us at it night and day all his life.'

'I wonder if that isn't part of the problem,' Kate said. They had Peter's scrappy notes before them, the back of a cigarette packet with some scribbles on it and an old envelope with figures that were indecipherable. He still lay in bed. 'He's seen us work too much and doesn't want it for himself.'

'That's the weakest excuse I've heard,' Aunt Bessie said. 'But you are his mother, I suppose we got to make allowances for you.' She put out a hand to her niece. 'You done your best, dear girl, we all did. I think maybe the boy isn't ... isn't made of stern enough stuff, and you'll have to face it.'

'But there's Tranter and Liscombe in Peter. How can he not be a fine man, one day? Perhaps he's too young still. There's time, isn't there?'

'Course there is,' Gideon cried. Aunt Bessie shuffled the envelope and cigarette packet together and tutted. Gideon said: 'I say we set it up for him, the way we think's best. Nightclubs is the quickest way to make money I ever saw. What if we stay in it a year or two, get the boy set up, then there'll be money enough for our retirement unless I'm mistaken – if we do it right, of course. There's clubs opening every day. We'll have to be quick about it and get established, and what's more we'll have to have something special about us to bring people, this Bright Young Things lot, rolling into us and not somewhere else.'

'Like Dorset food, Gideon?'

'Why not?'

By the end of the morning, plans were made and were presented to pale and fretful Peter when he went down to the parlour for his coffee. There would be nightclubs by Tranter's, but the Tranter's image would be part of them. They would take up some of the hotel for premises and use the Albemarle Street restaurant for a second.

'And, Peter,' said Kate, pouring his coffee, 'we've thought we might call them Tranter's Dog and Duck.'

'My God!' he shouted. 'What an idea! I said American, I said glamour, and I said not rustic!' He slammed a hand on the table and his coffee spilled into the saucer. 'I'm not going to be involved in some rustic idea. It won't work, I tell you.'

Kate, watching Gideon's face twist with hurt, felt her own heart twist too. There would never be any pleasing Peter. 'Gideon says we must be different,' she said. She felt very tired and wished there had not been any talk of nightclubs. She wished her son was safely at Oxford spending his allowance and not sitting before them at the table. The silk of the dressing gown she had bought him was dusty with cigarette ash. 'Give that robe to the maid,' she said automatically. To her astonishment, Aunt Bessie suddenly began to shout.

'You get yourself up them stairs and get yourself bathed and back down here.' She stood up and flicked at the papers on the table. 'You see these, my boy? These are pages of notes and calculations Gideon and your mother and me have been working on for days. You know what you've been doing? You've been swilling champagne, and the rest of the time you've been lying in that bed. You think we're fools? You get on up them stairs or I'll not answer for the consequences. You hear me?' She leaned across and pushed at Peter's

425

shoulder. Kate heard her aunt's harsh voice and saw the hectic patch of red on each cheek. Aunt Bessie had been angry before over Peter but never so violently as this. She could not find the strength to get to her feet and calm her aunt and the boy as she had always done, and it seemed suddenly that it did not matter, that it had been inevitable matters should come to this, that finally Peter should be told.

'I say.' He pushed at his aunt's arm. 'Leave off, do.'

'I've not finished yet.' Aunt Bessie gave him another push. 'And if I hear one word of complaint from you, one word against the work we've done for you – all for you, mind, we've no taste for nightclubs. We've done it because we can't bear to see your mother's heart broken over you. Not that you'll understand that. You've no heart, that's what I think, Peter. You've no heart in you and she's blamed herself for it. The very idea! You're not worth her pain. You're a fool and a wastrel and I wish I'd had nothing to do with your . . .'

'Bessie!' Gideon reached out to soothe her. 'Let's talk this over. Let the boy go upstairs. Get upstairs, Peter. Get dressed, then down here smartish.'

Peter took a gulp of coffee for the appearance of it and went, leaving behind him the heavy silence that only he ever caused. Kate sat breathless, hearing her heart beat; horror and relief filled her. She could not bear that Peter had been so scorned and by the woman who had loved him all his life. But Aunt Bessie had been right. The day had to come when Peter must be told.

When he returned, they had made their decision. He would join them in their plans for the nightclubs. Their planned choice of name and image and decor would stand. He would work with them. He would supervise the painters in their work, he would help them interview staff, he would work with the advertising agent on the advance publicity. His allowance would be increased only when he put in ten hours a day, as they did, seven days a week, and this would be his last chance.

Kate, watching Gideon issue this ultimatum to her subdued but still-sulky son, thought of her early dreams of him growing into a securely prosperous and contented man. He was to have no fears, nor any want. It had not been enough.

The three of them went into the nightclub project saddened by Peter and saddened for him.

At the two Tranter's Dog and Duck, barmen were dressed in shirt sleeves with waistcoats and corduroy trousers, and all the drinks were from stone jars, offering a mixture of hot cider and apple juice and tomato or French brandy made from apples. There were benches and deal tables and the band had no black American trombonist but men in big boots in their Sunday best country suits; they looked as if they might have played at Harvest Supper in the idyllic time before the war which people now thought of anew as the Arcadian dream. There was a place for the Arcadian as well as for American glamour for the whole of London began to party and partying stunts became the rage. Everyone wanted to go out dressed as someone or something else – as a baby in knicker-bockers or as a clown with a red nose – and the Dog and Duck in Albemarle Street and St John Street became ever more popular even as they opened. Kate had the idea of holding barn dances and the partying craze was satisfied then without much trouble. People could go as yokels and milkmaids. They got hold of boots somehow and stamped their feet to a mixture of countryside jigs and the latest tunes from

America. It did not matter, so long as they danced, so long as they dressed up, and so long as no one mentioned the war or pointed out the disabled and the unemployed who had suffered for such as they.

Kate moved in the evenings between the restaurants and the two nightclubs and saw the money go tumbling into their tills. Looking for Peter, always, to check that he was on duty and not drinking, not dancing, she too wore skirts almost to her knees and high-heeled strapped shoes with shiny stockings, like the other women, because she was still the figurehead, until Peter could see that it was his place. But seeing their customers in their frantic haste to drink and dance, hearing the music of their bands get louder and louder the more they danced and the more they drank, Kate knew she wanted none of this world. There was no taste, no class, no style, and certainly no glamour here, she thought. And could everyone have forgotten the war? There was frenzy, there was excitement; perhaps she was too old. Their restaurants had a glamour of their own, she could see that now, though she had not known the word before she created it. The glamour had been in the style she had created, in the special cachet of the way their look was carried through from the particular wood of the dressers, to the Willow Pattern china and the straw in the apple bowl.

The *Tatler* had printed a piece about their new venture. 'The energetic Miss Tranter never ceases to amaze us,' it said. 'No American club for her. Miss Tranter presents us with country inns in the heart of London, a stomping yokel band, and don't we love her for it.'

Reading that in her bedroom, Kate thought: But my heart is not in nightclubs or stomping yokel bands. I don't want to be Queen of the Nightclubs. It should be Peter Tranter they speak of. But Peter had made no impression on anyone. Few of their clients even knew that the man in evening dress ordering the waiter to serve champagne to the couples on the floor was not just another young customer. If Peter did not loudly boast, as he often did: 'Get that mess cleared up, don't you know who I am?' no one would know that Kate's own son was nineteen and nominally in charge of Tranter's Dog and Duck establishments.

Reading the *Tatler* at her dressing table, Kate felt she would not sleep now for worrying – about Peter and herself. She had a few faint lines about her eyes, and the mouth that had once been full was less so now. Kate put down the journal and switched on the light above the looking-glass. Yes, an older face. She had a son of nineteen and it did not matter to anyone that he had no father for she, Miss Tranter of Tranter's, was a success. But must she always work? There would be thirty years of work left if she went on.

Kate gazed at herself and unwound the pearls from around her neck, taking from her ears her diamond studs and from her dress the matching diamond brooch. Part of her persona, all of it. Plain Miss Tranter now, with a son of nineteen, young still but with no love in her life. Even Philip Waddington, so sweetly, gently patient; she had not known how to let herself be loved by him. And there could have been others.

She could not work thirty years more, but what else did she have? Kate felt a sense of panic make her heart beat too fast. She only knew how to work.

And last night, dreadful last night . . . She would not sleep now for thinking about that too. At the Dog and Duck in Albemarle Street, she had seen Daisy Liscombe, now Lady Berwick, lying on her dance floor. The staff had called her because there was a drunk on the dance floor, and since it was a lady they did not

429

know what to do. Kate had gazed down at the once-slender girl she had so envied. They had been quite alike then, tall with dark hair. Only now there was fat about her ladyship's chin. Daisy Berwick had a double chin and her lovely skin a yellow tinge as she lay in a drunken stupor on Kate's dance floor.

'Oh God, Daisy's done it again,' Kate heard a voice say. 'She's such a bore. I do wish she wouldn't hang about us so at her age.'

Kate signalled to the waiter to carry Lady Berwick discreetly into the office behind the bar. She herself combed back Daisy's red-dyed shingled hair that had once been her glory and held a bowl while Daisy was very sick into it. When Kate had wiped vomit and sweat and running mascara from a face which she now saw was lined under the eyes and puckered about the neck, Daisy sat up suddenly in the chair and said: 'Is it Kate? I wondered if I might see you one day.'

'Is there anything else I can do for you, Lady Berwick?'

'Oh, call me Daisy, do. We used to see each other, didn't we, at Liscombe and Harry used to cry for you. I've often been to your places. You've done better than I have, you know. Have you been happy, going up in the world, being so successful?'

'Sometimes,' Kate said, 'when I've been very busy. Have you been happy?' Suddenly it seemed important that she should know.

'Oh, God, happiness,' sighed Daisy. She searched in her jet-beaded bag for cigarettes and lit one. 'Is there such a thing? I just drink and dance my way through the days. I was never much good at anything, you see, not even women's things – you know, houses and so on. Never seemed quite to have the knack. Never had any children.' She drew deeply on her cigarette. 'Keep any

430

vodka here, do you? It's best, isn't it? You don't reek so afterwards . . .'

Kate went to the door and ordered vodka, but there did not seem to be much more that they had to say to each other. Daisy drank two full glasses and went tottering off on her high-heeled shoes.

'Got to see someone,' she said. 'Cheerio, Kate.'

The next day, a cold bright February day when the winter had set a cruel light on London and all its shabbiness and squalor, Kate thought, at breakfast: Dorset. I want to go home. I want clean air and clean working people who are sane. Last night she had seen Daisy Liscombe drunk. Horrible, mad London, since the war.

Aunt Bessie coughed through her first cigarette of the day. All that winter, the cough had troubled her.

'Time for Dorset, Aunt Bessie darling, don't you think?' Kate heard herself say suddenly. She did not know where the words had come from but they seemed so much the right ones.

'Dorset, girl? That old dream? Why not? I think my old bones are tired of this place.' She coughed again and drew heavily on the smoke. 'A bit of Dorset air might do my chest good.'

'What about Peter, you two?' asked Gideon.

Kate hesitated. 'I am not sure about Peter. I simply don't know what he wants, even now, though he has helped, hasn't he? He has begun to buckle down to work, don't you think?' She wanted it to be so.

'If you call only evenings work,' Aunt Bessie said drily, 'and them half spent drinking.'

'I just think I must go, we must go, away from here. We must ask Peter, for the last time, I suppose, what he wants. We must allow him that much and he must make up his own mind.'

431

Afterwards, they saw it had been as sudden as that, the decision, but of course Peter had no wish to be left with responsibility for the whole of the Tranter's operation. Gideon thought he would want the nightclubs but Peter made it clear he had other things in mind. He showed no surprise when they told him what they were to do.

That afternoon he said: 'I've got my eye on something quite exciting. I've been meaning to tell you. I'm not really cut out for catering.' He yawned. 'I don't know what made you ever think of nightclubs. They're nothing but glorified bars, are they? How did you ever think I'd be content with bars?' He sat before them at the table, yawning over his coffee and Kate felt the beginnings of the pleasure that she had known that morning, disperse before Peter. She had held it inside herself, not daring to believe that the decision was made, finally, that the Dorset dream could come true, that she and Gideon and Aunt Bessie could be free of their burden of work. Now Peter had spoilt it; she had let him spoil it. She heard him try again to cover his own failings with optimistic talk that would have no foundation in fact. She saw that the weakness in him, that she had taken so long to acknowledge to herself, was not part of his growing up, but part of what he was and would go on being. She saw Aunt Bessie's face grow red at the cheeks and heard her intake of breath. She saw Gideon's twisted sympathetic smile for her. She rose from her chair and said wearily: 'Peter, we shall help you to find something you will be content with, of course. We are going to Dorset. You may come with us if you wish and settle down with us there. Or not. I do not think I mind any more.'

But she did mind; the mother who had nursed him at her breast, who had watched with pride and love as he

432

grew from toddler to boy to man, would always mind. She hardened her heart against his grin, which hid, she knew, discomfiture and embarrassment and fear too, for his own future, and walked from the room. She must not let Peter stop her going home.

Tranter's Trading was sold very quickly. The restaurants went to a chain of teashops, the hotel to the proprietor of the adjoining one in St John Street, and the night-clubs were quarrelled over by the nightclub madam of the Tottenham Court Road and one in Piccadilly who had already been prosecuted for selling after-hours drinks.

Of the four of them, soon only Peter Tranter still went to the Dog and Duck in St John Street, there to pretend that he was the owner, and needing, he said, to keep up his contacts. His mother would give him some of the money they had and he would buy himself an interest in a business. He had no intention of going down to his rustic relations in Dorset.

By the end of February, twenty-eight days exactly after making their decision, they were all installed in a suite at the Imperial Palace Hotel, there to collect them-selves together and realize their extraordinary good fortune: no dawn rising, no working through the night, no staff problems, no food purchasing problems, noth-ing to disturb the short winter days but luncheon and tea served to them by someone else, someone else's waiter whose appearance and skill they had no need to inspect.

They ate and drank and felt more tired than they ever had before; they were too tired, yet, to pack up all their personal effects, find Peter an apartment and go down to Dorset to the new dream that had suddenly become possible, that they had suddenly made possible.

Peter Tranter came and went in the suite, ordering champagne and late-night sandwiches. He had been unable to find an apartment that was to his taste, he claimed, and his business contact was out of town.

Kate and Aunt Bessie and Gideon watched him come and go and offered neither scolding nor advice; they were too tired. They preferred to watch the mist rise over the Thames as they sat in their Palace suite at breakfast, and watch it fall again as they took tea.

In Liscombe valley where he had been raised, the other Liscombe and Tranter boy, Joe, sat at breakfast one day that February and asked his grandmother for a day off school.

'I've a sore throat, Granny, look.' He held his healthy red mouth open to Mrs Tranter.

'It's no sore throat you've got, my boy, you're wanting to go with your Uncle Johnny to a dratted horse sale again.' Susan Tranter gazed with solicitude upon her grandson, still in her mind baby Joe although he hated to be called it and was all of eleven years old now, standing as straight and firm as Beth Tranter had so many years before.

'Oh, Granny, can't I go? Do let me, just this once.'

'Whatever will your grampy say if I lets you off school again?'

'Gramps won't mind, you know he won't, Granny. He doesn't believe in any book learning. And no more don't I,' he added.

'Don't you go talking all Dorset,' said Mrs Tranter, 'and get that porridge down you. Your Auntie Kate won't want you speaking Dorset with the fine school she's sending you to.'

'All the fellows speak Dorset when there's no masters about, Granny.'

Joe Tranter gobbled porridge and gulped at tea, keeping an anxious eye through the kitchen window and up Liscombe Hill. He would have to be quick or his Uncle Johnny would leave without him.

'Bye, Granny, thanks.' He wound his muffler about his neck and put on his gloves to please her.

Susan Tranter watched her grandson go with a loving smile. He was the twin of Johnny Tranter in his ways and the image of his mother in looks, all but the eyes which were Harry Liscombe's. It was a wonder to her that no one ever saw it. She sighed and turned to the dresser where a photograph of her two dead children, Beth and Billy, smiled blankly at her through her long days. She thanked God that there seemed to be no Liscombe weakness in baby Joe, none of his father but those eyes. That boy had thrown away his life in saving the very Germans who had so devastated his own country's pride. All England's youth were gone but for a few of the strong like Johnny. Mrs Tranter had elaborated on the tale told by Johnny of Harry Liscombe going out into some strange place called No Man's Land to save the dying, and them Germans, and made it into a sign of Liscombe weakness. He could have saved himself and Beth might not have died of grief and Joe would have had a father. His father had gone as mad as his mother, in her opinion, giving away his wealth and pacing around the empty Hall. Liscombe weakness.

The dark November light seemed to press down from the hill into the cottage. There were hours yet for her to pass before Johnny and the boy would come running down for their supper. She felt the beginnings of gloom descend upon her; she had so little to do now that her romances could not fill the time.

She resolved to start upon their supper and, rooting

in her cupboards, found some Bramleys and set herself to peel them. An apple suet pudding was Will's favourite, and her two boys'. Before too long, they would set up their shout to her: 'Ma! Granny!' They would smell steamy clove and apple, running down, and bring their clumsy maleness around her kitchen door with their boots muddy and the fresh damp air wrapped about them. Then her loneliness would be banished; she still had three men to feed and glad she was of it. 'Apple pudding!' they would shout gleefully at the kitchen door. Tomorrow, she would make baked rice, their second favourite, and put it in the range early for the grains to grow fat with cream and sugar.

Johnny Tranter and his nephew Joe were late going down the hill for apple pudding that heavy February afternoon, for they had a new nag to consider. Johnny had jumped into the sale ring, when he had seen her beaten round by a gypsy trader. He had thrust a pound into the chap's hand and here she was, eating fit to burst and looking at them from the corner of her eye. Side by side in the stables that were Lord Liscombe's gift to Johnny, they noted her hanging head and the shrapnel scars, and the bones showing through her thin flesh.

'See those marks,' Johnny said, squinting through the smoke from his Navy Cut. 'The buggers have put a halter on her and someone's worked her since they bought her for a song. I bet they worked her before the shrapnel wounds were healed.'

'The buggers,' repeated Joe, weeping a little from pity and rage, as if he too had witnessed what his uncle had seen, in the war. The two of them were one as far as horses were concerned, and especially war horses. Joe often dreamed of the war, so graphic were his uncle's descriptions of it. 'She can't hardly believe she's somewhere safe, with us, Uncle Johnny.' He sniffed and looked up at his uncle's face beneath the cap. They'd be there some time yet, he decided, watching this poor creature. 'Uncle,' he said, 'why do they call me bastard boy at school?'

'Here.' Johnny threw away his cigarette. 'You want some more boxing lessons? You don't let anyone call you names. I'll come up to the school if you like, though it's maybe not the best . . .'

'No, no, it's all right, I don't mind. I give them a thrust to the chin like you showed me, but then someone else starts up and I . . . I just wonder why I am a bastard boy, that's all,' Joe finished lamely. He kicked at the stable door and whistled. He had wanted to ask the question for so long and now it seemed such a baby question, he wished he had not spoken. 'I'm all right really, Uncle Johnny. I don't mind.'

'It only means you have no father,' Johnny said, patting his shoulder awkwardly. 'There must be plenty of boys with no father since the war.'

'Yes, but it seems I'm different. Stirling hasn't got a father, nor has Jones, and yet they pick on me. Perhaps it's because I'm sort of a double orphan, eh, with my mother dead too. Is that it?' Joe looked up trustingly in the stable gloom to this man who was father, brother and uncle rolled into one.

'You could tell them your father was the very best there was, the very best. He saved a German in the war, and that's a fine and noble thing to do. Not many did, I can tell you. He went out into the most fearsome part of the battleground, on his own, to make one good gesture in all the mess.'

Joe paused. 'I don't think I can tell them my father saved a German,' he said. 'I'll say he was a war hero, eh? But not about the German.'

437

'Perhaps not, no one else is big enough to understand. You just say he was a war hero who died saving another soldier, and you tell 'em you've got a very rich auntie who's coming down. You tell 'em she's so rich she can buy a big manor house and you're going to live in it. You're going to be so grand when your auntie gets down here, those chaps'll soon by toadying round you. And you say your father nearly got a medal only the sergeant who saw him being so brave died before he could tell the story properly.'

'I don't think I want to be grand, Uncle Johnny, I just want to stay with you and the horses, and know my father was a good man.'

'All right, Joe, maybe we'll tell Auntie Kate we don't want to be grand, eh? We'll say we're all right as we are. We're happy, eh?'

'Do you think there's apple pudding for supper?'

'Let's get on down and see. This nag's still got some eating to do.'

Joe Tranter took the cap from his mop of dark brown hair, his mother's Tranter hair, threw it into the air and ran laughing down the hill to the stream where Mrs Tranter waited with her two favourites' favourite pudding. Tranter cheeks glowing red in the wintry air, narrow Liscombe eyes startlingly grey, Joe Tranter ran down Liscombe Hill shouting out his joy at the world. He had no need to worry now about the other boys' taunting. Uncle Johnny had made everything all right. His father had been a hero in the war. He would hold that in his heart and tell no one. It was enough for him just to know. And soon his Aunt Kate and Aunt Bessie and his cousin Peter would come down to Dorset to live; he would have a family.

The winter had passed into summer before Kate and

438

Aunt Bessie and Gideon felt able to make final arrangements to leave the city that had been their world for so long. But finally they bought a new car, a little Austin Seven four-seater. They did their packing and sent trunks off to the King's Arms Hotel, Dorchester – Peter's, too, for he had not been able to make the contacts he had planned for entry into business and did, he said, deserve a little holiday before he went up to Scotland for the grouse.

On the morning of their departure Kate rose from her luxurious bed in a gold and white Imperial Palace room that had reminded her of Paris, feeling happy. She was rested and felt lightened, as if the burdens of a lifetime had been lifted from her. Padding over to the window, she drew the curtains to see again and for the last time the sun on the Thames and the boats going down and the stone bridges that had been part of her adult life. In Dorset, the sun would rise on empty space and damp green grass and the cows waddling through mists to milking. She would not miss this, though there had been pleasure in it; she was ready for peace and clean air and a house on a hill in the sun. She had earned it, they all had, but first she must see that Peter had been forced from his bed or it would be lunch-time before they left and the best part of day would be gone.

Peter was not in his bed. It had not been slept in and there was a note propped against the pillows. Kate took it up; she felt no surprise. Peter had not looked at her these last days. He had been plotting something, she knew.

I cannot face the country, Mother, I have gone to stay with a fellow I know from school. Send £500, will you, to my account at Coutts? I've heard of a little business I'd like to get into since I have my

own living to earn, you say. I'm taking my hols first, you can't begrudge me that, but I can't stand Dorset.
Peter
P.S. Tell Gideon it's a perfectly safe investment and don't let him go investigating it and shaming me, Mother.

'The impertinence!' Aunt Bessie, reading this note supported by Imperial Palace pillows over her early tea, was otherwise speechless. Kate took the note to Gideon; they could not leave now, not until they heard that Peter was safe.

'I suppose the country really will never suit Peter?' she said. She had forgotten to put her slippers upon her feet. Gideon shrugged himself into his dressing gown. 'I should like us to find him a business down there, where we can keep an eye on him.' Kate rubbed one bare foot against the other. The day was spoiled now and her mother would be waiting. 'We cannot go without knowing where he is, anyway.'

'We'll have our work cut out keeping an eye on the boy,' Gideon said, pouring tea for himself. 'But you'll go on down, you and Bessie, I don't want you disappointed nor your mother. Let me stay. I'll find out where he is at least, and then we'll see.'

Bowling down to Dorset, Kate and Aunt Bessie only stopped once for tea and then not again until Kate finally drew up past the Long Trenthide Post Office before the turning into the hill, where first she had seen Lord David from their cart, with dust around her skirts and in her hair.

'The first time I was here,' she began, 'I was sitting on top of our removal cart and . . .'

'I'll maybe not recognize your mother, Kate.' Aunt Bessie was not listening to her. 'The last time I saw her she was younger than you are now, a lovely tall girl with your eyes and hair. Whatever shall we find to say to each other? I'll maybe not find anything to say. I've kept a bawdy house twenty years without telling her.'

'It will be all right, Aunt Bessie. You've written to each other every week all these years, you've not lost touch in a personal way.' Kate ground the car into top gear and turned at the top of the hill. 'I'll take the side path down the cow track, I don't want to go past the Hall. He's abroad now, his lordship, and it will be better that way, although of course we might meet one day. We should be able to do so, surely, with our past long finished?' Still her heart gave a little flutter of pain, seeing the line of Liscombe with its odd uneven shape and rows of empty windows showing black under the high sun.

Past and beyond it, waiting in a glow of warmth, was Stone Cottage. There was the stream and the faint pink from the sweet peas trailing around the blue door and the dark gold and yellow of mingled marigolds and king cups. There was her mother coming to blink up the hill from the doorway.

'Mother! Mother!' Kate drew on the brakes and threw open the car door, waving down to Stone Cottage. Nothing had changed here, thank heaven. Nothing had changed here.

Aunt Bessie sat heavily in the passenger seat, not moving. 'I can't get out, Kate,' she muttered. 'I can't get out. I've nothing to say to my own sister. Now I've come, I can't get out.'

'You can, Aunt Bessie, you can.' Kate walked round the car to put a gentle hand on her aunt's arm and ease her stout figure from the seat. 'Look, Mother's waving up to us.'

A figure very like her own, with grey hair and blue

dress and apron, stood down the valley, waving to them, but Aunt Bessie felt she could not move. It was too late. She had left it too late to go home.

'Come, dear, Mother's waving.' Kate saw tears in the blue eyes which seemed suddenly faded in the bright sunlight that was not like London sunlight.

Susan Tranter brushed the wisps of hair from her face. She saw her daughter's motor car rattle up to the top of the hill and Kate run round in her busy way to help someone out. She saw a stoutish figure in a blue dress and jacket with a cloche hat over her eyes. It could not be Bessie for she had always been so scrawny; their mother said she would go out like a sparrow if the consumption ever got to her. But it was Bessie for now she stood beside Kate and was waving down. Susan felt weak. Tears made the figure seem misty. She could not now think that she would ever find anything to say to this woman, a stranger, her own sister, not seen for forty years.

Kate made tea in the old way from the kettle on the range as if she were sixteen again. Her mother sat heavily at the deal table, whiter from the twenty more years of scrubbing since Kate had left, and Bessie stood awkwardly by the window with her hat taken off and her jacket but her shaky knees preventing her from moving across the room to sit down. The sunlight showed the dry red-dyed hair and the lines of age and fatigue about her eyes.

Kate poured three cups of tea into blue Willow Pattern cups. 'Where's your flowered one, Mother? Aunt Bessie still has hers.'

'Joe broke it playing at helping me, the dear love. He's too shy to be here and greet you. He's gone off up the hills with his Uncle Johnny, helping him.' She found the strength to look up at her own sister. Had she herself aged the same? She had a drawn face under a bit of London red hair and a look about her as if she were too tired to move. 'Sit down, Bess, do, by the fireside.' She watched her sister move slowly across the room and ease herself heavily into Will Tranter's chair. Bessie coughed. 'We'll soon get that London cough off you too,' she said.

Kate chattered nervously to cover the awkwardness of the two women. 'Mother,' she said, 'Aunt Bessie and I want you to be brave and come out with us in the little Austin. We want to go about here and find us a little manor house somewhere, on a hill. We do want to be on a hill – we've worked so long in London basements, haven't we, Auntie? And it was always my dream, do you remember? I used to stand here in this kitchen on my days off and say how one day I'd have a place on a hill so we'd always be in the sun? Do you remember, Mother?'

'You kids always was dreamers. What're you up to now?' Susan Tranter pushed aside her cold tea and said: 'You'd best take that London hat off, Kate, it don't look like you under it.' And Bessie did not look like her sister, not at all.

Kate laughed and pulled off the tight cloche that had concealed her shingled hair. Her mother had not noticed that. 'Mother?'

'I shan't say nothing about that hair if that's what you're waiting for. I'll only say it won't do for here-abouts.'

'I'm going to buy us a house on a hill, Mother, a grand one, and that'll give the neighbours something to talk about, the Tranters getting so grand, never mind my hair!' She glanced at her aunt, sitting so still and silent.

'Auntie,' she murmured, 'shall I make some more tea?'

'Yes, dear, do. I haven't seemed to touch this one.' Aunt Bessie gazed into the range where the warm glow of coals was taking the chill from her. She had felt cold from fear and strangeness, coming down the hill.

Mrs Tranter grumbled: 'We don't need no house, girl, we got this one. And don't you go off dreaming again, you're too old for that now.'

'You mean you and Pa have bought this house?'

'Yes,' she said vaguely, 'his lordship came down last week – years it is since he last came. He remembered and asked after you, and I said you was selling your little teashop business and bringing your auntie home. He said as how it was a shame he was off to Italy but he hoped to see you on his return. Lovely ways with him still though his mind have gone.'

'He's gone mad, Mother, really mad?'

'They do say as much,' Susan said staring at Bessie who was dozing gently. Steam from the second kettle put to boil drifted about her face. 'He were never right after the burning. He started mooning about and talking to servants and estate people, trying to make 'em go back to school, and those that went it never did any good to. That Bill Hawkins, he went to college, and then he was killed in the war so it did him no good at all, and the Beale boy went to the bad with drink.'

'Mother, have another cup of tea. You've told me all that before. You say his lordship has really gone mad and sold everything, and sold you and Pa the cottage?'

'No,' said Mrs Tranter sharply, 'he's given it to us. The deed things he brought down here we've locked up in the box under the bed. Them deeds say this is the property of Mr William Tranter, though I had to sign for it as Father couldn't, with no schooling.'

444

'So he's given it to you?' She thought: How will it be, to see him? Must I thank him for helping my parents when it was my place? He could not have learned how successful she had been.

'He have, for years of faithful service Will have put in, and for Johnny, so he shall always have a home when we're gone, his lordship says, since he tried to save his Harry and buried him in a proper churchyard like he did. Anyway,' she added irritably, 'it seems he wants the folk as have worked the land to own it. Them's Labour ideas. Can't be right, not on land that have been owned by the same family for generations. Now they say he's thinking of selling the Hall so the Trust can keep going after he's gone, and he's to be just a farmer.' She took up her cup and drank for the first time since their arrival.

'Susan?' Aunt Bessie stirred from her doze. 'I dreamed we were at home, you and me, with Mother alive and rambling on about something. Your voice was so like Mother's.' They saw her sit up and pick up her cup. She seemed livelier and smiled directly at her sister. Susan Tranter went to sit opposite her by the range and Kate heard them begin to chatter. It would be all right now.

She wandered across to the doorway. The sun was sinking behind Rookery Hill, giving a last glow to the golden stone of the Hall and its blank windows. Only servants moved about up there now that he was away. All those lovely rooms empty and unused and wasted, and he had gone mad, her mother said. She had often said it. Kate wondered if it might not be so and not just one of the usual rumours that abounded around the aristocracy. Country people watched their comings and goings and their marriages and their business affairs, and in the main condemned them.

*

The three of them spent several days talking in the kitchen, disturbed only by Aunt Bessie's cough and her extreme tiredness and the need to provide Will Tranter with his usual meals.

When finally the boy they still wanted to call baby Joe consented to join them, darting his shy smiles at them, a new contentment seemed to grow in the room. Aunt Bessie let her real self begin to show to her sister; Mrs Tranter overcame her sisterly resentment for all the years Kate had spent at Bessie's side instead of at her own; and Will Tranter went so far as to call his sister-in-law by her given name, addressing to her a remark about his cows.

After a week, Kate left the two women together and went off around Dorset in the Austin. Unusually, what she decided on the next days, she decided on alone. And could not sleep for her own daring. Her heart set itself into a rapid beat from the thrill she felt at an idea that had drifted into her mind one afternoon when her car drove round the lane and up on to Liscombe Hill.

The auction day came. Kate had decided not to tell her mother and aunt. They hardly noticed her going off daily for they were living in some time past, fifty years ago, in another Dorset cottage where they had spent their childhood.

Kate went alone to the auction and only Gideon knew of it, told by telephone in her nightly calls. She sat at the back of the hall though an agent was there to act for her. She was ready to leap to her feet if someone else should go over the limit she had set him. There must be no limit. But there were only very ordinary-looking farmers in the room who did not show much interest in item number three which did not include farmland. Kate did not want farmland.

She heard the man say: 'Now, ladies and gentlemen, our finest property on offer today ...' and held her breath.

CHAPTER NINETEEN

'Good morning, Miss Tranter.' Treeves bowed shakily to the new owner of Liscombe Hall.

'Good morning, Treeves. How nice to see you and Mrs Baker. How are you both?'

Miss Kate Tranter shook hands with her new staff lined up side by side to greet her in the great hall where once she had run with Harry, as his nursemaid.

Mrs Baker followed her new mistress up the polished oak staircase, past the bronzed pillars and the expanse of mullioned glass. Kate touched the warm places where the sun shone and went on up into the alcove where his portrait was and his father's, as dark-haired as David and as stern-faced as when she had first known him. She had seen David's face glow with love, looking at her, but she must not think of him, even though she now trod the same stairs as he had, and owned them. One day, Peter's likeness would be here in its rightful place, beside his father's.

'You'll start at the top, Madam?'

'Call me Miss Tranter, Mrs Baker.' Kate thought: She cannot call me Kate as she used to do but I cannot let her call me Madam either. It was going to be difficult. She felt her heart jump and settle itself too fast for comfort. She would have to be very careful not to hurt their feelings. Would she be able to carry it off, though she was as finely dressed as any lady who had lived at the Hall, and had hands as untouched by work, now? They, with so many years of aristocratic service behind them, could make her, the dairyman's daugher and kitchen maid, feel out of place, foolish, once more a country girl. If they chose.

She turned left on to the rich red pile of the carpet that she remembered, Mrs Baker in her place, just a little behind.

'The covering is worn, Miss Tranter,' Mrs Baker said. 'And the wallpaper will no doubt need replacing.' Kate touched the faded gold flock. Once she had stared to see such walls.

'Yes,' she said. 'But it does seem a pity, doesn't it, Mrs Baker?'

'It does, Miss Tranter, to see all the old things go.'

'I shall keep as much untouched as possible.'

'Yes, Miss Tranter.' Kate heard the relief in her voice.

She and Mrs Baker would be all right together once they had become used to this new status of hers. They both needed to get used to it, that she was the owner of Liscombe, with Aunt Bessie and Gideon. Kate Tranter and her aunt and a man who had begged in the street.

'Have all the bedrooms remained more or less the same?'

'His lordship didn't want anything touched. He had the East Wing shut off and used the guest rooms only.'

'Yes, I heard. So sad.'

'He spent much of his time working in the fields of Home Farm, until he decided to sell off all the farms to the tenants and get the Hall in good repair. For someone else, he said. He had no heart to live in it all alone.'

'Yes, yes,' Kate murmured, running her hand along the fine oak doors, opening one here and there – a red room, a room all in blue, one in gold. Which would Aunt Bessie and Gideon like to have – would they want them redecorated in a modern style or would they keep them as they were? There would be a lot of talking over it.

'I shall let my aunt and partner decide about the bedrooms, Mrs Baker, when they move up. For the moment, shall we just have the beds made up along both wings?' She really was going to move Gideon and her family into the rooms where Lady Blanche and he had loved and quarrelled and loved again, and where Lady Sarah had sat to write out her plans for the school. She felt strangely dream-like, standing there with Mrs Baker.

'Is the West Tower in use for the servants still?'

'Partly, Miss Tranter. There are so few of us now.'

'Yes, we shall have to discuss that later, Mrs Baker. Of course, we shan't keep such a large household. The time for that is past, isn't it?'

'Shall you want to be seeing the servants' rooms, Miss Tranter?'

'No, not today. I think I shall leave my old room where I slept with Letty for another day, Mrs Baker.'

The housekeeper smiled. Miss Tranter had mentioned it, so it was to be spoken of. It would be all right. Kate saw her relax.

'Your old room, Miss Tranter, is just as you left it. Letty did spread herself about a bit. She had it to herself before she went down to your mother.'

'She has a good place now with a family in Dorchester.'

It would be all right. She and Mrs Baker could not hide the extraordinary change in Kate's place in the world. They must simply accept that it was so and go on from there. Mrs Baker had been brought up with the aristocracy. She had good manners. It would be all right, although Kate's most difficult task remained: telling her family of the change that awaited them.

'Gideon? Can you hear me? It's a bad line. Yes, I have bought it, the house I spoke to you about. We own it, Gideon, us! Yes! Are you pleased? No, I haven't told

Aunt Bessie yet – I haven't dared! I don't know how she and Mother will take it. No, you must come down soon and see it. You've only seen it from the cottage, just the once . . .

'Well, how is Peter? Gone up for the grouse shooting with the Burnhams? That's nice of them . . .

'No, of course he mustn't buy goldmine shares, you're right. A gentlemen's outfitters in Bond Street is for sale? You think that . . .? Yes, I agree, look into it, do. He'll buckle down to it if it's all arranged for him. Yes, he always did like the best clothes. It should suit him . . .

'Don't leave it too long. We miss you. Goodbye, Gideon . . . Yes, you'll bring Peter down with you, I suppose, until the business is bought. Hurry home, Gideon. Hurry home.'

Kate put down the telephone in their suite at the King's Arms in Dorchester which they had only so far used for her business calls. It was done; telling Gideon made it seem more real, but she still had to tell her mother and Aunt Bessie. That morning she had opened her mouth to do so and could not find the words.

Susan Tranter, arm in arm with her sister Bessie, struggled up the hill to the Hall and round past the basement kitchens where the servants peeped up at them through the windows. Here they stood before the stone steps. Liscombe Hall. An old oak door with a brass ring in it. Mullioned windows warmed by the October sun, stretching along as far as they could see. A tower. A butler and a housekeeper coming down the steps. Liscombe Hall. Theirs.

'Well, I never did. What have that girl gone and done now, Bessie?'

Bessie could not answer. Kate had rushed at them so that morning, she had hardly understood her.

'Come on up to our new house,' she said, quite casually. And there they were. They had not had far to go.

'Her dream come true, Susan,' she murmured. Tears wiped away the London rouge she had had time to dab on her cheeks. 'Her dream, a house on a hill with the sun on it.'

'Well,' said Susan Tranter again, 'it can't never be right.' She had put on a new cloche hat which made her head ache, and Kate had been in such a rush that morning. For this. Liscombe Hall. Her father would not believe it, nor Johnny nor Joe. No one would believe it.

'Come on, Mother, Aunt Bessie, come on up.'

Kate stood beside Treeves and Mrs Baker, laughing down at them.

'We'd best go up then, Bessie.' Aunt Bessie coughed taking the steps up. Kate should have thought of that, Mrs Tranter decided. They were too old for steps. But they must not let her down, they must do things properly with the butler and everyone watching. They made it, arm in arm, breathless at the top of the steps, and there was the butler bowing and the old housekeeper graciously smiling.

'Welcome to Liscombe Hall, Mrs Tranter, Mrs Villiers.'

On they went past them. Susan Tranter offered a nod of the head, trembling a little. She felt Bessie tremble beside her. Kate had gone headlong into something which would end in tears.

'Shall we serve tea in the morning room, Miss Tranter?'

'Yes, Treeves, please. My mother and Mrs Villiers will no doubt make that their own little place in due course.'

'Yes, Miss Tranter.' Treeves bowed and slipped away.

Aunt Bessie looked around her. Dappled light from the long mullioned window played about the bronze pillars and lit the polished wooden floor and the staircase leading upwards. 'Kate,' she said, 'our dream has brought us this?'

Kate clasped her hands to her face and said: 'It has somehow happened though I am not sure how I have had the daring even to think of it. But here it is, here we are, and I feel it is not possible but it is. I keep touching the pillars and feeling all this lovely wood. Treeves calls me Miss Tranter and I can't believe it.' She wanted to sweep her mother and her aunt into her arms and hug them.

'This is where he was?' Aunt Bessie said.

'Yes. This is his house.'

'Will it be all right?'

Kate saw her look of love and concern, the look that had warmed her all through their years together. 'I think so, dear. He will not be here. He is abroad, and if he comes back it will be to a manor house somewhere near Dorchester.'

'He'll be back.' Mrs Tranter had heard them. 'And then what'll you do? It just ent right, Kate.'

'It is odd, sister, I grant you, but our Kate, she always does what turns out to be right in the end.'

Mrs Tranter felt the slight; her sister did know Kate better than she herself but it was not her fault. 'Where's this morning room then?' she said. 'You go first, Bessie.'

Kate watched, entranced, as the two sisters made their slow hesitant way across the wide stretch of floor and through the doorway of the small morning room where a lady would normally spend the first part of her day. They would soon get used to being ladies; she wanted them to get used to it, and enjoy it, and for the years of work and strain to leave them. She wanted them to be happy and learn how to take life easily.

But they were overcome now. She saw their backs hunched, arms pressed closed together, her mother's legs swollen over her new shoes and Aunt Bessie, thinner suddenly, with her skirt hanging crooked at the back. It made a little pain squeeze at her heart. It was too much for them; she had been clumsy and foolish.

Their faces were a joy to see none the less as they stood in old Lady Liscombe's room with pale grey silk on the walls, fat silk-covered pink chairs before little lacy cloths over three-legged tables. There was pride in their faces and wonder as they looked about them and watched Treeves slip into the room with the teatray.

Mrs Tranter felt the silver pots. Kate saw that she hesitated, wanting to ask if they had used boiling water and warmed the pots but not daring to do so.

Treeves closed the door behind him.

'Doesn't he know he should knock before coming into our private rooms?' Mrs Tranter sniffed. 'Milk's fresh,' she conceded.

'Butlers never knock on family rooms, dear, but I expect he will if we ask him.' It was going to be difficult to start with, but they would get used to it. Kate smiled at the sight of her mother with a silver tea pot and silver tray before a fire that was not a range and which she had not lit herself, bending on painful knees and puffing at damp newspaper.

Aunt Bessie sat wheezing in her chair, a little tearful, Kate saw, but beaming at her. 'You got your dream, darling girl. I can't hardly believe it. Look at that view, that sky out there. We ent never lived in so much space before. And them Chinese lacquer screens – worth a fortune they are. I always wanted some Chinese lacquer.'

'Our dream, Aunt Bessie,' Kate reminded her, 'though it's not a cottage, quite, is it?'

'Not quite, dear heart, but no doubt the vicar'll call.' She suddenly began to laugh, putting back her head and rocking in the pink silk chair. Her red-dyed fringe trembled and she spluttered. 'The vicar to tea, Kate! Won't we be respectable?'

Kate put up her hands to her face and laughed in joyful remembrance of the bawdy house. 'But not in disguise, Auntie, not with his dog collar off and a taste for . . .' She and Aunt Bessie laughed until the tears came, and even Mrs Tranter lost some of her stiffness over a joke she could not share.

'A vicar ent funny, you two,' she said, 'nothing less funny than a vicar. Maybe London vicars is different.' She poured tea into fine porcelain cups. Her hand shook as she passed a cup to Bessie, wiping away tears of laughter in her chair across the hearth. 'No doubt they'll have more of this sort?'

'Probably six dozen, Mother. You wait 'till you see the china room and the linen room and the silver there is.' Kate spluttered anew, remembering a certain bishop and Elsie Brownlow. Aunt Bessie's eyes sparkled back at her. 'Darling,' Kate ran to take her hand, 'we have done well, haven't we?'

'You have, Kate, you have.'

Kate had to leave the two sisters to nod over tea and the extraordinary change that Kate had brought about, for she had to collect Peter and Gideon from the station. Peter had consented to spend a period in Dorset and to discuss his affairs seriously with his mother; he had been in a little trouble, Gideon said, trouble which he did not want to specify. It had been dealt with and Gideon did not want to worry her.

'Now you ring the bell when you've finished tea,' she said, her heart warmed by the sight of them seated so cosily together, 'and ask Treeves to tell Mrs Baker you would like to be taken round the ground floor rooms.'

'I think we'll sit here, Kate, the shock's left us all of a heap.' Aunt Bessie coughed over her Madeira cake. 'You hurry back.'

'I shan't be long, the train's due in half an hour. I'll drive straight back.'

She must not be away long, she decided. They were too afraid to move. She had gone too far. She had bought unwisely. They could not make the change. It would be wrong to force it upon them.

Yet sitting in her little Austin, Kate thought: But it is so fine, this beautiful old house.

The long line of golden stone stretched before her. Autumn sun glowed on the windows; they did not seem black today. Someone was to live behind them. It was to be a home again. She would make it a home.

Kate revved up and swerved off across the Liscombe drive and down through the oaks that he had loved so much, the father of Harry, the father of Peter. One day, she would tell Peter that he was a Liscombe, when the time was right. He was not mature enough yet to take it in his stride, to behave like a gentleman and lord of the manor. Only it would be so difficult, telling Peter what he had a right to know and keeping such a thing from the world. Perhaps she would have to wait until Lord David died.

Thinking that, that he too would die one day and she could not resolve the problem of Peter, she thought: I must not think of it today, I must allow myself a little happiness today and not remember the pain of the past.

Taking the Austin fast up the hill to Dorchester station, Kate thought that she did not care about the past, for today she and Aunt Bessie and Gideon owned Liscombe Hall and they would never have to work again.

'Pop down and see if your grandfather wants to come up for his dinner after all, Peter.' Mrs Tranter was installed at Liscombe Hall but her husband refused to do so much as set foot upon the stone steps.

'He won't want to come, Grandma, you know he won't. He never does. Every day you send me down, when Treeves could go as easily, and all he does is grunt and chew on those doorstep pieces of bread he cuts himself. Where's Joe, anyway? He could go. I'm not a servant.'

'Peter, do as Grandma tells you.'

'Oh, damn!' Peter threw down his napkin and slammed the door behind him. An uncomfortable silence was left behind him, as it always was, at Liscombe.

'Gideon?' Kate turned to her old friend. 'Do you think we should send him up to London, give him what he wants?'

'We'll maybe have to consider it,' said Gideon, watching Mrs Tranter pick carefully at the liver pâté; her stomach could not quite get used to its richness.

'The boy's bad,' she said simply. 'I knew it as soon as I looked at him, no matter he's my grandson. Bad blood,' she repeated. 'The father . . .'

'His father wasn't bad,' said Kate irritably.

'Then it's the way he's been brought up. London ways,' said Mrs Tranter. 'And you always out at them teashops.'

'Oh, Mother!' said Kate. It was not the first time they had had this conversation. 'And we didn't have

457

teashops.' The little book of cuttings that Aunt Bessie kept in her black bag with the yellowing paper, opened and displayed so often, never made any difference to her mother's conviction that they had had teashops no matter how many times Aunt Bessie read out the newspaper headings. 'Miss Tranter, queen of the London restaurant scene', and 'Miss Tranter reveals her recipe secrets exclusively to *Daily Mail* readers'.

'I'll take Bessie in her tea and toast,' said Gideon. Aunt Bessie did not rise early now, for her cough troubled her at night and she slept little. 'Then we'll maybe see about Peter, Kate. He's doing no good here.'

In the small drawing room at Liscombe Hall that November afternoon, Mrs Tranter and Mrs Villiers sat with their tea-time guests. Firelight warmed the brass lamps and the little polished tables, reaching out to the gold of the Chinese bowls and the gilt of the picture frames about the walls.

'Cosy here, isn't it, Vicar?' Susan Tranter held out her little finger, sipping daintily at Jackson's best Indian tea.

'We always say the small drawing room's the cosiest for tea, don't we, Bessie?'

'We do, dear, and we like to see the nights draw in over the downs outside, don't we?'

'Of course,' Mrs Tranter took another sip, 'we do use the morning room of a morning.'

'Quite,' said the Vicar. 'I'll have a second cup if I may, Mrs Tranter.'

'Oh, where's my manners?' Mrs Tranter's saucer shook. 'Pass the Vicar's cup, Bessie.'

'Think of your indigestion, my dear.' The Vicar's wife, as thin and pale as he was stout and pink, sat stiffly beside her husband on a hard chair.

458

'Pass your plate, Mrs MacDonald, do. You must try a piece of Cook's Madeira.'

'No, Mrs Villiers, really. I have had quite sufficient.'

'I'll have a piece, Mrs Villiers. We mustn't let it go to waste, must we?'

Kate Tranter, flushed from her ride on one of Johnny's old war horses, strode through the Liscombe hallway and burst like spring air into the small drawing room and the collected company. 'Am I late? So sorry, Vicar, Mrs MacDonald, to rush in like this but it is lovely to see you again.'

'Shall I ring for the second pot, Kate? Is Johnny coming up?'

'No, Mother, one of his favourites is ailing, or so he thinks. You know what he is with his horses.'

'I always say it isn't Christian, Vicar, that lad and his horses. You'd think they was humans, you would. All he ever does is look after them horses, don't he, Bessie?' Mrs Tranter passed her sister sponge fingers and tiny almond tarts in a silver dish.

'It's the war that did it to him, sister, the war.' Bessie chose a sponge finger that would be scented with vanilla.

'Ah, yes, the war,' sighed the Vicar. 'But God was good, Mrs Tranter. He saved your son when so many were lost.'

'My other son he didn't save,' Susan Tranter began, 'nor my . . .'

'I'll have a cucumber sandwich, Mother, please,' Kate broke in. Tea with her mother and the Vicar did make her a little nervous. But she beamed across at her aunt, wiping delicately at the icing sugar on her fingers. Aunt Bessie beamed back. We've done it, each said to the other silently. We are respectable. Nothing could be more respectable than quiet tea-times with the Vicar in the small drawing room of Liscombe Hall.

*

459

Across the hills, Lord David Liscombe stood in the hallway of Manor House Farm.

'Er, yes, I shall be back for luncheon, no doubt, Mrs Dalton.' He adjusted his tie, took a last glance in the looking-glass. There was no sweep of flooring here, nor any bronzed pillars or patterned window stretching twelve feet into the stairwell. A tiny piece of coloured glass gave this hall its only light. Below it, Mrs Dalton had placed a vase of dried flowers. There had been no dried flowers at Liscombe. Until the last years, he had had a dozen gardeners and half an acre of glasshouses to supply fresh and exotic blooms. But he did not miss that, nor any of his past life. An empty Liscombe had mocked his loneliness and his losses. Now he felt he must see Kate; just once he must see her again.

He took another look at himself. The Italian sun had improved him a little, had darkened his skin, but it was still a worn face he saw. His hair was greying at the temples and forehead. What would Kate think, to see him, twenty years on? She would not have changed, only grown fuller about the face and figure, and taller with the confidence of her success. She would surely give him luncheon? 'Maybe I'll have lunch over there. They'll perhaps invite me and I shall not be able to refuse. Don't make me luncheon, Mrs Dalton,' he called.

Kate would hold out her hand to him in the hallway. He would be announced by Treeves. What an extraordinary change, to be announced into his old home by his old butler! He ran a nervous finger along his chin; already a slight shadow was showing, but he had not time to shave again for he had made up his mind to drive over to Liscombe that very day and he must not allow himself any excuses.

He could not go on, in the simple routine life he had

worked out for himself, without seeing Kate. It had given him a shock, seeing her name there on the sale papers.

'Liscombe Hall has been bought by a Miss Tranter, your lordship,' his agent had said. 'I believe she has two partners also. But it was she who signed.' And it was her name, in the rather elegant assured hand writing, Kate Tranter. She must have kept it as a business name. The husband would be her partner. No doubt he wanted it in her name. Her mother had only said his name was Gideon. A foolish name for a man. Rather grand for a tradesman. There was some gossip about the purchase of the house by a woman, and a kitchen maid to boot, but when Mrs Dalton tried to tell him at breakfast, he would not listen, not to calumny of Kate. The feeling of her purity was somehow precious to him though it was he who had first spoiled it. He did not think of that now, not often.

As far as Long Trenthide corner, he was all right, driving along, remembering, but coming up through his oaks – it was not that he could not bear they were no longer his – he simply found he could not go on. He could not go up the steps and ask for her. He would look too foolish, asking Treeves . . . Oh, God, he could not do it. She would look at him coolly, his Kate, and perhaps hardly remember, not being haunted all her life as he had been.

No one saw Lord David Liscombe turn his little Austin round in the drive of oaks and roar off back down the hill.

It was 1 February, as bleak and cold a day as any that winter had sent them. Kate had lived four long weeks alone in Liscombe Hall but for her servants. Aunt Bessie had gone to a sanatorium in Switzerland with suspected tuberculosis of the lungs; her mother had returned to the cottage, finding her days too long to turn around the empty rooms of the Hall without her sister; and Gideon was still in London with Peter, trying to settle him into some sort of business.

The country had not suited Peter. He rode Johnny's horses too hard, he used a gun carelessly, he treated the servants with arrogance. Kate had seen him leave Liscombe with both regret and sorrow; she had been ashamed of his behaviour, and she had fears for his unsettled future. Owning Liscombe would not suit Peter, and perhaps, she sometimes thought, did not suit her, not when she was alone in it. Mostly she set aside the plans for Liscombe – the rebuilding of the tower, the refurbishment of all the rooms – for without Aunt Bessie or Gideon the plans seemed pointless. Often she chose physical exercise instead so as to have no time or energy left for sitting alone in the small drawing room.

Today, she worked in Johnny's stables with a horse brush cleaning the sweat from Meggie, a battered mare she usually rode. Wind had blown fire into her cheeks and made her blood race. She had ridden down Liscombe Hill, round to Flush and almost to Dorchester.

'Shall you come up to the Hall for a hot toddy, Johnny?' she called to her brother working in the next stall.

'I've no time, sis, the vet'll be coming in to see Marlow. I don't want that swollen fetlock to go untended.'

'All right, Johnny, come up to lunch then, won't you? Bring Joe. Joe!' Kate called to her nephew who was earnestly, furiously, brushing down a horse the way Johnny had taught him. 'Come on up to the Hall with your Auntie Kate. I'll ask Treeves to bring you some gingerbread from Cook.'

462

'Not me, Auntie, thanks. I can't let Uncle finish up here on his own.'

'Well, mind you both come up for lunch then. I don't mind if you're a bit late.'

'Righto, Auntie.' Joe finished his brushing and ran off for water, his handsome glowing face with the Liscombe grey eyes so strange in Beth's face.

'Only you and me and Mother know who Joe's father was, Johnny, but I wonder the whole world can't see Harry in him.'

'I don't suppose anyone's looking for it, old girl.' Johnny lifted Marlow's left fetlock between his knees and frowned down upon it. 'Let's have a bit of light. Kate. Move over, away from the door.'

She moved away from the door and leaned on Marlow's stall. 'Your life is these horses now, Johnny. Won't you ever think of marrying, having a son, a boy of your own like Joe?'

'Joe's enough for me.' Johnny dropped the horse's leg and fumbled in his pocket for a Navy Cut. 'What woman'd stand for it anyway?' He lit his cigarette with a Swan match drawn down the stable door, pushing his cap to the back of his head. 'No woman'd be worth it, not to me. I'll never give up. I've got to do it, you see. I feel I must find the ones who are suffering, all the poor beasts that were taken out and went through it and had their nerves shattered and their flesh torn into – for men's sake, Kate! For bloody mad thinking that said we must get a bit more of that damn mud for ourselves.' He pushed at the sleeves of his jacket and rocked impatiently in fine leather riding boots. 'The world should have stopped for the madness out there. No one who ever lived through it will be able to forget nor live an ordinary life again. I feel if I save just one horse, one poor devil, it helps make up for one who suffered out

463

there and never came back.' He leaned on the stable door and drew on his Navy Cut. 'Harry would have done something if he'd lived,' he said.

'Did he suffer much?' They had never spoken of it. Kate saw Johnny drag his cap back down over his eyes.

'He suffered,' said Johnny. 'A long time it took for Harry to die.'

Kate followed his gaze towards the long slant of Liscombe, that should have been Harry's inheritance. She said: 'I remember Harry stopping his ears so as not to hear the dogs baying and the bugle sounding for the hunt.'

Johnny gave a kind of laugh. 'He remembered that,' he said, 'at the last. He was waiting to die. He managed to say to me, "It's like the foxes, Johnny," and then he died.'

All the windows of Liscombe suddenly seemed to Kate to be black and empty; Harry should have been living there, with Beth and Joe and the other children who would have followed. She thought: I must not remember Harry waiting to die, in terror. I must think of Liscombe and what I can do for Harry's son, Joe.

Johnny lit another cigarette. 'And it was his own fault, you see, a kind of weakness in him. He was both strong and weak, I suppose, strong enough to force himself out to save a bloody Fritz but soft enough to feel he must. As if it did any good! He died from it, one glorious action, and he wasn't the only one of his kind either. Half the sons of the aristocracy threw themselves into a glorious useless death and that's why half the stately homes of England are now owned by someone like you, our kind, the doers who worked and fought their way up to take their places. Natural justice it is and *right*, Kate, for their kind sent the rest of us out to die – and worse, never made them see the madness of it.

They made 'em think it glorious too. There was a chap from around here, no more than a boy. He'd sit in the mud with us and read out his letters home. "I'm going to try for a VC, Mother," he'd write. "I want you to be proud of me. I want my country to be proud of me." He volunteered for some sortie and only his paybook came back, there was nothing left to bury. We got up a bit of a deputation to the captain to put him forward for his VC.'

Kate held her breath. That boy had earned his medal for valour. His mother must have it now, brought out for visitors, for everyone to be proud and grateful.

'Said he couldn't have no bloody medal. No officer had been witness, you see. The rules had to be followed. I couldn't get a medal for Harry because no officer had seen him go out there.' Kate saw her brother's handsome dark profile held up to the Dorset sky. 'It was the same bloke who shot Sam Smith in the back for not going over when ordered to. A farmworker, Sam was, and he would keep on about his roses. "If only I could be home for a day, just one day," he said, around June time, when they were coming out. And he'd cry, you could see him crying, and write instructions home how to care for them. And then one day he'd a letter from home saying the roses had died and he couldn't stop crying then, and when he was lined up for the attack, he wouldn't go over. The officer shot him quick in case anyone else should have the same idea.' Johnny kicked at the stable door. 'All in all, I think they deserved to die themselves, and most of them did. Maybe our time has come, Kate. Natural justice you might call it. Look at you, owning a stately home, and you once a kitchen maid, meant for scrubbing floors. If you haven't beaten the caste system, I don't know who has. You must do something useful with it, something satisfying, not just use it as they did. Or else keep some people employed. They did at least do that.'

'You can have some more of it, Johnny,' Kate said eagerly, leaning her cheek against the rough wool of his jacket, finding comfort in the familiar male smell of tobacco and horse and cologne. 'I'll get you more land. You could build up a real stables, start breeding. They're good stock, some of your horses.'

'We'll see, sis.' Johnny turned his handsome brown face to her. 'You mustn't dissipate your capital, you know. You must make it work for you. I'm grateful enough to you for helping me already.'

'Yes,' said Kate, 'I must be sensible about it, but what will it be for, if I make more money?' Behind them Marlow snorted and his companion let out a bellow which set up a clatter of hooves along the row of stalls. She felt a return of the slight sense of panic she sometimes felt in the long evenings when she was alone. 'Perhaps I had better do some charitable work again. I enjoyed working at the soup kitchens, I felt I was doing something positive, although to see the men's faces sometimes . . .'

'You're an emancipated woman, sis, one of the first you were, and without any fuss. You emancipated yourself, like that *Daily Mail* said. You can't just hang about here and wonder what to do with your money.'

'No, dear, no.' Kate felt that she must move or the chill air would reach into her bones. 'Well, come up to luncheon when you and Joe are ready. I don't mind waiting.'

'Righto, sis.'

Kate walked back across the courtyard and up the drive, through the oaks to her oak door with the brass ring in it and Treeves holding it open for her. She went, still in her riding habit, down the empty East Wing to the study where once she had stood before Lord David and first felt his gaze upon her. She had had all his old things put back, the ones he had not bothered to take with him: an old brown photograph of him at Eton in 1885, a long stuffed fish in a glass case, a pipe. She sat for a moment at his desk, running through the letters from that morning's delivery. There was an estimate for the rebuilding of the East Tower, one for the repainting of the dining room, a cattle feed price-list addressed to him. She owned and occupied his house now, a house on a hill in the sun, and she was alone, sitting in it waiting for Gideon and Peter to return from London and Aunt Bessie from Switzerland, to ease the emptiness about her; waiting always for the next meal so that she might have the company of Johnny or Joe or her mother. Today they would come and she would not eat alone.

Gazing unseeing at an estimate, Kate felt a sudden catch at her breath, a longing for the time past when she was never alone, when she was not enough alone. A house on a hill had been only a dream. She had had work to do and so much lay before her. Now she owned land, part of the downs rolling out beyond the window. She was a landowner. Kate put the estimate on a pile of unanswered letters. Millions of men had suffered and died over land. She was ungrateful! She had a great house and a stretch of land, and she sat alone wondering what to do alone in the space and the time she had, with no more work. She was unworthy, Kate told herself. She must pick up her pen and answer her letters and telephone the solicitor in Dorchester to make a Will.

Kate picked up her Waterman and took up a sheet of fine cream paper which bore the simple legend:

Liscombe Hall, Dorset. Today she would write and tomorrow she would make her call to the solicitor and by then she must have decided who should inherit Liscombe in the event of her death. Peter or Joe? It was a dilemma she did not want to face. Neither, she supposed, had a legitimate right to it, but who had the moral right? If Aunt Bessie were home, she would have been able to talk it over with her.

Under her hand, not red now but a lady's hand, there was cool leather that he had touched. It reminded her of the day she had first seen this room, standing before him in her old black boots and good blue dress. He had sat behind the desk with his arms upon it and there had been a smell of cigar smoke and cologne and his face had been angry and shadowed. She had been afraid of him.

Kate put down her pen. She could not write here. She seemed to catch a drift, a kind of memory, of the smell of his cigars, and the image of his face and her fear; sixteen years old she had been and overcome with the power of his male presence, coming towards her over the carpet with a small thud of his boots. She had held her breath and he had come towards her across the very same room and it had all begun.

She began to read again the letter to which she had already composed a reply in her mind. 'Dear Miss Tranter,' it said, 'we are a small charity . . .' She could not see the words for the blur of tears that seemed to have been waiting to fall. Kate put a hand to her mouth. She must not cry for she would not be able to stop. 'Dear Miss Tranter,' she read again.

She could still feel the way her heart had stopped as he rose from his chair, this chair where she sat, and came towards her. She was still sixteen; she had learned nothing for she could still feel that and if he came to the door of the study at that moment it would be as if the whole of her adult life had never existed. 'We are a small charity,' she read again, and cried out at the sudden knock that seemed to sound in her heart. It could not be ... She dropped her letter and turned round. It could not be him, but if only he would come!

Treeves slipped into the room with coffee on a silver tray and murmured: 'There is a policeman to see you, Miss Tranter.'

Kate's heart leaped again. 'An accident, Treeves? My son, my mother? My aunt?'

'He did not say.' Treeves placed the tray on the desk beside her letters. 'I have put him in the morning room and informed him that you are taking your coffee and will be with him shortly.'

'Thank you, Treeves.' Kate poured black Kenyan coffee and allowed the scent of it to drift up to her. It might be an estate matter. She would drink her coffee and go down calmly, as Miss Tranter, and leave behind the sixteen-year-old self that had crept up on her. But her hand, raising the cup to her mouth, trembled. She had a sudden chill feeling about her shoulders though the fire in the grate burned as brightly as it always did.

She ran downstairs and into the morning room where a man stood holding a trilby hat.

'You are Miss Kate Tranter?'

'Yes.' She was conscious of a thumping at her temples. He was a London policeman, from his accent.

'Detective Inspector Bowman,' said the man. 'You are the mother of Peter William Tranter?'

'I am.' The thumping moved to her chest.

'I am sorry to inform you, Madam, that your son has been arrested and is being held in custody at Cannon Row police station in London.'

Kate said: 'Has my son been stealing ... or something?' It was not a surprise to her, not a surprise at all.

'It is a rather more serious matter than that, Madam. I suggest that you collect an overnight bag and come along with us to London.'

They took Kate to a hospital in Paddington. Afterwards, she remembered nothing about it, only climbing some stone stairs and the smell in the long room, urine and disinfectant, where Gideon lay in a bed by the door. There were bandages about his neck and chest. Around him, two nurses moved and a doctor said: 'A minute only, please.'

Kate saw Gideon's dear twisted face that had always been there, watching her, loving her, supporting her. More than twenty years Gideon had been part of her life and now he lay, a tiny bent body, dying. There was a bubble of blood at his mouth. She leaned forward and kissed his forehead.

'Gideon, darling, it's Kate.'

'Kate,' he said. One clear word. His eyes flickered open.

'Gideon – my son! How can you forgive me?'

'Not yours, Kate.' His breath, a quiver of life, seemed suddenly to come in gasps. 'I bought him – two guineas – East End. Long time now.' The words were only a whisper between breaths. Blood was seeping at the wound in his throat. 'Ask Bessie.'

The doctor said, taking Kate's arm, 'That's all now, please.'

But she pushed him away. Gideon! She leaned forward again and put her arms around the bandages wrapped about Gideon who was dying. Peter not her son? She had not borne Peter?

'Peter is not mine, ours, Gideon?'

'For love – we did – you wailing for baby . . .'

'Leave now, please. I must help this man.'

'He is beyond help, isn't he?' Kate heard her own voice saying. And she went on because Gideon could not live and she must know: 'I love you, dear Gideon, do not leave me.' She wanted him to hear her voice although it was too late, to know that she had loved him though the words had never been said.

She leaned her face against Gideon's closed eyes, and held his head where his hair grew crookedly too. And she must say more for it could not be that Peter was not her son.

'My baby died, Gideon? And you and Aunt Bessie got me another?'

She felt a nod of his head between her fingers. A faint trickle of blood came from his mouth. The doctor took up his wrist and put a hand against his heart over the bandages.

They let Kate stay until the warmth of life left him and the policeman came to take her away. She spoke to the man; she spoke later to a lawyer; she made arrangements to stay in London. And all the time the heart said: I am not Peter's mother; the boy I held to my breast was not the one I bore. He is neither Liscombe nor Tranter. The love that Gideon and Aunt Bessie had felt for her was enough for them to commit a criminal act, to live out a lie. She thought: All the times when I watched him, wondering about his stealing and his mean ways and thought them my fault, it was something in him that was alien. But she could not blame the others. It was done, and Peter had murdered Gideon. She must go on and behave like his mother. She must try and understand him; she must get him freed. She loved him. He was her son in all but flesh and blood. Any fault in him was hers.

'Miss Tranter! Miss Tranter! Have you told his father that Peter Tranter has been accused of murder?'

'Miss Tranter! Who is your son's father, Miss Tranter?'

'Look this way, Miss Tranter!'

They were flashing cameras in her face, pushing at her, pulling her arm. Kate stood rooted to the pavement before the Imperial Palace Hotel and felt she could not move; she would never move again. There would always be about her these men in Homburgs and swinging overcoats, shouting and grinning at her – a murderer's mother. Uncertain, trembling, she looked beyond the newspapermen and the cameramen and silently begged the Palace doorman for help. She could not move herself; he must come and help her.

'Please,' she whispered uselessly, 'please, leave me alone.'

'Here, get out of it. We'll call the police. Get out of it.' A strong uniformed arm seemed to pick her up and lead her into the sweet warm darkness of the Imperial Hotel's back entrance.

'Get out of it!'

'Please, Miss Tranter, look this way one more time! Does his father . . . Miss Tranter!'

Kate took in stifled panicky breaths. Safe here, a little quiet here.

'We have given you your usual suite, Miss Tranter.'

'Thank you so much.'

'Shall you be staying with us long, Miss Tranter?'

'I cannot tell.'

'No, of course not. Shall I have a tray of tea sent up, Miss Tranter?'

'Yes, please.'

Let them send tea, whatever, it did not matter. Kate let herself be led dumbly into the lift and along the silent corridors into the suite which once, such a short time ago, had seen their happiness. Here the three of them had taken tea together, as she was now. Only she was quite alone. In her pocket was the telegram from Aunt Bessie's doctor. She was not yet fit to travel home.

Kate sat in the hotel sitting room and gazed out across the river. Happy, they had been so happy, making plans for a good life to come after so much hard work: the country and the Vicar to tea in a house on the hill in the sun.

A cold wintry sun filtered now through the London air outside. There was no real light in it, no warmth in the London sun. Kate tried to pour herself a second cup of tea though her hand shook. They had sat here on warm July days only last year and they had laughed together, planning.

Now Aunt Bessie was sick, Gideon dead, murdered by Peter, who was not of her blood though no one must ever know it except her mother. Her mother would be glad he was not Tranter and Clarke, and she must share the knowledge with someone. She could not bear to hold it for ever within herself.

It was a nightmare only she was awake, for here was the telephone ringing. She must answer it. Her arm, reaching out, felt as if it held a heavy weight in it.

'Hello?'

'The *Daily Mail*, Miss Tranter. Do you . . .'

'I have nothing to say.'

Kate sat on, watching the cold sun fade away and leave dark winter night over the Thames. She had not the strength to move.

'Why, Peter?'

Kate Tranter sat watching him in a room somewhere deep inside Pentonville prison. She could hardly see his face for the darkness there and the iron grille which separated them, which would always separate them now.

'How could you kill Gideon when he loved you so, when he brought you up? He taught you to read, Peter.' How weak her voice sounded. She had hardly the force to speak and the words meant nothing. She said them only because she must say something sitting here with her son.

'He watched me, he was always watching me all my life, and you never cared.'

Peter sat helplessly sobbing through his words. There was no point in his saying it, any of it, for Gideon was dead and he a condemned man. The evidence was clear enough.

'But what . . . what made you, Peter? You must tell me.' She did not want to know.

'He was watching me, I tell you! I couldn't stand it any more. He said I must go into business and do something with my life, for your sake. He wanted me to be a gentlemen's outfitter. Me, a tradesman, Mother. Can't you see?'

'*I* wanted that for you too, not just Gideon. It was a safe business and there aren't many now with the state the country's in, the strikes and so on. Business will be hard, Gideon says . . . Gideon said we must put you into something safe. Since the General Strike, Peter . . .'

'Oh, what does it matter, Mother? I'm a lost man now. Save me, Mother. Save me.' He put his plump hands around that pale unhealthy face and gave out a kind of wail. His hair, such thin limp hair, was dark with the sweat of his fear.

'I have naturally engaged the best lawyers. There is nothing else I can do.'

They sat with the sound of his sobbing between them.

'Why did you kill him, Peter?' She must know, for Gideon's sake, for the memory of him she would hold in her heart. She must, in her heart, ask Gideon for forgiveness, to forgive her.

474

'He found me.' Peter seemed to quieten, looking past her through the dim light to the square of grilled window.

'He found me and said he would tell you this time, that you must know what I was. So I took up the knife he'd given me – you know, the Swiss one with a cross on it. I always kept it about me. He used to say . . . he used to joke about it. There was a tool in it for taking stones from horses' hooves, and he said you never knew when you might have a horse with a stone in its . . . I didn't mean to kill him, Mother, I don't think I did. Only when he crept into my room in the hotel where I'd gone for a bit – you didn't want me at Liscombe, did you? Don't think I didn't know. And then I had to meet a few fellows about some business, you have to have a decent place to meet fellows – and then he came creeping up the way he used to do always, and he found me.'

'Found you, Peter? With a girl, do you mean, in your room? Is that what you mean? Gideon would not have minded that.'

'No, not a girl. I only wish it had been.' She saw him slump back in the prison chair. His skin was grey with shadows under his pale blue eyes. Sometimes he would not turn his eyes to look at her and she knew then he was being deceitful.

She had never had enough time for Peter, that was the truth of it. She loved him so much, she had thought he was part of her, but she had never had enough time. Now she must pay for that. He had begun a high kind of snivelling like he had used to do when he wanted something as a child and could not have it.

'It's all your fault, Mother! If you'd given me a normal home. What was there for me, always alone except for Gideon watching me, and those girls? Do you remember the girls who used to play with me? The upstairs girls?'

475

'What does all this have to do with Gideon's death, Peter?'

'All right, I'll tell you. Yes, you ought to know. You're my mother and you never knew and I used to do it all the time – I used to go up to your room and dress in your clothes, and the girls' clothes. I liked it and I used to do it whenever I could. He knew about it, the dwarf, and he used to threaten me he'd tell you. And then when he came up this time to my room and found me, found me like it, I had on . . . some clothes, a dress, he jeered at me. You wouldn't understand, you're so normal, Mother – you are. You wouldn't understand but that dwarf did, he understood. It was as if he understood everything about me and he was jeering at me. He would use what he knew of me, somehow, I knew he would, so when he found me this time, I put the knife into his neck and chest and he bled all over me. It was awful, his blood, and so I screamed and someone came.'

Kate watched with her heart stopped as Peter stood up against the prison door and banged upon it, sobbing. He sank to the stone floor. A guard was looking at them through the hole in the door. She could not breathe. Her heart had stopped.

'Time's up, Miss Tranter. Come on now, lad.'

It was all over and here she was out in the street. Someone had led her there and now she must move; she must call a cab and go to the lawyer's office and there be calm and determined. They must do everything they could to get Peter freed, she must say. She must go now, move forward and walk along to the street until she found a corner where a cab might pass. It was quite simple, she must just get herself to move. Only she could not.

*

476

The day before they hanged Peter, the headlines screamed out 'No more appeals – Tranter son dies tomorrow'. The news of the falling shares on Wall Street was wiped from the billboards. The Tranter name sang out.

Kate walked the London streets alone, up and down Bond Street and along the Strand, across to the river. She could not stay in her hotel room, she could not stay still anywhere, everyone was watching the mother of a murderer.

Alone, the beautiful, successful Miss Tranter walked the streets waiting for the time to pass before they hanged Peter. She had one last visit to face tonight, now, and she would walk there.

She had not let Johnny come up to be with her and the lawyers she had sent away. They could be of no use now and she had known they would never be of any use. No matter what kind of evidence they had produced as to his mental state, Peter Tranter was guilty of murder and would hang.

Kate walked alone through the London streets towards the condemned cell of Pentonville prison. There was of course the little crowd of newsmen at the door. Might there not be a final last-minute reprieve?

'Any hope, Miss Tranter? Did you see the Home Secretary personally?'

'Miss Tranter!'

They parted to let her pass, silent, suddenly, perhaps sympathetic; it did not matter. Kate felt nothing, saw nothing, only the great door and all those other doors with their keys turning to let her pass. Miss Kate Tranter, the mother of a murderer, the mother of . . . all those names they had called him.

She had no strength for any words for him, but sat beside him in his condemned cell. His skin was quite grey now and his shirt hung loosely on him. He had lost weight. All along his jaw there was a line of dark stubble. He had not shaved today. Would he ever shave again? Would they shave him, tomorrow, before they hanged him? Once she had fed him from her breast and thought him her son.

Kate sat, not breathing, not feeling, beside her son.

'Mother!' he said. 'Save me, Mother.'

She could not touch him. The guard would not allow it, probably, and it did not matter, for she could not.

'I cannot.' All the life in her was gone, waiting for him to die. 'I am sorry, son.' Silent tears seemed to be warming her cheeks. 'Forgive me.'

He sat shivering, silent now, not sobbing; he could have no more strength for it. He would not struggle when they led him down tomorrow. I hope he will not struggle. The vague faint hope came to her, that he would go silently, quickly, down to die.

'The time is up. I'm sorry, Miss Tranter.' The guard was polite, solicitous for the mother of a condemned man.

'Oh. Yes.' She rose on legs she did not feel. She seemed to move across the cell and back again, standing before him.

'Goodbye, Mother.'

She seemed to reach out and touch his hair, his shoulder, and the cold skin of his hand.

'I'm sorry, Miss Tranter.'

'Goodbye, son.' Son. She must go on pretending that he was her son. He had no one else. It was part of her suffering that she must not let anyone know that he was not her son.

A long wail of despair sounded along the corridor as she walked away. She seemed to be floating for surely her body was not her own. The long slow wail reached her but she did not turn back.

*

She did not return to the Imperial Palace that night;
they would be waiting for her there, the newsmen.
Instead, she asked for a room from the new owner of
Tranter's Hotel in St John Street and there she hid,
alone, waiting, in a room on the second floor. They had
kept the Dorset country-style bedrooms, she noticed
vaguely, but did not see things very clearly. Her mind
was on the past. Here she had slept and bathed and
dressed whilst Peter had played with the silks and lace
of her underwear and the maids'. How the newspapers
had loved that, how they had revelled in it.

Only she would not think of it now, she would think
back to the good days, happy days when there had been
such work to do and so much planning. And Peter had
sat up here, ignored, playing with underwear.

She had not cried for it, she could not cry.

She sat at the window fully dressed and heard the
clocks striking the hours.

At six, she ordered a cup of tea and was able to drink it.

She dressed in the plainest black outfit which she had
ordered by telephone from her old dressmaker. But she
had had it made up to her old measurements. The skirt
was loose about her waist, the jacket sat awkwardly on
her shoulders. It did not matter. There would be no
point in pulling her hat over her eyes. They would spot
her today, the newspapermen, she would not be able to
walk the streets. Perhaps she should have ordered a car?

Too late now. If they had let Aunt Bessie come home,
she might have been able to bear it; they would have
walked together.

There was a faint misty drizzle in the air. Kate stood
at the hotel steps where she had so often stood proudly
before, and hesitated. She felt her heart beating too fast.
She had not felt that for a long time. It was a long time
since she had felt anything.

'Allow me to drive you, Miss Tranter.' A discreet cough behind her. The new owner of Tranter's stood there, a kind, concerned face only trying to help, wanting to help.

'Thank you, yes. Only do not stay with me, just let me . . .'

'Of course, Miss Tranter. Come this way, my car is waiting. I've had it waiting since last night in case I could be of use to you. Such a terrible business, the newspapers . . .'

'Yes, thank you.'

There was a little movement outside the prison by the great door. They were there already, waiting for her with their cameras.

'You cannot stand there with them,' the man said, moving his car along the street.

'No, take me a little further down, to some doorway somewhere.' It did not matter.

He did not want to leave her, but Kate insisted. She could not remember his name.

'Thank you. I shall be quite all right.' They did not see her; no one saw her.

She waited in a dark silent doorway that smelt of cats. It did not matter. She waited.

She seemed to be able to hear a clock ticking. It matched the beating of her heart. It seemed to get slower, waiting, like her heart.

She knew it was almost time when a murmur reached her from down the street where other people waited for the second that would bring Peter Tranter's death. A thudding in her chest. A louder murmur, down there, by the great door. They were moving, there was movement. Dong, dong. A distant clock struck eight times with the beating of her heart. Peter was dead.

*

480

'Get in quickly, Miss Tranter. Quickly!' A voice spoke from behind the wheel of the car in the street before her. It must be the hotel man.

'Thank you,' she heard her own voice say.

But it was not the hotel man. This man was dark, he had dark hair grown grey at the temples, she saw that much, and there were dark hairs on the hands at the wheel. Who was he? A newspaperman? She had been caught.

'Who are you? Let me out!'

'Kate,' the man said, a long-forgotten voice, remembered now.

'Lord Liscombe?'

'David, please, Kate. Where would you like to go? I can take you anywhere – home if you like. Just say.'

She could see his profile, the straight firm nose, the firm chin and those grey eyes that once had looked at her with love. The same.

'I saw in the newspapers . . . your son. I am so sorry about your son. I thought you might need help. Johnny said you didn't want him up but I thought . . . Forgive me, rambling on. Let me just get the car out of London, then the cameras won't find you. My dear, your son. I am so sorry.'

A mist of grey streets passed in the grey light; little doorways, poor streets, a dog scavenging in the gutter.

'Not my son,' she said, 'but my fault.'

He seemed to be driving her home, silently, all the way to Liscombe. She watched his steady hands on the wheel beside her and thought of nothing. They seemed to stop at some country inn and he put coffee and brandy before her and she drank, still silent, watching his face, seeing in some distant part of her mind that he had aged but was handsome still, and his once so-loved face was watching her, seeing her too no doubt aged. They did not speak, he simply took her arm and guided her in and out of the car at the inn and, finally, at the top of Liscombe Hall steps where the door was open to receive her. Treeves stood there, and Mrs Baker and her mother, they all stood there, weeping, she thought, but she could hardly see them through the mist that seemed to be in the air.

'No newsmen here then, Treeves?' she heard him say. She walked up the steps on his arm and he gave her up to her mother who was sobbing. She could hear her mother sobbing but perhaps it was herself.

Long days she sat in the morning room. She dressed and went down the staircase at breakfast time and sat in Aunt Bessie's place by the fireside, until finally her mother stopped moving cautiously around her and said firmly: 'You ought to be out of that chair, our Kate, you ought to be up and doing. Tisn't no good you sitting there. What about the dining room walls? The man's here to start the painting.'

'Yes, Mother, tomorrow,' she heard herself say. There was a faint frozen smile on her lips; she could feel it.

Treeves and Mrs Baker moved behind her mother like black shadows.

'Shall the painter be told to start, Miss Tranter? Shall we get an estimate in for the rebuilding of East Tower?' they said, as if together.

'Yes, tomorrow.' She could hear her own voice saying it quite clearly, and they went away to whisper behind the door.

Then her mother sent in Johnny and Joe. A gust of cold air came in with them, and they cried out because they had been told to: 'Coming out for a ride? Meggie needs a gallop. It's a lovely day, nice breeze out there, sis.'

'Do come Auntie!'

Johnny, embarrassed and awkward, waited for her answer, fidgeting round the room. Poor Joe looked at her with anxious love. 'Come on, Auntie.'

She heard herself say: 'Tomorrow, darling. I'll come tomorrow.'

The second or third time that Lord Liscombe tentatively invited himself for tea and sat there before her in her mother's chair, while Treeves, shaking a little, brought in the tea things, she began to talk. She talked of Paris and her journey home, and on through the London days, her cooking and the baby's birth, their son's, and his death. And then Peter whom she thought was theirs, whom she had loved as if he were.

David stayed on until night-time. She watched his face, his handsome face with the two deep lines about his mouth and the darkness under his eyes, and it seemed to grow younger as the light slipped away and no one came to light the lamps. It was the face she had known before: concerned, serious, laughing at her in the Paris bedroom. 'Kate, Kate, it will be all right. I'll buy you a little apartment, you will be happy.'

'I was happy working,' she said. 'I was happy working with Aunt Bessie and Gideon, so busy, achieving what I thought was something special. I felt proud sometimes at what I had done, what I was doing. I used to think: Once I was a kitchen maid with one good dress. Once people gave us things because we were so poor. I was thrilled with my own achievement, and Aunt Bessie's and Gideon's, and all the time Peter was as he was.'

'You cannot blame yourself. No parent can be fully responsible for the children they have. Obviously there was bad blood in him, it had nothing to do with the way you brought him up. You cannot be blamed for that. You had your living to earn, and his, and that was my fault, all mine.'

'But I was not a good enough mother. I could not have been.'

'If it's anyone's fault then it is mine, for taking you in the way I did, not thinking beyond what I felt for you. The fault must be mine that a baby was born. And then, what Peter actually was, that unhealthy streak in him, was just an accident. He could have been a fine chap, in spite of his birth. Who can explain these things – mental illness, deformity? And as for upbringing, look how Harry was neglected in that nursery – a drunken Nanny, an uncaring mother – all quite usual in our circle. I would do it differently if I had my time again.' He bent forward to stir the fire into life. 'You see, then I suppose I expected to have everything I wanted. I wanted my pleasant free life at Liscombe. And I wanted you very much. I wrote many times to you, didn't I? Surely you must have realized it was more for me than a night of pleasure?'

'I did not read the letters until after Gideon died and Aunt Bessie sent the key for her black box, with a letter, from Switzerland.'

'She kept them from you? Then, darling Kate, you did not reject me? You did not want to hurt me?'

Outside an owl called across the downs.

Kate said, turning her head towards the dark window: 'She meant well, she wanted to protect me and wanted me to be the kind of woman that she might have been. She meant well for me. She loved me.'

She turned to see his face watching her, his remembered face with the two lines deeper down to his mouth, and his grey eyes, Harry's eyes, seeming darker today in the firelight.

'And you achieved what she wanted, what everyone

wanted, Kate. It has been a remarkable achievement. You must place that beside what you think of as your failure with Peter. And, Kate, you did not reject me, did not stop loving me? If I could only believe that!'

Over the hearth a clock ticked, its tiny pendulum swinging to and fro. 'All those years apart,' he said.

Kate did not seem to hear him but gazed into the fire; the glow from it coloured her face and the golden skin of her neck above her black dress.

'Mother says wanting grand things means you'll suffer,' she said, as if in a dream. Her voice seemed to come from far away.

'Perhaps your mother is right, if we want something which means someone else must suffer for it. Me wanting you. Blanche wanting, God knows what.'

A murmur of voices outside the door. They would be standing there, wondering if they might come in, David thought. He said: 'But I should like to think that you had been happy, at least some of the time.' He felt the fire's warmth reaching him and his heart was thudding; Kate had not rejected him all those years before.

'Some of it, when I was working. Now I wonder how it has come down to this. Myself alone in this great place. Aunt Bessie sick, Gideon and Peter dead – and I wanted it for them too. Before – the murder, I used to stand and look out over the downs and wonder what I should do all alone, without even Aunt Bessie or my mother with me. I suppose I must begin wondering it again once . . . once I can begin to think properly.'

'I will help you, Kate, if you will let me. I will come again tomorrow, and every day, until you don't need me any more.' He would not trouble her with his own feelings, not yet; he would simply be there.

She did not answer. Perhaps it did not matter whether he came or not. She watched him rise and walk across the dark room. Was it time now to go up and let sleep release her? He had helped the time pass. Let him come tomorrow then.

Her heart said: I want him to come tomorrow. I want his dear tired face pressed into mine. I want to feel his arms about me, I have waited so long to feel his arms about me.

When he came the next day, and the next, she watched him and waited for him to know that she wanted him to hold her. It would be soon when the suffering was enough and she could feel the life begin to start in her again, when the image of Peter's face, the grey drawn face that he had, waiting to die, ceased to be always where she was and the sound of his long wail did not echo down the empty Liscombe corridors and inhabit the room where she slept.

CHAPTER TWENTY

'A new spring, Kate, my darling, a new start!' Lord David Liscombe reined in his horse Jasper at the top of Rookery Hill and turned to catch Kate's grey, Meggie, wheeling round behind him. He thought: Oh, the look of her this morning, her lovely neck and her head up in the Dorset air! Liscombe was healing her slowly, and Kate was healing the long-ago break in his own heart.

'Aren't we too old to be making new starts?' She was almost smiling, reining in the horse with an expert hand. She seemed no more than twenty.

'Kate, listen.' He leaned over and held Meggie's bridle. 'Marry me, please.'

Her eyes seemed to grow darker in the sunshine. 'Marry you?'

He had said it too soon, but he could not stop now. 'Lady Liscombe of Liscombe Hall, Kate?'

'I don't want . . .'

'No, nothing grand, I know. Just Mr and Mrs David Liscombe of Liscombe, if you like, or even of Home Farmhouse, I shan't mind! Please. I am so lonely without you. I cannot bear to walk down the steps when you send me away after tea.'

'Mother would like to see me decent and married at last.' She seemed to be thinking it over, gazing down to the stream and Stone Cottage.

He held his breath. 'Quiet, Meggie,' he whispered.

'I am lonely too,' she said, 'I am so lonely, even with Aunt Bessie home at last.' There were tears glistening in her eyes. 'I don't know how to get through the days even with her and Mother and Johnny and Joe helping.'

She began to sob helplessly, sitting on Meggie's back. 'Peter and Gideon . . . my fault . . . haunting me. All my fault.'

'Kate.' He got down from Jasper and pulled her gently from her saddle. 'Kate.' She could not stop. It was all coming out, all the sorrow that she had held to herself for so long.

He put his arms about her and felt again the slender straight body against his, the silky skin of her face against his. So long, he had had this dream; holding Kate again. He put his face into her hair and breathed in the sweet remembered scent of her. 'It was worth it, Kate, all the waiting, all the dreaming, to feel you here.' He felt himself begin to sob along with her. 'I could not bear life without you,' he said. 'I cannot bear it. Please marry me, Kate.'

'Peter and Gideon are everywhere I go.'

'Cry, darling. Cry until they are gone.'

They must have sent for Aunt Bessie and her mother to put her to bed. She could hear them moving about the room and whispering. A doctor had called and given her something to help her sleep but Kate felt that for once, lying there, she would not sleep, did not want to sleep any more. Her body felt light and empty from crying. She lay in the bed that once had been Lady Sarah's. From the window she could glimpse Rookery Hill; tiny black specks moved against the sky, the birds swooping the way she remembered. She had forgotten the birds. She had forgotten the hills. She had been living, moving about Liscombe, talking to people, her family, David, and she had been riding in the wind, but it seemed it was only now, tonight, that she realized she had been doing these things. Had months passed since they had hanged Peter, a year or more since he had killed Gideon? This evening, lying here, sleepless, she could not see Peter's fretful, accusing face. Suddenly, she could not remember his face.

'Gideon?' she whispered. Gideon had always been standing behind Peter. These long months he had been standing behind the boy with his most loving expression, forgiving her. She must let him forgive her, if she wanted to live.

'What time is it, Mother?'

'Tea-time.' Mrs Tranter moved heavily to the window and looked down over the valley. 'Father'll be home, and Joe, wanting their teas, and Bessie's got to go for her rest.'

'You go, Mother, I'll be all right. I feel . . . better.'

'I don't know as I . . .' Kate saw her tired face shadowed in the evening light. 'Shall I let *him* up?'

. 'No, not now, tonight.' She wanted to be alone, to feel herself living. She must face Gideon's memory and let herself be forgiven. 'Tell him tomorrow, in the morning.'

'I do hope as how you'll be sensible over this, our Kate.'

'Sensible, Mother?' She felt herself give her old smile at the dear tired face of her Aunt Bessie leaning over her, thinner now since Switzerland but filled with love for her, as always.

'You'd be respectable, that's all I got to say. And it's time, with all we've been through, ent it, Bessie?' Mrs Tranter pulled at the bedsheet. 'I just want our Kate to do what *she* wants.' Aunt Bessie took up Kate's hand. 'The rest of us have got no say in it. We done enough, we have.'

Kate held her aunt's hand and gave her a look of wordless understanding. Once, after Aunt Bessie's return, they had talked of the matter of Lord David's letters hidden so long in the basement safe. There had been no reproaches. Kate had wanted none. Her aunt had done what she thought was necessary at the time, to save a girl of sixteen from ruin. 'I could be respectable, Auntie. Lady Liscombe,' she whispered. 'I could be happy. Will Gideon forgive me if I am ever happy again?'

'Forgive you, dear heart? That man only lived for you and me. If we could find a bit of contentment now, a bit of peace, he'd be up there rejoicing, he would.' Aunt Bessie wiped the eyes that had cried enough in the hospital bed in Switzerland and gave a laugh. 'What'd he say to see me without no cigarette, nor no drink for me comfort?'

'He'd be glad to see you looking so well, Aunt Bessie.'

'And to see you Lady Liscombe, that's what I think, my girl.'

The ceremony at the Dorchester Register Office was a simple one; only Tranter and Liscombe family members were present. With so much tragedy and scandal in the families, the local people agreed it was not surprising that the event should be a subdued one. A few of them, gathered around the office courtyard, whispered about it. Kate, coming down the steps on the arm of Lord David Liscombe, saw the hats nodding and imagined wryly the comments. Her hand tightened on David's arm; they could not hurt her. She would have no more of hurt. She had earned her happiness in suffering.

She wore dark blue crêpe-de-chine, the exact colour of her eyes, chosen in London, with a wisp of net over her chestnut hair. Around her neck was a double row of pink pearls David had kept from Blanche, and he had placed his mother's gold ring upon her finger. She said, blinking into the sun behind the cameraman: 'I feel we are waking from a nightmare that has lasted most of our lives.'

'Let us hurry home, darling Kate.' Her husband held her arm tightly beneath his and dropped his top hat. The families behind them giggled and the crowd murmured in amusement. The atmosphere lightened.

Aunt Bessie, daringly in day-time red with her hair newly hennaed and a saucy feather in her hat, winked across at him, and his daughter Lulu Browne, formerly Liscombe, smiled into the camera from under her sensible felt hat, so unlike Aunt Bessie's. Her tweed suit was stretched about her waist, for she was expecting another child, her sixth; she had found the way to feel loved and to give the love that was in her. Her husband, in hired morning suit, was harassed by the thought of the work that awaited him at the small charity hospital his wife's dowry had founded; even his moustache had an air of being grown in a hurry.

Behind him stood Lord Berwick, husband to Daisy; he was to show as only a blur in the later photograph for his head had jerked in nervous anticipation of the cameraman's order to smile. Lord Berwick was not often in public; his epilepsy had weakened his body and his command of himself.

The youngest of the Tranters stood near his aunt. Thick chestnut hair was smoothed down with Brylcreem like his Uncle Johnny's and the same tuft of Tranter hair resisted it, sticking up at the back. He smiled shyly into the camera, standing straight for his aunt's special day for she had promised him he might stay at the grammar school and not have to suffer the tortures of Harrow or Eton or Winchester and his time could still be for horses.

'Smile, please!' The camera clicked under the black cloth.

Lord and Lady Liscombe, each as tall and handsome as the other, lifted their faces to the sunshine and smiled. 'Good morning, Lady Liscombe,' he said, his arm tightly under hers.

Mrs Tranter, pale and stout, dressed in pink with her favourite black straw hat and matching rose, gave a loud sob. Her husband, standing stiffly beside her in his new wedding and funeral suit, frowned beneath the unaccustomed top hat and longed for his end of cigarette with the tobacco strands burning his lip. As darkly good-looking as his father, Johnny Tranter fidgeted and scraped his boots upon the stones, very much as his own horses did when agitated.

'Smile, please!'

Daisy, Lady Berwick, obediently pulled her stole about her and smiled. Diamonds flashed at her fingers and neck. The lovely eyes she had inherited from her mother gazed vaguely into the Dorchester street, where the crowd of local people had increased. God, she thought, the country doesn't suit me. She hoped Treeves had got in some vodka.

Lord David called for a final photograph of his wife and the party broke up, wandering down the steps and into the waiting cars, ushered by Johnny and Joe according to instructions.

The limousines took them up the lane where the primroses were fading, a pale gold patch under the hawthorn. Soon all Liscombe would be budding into life.

Stepping from the car on to the gravel drive, Kate, suddenly her old energetic self, shooed them up the steps to the waiting Treeves and Mrs Baker with champagne on silver trays.

David, lingering behind, caught at Kate's arm to hold her back.

'Darling,' he said, 'stand with me for a moment on Liscombe steps. I used to dream of us here together.'

They stood linked, the murmur of their families behind them. Sun lit the downs, a stretch of hill and vale which was theirs, and warmed the stone pillars of the terrace beside them.

'All this,' he said, 'was nothing without you. It was nothing to me. The only good I ever did with it was to send three village girls to teacher training college in memory of you, Kate, and then two of them immediately married. So I just hung about waiting, hoping against all sense that you would one day come to me. And you did.'

Kate said: 'I don't know that I should have been able to bear it if you had not come.' The sun made dark shadows of the oaks on the drive and the tower of Liscombe Church. 'If you had not finally come to me.'

'Just you and me together, now,' he said. 'How could I not have come?'

Kate felt her heart turn over as his handsome, tired, beloved face, at once grave and smiling, looked down at her. 'I've been thinking,' she said, 'this would make a marvellous hotel.' The words just slipped out; they hardly seemed to matter. She barely knew that she spoke for he was there beside her.

'A hotel? Liscombe Hall?' His face had no question in it; the words did not matter to him either.

'Liscombe Hall Hotel,' she said. 'We could offer hunting and golf and the country. It's what people still want – more, perhaps, after the war.' She was smiling up at him. She had come to life again only in the past days. 'I was happy working,' she went on, to tease him. His eyes had the same loving look of twenty years before. 'Perhaps I had better work in case something happens to take you away again?'

'You could be lady of the manor and do a lot of good in the district, Kate.' His arm was so tightly about her that she could not move; she did not want to move. She said: 'Johnny says the old feudalism is all gone.'

'Did you say something might happen to take me away? I cannot hear the words you say, or else I hear them and then I forget because they do not matter, not today. If anything happens to me, you shall know it for I shall be near you at the time.'

Kate leaned into the warmth of his arm. She would never be alone again.

A querulous voice sounded from the hall. 'Aren't you coming, Kate? I do think a bride should be present at a wedding.'

David took his place at the bottom of the table and Kate hers at the top where Treeves waited to serve the mistress of the house, her ladyship. Behind them was the glowing portrait of old Lady Liscombe in blue with a haze of pink Dorset sky behind her. At last, David thought, holding up his glass to his wife, a fitting mistress for this room and house. His Kate sat in a glory of golden skin and chestnut hair and eyes so blue he could see them from his place; grief and sadness and a lifetime of work had not lessened her beauty but only enhanced it. The shadows in her face made his heart turn over with love and tenderness. She would suffer no more.

Kate saw her husband raise his glass and knew what thoughts were being sent across the long expanse of linen and the Liscombe silver and the platters of Dorset salmon. She knew that he would not eat, from happiness.

On each side of her, between them, sat Tranter and Liscombe, once divided into hill and valley people, upstairs and downstairs, by class and tradition; now

494

they were joined. She remembered with familiar sorrow her son Peter who should have been there, Harry Liscombe, dear Gideon, her sister Beth, her brother Billy.

She drank a little champagne and reminded herself that today she was to leave her grief and her sorrow behind her, part of her past. Today was the first day of her new life. She lifted her glass to Aunt Bessie who beamed back at her through tears. David too lifted his glass to Aunt Bessie and whispered: 'All forgiven?' Aunt Bessie could do no more than nod and whisper back: 'Worth waiting for,' the words that David had said to her that morning.

The salmon was eaten, the pheasant served, and the conversation became general. Drinking steadily, Daisy, Lady Berwick spoke of childhood days when they walked together, Tranter and Liscombe children, and lessons had been shared. 'We used to envy them their stews and their hot bricks,' she said, and there was no embarrassment around the table.

Lulu Liscombe, now Mrs Louisa Browne, recounted her new life as a doctor's wife. Johnny told the table how war horses had been treated, until a hiss from his mother warned him that he had talked too long. His father watched him for reminders about which knife and fork to use, and swallowed champagne that he did not care for.

Opposite him, Susan Tranter put her fingers delicately around her champagne glass and watched the two Liscombe girls. She thought that they were nothing to be proud of, for all their advantages. Was it, she wondered, quite in order for a lady to drink so much? And Miss Lulu had the air of a vicar's wife, an air about her of making-do. She thought with pride that Kate had long since passed the days of making-do. They were Kate's step-daughters. No one had mentioned this extraordinary fact and it was better that she should not do so. She took in the sight of the laden table with a display of fresh flowers reaching three feet from its bowl, and candles the exact colour of Kate's dress massed into the rows of candelabra. Now it felt to her that all was as it should be at Liscombe Hall, for Kate had married into it and had her proper place as a wife there.

They all sat on until tea-time when the bringing in of the silver trays and the steaming pots to the drawing room seemed to make a natural break in the events of the day, and soon afterwards everyone began to make preparations to depart.

Kate and David Liscombe stood on the terrace, watching their guests leave, Mrs Tranter last, moving carefully down the steps behind her husband. The sun was going from Liscombe Hill; a chill winter breeze had started up but they did not feel it. Wind stirred at the Liscombe oaks and a familiar distant sound reached them: horses' hooves thudding on dry earth. Johnny, having left the party early to tend his beasts, was a dark patch moving across the bottom hill, followed by Joe on his pony. A shout drifted up: 'Whowee!'

'That's Joe shouting out for joy,' Kate said, 'just like Johnny used to do.' She felt a little faint, feeling David beside her, for the moment that had at last come: he and she together after such long, long years of waiting. She had not known she had been waiting. She had thought she had simply closed up her heart and would not love again. It was only now she knew that she had been waiting. His arm was in its rightful place, around her, and she leaned into her place, her face against his.

'Maybe, Kate . . .' David swung round and hugged her to him. 'Maybe there'll be another Joe, Tranter and

Liscombe, yours and mine. And we'll love him the way we love each other.' At last, he thought, at last today, tonight, Kate would lie with him again, where she belonged.

'Oh, I don't think . . .' Kate laughed. Upstairs their room, their bed, and their old memories lay in wait. She put her arms about him and breathed in male warmth and the remembered scent of cedar cologne.

'Come on, Lady Liscombe.' He lifted her and strode with her up the steps and on past the bronzed pillars, warmed by a last gleam of sunlight through the Liscombe windowpanes.

Published or forthcoming

Lilies of the Field

Maureen O'Donoghue

Invited back to Trewythian, her long-lost island home, Sally leaves the sophisticated charm of London for the golden memories of her childhood.

As she is drawn into the warm embrace of the villagers, and intoxicated by a new romance, Sally's homecoming promises to be a joyous occasion. But the idyll turns sour when she stumbles upon a shocking secret from her family's past − a secret shared by a murderous assailant who stalks the island determined that she will never leave Trewythian again.

Unfolding against the sweeping moors and boundless skies of a gaunt and beautiful island, *Lilies of the Field* is a stirring, sensual tale of romance and adventure.

SIGNET

Published or forthcoming

THE GLITTERING STRAND

Judith Lennox

The Levant trade of the 1590's offers wealth and danger in equal measure. And, always, dreams …

A dream for Serafina Guardi, captured by corsairs and sold into slavery *en route* to her profitable betrothal, struggling with the intrigues of the Italian cloth trade to reclaim her heritage – and revenge herself. And for Thomas Marlowe, the English pilot wrecked on the Barbary Coast, dreams of a ship such as the Mediterranean has never seen and wider seas to sail her in.

Chance and treachery conspire against their hopes while irretrievably entangling their fates. There will be long, hard years before either Serafina or Thomas comes near to their dream – only to find the dream is no longer the same…

The Stars Burn On

Denise Robertson

On New Year's Day 1980, Jenny and seven friends watch the dawn from a northern hill. On the brink of adulthood, confident of their futures, they vow to meet there again at the end of the decade. Just two weeks later, one of the group is dead. The others, irrevocably affected, go on to pursue careers in the law or media, and make new lives for themselves as husbands, wives and parents. Jenny, who establishes herself as a successful journalist in London, remains their lynchpin – and only Jenny knows that the secret that binds them is a lie.

'A saga that'll keep you turning the pages … told with perception and humour' – *Prima*

'Her prose has a fine flow, her knowledge of the region is deep and instinctive. Above all, her compassion and great understanding of life show in all she writes' – *Evening Chronicle, Newcastle on Tyne*

HAVING IT ALL

Maeve Haran

Having it All. Power. Money. Success. *And* a happy family. Liz really believed she could have it all. So when she's offered one of the most important jobs in television, she jumps at it.

But Liz discovers that there's a price to be paid for her success and that the whole glittering image is just an illusion. And one day she's faced with the choice she thought she'd never have to make.

Liz decides she *will* have it all – but on her own terms.

'Will touch cords, tug heartstrings. Every woman's been here' – Penny Vincenzi, author of *Old Sins*

'Realistic, compassionate, but still as pacey as they come' – *Cosmopolitan*

Published or forthcoming

TRIAL

Clifford Irving

They called it suppression of evidence and dis-
barred him from the 299th District Court for
two long years.

Criminal Defence lawyer Warren Blackburn
came back from the wilderness to pick up the
crumbs – and found two cases just like the one
that brought him down.

But this time he was ready to back his judgement and fight. Fight for justice and a fair trial
against a legal system that would do anything
as long as it got a deal...

'Riveting legal edge-of-the seater ... Has
Texas and American Justice systems by the
tail' – *Daily Telegraph*

SIGNET

Published or forthcoming

FADE THE HEAT

Jay Brandon

Mark Blackwell is District Attorney of San Antonio, city of favours and pay-offs. His success has cost him his marriage and family life. Now his son stands accused of rape.

During the trial that follows Mark is torn apart, caught in the judicial wheel that he has set in motion. As the pressure builds, the media and his rivals move in for the kill. Suddenly he has everything to lose and nothing to gain...

'A clever plot, a gripping novel' – Tony Hillerman, author of *Talking God*

'Tension radiates from every page ... guilty of being an enthralling read' – *Today*

Published or forthcoming

38 NORTH YANKEE

Ed Ruggero

When an unarmed convoy of American troops on a training exercise is ambushed by North Koreans near Hongch'on, the fragile peace that has existed since 1953 is shattered, and once again the US Army is in the front line of a war on foreign territory.

38 North Yankee is the blistering story of the men and machines on both sides as the powder-keg of Korea explodes into a bloody and ruthless struggle for military supremacy.

Blood Knot

Sam Llewellyn

Bill Tyrrell has locked the door on his crusading past. As a reporter, he's seen conflict and pain close up – and not once have his words ever saved a life. Now he's back in England, living on the antique cutter *Vixen*, the only legacy from his long-vanished father. But the journalist in him can't be buried. Not when a Russian sea cadet gets wrapped round the *Vixen's* propeller under the eyes of a Cabinet Minister – and Tyrrell becomes the scapegoat...

It is the first in a series of harrowing accidents. And suddenly the past begins to open up all over again, as Tyrrell's battle-hardened reporting reflexes lure him into a dark maze of political cover-ups and violent death...

'The best seabourne thriller in many a tide'
– *Daily Mail*